The
Debutante
Divorcée

The Debutante Divorcée

A NOVEL

Plum Sykes

miramax books

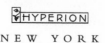

NEW YORK

ISBN 1-4013-5244-8

First Edition
10   9   8   7   6   5   4   3   2   1

For Toby

1

Lost-Husbands Edition

Married girls in New York these days put almost as much effort into losing husbands as they once did into finding them. It's not uncommon for husbands to be mislaid almost as soon as the honeymoon begins. This is a particular hazard in locations like Capri or Harbour Island, where the glamour quotient of the early-morning beach gang rivals that of a front row at a Valentino couture show. Some husbands, like Jamie Bellangere, get forgotten as early as Barbados airport, an airline terminal so social it is considered perilous for new spouses to pass through even a whole year after marriage. As the twenty-six-and-a-half-year-old former Mrs. Jamie Bellangere always says in her defense, *of course* she forgot to get Jamie into the hotel's courtesy car! The concierge from Sandy Lane had just called her with a message from the Douglas Blunketts saying that they expected her on "the tub" for dinner at eight! ("the tub" being Blunkett slang for their 150-foot sailing yacht, *Private Lives*). Meanwhile, that lethal little airstrip in Mustique is even more notorious than Barbados: marriage vows tend to slip a new bride's mind right at the bamboo baggage carousel. This is usually because Mick Jagger has just invited her to dinner, which tends to happen the second a new wife's plane has landed.

The social demographics of Careyes, Mexico, are such that there is no place better suited to the exotic pleasures of the Divorce Honeymoon. A sexually scandalous vacation is the newfound, but nevertheless inalienable, privilege of the debutante divorcées—New York's young, social, newly unwed girls. It must be spent in a spot where the atmosphere is uplifting, the views are spectacular, acupuncture and exercise facilities abound, and conversation topics are lighter than a soufflé. Popular subjects range from "How far did you swim today?" "Did you get to the island?" to "Can I wear white jeans for dinner?" and "Are you invited to the Goldsmiths' for New Year?" There are so many parties every night it's literally impossible to stay home unless you are the one throwing the party. Then, everyone's permanently drunk because the only thing anyone drinks all day are miceladas—a make out friendly mix of beer, lemonade, and tequila. To be blunt, Careyes is the ideal spot for the gorgeous divorcée because she can have sex with a different hedge fund manager every night if she wishes.

I met Lauren Blount on the beach on Labor Day. You know how it is in Careyes. You're best friends in five minutes flat because you're both wearing Pucci bikinis. Lauren was one week into her Divorce Honeymoon, and she told me everything in a minute. Still, that didn't mean I really knew a thing about her.

"The day of my divorce was sort of glamorous, actually," said Lauren from under the wide-brimmed black sunhat she had found in her canvas Hermès tote. "Like the hat? Yves Saint Laurent gave it to my mom in 1972."

"It's gorgeous," I said.

Lauren's beach look was impossibly chic. Her lithe, petite body was a delicious cocoa brown, which set off to perfection the chocolate and turquoise geometric print of her bandeau bikini. Her toes were manicured an understated flesh pink, and her brunette locks, gleaming like espresso beans, fell in loose waves around her shoulders and grazed the sand when she moved. Six long strands of tiny seed pearls dropped gracefully from her delicate throat, and she had three gold bangles that she'd bought in the souk in Marrakesh pushed up around her forearm.

"Mama would murder me if she knew I was wearing her pearls on the beach," said Lauren, noticing me looking at them. "The saltwater ruins them. But I just felt very *Tender Is the Night* when I woke up today, and I had to wear them. I'm totally into 1920s Riviera chic, aren't you?"

"I adore it," I agreed.

"God, it's so hot. There's too many people here," sighed Lauren, gazing along Playa Rosa. There were maybe three people on the beach. "Why don't you come up to the house?"

"I'd love to," I said, getting up from my lounger.

"We can have lunch and hang out all afternoon. The Casa's got the most divine sunken living room. It's to die," she said, gathering up her tote and slipping on a pair of gold leather thong sandals.

It's generally agreed in Careyes that without a sunken drawing room one *would* die, socially. Not a soul will visit if you don't have one. If you do, it must simultaneously offer shade from a partial, immaculately thatched roof while being open to the breezes of the ocean, even if that means the Moorish antiques are eaten away at an alarming rate by sea salt.

Casa Papa, as Lauren nicknamed her father's house, is a whitewashed, sun-bleached Mexican castle with a bright blue pool washing around it like a moat. When we arrived, Lauren led me through the house and out into the sunken drawing room. That second, a maid dressed crisply in a blue-and-white-striped uniform—she would have looked more at home on the Upper East Side—appeared with a turquoise chiffon robe in her hand that Lauren threw straight over her bikini. Moments later another maid arrived bearing a tray filled with just-made quesadillas and guacamole, glass plates, and candy-pink linen napkins.

"Mmmmm! Thank you, Maria," said Lauren. *"Puede hacer nos el favor de traer dos limonadas heladas?"*

"Si, señorita," nodded Maria.

Maria bustled about setting a low lacquered table, then disappeared inside to track down the lemonade.

"God, this is nice," I said, throwing my beach bag on the floor and flopping onto a deep sofa while Lauren curled up in a wicker chair. In the center of the room the huge red trunk of an ancient, twisted *candelabro* cactus grew up to the ceiling. From where we were sitting we could just make out a tiny figure sunbathing on the terrace of the house opposite.

"That's my cousin, Tinsley Bellangere," said Lauren, squinting. "I can't *believe* she's lying out like that—so dangerous in this heat. And after her whole family died of skin cancer! She's had all her freckles lasered off. Tinsley's on her divorce honeymoon too, which is nice for me. I call her Miss Mini-Marriage. She was married to Jamie less than three days, which is something of an achievement, no? Anyway, do you still want to hear about the divorce day?"

"Absolutely," I replied. Who could resist? There's nothing like hearing about another girl's love life to make three hours pass in three seconds.

"I got my divorce papers signed. I guess that was three weeks ago now. The biggest thing in the divorce was the dog, Boo Boo. That took months. I got him. Anyway, that night I decided to celebrate with Milton Holmes—he's the family decorator, and my best friend, sort of. Milton was obsessed with going to the private room at Harry's Downtown, even though it was like, August twelfth and I knew there wouldn't be a soul there. I was dressed head to toe in black frayed Lanvin with my great grandmother's ivory barrette in my hair. I thought I was absolutely it—but when I look back it's like I was dressing for a funeral—oh, thank you so much," said Lauren as Maria returned with a jug of iced lemonade and two tall glasses. "Sorry. God, I'm going to have to have a cigarette."

Lauren delved into her tote and pulled out a little green crocodile case the size of a lipstick holder. The silver-lined box contained two "platinums," as she calls them—two Marlboro Ultra Lights. She lit one, then left it untouched on the side of the ashtray.

"So here I am in my divorcée look, and Milton was like, 'We *have* to be upstairs, *everyone's* upstairs,' when actually there wasn't a soul up there, except Beyoncé or Lindsay Lohan, or some other girl of the minute everyone's so tired of they don't even count. Well, actually, I *love* Lindsay Lohan again. I want to be Lindsay Lohan most of the time, don't you?"

Lauren paused and waited for my answer. This was obviously a serious question.

"Wouldn't it be exhausting to be Lindsay Lohan *every day,*

though?" I said. That many changes of sunglasses must be punishing.

"I'd love the attention. Anyway, I digress. Milton and I went upstairs, and I ordered strawberry tequila after strawberry tequila and . . ." Lauren paused and looked around, as though making sure no one else was listening. Then she whispered, ". . . and next thing I know, this complete stranger sent over a glass of vintage champagne."

"Who was he?" I asked.

"Well. It was . . . you're not going to believe it. It was Sanford Berman."

"No," I gasped.

"Totally. And he was celebrating his third company going public or something crazy like that, but I had no idea who he was because I stopped reading the papers recently so I don't have to read about my divorce. Milton was flipping, Sanford's his total icon. Milton said, 'Everyone thinks Rupert Murdoch's huge, but Sanford's so huge *he* owns Rupert Murdoch.'"

Lauren's cell phone started beeping. She picked it up and turned it off.

"It's him. It's *always* him," said Lauren ever so blasé.

"You should have answered. I don't mind," I said.

"Actually I need a break from him for now. Here's the thing. He's getting way too obsessed with me. Sanford is seventy-one and a half years old. I can't date an antique. Sure, I like antiques, but not as boyfriends. So, where was I?" asked Lauren.

"The drink from Sanford came over," I reminded her.

"Well, I downed that glass of champagne, and then Sanford himself came over and started talking to me. He was so charming—in the way that old things are. He thought it was very 'modern' that I was partying like that on my divorce day. So I was like, 'Ok, let's get another round of shots.' I can't really remember the night well at all," she said, with a coy expression, "except it turns out Sanford's married, but he's asking if he can take me home. So I let him give me a ride. On the way he asked me what I do, so I told him about how I occasionally buy and sell one-off estate jewelry, and he said he wanted to buy some for his wife. I thought that was sweet."

Sanford had called Lauren at 8 A.M. the next morning, asking to view the jewels. He showed up at her place at half past ten that night. They hung out until midnight, and finally Lauren asked Sanford if he wanted to see the jewels.

"He said to me, 'Not really. I just think you're amusing.' Can you *believe*?" said Lauren, her eyes widening cartoonishly to exaggerate the point. "God, I have to actually *smoke* a cigarette at this moment in the tale," she added, starting over with another. "Then he started sending his driver over every morning with the *Wall Street Journal*, a latte, and a warm croissant from Patisserie Claude, at which point I decided being a newly unwed sucks a lot less than being a newlywed. God, my divorce honeymoon is the *best*," she sighed contentedly as she sunned herself. "I *love* being divorced."

❦

It would be impossible *not* to love being divorced if you were Lauren Blount, of the Chicago Hamill Blounts, who pretty much invented Chicago, depending on who you ask. (There's the Marshall Field's camp and the Hamill Blount camp, and never the twain shall dine in the Chicago Racquet Club together, if you get my meaning.) The rumor is that the Hamill Blounts own more art than the Guggenheims, more real estate than McDonald's, and that Lauren's mother's jewelry vaults are the reason Colombia is running low on emeralds.

It had only been three weeks since Lauren's divorce, but ever since, she'd been going out like crazy. It amused her to dress up in her Chanel couture rehearsal-dinner dress, which was very heavy on the white Lesage lace, and one of her three engagement rings. She was instantly nominated for the Best Dressed List but brushed it off as a silly joke. However, it was actually the consensus among the Pastis set that Lauren truly deserved the honor. (Most of the time a sickening combination of admiration and envy makes the girls who hang out at Pastis physically unable to admit that anyone deserves to be on the BDL, especially if they were in the same class at Spence.)

Lauren oozed rich-girl chic. She wasn't extremely tall, but because she was so delightfully proportioned, with tiny fine wrists and arms, she could pull off virtually anything. Her exquisite legs, which drew so much envy among her set, "reflect years of private ballet instruction," she always said. She looked rather like a cleaned-up, freshly laundered version of her icon—the young Jane Birkin: she had the long chestnut locks, the eye-grazing fringe, and the year-round tan (easy when there's a family home in every resort from Antigua to Aspen). When casually dressed she exuded a natural glamour that was low on bling and high on class. Her daytime uniform consisted of long, skinny pants from Marni, little lace blouses by Yves Saint Laurent, and minuscule, shrunken leather jackets from Rick Owens. If she wore vintage, it had to be Ossie Clarke or Dior, and she would fly to London especially to stock up on the best things at the Dover Street Market.

Dressing up, though, was Lauren's real obsession. If you dropped by mid-afternoon, she was just as likely to be clad in a cerise organza cocktail frock by Christian Lacroix as she was to be in her Pilates leotard (a hangover from the ballerina days). Her collection of ball gowns—Balmain couture, McQueen couture, original Givenchy couture—was a matter of some envy among New York's social set and was stored in a climate-controlled walk-in closet that was the size of a small studio appartment. Gowns were "gifted" to Lauren on a weekly basis by everyone from Oscar de la Renta to Peter Som, but she always returned them, however beautiful. She felt it was tacky not to pay for clothes, saying, "I give to charity. I don't take it." Her great weakness, though, was real jewels, particularly when they were most inappropriate—there was nothing that amused Lauren more than wearing a priceless Indian ruby in bed.

❧

"Maybe I should invite Tinsley over here so she can get some shade. She's crazy to be sunbathing like that," said Lauren a little later. "It must be the divorce. Tinsley thinks she's having fun, but she's getting more deranged by the second. She's changing bikinis seven times a day now, which has got to be a sign of mental instability. I love her, and I want her to be OK, not getting chemo."

Lauren clicked open her little silver cell and called Tinsley, who said she'd be over in ten minutes. The bikini-clad figure waved from her terrace and disappeared from view.

"They always take that place over Labor Day. You'll like her," said Lauren. "What are you doing here in Careyes anyway?"

"I'm on . . . honeymoon," I said unsurely.

"*Real* honeymoon?" asked Lauren.

"Yes," I answered reluctantly.

"Alone?"

"Sort of," I mumbled, lowering my eyes. (The floor is an excellent place to look, I always find, when admitting one has lost one's husband about three seconds after the wedding.)

"Sounds a lot like my divorce honeymoon. It's really immaterial whether you have a husband with you or not."

Lauren giggled and caught my eye. When she saw my face she abruptly stopped. "Oh! I'm sorry! You look so upset."

"I'm fine," I insisted. Hoping she wouldn't notice, I wiped a stray tear from my nose with the back of my hand.

"What happened?" said Lauren sympathetically.

"Well . . . huh," I sighed.

Maybe I should tell Lauren the whole hideous story. She was almost a complete stranger, but then lots of people pay a fortune to tell a stranger their most intimate thoughts in therapy every week.

I was beyond embarrassed, I realized, as I told Lauren my sorry tale. The fact was, my "honeymoon" felt about as romantic as solitary confinement right now. My new husband, Hunter, had been forced to leave on the second day of our vacation to close a business deal. Now, I have never been one of those girls who dreamed about her wedding day all her life, but I *had* dreamed about my honeymoon: it was meant to be the most delicious, sexy two weeks of your life, the vacation version of heaven. When Hunter had explained that he had to leave, in a terrible rush, I behaved in a very grown-up way, I thought, and told him I understood. But inside I was desolate. Hunter promised to deliver another honeymoon, but a subsitute vacation held no appeal. How do you get that blissed-out, just-married feeling six months after the wedding? By definition, you can only feel just-married for about a minute. Honeymoons have a small window of opportunity, bliss being as transient as it is.

Hunter had been gone three days now, and having felt stoic for about three hours, I had quickly evolved to feeling utterly tragic. The trouble with being alone on your honeymoon is that there is oodles of time to wallow. Reading trashy magazines full of celebrity breakups doesn't help.

My self-pity was only exacerbated by the maid at our beach house bringing romantic breakfast trays for two each morning, covered in flowers and Mexican hearts wishing us good luck. I couldn't face telling her that Hunter had left and might not get back. I was so ashamed about the whole thing, I hadn't even called a friend to commiserate. What would people think? Hunter and I had known each other only six months and had gotten married on the spur of the moment, in Hawaii. I could imagine the gossip already: *she didn't have a clue what she was getting into; she hardly knew him; apparently he left some other girlfriend on vacation* . . . My mind was bedeviled by hideous thoughts—and disappointment. Ah! Disappointment! It's the worst affliction. It's so dreary, and you can't do anything to improve it; it just has to fade away . . . over years, I told Lauren gloomily, maybe decades . . .

"Stop overreacting. It's not that bad," interjected Lauren. "At least you've got a husband. This is an exercise in ego-loss for you and you're indulging yourself."

Ego-loss? What about husband-loss?

"You're the first person I've told," I admitted as tears suddenly flooded my eyes. "It's such a ghastly start to a marriage. I'm bloody furious, and so angry with Hunter. I know he has to make money, and work, but . . . oh, God."

"Here," said Lauren, rummaging in her tote. She handed me a lace-trimmed, white silk handkerchief with her initials embroidered on it.

"Thanks," I said, taking it. It was criminal to wipe one's nose on such an exquisite item, but I went ahead. "This is so pretty."

"You get them at Leron. Special order. They fly to Chicago

to see my mother. It's all by appointment only. You should see the linens. Blissful. Why don't I order some for you next time? Would that cheer you up?"

"I guess," I said. That was sweet of Lauren, I thought. If I was destined to spend my marriage in tears, I supposed white lace would be much more pleasant to weep into than Charmin toilet paper.

"Look at it this way: most marriages start with an in-credible honeymoon and go downhill from there. At least this way the only place you can go is up. I mean, it can't get any worse, right?"

I dabbed at my eyes with Lauren's handkerchief. Through my tears, I somehow managed a laugh.

"Don't obsess about this, or you'll really ruin things. Honeymoons are seriously overrated. They're just so pres-sured, like birthdays. You're supposed to wake up excited every morning, and feel crazy in love and all floaty every minute of it, and guess what? You've got menstrual cramps that day, or you've been eaten alive by mosquitoes, and the *last* thing you feel like is fucking each other like mad, like you're supposed to want to."

"Hey, Lauren," came a girlish voice from behind us.

Tinsley Bellangere, ex-wife of the mislaid Jamie, appeared at the archway to the sunken drawing room. She was outra-geously pretty, like a milk-fed farm girl with class. She was twenty-eight years old, had flat blonde hair to her elbow, a few perfectly located post-laser freckles, and sky-blue eyes. Her skin was evenly tanned, and she was wearing a fitted yellow satin cocktail dress with a slashed skirt that streamed beauti-fully about her legs in the breeze. She wasn't dressed for the beach; she was dressed for a benefit.

Lauren made the introductions and then said, "Sylvie just

got married." She patted the seat beside her. "You always look so pretty, Tinsley."

"You look better," said Tinsley as she flopped down, all legs and satin and hair. Then she looked at me and said, "You want to hear my secret of a happy marriage? Agree with your husband on everything. Then do whatever you like. It worked really well for Jamie and me. We separated *very* amicably."

With that Tinsley stood up and made her way over to the drinks tray in the corner. "I'll be having a neat tequila. Anyone else?"

"Love one," I said. Maybe being drunk in the afternoon would improve my non-honeymoon.

"Everyone thinks I'm crazy when I drink these in the tea area at The Carlyle at noon," said Tinsley, handing one each to Lauren and me. Then she tossed her blonde mane back and downed her shot in one.

"Let's go for a swim," said Lauren. "I'm baking."

"I can't. I'm too tired," said Tinsley with a wink. She stretched out on a huge white mattress piled with giant cushions on the floor. "I'm going to lie here and watch you exhaust yourselves while I eat cactus ice cream or something."

"I'll come," I said, following Lauren into the water.

Maybe a swim would help dissipate my grim disappointment, I thought, as I splashed into the pool. The water was blood-heat hot, the kind of hotel-pool temperature that girls love and men abhor.

"Twenty loops round the house!" commanded Lauren, splashing off.

"Twenty?" I shouted after her, surprised.

"Absolutely. You've *got* to have goals in life. Personally I am a very goal-oriented person," said Lauren, between strokes.

I caught up with her, and we swam leisurely side by side. Lauren barely drew breath as she paddled and continued chatting.

"I mean even after my divorce and everything, which, by the way, is freely available for the entire world to read in great detail on Google, I said, me being me and goals being goals, I've got to set myself a post-divorce goal. You know, a serious purpose in life. Something to aim for."

As we swam around the moat, I peeked into the guest rooms that opened out onto it. They were whitewashed, and mosquito nets were draped over immaculately made-up beds. Some of the rooms had bright yellow flowers climbing around the windows, or antique Mexican icons on the walls. I started to feel a little cheerier—who wouldn't?

"So, Lauren," I said, perking up, "what is your goal?"

"To date like I'm in college again. No relationships, no falling in love. I just want to have fun, and not think beyond that."

Her reply had an unwavering certainty about it. Lauren stopped paddling and turned around to face me. Standing in the aqua water, she looked both amused and determined, as she said, "So, my *specific* goal, and I am very clear about this, because it's insanely straightforward, is that I must make out with five men between Labor Day and Memorial Day. Five ultra-diverse, top-quality, commitment-free make outs. And I shall celebrate each one in an appropriate manner. With a jewel. Or a piece of art, or a fur coat. I've already put this heavenly Revillon sable on hold in Paris, as a matter of fact. One kiss and it's mine."

With that Lauren dived under the water. When she resurfaced, the drops on her face twinkling in the sun, I asked, "God, do you think you can find *five* make outs?"

The fact is, Lauren is beautiful and sexy but she was thirty-one years old—antique by New York standards. After the age of thirty-three or thirty-four, the Manhattan male abandons his peers altogether, seeking out girls in their early to mid-twenties at the absolutely most ancient. The really sad ones give up on the New York girl altogether and exclusively date nineteen-year-old models from South Beach. Anyway, my point is that literally no one I knew over the age of thirty was getting to make out with one man over the space of six months, let alone five.

"I'm setting myself a realistic target. But I have heard," replied Lauren, gliding her fingers rather aimlessly in a circle in the water, "from other divorcées, some of whom are my friends, that it may not be overly optimistic to expect *in excess* of five. Oh! Wait! My other big ambition is to connect my own surround sound. Louis used to do all of that. I'm absolutely convinced I can do it on my own, however long it takes. Now, what's your goal?"

That was one thing I was very clear about.

"I want to be like the Eternity couple," I laughed.

Secretly, I'd always hoped that matrimony would be like the Eternity ad: a very gorgeous you, a hot him, and oodles of vanilla-colored cashmere sweaters. If possible my whole marriage would take place on a beach in East Hampton, preferably in a flattering black-and-white palette.

"If only I had had such *noble* aims, maybe my marriage would have lasted," shrieked Lauren. She hooted with laughter. "I gave up the Eternity dream at age eight. You are so cute. But I've got a tip for you."

"What?" I asked.

"Your goal should be keeping your husband away from the Husband Huntresses."

I frowned at her, confused.

"You know," explained Lauren. "Those wicked girls who *only* pursue husbands. You only become aware of them once you're married."

"Stop it." I giggled.

"Be warned."

Our swim had now come full circle, and we were back in front of the sunken drawing room. Tinsley beckoned to us to come in.

"Mojitos await," she yelled.

"Well, that was only one lap, but let's go hang with her or she'll start hyperventilating," said Lauren, climbing the shallow steps up to the drawing room. She grabbed a towel from a neat pile on a wicker table and handed one to me.

"God, that swim was lovely," I said, drying myself off. I took one of the mojitos and sipped it. It was so refreshing.

"Isn't the pool genius?" said Lauren.

She curled up in her towel onto the couch opposite Tinsley, and I sat in a rocking chair painted a hot Latin blue. I noticed that the back of the chair was inlaid with exquisite mother-of-pearl.

"What do you do, Tinsley?" I asked. Tinsley seemed like such a character, I wanted to get to know her.

"Nothing," she said brightly.

"Don't you want a job?" I asked.

At this Tinsley shook with laughter. Then she said, dead serious, "I can't work, because I can't dress for day. I can only dress for evening. So obviously office life doesn't work for me. I can only dress either for the gym or for a party."

She stood up and twirled around in her cocktail frock.

"I mean, look at me. It's two o'clock in the afternoon, and this is the most low-key I can go. The only career I could do is be an anchor on MTV, but I don't really aspire to that. It's so *old*. I mean, whereforart Serena Altschul now? The other thing that's really in the way of my career is my mom. I have to be available for two-hour conversations every day to discuss family problems, then I have to be available to go to Palm Beach at a moment's notice. I tried to have a job once working for Charlie Rose, but I was hardly ever there, and on the few unfortunate occasions that I was, I was making personal calls the *whole time*."

I laughed, and as I did, a pang of guilt hit me. Here I was, 100 percent amused on my non-honeymoon. Gosh, I thought as I sipped my mojito, shouldn't I be feeling more wistful right now?

"It's *terrible* for her, isn't it, Tinsley darling?" joked Lauren. Then she turned to me and said, "So. When do we get to meet Hunter? Is he ever coming back? Or is it reckless abandonment, honeymoon-style?"

"You'll meet him in New York. But he's going to be traveling a lot to Paris for the TV show he just did this deal for," I said. With a hint of humor I even managed to add, "the deal he wrecked our honeymoon over."

"We can keep each other company while Hunter's gone. Whatever anyone thinks, I get lonesome sometimes," said Lauren, looking suddenly vulnerable.

Later on, when the sun had started to set, and, I must admit, we were all slightly tipsy from the cocktails and heat, the conversation got more intense.

"Do you ever think about getting married again?" I asked Lauren. She was lazing in a hammock, being rocked gently by the wind.

"Yes. I think I won't," said Lauren.

"Quite right," agreed Tinsley, who was mixing yet another cocktail. "Married couples are *so dull.*"

"I know," I agreed. "It's terrible."

The fact is, a married girlfriend is never as fun as she was when she was single. One of my secret—and, I admit, terribly superficial—fears about getting married had been that I would become as dull as my dull married girlfriends.

"So, Lauren, why did you break up with Louis?" I asked.

Lauren sighed. Then she said, "We broke up . . . because, hmmm . . ." She paused, as though unsure of the answer. "I guess I thought I was getting married for the right reasons—because I was in love, and Louis had gotten me a darling Van Cleef ring, but the truth is, no one should get married just because they are in love."

"That's not very romantic," I said.

"Marriage isn't a very romantic proposition," declared Lauren. "It's a practical arrangement. Sorry, but it's the truth. I figure if I avoid the marriage bit, I can still have the romance. But you look like you are so in love. Don't listen to a word I say. It's different for everyone. I don't have a clue."

"I'm sure you do," I said.

"OK, well if you want to know what *not* to do," continued Lauren, "I'd start with don't have a wedding for four hundred. It completely clouds your judgment. I knew the whole thing was going be a downer the day of the wedding. Can you believe?"

"How?"

"There we all were up in Maine, at this nice sort of private hippie island my mom's family has had forever. It's got a couple of cute cottages. I remember looking out to the ocean the day before the wedding and seeing a crystal chandelier going by on a barge for the tent. It looked like they'd stolen it from the ballroom at the Waldorf. The thing is, I *hate* chandeliers of a certain type—I had to literally move out of my parents' place on Park when I came to New York because there were chandeliers everywhere—and here I was getting married and trying to leave the chandeliers behind and the chandeliers were still coming after me," Lauren recalled. "It was *all wrong*," she shuddered. "The whole thing was just crazy."

Lauren slid languidly off the hammock and started rummaging around in her bag. A few seconds later she held up an exquisite pair of Victorian cameo earrings. She expertly pushed the posts through her ears, saying, "I do love wearing my baubles on the beach. Don't you think these are very Talitha Getty, Tinsley?"

"*So* Talitha. I worship her style. If you are going to die, make it an overdose and everyone will worship your fashion sense forever," she declared.

"That's an awful thing to say," insisted Lauren. Then, looking slightly nostalgic, she returned to the subject of her marriage, adding, "Finally, one day I went on vacation and . . . well, the truth is I just never came home. Everyone was frantic. When I think back," she concluded, with a mischievous smile, "I'm really appalled at my own behavior. I've never met anyone as terrible as me."

2

The Consolation of a Fabulous Husband

"I wanna know everything, how you met, what he's like, can he kiss . . ." said Tinsley a few days later. We were with Lauren on Tinsley's father's boat, an old sloop, taking a sail out to the little island off the beach. We were all lying out on the sundeck at the back of the boat. It was sunny and breezy, ideal for tanning. Lauren and Tinsley were both wearing white string bikinis which they reserved strictly for sunbathing. They'd also brought a huge bag of alternative boating outfits, including specific Hermès swimsuits for diving, water skiing, and back flips.

I had met Hunter, I told them, only six months earlier, at a wedding (isn't that always the way?). My old high school friend Jessica was getting married on the beach in Anguilla in March. Jessica's wedding was beautiful: she had cool raj tents, long refectory tables covered in pink bougainvillea, and a small group of rather glamorous-looking guests.

Hmmm, I remember thinking to myself as I saw a tall, dark-haired man approach my table, check the place cards, read his name—Hunter Mortimer—find his seat, and lay eyes on me. *Gorgeous*, I'd declared secretly to myself, noting that this man was a little tan and was wearing an agreeably casual, pale summer suit. *Not bald*, I'd noted happily, noticing his generous mop of brown hair, a blessing many thirty-four-year-old men are sadly without. *Devastating smile,* I'd thought, blushing inwardly as he shook my hand. He had an easy, joyful expression, and his green eyes twinkled mischievously. *At least six foot two,* I'd calculated, looking up at his frame. I suppose, subconsciously, I was saying to myself, *Nice gene pool.*

"Isn't this a wonderful wedding?" he'd said when he sat down next to me. He looked at my left hand, smiled and added, "Although there's nothing better than being single at a wedding, is there?"

"So flirtatious," said Lauren, sipping an orange blossom water, her new favorite drink. "It all sounds so perfect."

"It was," I sighed. "He just . . . appealed to me, immediately. It was the most delicious moment, I *knew* it was going to happen. I'd like to say it took me ages to get to know him and fall in love, but actually, it was all over the minute I laid eyes on him."

It turned out he lived close to me in L.A., and we started dating a few weeks after the wedding. Five months later Hunter asked me to marry him. We'd never lived together, but I wasn't worried. Hunter was a happy, uncomplicated, unselfish person to be around. There was no self-obsession, no self-doubt, which set him miles apart from other recent boyfriends of mine. He didn't get hysterical. He didn't freak out. He sorted out a problem with a minimum of fuss. He didn't over-analyze, a trait not readily available among American men. I blame James Spader. I've always thought social acceptance of male self-torture can be traced directly back to *Sex, Lies, and Videotape.*

Hunter did things quietly, even secretly, and didn't particularly enjoy being singled out for congratulation. I suppose you could say that although he was a confident person, he was very private, which I admired. I also found it rather sexy that he was sometimes mysterious about things. He was incredibly romantic, but not in a silly way. When he said *I love you*, he meant it.

"Soooo cute." said Tinsley. "More, please."

There was one thing Hunter did, a few months after I met him, that turned a madly in love girl into a deeply in love girl. My housekeeper in L.A. had a minor car accident. She had a couple of broken bones—nothing too serious—but she had no health insurance. I didn't know how she was going to pay her medical bills, and I offered to help, but she told me someone had taken care of it all. A couple of months after she recovered and was back working at the apartment, I told her I was going to marry Hunter. At this news she wept, declaring that Hunter was the kindest man in all of America. What I learned that day was that Hunter had paid all her medical bills and had asked her not to tell me. He'd never said a thing about it. I call it his Mr. Darcy moment.

That was very Hunter. There he was, a successful young producer—he'd had a big success on MTV with a rock show he'd produced, and he was being courted by all the major networks (hence the canceled honeymoon). He didn't need to be nice to anyone, but he was, because he felt that's how human beings should behave.

"He sounds like a saint," declared Tinsley. "A handsome saint. I bet you've forgiven him for the honeymoon disaster already. It doesn't matter that much, does it?"

I nodded, smiling. Tinsley was right. The non-honeymoon wasn't the end of the world. However hard I tried to maintain my fury at Hunter, it just wouldn't stick. He had been calling all the time, to check that I was OK, and, the fact was, whenever I thought of him, I melted. Deep down I knew the marriage was the important thing, not the honeymoon.

"I'm trying to stay angry, but he's so sweet," I said. "It's impossible. I just want to be a great wife to him."

"I hope you've got something else to focus on aside from being the Eternity wife. Look what happened to Jessica Simpson," giggled Lauren.

Luckily, I did have something else. Just before we'd run off and gotten married, Hunter had decided to move his company to New York. He loved it there, and since I'd grown up in the city I was thrilled to be going back. We'd lucked out and found a great apartment downtown. Now that he'd struck this latest deal to make a TV show set in Paris, it made even more sense, since he'd be traveling to Europe frequently. Meanwhile, my old friend Thackeray Johnston—who'd snuck off to Parsons when everyone else had gone to the East Coast colleges—had contacted me and asked if I wanted to run his fashion house. I'd been working for a big European designer in L.A., dressing actresses, and was ready for something more. Thackeray was making a name for himself as one of the cooler young designers in New York but couldn't handle the business side as well as the designing. In return for crazily low pay, he'd offered me 5 percent of the company, which we hoped to sell one day. Now that I'd met Lauren and Tinsley I was looking forward to being back in New York even more.

"My God, how fun. I've seen Thackeray's stuff. It's awesome. I think he's really talented. I don't think you're life's too bad, Sylvie. You may not have had a honeymoon," said Tinsley, "but you've got the best consolation: a fabulous husband."

"Agreed. Although I," declared Lauren wickedly, "would *far* rather end up with the honeymoon than the husband."

3

Legendary Lovers

"*C*an you believe John Currin and Rachel Feinstein have come . . . *as themselves*!" said Lauren the night of her birthday party. "They're so existential, I feel like a retard."

We were now back in New York, and the first time I saw Lauren Blount after Careyes was at her thirty-second birthday party in her West Eleventh Street townhouse (it's that crisp, double-width, white-and-brick Greek revival affair between West Fourth street and Waverly Place). Like all Lauren's birthday parties, this one, in mid September, was a costume party. The theme was Legendary Lovers, and Lauren said it didn't matter whether the couple you went as were still together or broken up, alive or dead, because she said no one could remember that sort of detail about those sort of people anyway. She liked her theme because guests could come as Sylvia Plath and Ted Hughes if they wanted to make no effort at all, or Marilyn Manson and Dita Von Teese if they felt like going completely over the top.

While Hunter was dropping off our coats, I headed upstairs, where Lauren was welcoming guests at the doorway to the first-floor drawing room. She was wearing minuscule hot pants of primrose yellow terry toweling and a candy-pink tee. On her head was a blonde wig tied in perky pigtails. Her feet were clad in glowing white bobby socks and brand-new white leather roller skates. To all intents and purposes she was Rollergirl; however, the one thing that made her very *not* Rollergirl was the diamond Cartier bracelet fastened to her left wrist. It glittered alluringly in the light cast from the temporary disco ball twirling in the center of the room.

"It was the Duchess of Windsor's," said Lauren, twisting it around her wrist. "Isn't it heaven? Uncle Freddie sent it down" ('Uncle Freddie' being the name Lauren used for the totally unrelated Fred Leighton, of Madison Avenue jewelry fame).

"It's so beautiful," I remarked.

"I was thinking of dressing as Bianca Jagger, and having Milton come as Mick tonight," she said, regarding her outfit. "But then, I realized, I go out every night dressed as Bianca Jagger already. So I'm Rollergirl, which has nothing to do with anything except it guarantees me maximum attention. Does it look like a rollerrink in here?"

"Not exactly," I said.

With its walls upholstered in antique pink satin, the Cedric Gibbons furniture inherited from one of Lauren's movie starlet grandmothers, and the Rothkos and Rauschenbergs, Lauren's drawing room feels like an avant-garde boudoir. It's usually immaculate, but tonight the room was strewn with glam couples dressed in witty takes on the party's theme. Two gorgeous teenage boys, leaning nonchalantly on the front balcony overlooking the street, were dressed as Jean Harlow and Marilyn Monroe, in platinum blonde wigs and crystal-studded gowns. Over by the fireplace, right underneath a huge Gilbert and George collage, stood two cool girls in gray suits and glasses, dressed as the artists. There were Bogie and Bacall couples lounging on black lacquer and gilt chairs, and a very convincing Jean Shrimpton and David Bailey duo were giggling by the bar. A Penelope Tree and Truman Capote pair sat cross-legged on the floor talking intensely, while a Halston and Warhol combo stepped coolly over them. On Lauren's sofas, which had been recovered in old 1930s Japanese kimono fabric, three sets of Johns and Yokos sat gossiping as hard as though they really were John and Yoko. People seemed to be having fun, which, I have to say, was something of a surprise: the glamorous parties in New York full of gorgeous people usually resemble a death march.

"Gingertini?" asked a waiter, offering us a tray of electric-orange drinks. Like all the other male staff that night, he was dressed as Donald Trump in a tuxedo, hairpiece, and fantasy tan. The waitresses were multiples of Melania, their hair teased into skyscraping brunette beehives, their bodies squeezed into wedding dresses so tight they threatened to suffocate them. The real Melania is a miracle of human survival. By this point in her marriage she should have suffered death by Dolce and Gabbana corset.

"Don't you adore my Donalds?" said Lauren, taking a gingertini from the tray. "He and Melania are the ultimate tabloid couple."

Just then, Hunter appeared. He kissed me on the cheek and then held out his hand to shake Lauren's. Lauren took it, gasping, melodramatically, "Hunter! The disappearing, divine new husband. I am so thrilled to meet you." She flung her arms around Hunter and gave him a huge hug. "God, you're *so handsome*. I can't stand it!"

Hunter extricated himself. I could see he was amused.

"The divine new friend, I assume," he said, kissing Lauren on the cheek.

"Oh, wow, you're so charming I want to faint. God, Sylvie, you must be so, like thrilled with this . . . *thing*."

I smiled. Lauren seemed genuinely happy for us. She drew back as if to observe us.

"Oooh. Frida and Diego. So romantic." she cooed. Having just been in Mexico, it hadn't been hard to rustle up my scarlet Frida Kahlo flamenco dress. Meanwhile Hunter was in paint-spattered overalls that he'd created himself. "I, on the other hand, am enjoying my one night as a tacky coke addict. You must come downstairs and meet Milton, who I was telling you about in Careyes. My interior decorator. He's going to die over both of you."

With that, Lauren wove her way through her guests, leading us through the crowd, blowing kisses as she went. When we reached the stairs, Lauren removed her roller skates and skipped down ahead of us. On the parlor floor, Lauren put her roller skates back on and then we headed toward the back of the house into Lauren's "morning room. Well, that's what Milton calls it. I call it the White Room. I mean, I'm not Marie Antoinette . . . yet. Milton's so pretentious," she moaned. "But I adore him all the same. I mean this floor he made me do," she said, gesturing to the polished wood floor of the corridor. "Parquet de Versailles. It's real. Can you imagine? Daylight robbery."

We arrived at two mirrored French doors, and Lauren pushed them open into the "shoes-off" white room. (All-white rooms are so in right now in New York that you're barely able to keep your shoes on at night at all anymore. That night, though, everyone was allowed to keep their footwear on, thankfully.) Even though the room was packed,

I could see six pairs of white-painted plaster palms along the back wall, separated by six sets of French windows that opened onto a formal planted garden that had been floodlit for the night. It was more like Venice than West Village. At one end of the room was a very rock 'n' roll white baby grand piano, watched over by a Tom Sachs "White" collage. The floor was pure white marble, and in case you don't know much about marble snobbery, the plain white kind without veins is more pricey than the kind with veins. That's very now, to pay more for less—or rather, to pay a lot more for a lot less.

"There he is," said Lauren, gesturing at a woman perched on the end of one of two deeply tufted white silk chaise longues.

Milton Whitney Holmes (real name: Joe Straaba) was dressed as Iman, in an homage to a former owner of the house. The vintage Alaia dress and Afro wig he was wearing looked bizarre on him, since he's rather petite and white, so he'd hung a name tag from the dress which read MRS. DAVID BOWIE, in case no one recognized him. (They didn't.) Milton was chatting to a slight girl dressed in a prim-looking outfit consisting of a tweed skirt and Fair Isle sweater. Her main accessory was a tube of pale-pink lip gloss that she squirted at her mouth every five seconds. Her complexion was invalid-white, and her blonde hair was almost as pale.

"Drat, Marci Klugerson's got to him," sighed Lauren as we approached. She turned and stopped us for a second. Then she lowered her voice and whispered, "Be nice to Marci. She seems perfectly innocent, but she's a terrible gossip—she hears everything, and always gets it slightly wrong. Anyway, she seems really uptight because she thinks she has scoliosis, which she doesn't, by the way. We all think she's on her way to being a divorcée, but she doesn't know it yet. She forgets she's married all the time. I call her the careless wife."

"I think I went to college with Marci," I said. I felt as though I recognized her name. "Was she at Brown?"

"I think she was, yes," said Lauren.

Milton waved from the sofa. When we got over there, Lauren introduced everyone.

"Where have you *been*?" said Marci Klugerson when she clapped eyes on Lauren. This is what Marci always says when she sees Lauren.

"Oh, God, I don't know," replied Lauren nonchalantly. "Where have you been?" This is what Lauren always says to everyone when they ask her where she's been.

"Well, you must have been *somewhere*." Marci seemed a little annoyed.

"You'll never get an answer," said Milton solemnly.

"I guess I was on my father's ranch for a while. Then we were on the boat. You know," said Lauren vaguely.

"We?" asked Marci.

"Oh, no one," said Lauren mysteriously.

With that, she skated off. Marci looked after her, rather forlornly.

Lauren's never been anywhere she can tell you about, she often says when she returns from one of her frequent disappearances. Then you read somewhere or other that she's been at Mr. Revlon or whoever's place in Barbuda and he's been asking her what companies he should buy or what she thinks about hedge funds or distressed companies in Russia. Later you hear that while she was down there some rock star was staying with Mr. Revlon too. But the fact was, he was totally bored by Mr. Revlon and was only there for Lauren, who barely spoke to him and told him she'd never heard his music, which made him crazy for her.

"Marci, I think maybe we were at Brown together," I said.

Marci looked at me curiously for a moment and then said, "Sylvie . . . Wentworth?"

"Yes," I told her, "Well, it's Sylvie Mortimer, now I'm married to Hunter."

"Congratulations," said Milton. "You make a cute couple."

"I hear you're absolutely best friends with Lauren," said Marci. Suddenly she looked troubled as she added, "Well, actually she says you're her second best best friend. I'm her *best* best friend. Officially."

"Darling, *I'm* Lauren's best friend," declared Milton dramatically.

"Well, I only just met Lauren, in Careyes," I said, sensing an atmosphere. "I barely know her."

"I know. Lauren told me all about you. She says you're the most wonderful influence on her," said Marci, slightly grudgingly.

Suddenly Marci seemed nervous. She scanned the room, tugging awkwardly at her tweed skirt.

"I'm so unoriginal, aren't I? The only thing I could be was Bridget Jones Two because I'm so enormous. And don't tell me I'm thin because I know I look like a museum. But at least my husband looks like Mark Darcy—well, Mark Darcy with red hair. Ha ha ha!"

"Darling, I've just spotted an old acquaintance over there," said Hunter, "I'm just going to pop over and say hello, all right?"

"Sure, sweetie," I said, as Hunter headed over toward a group in the far corner.

Milton patted the sofa next to him, and Marci and I sat down.

"How's married life?" asked Milton.

"It's so nice—" I started, but Marci interrupted me.

"Being married has got to be the draggiest drag of all time," she groaned. "My self-esteem will never get over it. I love and adore Christopher and everything, but marriage is totally hideous. The only girls I know getting any sex are divorced."

I must have looked surprised, because the next minute Milton was nodding his head and saying, "Absolutely true."

"Milton, is it true that Axel Vervoordt escorted the parquet in the corridor from Holland? *Personally?*" said Marci. "I heard Lauren's converted the wine cellar into a fur vault. Apparently it's colder than Alaska down there. Or is that just a rumor?"

"I couldn't possibly divulge my clients' secrets," said Milton, suddenly sphinx-like.

There was an awkward pause and Marci went bright pink. "I didn't mean to pry—"

"Now, what's happened to that fabulous husband of yours?" he interrupted, looking at me and changing the subject.

"He's—"

I looked around. I couldn't see Hunter anywhere. Then I spotted him standing over by the piano. He had his back to me and was chatting to two girls dressed as white-faced Harajuku twins. One of them was very plain, the other noticeably beautiful, with such extraordinary cheekbones it was hard not to stare. The ordinary one soon moved off, and I could see Hunter still chatting to the cheekbones. The girl's face was framed by a gleaming wig of straight Japanese hair. She was wearing a white shirt, a black tie, and a mini-kilt. Her legs were of the insanely long, rangy variety indigenous to summertime Sardinia. On her feet were extremely high platform shoes and knee-high white socks. She looked weirdly chic actually, especially with Lauren's all-white room as a backdrop.

"There he is," I said, pointing Hunter out. "Let's go over and get him."

We all got up. But the second Marci laid eyes on the Harajuku girl, she stopped and stared.

"*Un*-be-liev-able!" uttered Marci. She sounded incensed. "He's with Sophie D'Arlan. Look at her! Touching his arm like that," she whispered as we all crossed the room toward them. "She's an outrageous flirt. I don't like to gossip, *at all*, you know, I think it's evil, but apparently Sophie is always having an affair with several people she shouldn't be. You'd better watch out for her."

"Marci, we got married four weeks ago. I don't think she'll go after a newlywed," I said, unconcerned.

"Don't think the fact that you're married is going to stop Sophie. She *only* dates husbands."

"Stop scaring Sylvie," retorted Milton, hobbling behind us on his high heels. "I'll see you later. I've just spotted the real David Bowie."

With that, Milton wobbled off toward the garden. Meanwhile, when Marci and I reached Hunter, Marci hugged and kissed Sophie in a friendly way, despite what she had been saying a few seconds before.

"Sophie, do you know Sylvie?" said Marci, turning toward me.

"I don't think I do. Hi. I'm Sophi-*a* D'Arlan," she said, extending her hand. She spoke with a trace of a rather exotic French accent. "Marci, quit calling me 'Sophie.' "

"Sylvie's *married* to Hunter," added Marci, exaggerating the word married in an unnecessary way, I thought.

At this news, Sophia seemed to visibly pale, despite her

powder-white face. She put her hand out toward the piano, as though to steady herself.

"You got . . . married? Hunter?" said Sophia, looking at him accusingly.

"They're wearing matching wedding rings, Sophie," said Marci pointedly. "But I guess it's too dark for you to notice, Sophie."

"It's Sophi-*a*," she said. Then, with a loud sigh of disappointment, she added, "Anyway, congratulations, Sylvie. I've known your *gorgeous* new husband, God . . . forever, since high school. We were like *that*," she said, crossing her index and forefinger together. Then, glancing at Hunter, she added, "Hunter . . . I can't believe you didn't tell me you were taking yourself off the market. Who knew?! Married."

She seemed to stare at Hunter for a little too long, eventually turning to me and saying, "Hunter is being so nice. He's helping me with something I'm working on. So sweet."

"He is sweet, isn't he?" I said, smiling at Hunter. I felt him loop his arm around my waist and squeeze me affectionately.

"Yes, he's a very *attentive husband*," said Marci, quite obviously directing this at Sophia.

"Hey, girls, enough of that," said Hunter, looking embarrassed.

"Would you be sweet, Sylvie, and just let me steal Hunter for another five minutes, to discuss my project?" said Sophia.

Without waiting for an answer, she steered Hunter off toward the fireplace. Marci looked after them, her expression sulky.

"I'm probably being paranoid," she huffed.

"Talking of husbands, Marci, where's yours?" I said in an effort to change the subject.

"I don't know," said Marci. She didn't appear to be at all disturbed by this revelation.

"Marci, what do you mean you don't know?" I laughed.

"I forget."

"Marci!" I protested.

"Oh, who knows . . . Christopher's probably off somewhere ghastly like Cleveland selling something. I can't possibly remember. What does it matter anyway?"

Just then Lauren reappeared, skating expertly across the marble with a small silver tray balanced on the palm of her left hand.

"Tequila shot, anyone?" she asked, setting the tray down on a little side table. Marci took one and downed it in a single gulp.

"Where's Hunter?" said Lauren, looking around. "I want to get to know him better."

"Over there with Sophia D'Arlan," I said, gesturing toward the fireplace, where Sophia was still talking with Hunter, with a serious look on her face. "Apparently they're old friends."

Lauren pirouetted expertly on her roller skates and then bent double and touched her toes. From this position she said, "Sophia says that about everyone's husband."

"Hunter's helping her with some project she's working on," I said.

"Believe me, Sophia D'Arlan doesn't need anyone's help. She's better connected than Verizon. Her mom's a de Rothschild or something, and her dad won the Nobel Peace Prize for some deathly boring French play he wrote."

"Oh," I said. "Well, Hunter's just nice like that. He's good to everyone."

Lauren stood up and surveyed the crowd.

"Even if my husband were a saint I wouldn't let Sophia near him. What did I tell you about those Husband Huntresses?" said Lauren, eyebrows raised. "Oh, God. Here we go."

Before Lauren could tell me anything else, the DJ struck up *"Good Times"* and everyone was dancing. I barely noticed, but I must have been dancing for almost an hour when out of the corner of my eye I saw Sophia kissing Hunter on both cheeks, French style, I guess. Then she threw both her arms around his neck and hugged him, before making her way off. Hunter immediately headed over to us, weaving his way past a glamorous couple dressed as Liz Taylor and Richard Burton who were dancing with two girls dressed in white Carolina Herrera wedding gowns. They were both blonde, barefoot, and holding bouquets of white roses.

"Here comes Hunter. Mind the Renée Zellwegers!" cried Lauren as he approached. When he reached us, she continued dancing and said, "You've been missing all the fun. How was it over there?"

Hunter wrapped one arm around me and let the other fall over Lauren's bobbing shoulders.

"Not very thrilling without you two," said Hunter. "Shall we get a drink? I'm parched."

A few minutes later as we sipped at our Saccotinis by the bar Hunter said, "Now, I had a great idea. How about I set Lauren up with my best friend? He's my oldest college buddy."

"Who?" I said.

"You haven't met him yet, darling. He's out of town on business a lot. He'd be perfect for Lauren. He's incredibly smart, and definitely glamorous enough for you—"

"That's really dolly of you, Hunter," interrupted Lauren. "But I don't do blind dates. I think they're tacky."

"We could all have dinner next time he's here," insisted Hunter.

"Don't do setups either. I only do anonymous hot sex," she replied, deadpan. "But thanks. You're very sweet, as your wife says."

"I may have to take matters into my own hands," sighed Hunter, with a knowing smile. "You two would be a great match."

"You sound like that guy on *The Bachelorette*," wailed Lauren. "Gross!"

"I can't interest you in a glittering marriage, then?" said Hunter, refusing to let his enthusiasm be dampened.

"Now you sound like my grandmother. I can't think of anything worse than being glitteringly married." Lauren suddenly looked embarrassed. "I mean, unless I was you two. Sorry."

Suddenly Marci appeared, looking irritated.

"Where have you been all night—" she started.

At that moment Lauren's cell rang. She glanced at the screen, smiled, then set the phone on the marble slab and left it ringing.

"That's probably, like, Jay-Z or someone calling to ask if they can come to the party," said Marci, whose gaze seemed glued to the phone. "Why don't you answer?"

At this, Lauren just shrugged and skated off.

A little later, when the party was thinning out and we were all pretty relaxed, I was lounging on a sofa with Hunter when Marci came and plopped down next to us. In a slightly rambling, drunken manner she informed us that one of the main reasons she and just about everyone else in New York is obsessed with Lauren is because she never answers her cell. She only returns calls, never takes them. Apparently no one has ever seen Lauren so much as dial a number. So you can only speak to her if she returns your message. It's rumored that she's never given her landline number to anyone except her maid. She doesn't care if a man calls her back—which means they always do—and then she doesn't call them back for three weeks. Some girls in New York—the ones who are jealous of her—dismiss Lauren as rude. But Marci says she's "scared, like Greta Garbo," and that's why she doesn't return calls.

"I've heard people say really cruel things, like that Lauren gets home after all the parties and stares at the fireplace and cuddles her dog all night in bed because she's so lonely. But that's just mean. She's so sweet and no one really knows how ghastly it was with her sister being killed like that so young. She smiles through everything, even with family tragedy. Lauren's got a heart of gold, even if she is frivolous. Anyway, most people here are just too available," continued Marci. "Too available for dinners, or for magazine shoots, or for TV appearances, or for sex. Lauren's never available for anything."

The fact is, Lauren can be counted on to cancel an eight o'clock dinner that other girls would die to be at, at precisely eight o'clock, and get away with it. New York hostesses take the long view: the philosophy has to be that if she didn't show this time, maybe she will the next, but not if you get angry with her. Then, she's always canceling for such exotic reasons—*I gotta go see Dad's soccer team in L.A. / I'm stuck at the airport in Aspen / BooBoo (a Hungarian Vizsla) has got allergies*—that it's impossible to be angry. If you complain, it might look like you are jealous of her dad / place in Aspen / dog. Lauren is so unavailable that even when you visit her, the door is always answered by someone else. Often it's her maid, Agata, who is Polish and wears all white—white shoes, white pants, white shirt—and tells you, "Miss Lauren will be down shortly. Who can I say is calling?" as though no one was expected at this unforeseen moment. While you're waiting, Agata offers you fresh sage tea. There's always a pot of it warming on the kitchen stove in case Lauren feels like some at 3 A.M. Agata worships Lauren because she lets her wear her jewelry around the house when she's cleaning.

"Maybe we should go and see if there's some down there now," added Marci. "A shot of sage tea might help my impending hangover."

Just then Lauren roller-skated back over to us. She perched on the arm of the sofa.

"Someone talking about Agata's sage tea?" she said. "It's on its way up."

"Delish!" exclaimed Marci, her eyes glowing with excitement. She obviously worshiped Lauren even more than Agata did.

"So, Hunter, Sylvie was saying you're leaving for Paris this week," said Lauren.

"Yup, I'm off for a few weeks, actually," said Hunter. "Can you look after my darling wife—"

"—did I hear someone saying they're going to be in Paris?"

It was Sophia. She was suddenly standing there, looking straight at Hunter. "I'm going to be there too. Maybe we can meet for a *verveine*? At the Costes? I get so lonely over there. . . . Anyway, I just came over to say good-bye to both of you. You make the most gorgeous couple. Of course, I'm *devastated* for me."

"Why are you leaving now?" asked Marci. "There's still a lot of party left here, you know."

"I have a *very* busy night ahead," said Sophia, with a wink.

She turned to go and then paused, looking back over her shoulder, saying "Hunter, I'll call you in Paris."

Lauren shot me a quick warning look. I looked at Hunter, but he seemed unconcerned. Sophia appeared to be living up to her reputation, but my darling husband seemed to be completely incorruptible. Tabloid couple we were not.

4

Professional Friends

According to absolutely everyone who is an authority on such matters, the invitation of invitations that fall in New York was from Alixe Carter. It arrived at terribly short notice, a few days after Lauren's birthday, and was hand-delivered. No one mails anything anymore in New York. A mailed invitation is a sign that the hostess is ambivalent about your presence at her event; if she wanted to be sure of your getting the invitation, and a prompt response, she would have messengered it.

The paper of the envelope was the same pale gray as the Dior salon is, and the script on the card was letter-pressed in old-fashioned white type. Though it looks plain, this is the most popular style of invitation going in New York City, even though, or perhaps because, white script is double the price of the pastel pink ink at Smythsons, which is double the price of the "standard" colors.

I read the card.

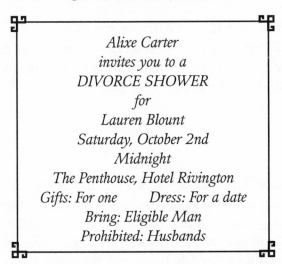

Alixe Carter
invites you to a
DIVORCE SHOWER
for
Lauren Blount
Saturday, October 2nd
Midnight
The Penthouse, Hotel Rivington
Gifts: For one   Dress: For a date
Bring: Eligible Man
Prohibited: Husbands

That was very Lauren, I thought. To have a "shower" thrown for her just at the moment when every thirty-two-year-old girl in New York had sworn off wedding and baby showers, due to an allergy to the phrase "dilated ten centimeters." "Dilated" is a horrific word. They should change it. I noticed there was something else in the envelope: another engraved card, this one with gray type on a white card. It read:

Lauren is registered at:
Condomania, 351 Bleecker Street, Tel 212-555-9442
Agent Provocateur, 133 Mercer Street, Tel 212-222-0229

As usual, no one had heard a word from Lauren in days. I'd tried to call her a couple of times to thank her for her birthday party, and had always been greeted by the words 'This. Voicemail Box. Is. Full." You couldn't even leave a message. And then out of the blue she'd come up with this divorce shower thing that everyone thought was hysterical.

Although no one was quite sure exactly what it meant,

that didn't really matter. After all, no one's quite sure about Lauren Blount's anything. The only thing, in fact, that anyone is certain about is that Lauren's life is beautifully arranged: she's very rich, very young, very thin, very pretty—and very, very divorced.

Professional Friends are the newest kind of acquaintance to have in New York—subconsciously, that is. In that, if you have one you are 100 percent unaware of it, it being the nature of Professional Friends to act as genuinely warm and smoochy as Real Friends. Interior designers, art consultants, financial advisers, gyrotonics masters, or party decorators, Professional Friends lurk invisibly on the payroll of the Manhattan heiress, spending her money, skimming off their 15 percent commission, and being the ultimate best buddy. Who else understands "how stressful everything is" and will understand it at half past five in the morning, the hour at which New York princesses generally start to freak out about "how stressful everything is"?

Feared by their married counterparts, unable to trust straight men, frequently in need of a walker, the Debutante Divorcée is easy prey. Charming Milton, I soon realized, is the most professional of the Professional Friends. You'd never have a clue that he's not a real friend. Fairly often he messengers little baskets of vitamins to all his girlfriends with a note saying he's "worried" about them. Milton even telephones Lauren, and his other benefactresses, if it's chillier than usual and warns them, "Don't go out. It's cold." Naturally, they feel like they'd die of frostbite, or rickets, without him.

It was no coincidence that the day after Hunter left for his long trip to Paris, a spectacularly elegant parcel arrived at our apartment early in the morning. It was wrapped in glossy black paper and had a white grosgrain bow tied around it with geometrical precision. I tore the envelope on the top open. Inside was a thick white card with gold edging and the name Milton Holmes engraved in orange across the top. Written in beautiful sepia ink were the words,

Dearest Sylvie,
A little piece of Paris for One Fifth Avenue.
Adored meeting you. I'll be over at six to see you.
Hugs, Milton

Over at six? How did Milton know where I lived? Maybe Lauren had told him. But what did he want?

I unwrapped the package between sips of espresso. Inside was an Assouline book entitled *Paris Living Rooms*. Several pages were marked with powder blue Post-it notes. I opened the book to one of them. The page showed a huge, white paneled drawing room filled with antique white chairs, tables, Deco glass lamps, and vases filled with lilacs. Underneath the photograph the text read, "Ines de la Fressange, fashion designer, Elysée district." On the Post-it, Milton had scribbled, "I like the wide herringbone flooring."

I was fully aware that I was being professionally stalked for an interior decorating job. Before we had moved to New York, we had found this charming, fairly large, and very old-fashioned apartment on the fifth floor at One Fifth Avenue, a 1920s building. Our apartment looked over Washington Square Park, and even though it was still only half-decorated, I loved it. Milton would be expecting me to be vulnerable to his charms now that Hunter was out of town. But, I reminded myself, I wasn't the kind of girl who went out and hired a decorator. I'd never had that kind of money in the past, and even if we did now, that didn't change things as far as I was concerned. I did things myself. I often think that girls in New York generally don't do enough things for themselves, and I wasn't interested in that kind of life. This is twenty-first-century New York, not eighteenth-century Florence, though many women here seem blissfully unaware of that fact. Apparently there are still girls on the Upper East Side who don't even brush their own hair.

I had no idea when I'd have time to finish doing up our place, but I'd figure something out. I had weekends, and now that Hunter was away, I definitely had fewer distractions. Still, I realized as I walked from the hall out into the drawing room, we had a lot of space to make beautiful. I had to admit to myself that it was intimidating.

Just then the phone rang. It was Milton.

"Are you obsessed with the book?" he said perkily.

"Milton, I loved it—"

"—could you just move the chaise, maybe . . . six and a *half* inches to the right? No, a little more, yes, a *smidge-ola* toward the terrace . . . that's it. Stop! Sto-o-op!!!" he howled. "Sorry, I'm on site."

"Shall I call you back?" I asked.

"I'm always on site. Anyway," Milton asked, "do I get the job?"

"I'm sure you don't have time," I said, trying to put him off politely.

"How are you ever going to do that place alone?" said Milton. "It's huge, and you won't be able to get a yard of decent fabric unless I take you to the D&D building. Are you awfully lonely without Hunter—"

"He calls all the time," I said.

He did. Hunter had only been gone twenty-four hours, but he'd called from JFK and from Charles de Gaulle, and he even left a sweet love-you-miss-you message in the early hours this morning on my cell. I couldn't have wished for a more attentive husband.

"Anyway, I'm coming for coffee later. There's nothing you can do. See you at six."

With that, he put the phone down. What was I doing at six o'clock tonight? I quickly flicked through my diary: I had a meeting with Thack and the senior buyer from Neiman Marcus this afternoon. It would be heavy going—I was sure Neimans would barely order a thing from the new collection. Maybe it was a good thing Milton was coming over later, I thought. He would definitely cheer me up after that meeting. It didn't mean I had to hire him.

⌘

"We love the gowns," said Bob Bulton, the Neiman Marcus buyer, wrapping up his order and flicking the elastic around his folder.

Bob Bulton was one of the most influential fashion buyers at Neiman Marcus, though his appearance would not necessarily have led one to that conclusion. He was extremely large, nearing retirement, and clad in a bespoke Thom Browne suit, the most noticeable feature of which was the way the cuff of the pants stopped far enough above the ankle to reveal his lilac cashmere socks. Despite the fact that Thack's Chrystie Street studio was crammed with stock, sewing machines, F.I.T. interns, and Chinese seamstresses, Bob hadn't seemed to mind the chaos at all. He delicately eased his squishy behind off the dainty antique chair he had been sitting on.

"But we can't commit to more than fifteen looks until we start to see some press," he added. Then he looked Thackeray in the eye and said, "You gotta get press."

"Absolutely not an issue," said Thackeray coolly.

Thack was smiling in an easy way, perched on the edge of the old French sofa at one end of the studio. He looked completely relaxed, dressed in a 1960s Saville Row suit and a sharp, white, handmade shirt. A diamond and pearl rose brooch, which had once belonged to his mother, was pinned to the lapel of his jacket. Suddenly he looked at me, saying, "Sylvie here is very connected in New York. She's already got at least three really beautiful young girls who have signed on to wear gowns at . . . Alixe Carter's New Year's ball."

Like many fashion designers, Thackeray was more deserving of an Oscar than most actors. What an absolute, wretched lie, I thought, nodding and smiling and saying, "Isn't that great news?"

No doubt I would be punished for perjuring myself later.

"Well, I have to congratulate you," said Bob, looking impressed. "You've nailed those girls down *very early*. We'll add two of each of the dresses that will be worn at the party for our pre-spring order." He seemed to be opening his folder again. "If they're photographed they'll fly out of the store. Do you think Alixe herself will wear a dress?"

"Her fitting's in two weeks," said Thackeray, in an inspired spurt of fibbing.

"Well," said Bob, "I will have to congratulate Alixe on her taste. She's an extremely close friend of my wife's, you know."

"How lovely," I said, feeling slight chest pains. "So will you be at the ball then?"

"Wouldn't miss it for the world. Congratulations, Thackeray," said Bob warmly.

Alas, I thought, *alas.*

The minute Bob had gone, I dragged Thackeray into the very humble restroom. It was the only place we could speak in private. It was so grotty we lit it only with candles so clients couldn't see how utterly hovel-like it was in there.

"My God, Thackeray! What was that?" I blurted in the dark.

"You can get me those girls, can't you?" he said. "We've doubled the order based on those girls wearing my gowns at Alixe Carter's party—"

"Thackeray. Can I remind you of something? *No one* is wearing your dresses at Alixe's party. You made that up."

"Sylvie, this is serious. You can carry it off."

This was typical Thackeray. He promised his buyers the earth and then always somehow persuaded me to deliver it. Much as I didn't want to spend my time squeezing thin women into sample-size dresses that made even the size zeros feel obese, Thackeray was right about business. He had just sold another six gowns. We had to dress as many girls as possible at Alixe's fancy New Year's party. Suddenly I had an inspiration.

"Lauren!" I exclaimed. "Alixe is having this crazy divorce shower thing for her. I just got the invitation. Lauren must be really close with Alixe."

"Not Lauren Hamill Blount?" said Thackeray. "God, she's glamorous."

"Exactly."

"Lauren's *so* chic. Could you arrange for me to dress her too?"

"I'll try," I sighed.

If I could ever get hold of her, that was.

❦

I'd called Lauren again after getting the divorce shower invitation. Although I'd been able to leave a message this time, she'd never called back. I'd almost given up on her, but with this Thackeray–Alixe business I tried again. I left her another message later on that day but expected to hear nothing, and went home, as I'd predicted, having not heard a peep from her. However, I imagined that Milton, being her "best friend," would be able to pin her down. I zipped home from work to find Milton already installed on the one, shameful-looking sofa in my drawing room. He was wearing a heavy orange kaftan thrown over white linen pants, in the manner of a 1970s Palm Beach hostess. When I walked in, he raised his eyebrows pitifully, inclining his head toward the dismal seating arrangement.

"I can't believe you persuaded the doorman to let you in." I said when I saw him. I flung my bag on the floor and collapsed next to him.

"I would describe your furniture as exhausted, but this place is . . ." Milton paused and looked around the airy drawing room, taking in the high ceilings and the original fireplace, "chicenstein. Totally chicenstein."

The apartment might have been empty, but it was indeed chicenstein, to quote Milton. Aside from the huge drawing room, there were three bedrooms, a maid's room, several bathrooms, a dining room, a library, and a good-size kitchen.

"What a space." said Milton, rising and pacing the room. "Three exposures! Good lord. What do you want herringbone floors for when you've got original terrazzo down here?"

"I don't really know where to start in here," I said, suddenly feeling overwhelmed by the work ahead.

"This is a beautiful room with great bones. What about eighteenth-century-Italian-inspired pale celadon wallpaper, hand blocked with silver bouquets of roses?"

"That sounds lovely . . . but maybe a little over the top for us." I replied, trying to be polite. I felt a little perturbed: hand blocked anything sounded alarmingly pricey. "What else can we do?"

"Sylvie, I have a better idea. Farrow and Ball Pink Ground—

I'm obsessed with it. It's the softest pink paint from Eng-land, it would look so . . . *Chatsworth* in here. We shall not go wallpapering in this room. The view is the décor. Look at it!"

Milton, of course, was completely right. I walked across the room and unlocked the French windows, which open onto three delightful little ornamental balconies. From there all you see is the breezy, sun-blanched treetops of Wash-ington Square Park and, above that, endless blue sky. Still, this had gone too far, I thought. I did not want a decorator, I reminded myself.

"Milton," I said, "I don't think I can afford you." Surely that would put him off.

No answer. I turned to find that Milton had left the room. A few moments later I found him wafting like an orange cloud around the master bedroom.

"I think that look—done but not *done*—undone done—is what you want. Unstudied. Like you did it yourself. But you did it yourself with utter perfection. You need an antique headboard in here, hand-painted Chinese wallpaper, and Jan Sen side tables—"

"—Milton, I can't possibly hire a decorator," I said. "I love your ideas, but I'm just not that kind of girl."

"Well, I'm a gift from Lauren, so you have no choice about it anyway," he replied, heading toward the kitchen.

"What?" I said, following him in an alarmed fashion.

"I'm decorating your apartment. Lauren knew you'd never hire me yourself, so she's hired me for you. Isn't that adorable of her? Not to boast, but I'm brilliant at it, so it works for all of us. Glass of champagne?" he said, opening the refrigerator in the kitchen.

Without waiting for an answer he popped the cork on a bottle. He poured two drinks. We clinked glasses.

I took a sip, resigned: the Milton Effect was operating at

a high level. It's amazing, isn't it, how little it takes to be persuaded that something you have long opposed is actually the best idea ever. Milton had me seduced within minutes, mainly by convincing me how lovely it would be for Hunter if he came back from Paris to at least three properly finished rooms—the kitchen, master bedroom, and the drawing room—and pointing out that I couldn't possibly achieve that myself in under a month. He was right. Milton, I knew, was manipulating that part of me that wanted to surprise Hunter with some old-fashioned, non-career-girl, newlywed-style homemaking. I knew a comfortable home would make Hunter happy, particularly if he wasn't expecting it, but I also knew that I didn't have the time to pull it off. I had to admit to myself that the Chinese wallpaper did sound divine, and Milton told me he had the most amazing secret sources for wonderful furniture. In my head I was already planning a surprise birthday party here for Hunter—it would be a great entertaining space when it was finished.

"Well," said Milton, draining his glass, "this is going to be a breeze. It's really just a cosmetic job. I think we can complete the main rooms by the time your husband gets back. Where is Hunter, anyway?"

"He's in Paris. He's working on locations for this new show," I replied.

"How marvelous," said Milton. "I must hook up with him when I'm over there next week. I'm going on a buying trip and then to visit Sophia. She has the most *fabulous* family place on the Ile St. Louis."

"I'm sure," I said.

"She's going to show me the Bourbon Palace in the countryside. No one's been in it for forty years, but she *is* secretly a Bourbon, so she's arranged it. You know she'd be queen of France if it wasn't for all that ghastly business in 1789."

"Milton, are you seeing Lauren at all?" I asked, changing the subject. The mention of Sophia was an unwelcome one, and I had other things on my mind.

"I'm going over there tonight before I leave for Paris."

"Can you get her to call me?" I said. "I really need her help with something for work, but I can never get hold of her."

"I'll tell her to call the second I see her," said Milton. "She's probably sitting in her house at this very moment all lonely, not returning calls."

5

Friends You Can't Count On

That night my cell phone started ringing at something like half past God knows what time. Maybe it was 3 A.M., I don't know. I dozily picked it up, hoping it was Hunter calling from Paris.

It was Lauren. She sounded wired.

"God, he's just left," she gasped. She was wide awake.

"Who?" I asked sleepily.

"Sanford, of course."

"No!"

"I know. It's way too late for a married man to be at a divorced girl's house. Especially a cute divorced girl. I had to virtually call his own security to get rid of him. Do you like that new gardenia oil everyone's suddenly wearing? It makes you smell like Hawaii."

"What?" I said.

"Do you notice how I constantly A.D.D. from one subject to the next?"

"What did Sanford want?" I switched on the light and sat up a little in bed.

"Oh, you know, *that . . . Of course,* I didn't do a thing, which made him crazy. I don't do married men, I think it's un-chic. God, I'm sorry it's taken me so long to call you back. It's totally my fault. I've been really sick actually, couldn't do a thing. Anyway, what do you think of this whole gardenia oil thing?"

"I love it, but I don't know where you get it," I said.

"Bond No. 9. You can have mine. I really can't stand that everyone's gone all gardenia crazy downtown. Milton says I have to wear a gardenia in my hair the next time I throw one of my dinners, and that I should go barefoot. You should come to the next one."

"I'd love to—"

"—sorry," she interrupted. "Can you hold on a second?"

Lauren broke off. In the background I could hear another phone ringing. Lauren picked it up.

"Yes, darling . . . I miss you too," I could hear her saying. "Oh, Noopy-Noo, no . . . can I call you back? What time is it there? . . . OK? Later."

She came back to the telephone.

"Oh! Drama-erama." She sighed.

"Who was that?"

"Why don't we have lunch tomorrow?" said Lauren, ignoring my question.

"Sure," I said. I could ask her about Alixe Carter then. "Where?"

"Let's decide in the morning. Can I call you at eleven?"

Lauren called me absolutely on the dot of eleven the next morning at the studio. Frankly, I found her punctuality surprising and somewhat encouraging. Maybe Lauren wasn't as terrible as she claimed, after all.

"God, I'm not late, am I?" she said when I picked up.

"No. It's literally one minute before eleven," I answered.

"You're going to think I'm absolutely the flakiest girl ever, but I have to cancel our lunch. I'm so gutted."

So was I. What was I going to do about Thackeray's dress project?

"Is everything OK?" I asked.

"Oh, God, it's totally fine, but, well, it's complicated. Lunch just isn't even vaguely possible."

"I was wondering if you could help me with a work thing? Do you want to go for tea instead?" I suggested hopefully.

"Oh, that would be so nice. But I can't. I'm stuck in Spain."

Lauren was in Madrid. Of course she was. Lauren, I soon came to realize, found staying in any one place longer than a heartbeat physically and emotionally impossible. Still, it was certainly ingenious to be in New York in the middle of the night and in Madrid the next morning. How had she gotten there?

"Privé," she said in a low voice. "It wasn't Sanford's plane or anything. It's this friend of mine. He booked a plane to go to Madrid last night and kept bugging me to go, and I guess at like 3 A.M. I thought it might be nice to spend the weekend in the mountains here. They've got the most fabulous horses, and I was desperate to ride, but now I'm here I wish I was having lunch with you. I'm sorry. Do you hate me?"

"No, don't be crazy. What are you doing there?"

"Put it this way. Phase one of the Make Out Challenge is

accomplished. One down! I had a Make Out with a Matador. I'm *totally* over him already."

Lauren was as giddy as a schoolgirl. This was certainly rapid progress. Then she sighed and said, "The thing is, Mr. Madrid, who really is a part-time bullfighter, looked divine over the kedgeree on the plane last night, but now I'm in his weird house in the hills with him, and the plants are giving me total claustrophobia. There're so many palm trees in the courtyard it's like *The Day of the Triffids*. But in the pursuit of my goal I must suffer it." Lauren now sounded as solemn as a nun who has just taken a vow of celibacy. "He's the first Make Out of my plan."

"What was he like?" I asked her.

"Put it this way. Matador Make Out really took it out of me. Kissing a Spaniard is icky. They literally suck your tongue, like they want to swallow it. Ugh! I'd have an American who did that arrested. Needless to say, the shaved sable from Revillon, you know, the little pea coat with the antique buttons, is en route from Paris. I'm hoping it'll be back in New York before me. I must mark each Make Out with a huge surprise for myself, *n'est ce pas*? After all, kissing a strange man is *agony*. The foreign saliva and everything . . . it's like lukewarm oatmeal."

"Ugh!" I laughed. "You definitely deserve a major fur."

"God, I have to get out of here," declared Lauren, "I'll call you the second I'm back in town. Sending you a big kiss."

I don't usually mind about a girl being flaky, or canceling lunch, but Lauren took the Flaky New York Girl thing to the edge of acceptability. Let me explain. A certain amount of flakiness, last-minute canceling, letting-down, and general uselessness in the friendship department is the norm in New York among a certain set. The fact is that very pretty, well-to-do girls are allowed to let everyone else down more than their less attractive, less liquid counterparts. Lauren had taken the art of flakiness to another level. She constantly let people down, but with such charm that her flakiness was not only widely accepted but considered rather alluring. Still, what wasn't at all charming were the next two days I spent at the studio, with Thackeray constantly asking if I had gotten hold of Alixe Carter yet.

The next thing I heard from Lauren, a few days after Milton had come over, was via messenger. That Thursday I was working from home and keeping an eye on Milton's army of workers (who, I must say, had done wonders in only a few days) when a package arrived with a lilliputian envelope on top. It was of the palest pink, and inside was a matching postage-stamp-size note on which was written, in hot pink ink,

Sorry! Lunch 1 pm Blue Ribbon? xxxx L

There is nothing like composing an apology to leave a New York girl feeling slightly unhinged. This surely explains the current vogue for monogrammed note cards of dimensions so diminutive (2″ by 3″ is the smallest currently available) that they are barely able to contain more than four words. *Divine dinner darling! Cecile x* is about the most you can get on a card, and that's if you use both sides. Some unkind people have started to say that Manhattan girls favor minuscule writing cards with no room to say anything because they have nothing to say.

The thing about Lauren's flakiness is that it's all-encompassing. It's not just about canceling. It also includes making brand-new arrangements that are as last-minute as last-minute cancellations. When a flake springs "plans" there is no recourse, because they are probably plans you are extremely interested in having.

For a moment, while reading Lauren's chic little card, I felt like telling Lauren that I already had plans. Meanwhile, I grumpily unwrapped the little package. Inside was a heavy glass bottle of the Bond No. 9 gardenia oil perfume—named, incidentally, New York Fling. There was also an old-fashioned atomizer, very chic, covered in orange calfskin with a bright green squirter on top. I couldn't help being thrilled by such a decadent item. I decanted the perfume into the atomizer and sprayed a little on my wrist. It smelled delicious. Maybe I didn't have plans after all.

I called Thackeray and warned him that I might be gone the whole afternoon. He thought it was worth it if we could get Alixe into a fitting in the studio. God, I thought, as I dressed for lunch later that morning, I hardly knew Lauren, and now I was going to have to ask her to help me out of an embarrassing situation involving her very close friend. I threw on a new pair of chocolate brown velvet Hudson jeans and a white cashmere car coat. If my emotional state was anxious, I hoped my outfit disguised it.

Much to my surprise, Lauren was already at Blue Ribbon, on the corner of Downing and Bedford, when I arrived. She was sitting at a round table by the window of the cute little restaurant. She was draped in a ruffled mocha-colored chiffon dress. Despite the autumnal chill in the air, her legs were bare, and she had pastel pink Jimmy Choo alligator mules on her feet. A soft green fox fur stole was thrown casually over her seat back. She looked remarkably rested for someone who had flown across the Atlantic twice in as many days. As I walked over to her, I scanned the restaurant. There were at least four girls in white car coats, I noted, disappointed in myself. In New York the fashion cycle is always on fast forward. In any other American city it takes at least a season for something to be "over." Here, it takes just one lunchtime.

"You look like Jackie O," said Lauren when I reached her. She got up, hugged me, and kissed me on both cheeks. "I *love* that coat."

"It's hideous. *You* look amazing," I replied, kissing her back.

"Ugh! I look horrible," said Lauren, pulling at her dress. "I feel like a hog."

Although both of us looked fine, it is compulsory for lunching girls, wherever they are in America, to swap compliments on the other's incredible fashion sense. They must then swap remarks of a self-loathing nature about their own style. You learn the script in high school, right after the pledge of allegiance. The main point is never to ad-lib and mistakenly accept a compliment.

When that was out of the way we sighed simultaneously and sat down. A waiter came up and took our order—two Cokes, steak frites, no salad.

"I'm starving." said Lauren. "Let's get right down to it. What can I help you with?"

"Well, it's about your friend, Alixe, the one who invited me to the shower."

"That's so weird. *I* was going to ask you something about Alixe," said Lauren, looking surprised.

"What?" I said, suddenly intrigued.

"No, you ask first," said Lauren, smiling.

I just came out with it and told Lauren the whole sorry story, from start to finish.

With that, Lauren picked up her cell phone, dialed Alixe Carter, and ordered her to wear Thackeray Johnston to her ball in January. From what I could gather from the conversation, Alixe Carter did whatever Lauren told her.

"Done. Alixe will be at the studio for a fitting this Monday, September 20th, at 2 P.M. I'll wear Thack to her ball too if it helps," she promised, snapping her phone shut. "Oh, God, delicious, thank you," said Lauren as a waiter appeared with two Cokes. Lauren drained hers in two seconds flat, as though she hadn't drunk in month. "Isn't Coke the most delicious thing in the world? I've tried giving it up a thousand times, but I absolutely can't. It's easier quitting smoking, which I also can't do."

A few minutes later, the waiter brought our food and set it on the table. Lauren looked at hers and said, "Can I just get a radish salad?" and handed it straight back to the waiter. Then she said, "I was going to ask you a huge favor, to help me out with something—"

"Of course," I said. "You've just done me the biggest favor ever."

"I want you to be my maid of honor," said Lauren with a sweet smile.

"You're marrying Matador Make Out?"

"No. For my divorce shower."

"I'd love to," I said. It sounded hilarious.

It soon became clear that Lauren's main directive for the maid of honor was for her to ensure that no husbands were brought to the event. Each guest must bring one eligible man, as specified on the invitation, but a "good one," as opposed to one of a handful of known walkers who reappeared year after year on the party circuit, mainly because they were unmarriageable. A "good one" was defined as a man in possession of an interesting, high-paying career, although the higher paid the career, the less interesting it needed to be.

Computer work was OK, for example, if you were Mr.
Skype. Other requirements included a full head of hair, real
estate ("No renters," Lauren decreed), and, if possible, an in-
heritance.

"Not that I'm looking for a husband," said Lauren coyly.
"I'm only looking for Make Out Number Two. The main
point is that the divorce shower is a smoocherama where
the divorcée finds herself in a room of married women and
single men. Zero competition. Oh, except I might have a se-
lect few of the Debutante Divorcées there . . . Salome, and
Tinsley . . . they're *so* fun. God, I hope you don't mind organizing this at the last minute. I can give you a list of guys.
I hope I'm not being too . . . *flaky*," she said.

"It's not flaky *at all*," I said, thinking, *How could anyone be
flakier?*

6

Husband-hunting

*W*as there something slightly dangerous, I asked myself later that Friday night, when I'd got home after my impromptu lunch with Lauren, about a new wife like me organizing a husband-free party that was celebrating a divorce? Something was bothering me. It wasn't that I felt guilty exactly, but I did have some sense that it wasn't quite appropriate for a newlywed to be involved—or to be quite so thrilled with her role. The truth was, I secretly found other newlyweds insufferable. The divorce shower, I thought, would be a marvelous antidote to the bourgeois fixations of newly married couples, who seem unable to discuss anything other than the Waterworks tiling in their new kitchens or their attempts to "try" for a baby. Episiotomies and ovulation cycles should be banned as conversation topics after 7 P.M. in mixed company. It makes everyone feel queasy.

Early that evening I called Hunter—it must have been eleven o'clock his time—to tell him about the divorce shower.

As long as my husband knew what I was up to, I was doing nothing wrong. And if he said he didn't want me involved, I'd quit as maid of honor.

"Darling, can I call you back later? I'm still at dinner," he said when I got through on his cell.

I could hear lots of jollity in the background, and several American and British accents. It sounded as though Hunter was having fun.

"Yes, of course. Miss you, honey," I said, putting down the phone.

I wasn't going out that night, so I decided to eat dinner in bed, watch an episode of *Entourage* I'd missed, and wait for Hunter to call back. This felt deliciously decadent. Hunter absolutely forbids eating in bed—he thinks it's indecent or something—but I think it's unbelievably civilized. It felt amazing to be bed-bound, eating Chinese food in a vintage silk nightdress, with no one to worry about. Before Hunter could call back, I had fallen asleep. He must have known not to disturb me, because when I woke up that Saturday morning, he still hadn't called.

As soon as I had roused myself I called Hunter at his hotel. He was living—in some style, I imagined—at the Hotel Bristol when he was in Paris. It's one of the nicer old hotels there.

"Monsieur Mortimer is not 'ere," said a rather curt Frenchman at the other end of the line. "'E not 'ere all day."

I wondered what he had been doing. Wistfully strolling the streets of Paris thinking of me, I hoped. Maybe he was buying me unbelievable handmade lace camisoles at Sabbia Rosa. Except I hadn't told him about Sabbia Rosa, and we all know that husbands have to be told exactly what to surprise their wives with. I made a note to myself to mention it, extremely casually, the next time I spoke to him.

"Can you give Monsieur Mortimer a message when he gets back?" I said.

The reception desk put me through to a voicemail, where I left an overly long, lovey-dovey, missing-you type message involving sending many smooches over the line to Hunter.

"Kiss-kiss-kiss darling."

Next I called Hunter on his cell. It rang a few times, and then there were three beeps and a voice said, "Please. Try. Later." I called back a few times, but the phone obviously wasn't working. Maybe the French made it impossible for U.S. cell phones to function there, just like they did everything else American. Oh well, I'll email him, I thought. I sat in my dressing gown at the desk Milton had provided for Hunter in the library and typed the following:

Dearest darling husband,

Your wife misses you very much. She has been sucked into a terrible Debutante Divorcée plan involving non-husbands and hopes you don't object. By the way, if you are in the Rue Des Saintes Pères and are uncontrollably drawn toward a store called Sabbia Rosa, do follow your instincts and go in, as your wife loves Sabbia Rosa–type surprises. Call me, baby!

xxxx S

Having come clean about the divorce shower, I went to bed dreaming of Sabbia Rosa satin. On Sunday morning, Hunter still hadn't called, so I rang the Bristol again. The hotel operator took a little while trying to find Hunter's room, and then announced, "There is no Monsieur Mortimer staying here. He must have checked out."

"No, he's definitely there," I insisted. Where else would he be?

"I check again . . ." there was a pause and I could hear the operator tapping at computer keys. "No. It says here he checked out on Friday. 2 P.M. *Au revoir.*"

The line went dead. I slowly hung up. My stomach suddenly felt like a cement mixer. Hunter had checked out? Where was he? That Sunday, for the first time in my brief marriage, I started to seriously wonder about Hunter. I adored him, but did I really know him after six months? Hunter had only been gone a week or so, but could I trust him? I felt myself sinking into a ghastly Sunday-ish depression as the day went on. Even a chirpy call from Milton saying he'd found the most beautiful antique chandelier at Les Puces didn't cheer me up. Who cared about lighting your house with Venetian crystal when there was no husband to be lit by it?

"Have you seen Hunter?" I asked.

"Er . . ." Milton stuttered.

"What? What is it?"

"Haven't even caught a glimpse of him. The chandelier is wonderful—"

"—if you see him can you, maybe, the thing is . . ."

Completely unexpectedly, I burst into tears.

"Sylvie, what is it?" said Milton, concerned.

"I just need to speak to him. I can't find him, and it's all suddenly really stressful, this whole . . . being married thing."

"Well, I know we're seeing him tomorrow."

"We?"

"Sophia's arranged it."

Sophia. The Harajuku-slash-almost-queen-of-France girl, with legs.

"Why has Sophia 'arranged it'?" I asked, slightly peeved.

"We're all going to some restaurant in the rue Oberkampf. I think she got the table."

⋙❦⋘

Monday was not a good day. Hunter still didn't call, I couldn't track him down, and on top of that Alixe Carter never showed up for her fitting. I was sure I'd heard Lauren confirm the date and time—2 P.M., Monday September 20th. But Alixe didn't telephone, she didn't email, and her cell went straight to voicemail. Annoyed, Thackeray spent the entire day angrily sketching gloomy Oscar gowns that, hopefully, no actress would be doomed to wear. I, on the other hand, buried my head in the accounts in a poor attempt to distract myself from my own anxiety.

By the time I finally heard from Hunter that evening I was into the emotional false-positive stage of the whole not-hearing-from-your-husband drama, where you have cried and fretted and finally emerged relentlessly cheerful. I'd even told myself a million times, to the point where I almost believed it, *I don't need a husband anyway*. It was almost seven in the evening when he called.

"Hello, darling," I said cautiously when I heard his voice. My heart was beating a million miles a minute.

"I've been missing you like mad. Where were you all weekend?" he said.

"Where was *I*? I was wondering where you were. I called you, like, fifteen times. Where did you get to?" I said irritably. I felt a little annoyed suddenly.

"Here," said Hunter. "Where else would I be?"

What? This was bizarre.

"The hotel said you checked out," I replied.

"That's odd. I was here all weekend. I couldn't call when

I wanted to because . . . I had endless business . . . meetings and then with the time difference . . ."

"I wonder why they said you weren't there," I said, trying not to sound accusatory.

"The hotel must have made a mistake," said Hunter. "Now, about that divorce shower of Lauren's . . . I think you should definitely be the maid of honor. And I want a full report of all the evil goings-on that night."

"Oh, absolutely." I laughed. Maybe everything was all right.

"And about that other item . . . Sabbia Rosa . . . nice store—"

"—did you get me something?" I asked excitedly.

"I couldn't possibly divulge, darling . . ."

"Darling, I'm sorry," I said.

"For what?"

How could I have not trusted Hunter? Going to Sabbia Rosa like that after only one tiny email hint was admirable husband behavior. The mixup this weekend was obviously the hotel's fault. Still . . . it was *odd,* the whole thing. But . . . well . . . what did it matter? I was probably just being overly paranoid with Hunter away for such a long time and everything.

"For missing you so much," I lied.

"I think about you all the time. I keep thinking Paris isn't really Paris without my beautiful wife beside me."

"You're my favorite," I said. He was. Period.

"So, listen, I found the most amazing location last week for the country house scene. It's this fantastic old chateau, about two hours north of Paris."

"How did you find it?"

"Milton. He called out of the blue last week, and we had breakfast at Café Flore. We got chatting about interiors. He mentioned that Sophia had shown him this incredible space, so I took a look. The whole team's up there now working on it."

"How nice of Sophia," I responded—very generously, I thought.

Then something struck me. Hadn't Milton just told me yesterday that he hadn't seen Hunter yet? Maybe I'd misheard him. Still, I felt a little peculiar suddenly.

"Yeah. She's a useful contact here. Look, I must run to dinner, we're all meeting up. I'll say hi from you."

"Lovely," I said and hung up.

Why was everyone, including The Woman Who Only Dates Husbands, having dinner in Paris with my husband when I was in New York? This was all wrong. I must plan a weekend in Paris, soon.

7

The Divorce Shower

Alixe Carter's parties always live up to her nickname: Spenderella. Spenderella is the only girl in New York under thirty-five who can honestly say that she has a ballroom, which is the location for her annual New Year's ball. She says, and honestly believes, that she paid for her palace on Charles Street with royalties from her Arancia di Firenze soap line. Even though everyone knows that Alixe's husband, Steve, actually pays for everything with revenues from his chain of casinos, this is never mentioned by writers from women's magazines or Alixe's coterie of slavishly devoted girlfriends, a.k.a. the ladies in waiting.

"Did I overdo the pear blossom? Or underdo?" she asked with a worried expression as Lauren and I arrived, just after midnight, at the penthouse suite of the Hotel Rivington, the location for the Divorce Shower. She was wearing a white Ungaro gown, printed with crimson poppies. It perfectly suited her floral theme. "If anything's wrong, I *completely* blame Anthony Todd, whom I *adore*. He did the flowers, you know."

Anthony Todd, had, as usual, wildly overcompensated on the $60-a-stem pear blossom front. The absurd price was justified by the fact that pear blossom is completely out of season on October 2nd, which was, of course, the main reason Alixe wanted it. (Now that status handbags were gauche accoutrements, status blooms filled that gap in her life.) The rumor was that she'd done more damage to New Zealand's pear orchards to create her spring garden than McDonald's ever did to the rain forests. "Rebirth!" declared Alixe, explaining the reason for creating a spring blossom orchard in the fall, although everyone knew the only criterion Alixe ever used for deciding floral themes was that the latest one should be more glaringly costly than the last.

"It looks amazing, Alixe," I said, reassuring her.

"Sylvie Mortimer? So thrilled to finally meet you. Bon divorce, girls," she squealed, turning to greet another guest.

Alixe didn't mention the missed dress appointment. Nor did I.

"Right, let's get alcohol fast," said Lauren, leading the way to the bar. "Two champagne on the rocks, in tumblers," she said when we arrived. "I read somewhere that Fred Chandon used to drink it like this. Isn't that glam?"

The barman poured our drinks, and Lauren handed me one.

"Can you see anyone cute here?" she asked as her eyes scanned the room. "Do I look tacky?"

Lauren's flawless outfit conformed to the unspoken dress code of the Hotel Rivington—unreconstructed black tie. She was wearing a cloud-gray, floor-length, ruched Tuleh dress, with tiny white polka dots. A jacketini—a small, barely shoulder-length garment made of approximately half an inch of illegal monkey fur—covered her shoulders. Her eyes were framed by false eyelashes and lashings of kohl, and her hair was falling in unbrushed waves around her shoulders. I, on the other hand, was dressed in one of Thack's most demure white lace dresses. I wanted to make it quite plain that I was not on the prowl for cute guys.

"You look really great," I told her.

"I feel weird," she said, her eyes darting around the mass of guests. "It's all way too cool in here for me."

The party wasn't exactly your typical girly shower (thank God). The wraparound glass windows of the penthouse, through which you could see the streetlights shimmering red and orange below, were a glittering backdrop for the party scene. Here and there I could make out silhouettes of men with their arms wrapped around girls' waists, little groups perching on tiny sofas that had been brought in for the night, and intimate twosomes lounging on giant fur poufs that were scattered about the party. There was even already some kissing going on beneath the pear blossom, whose blooms were so lusciously puffy they looked fluffier than whipped cream.

"Who's *that*?" I asked.

Right next to me a very exotic-looking girl was propped up on a bar stool, frantically kissing a dark-skinned man. She was edging him farther and farther back against the bar. It looked incredibly uncomfortable for him. As he was pressed backward, a skullcap suddenly fell off the back of his head and plopped onto the bar. He didn't notice, and Lauren and I tried hard to stifle our giggles.

"That's Salome Al-Firaih. She's known," whispered Lauren archly, "as the Middle East Peace Plan Divorcée. She's never not kissing someone of the opposite religion. She's unbearably cool. I'm modeling myself on her."

With that, Lauren stepped over to Salome and tapped her on the shoulder, saying,

"Salome. You should be careful. This isn't Geneva. This is the Hotel Rivington."

"Lauren! I'm *busy*," hissed Salome, barely unlocking her lips.

Salome resembled a Middle Eastern Sophia Loren. Her skin was the color of an overpriced Fauchon praline, and her shoulder-length black tresses glistened like an oil slick. Bambi-length eyelashes framed her jade irises, and her décolletage was corseted into a very revealing frock. She had the classy Arabian bombshell look down.

"Salome, you've got to be discreet," said Lauren to Salome's hair. She sounded slightly bossy.

Salome glanced up momentarily and winked naughtily at Lauren.

"Darling, happy divorce!" she said. "Why be discreet when everyone knows everything anyway?"

The "everything" that "everyone" knows is that Salome, a twenty-eight-year-old Saudi princess, had married Harvard-educated Faisal Al-Firaih, a nephew of the king, when she was twenty-one, in an arranged marriage. A few years after they wed, he brought her to New York, where he was taking care of family business. About a year ago he'd had to go back to the Middle East for three months, which was when Salome discovered Bungalow 8, the after-2 A.M. private club favored by downtown royalty. Meanwhile, Manhattan disovered Salome, and Salome discovered she loved being photographed. Although she looked as sophisticated as a panther, Bungalow 8 was only the second nightclub Salome had ever been to. She went man-crazy and vodkatini-mad, and hoarded Bungalow 8 slippers as though they were art. One night she was spotted making out with Shai Fledman, an American–Israeli property guy. Unhappily, Faisal read about his wife the next morning in Page Six Online under the extended headline "The Saudi-Princess-Israeli-Hunk Diaries." He called Salome from Riyadh, said, "I divorce you. I divorce you. I divorce you," and that was it. Under Sharia law they were instantly divorced. Now Salome's dating the Jewish guy. Her parents won't speak to him. His parents won't speak to her. Salome's parents won't speak to her either, which is why Salome calls herself the One Woman Road Map.

I couldn't stop staring at Salome, partly because of her show-stopping performance in the kissing department, but also because she seemed to glow from within. Thackeray, I thought, would love to dress her if Alixe Carter didn't work out, which was looking less and less likely. Salome was far more intriguing than a movie star or TV celebrity.

"She'd be great for Thackeray," whispered Lauren.

"Exactly what I was thinking," I said under my voice.

Lauren literally dragged Salome off Shai, amid much giggling and hysterics. She gestured toward me.

"I want you to meet my friend Sylvie," said Lauren.

"Hi," said Salome. "I love your dress."

"Thanks," I said.

I would call Salome next week and get her into the studio. I had to be smarter about this one than I had been about Alixe. A waiter glided by with a tray of champagne.

"Want some?" I asked Salome.

"Nope. Champagne doesn't do *anything*. I only drink spirits. Vodka shot, please," she said to the waiter.

"Coming up," he replied, and headed back toward his station.

Just then, a very in-proportion pregnant person—as far as I can gather, the only kind of pregnant people allowed out at night in Manhattan—appeared. She had a glossy ponytail and was wearing skinny jeans and a ruched peasant top. Her belly was as neat as a cantaloupe underneath it.

"Lauren! My eligible man's already with someone else!" she said excitedly.

"Phoebe Calder. God, I so appreciate you being here. Midnight's really late for a pregnant lady. You look really thin," lied Lauren.

"I feel like a sideways camel," lied Phoebe.

"I wouldn't even know you're pregnant," lied Salome.

Just then the waiter appeared with an entire tray of vodka shots. He put them down on the little table beside us. Everyone except Phoebe took one. Shai, miserable now he was no longer glued to Salome, took two.

"Phoebe, have you met Sylvie?" said Lauren.

Phoebe smiled warmly at me. I hadn't met her before, but her name sounded familiar. She blinked a little shyly, and then said, "I've known Hunter since I was a debutante. I heard you did the secret wedding thing. Congratulations on nailing him. He's devastatingly handsome. What a player he was. Ooooh, he was wonderful."

"Yes, he's pretty wonderful," I agreed, ignoring Phoebe's other observations.

Salome, who, I decided, was a more sensitive soul than her appearance would suggest, rapidly changed the subject. "When are you due?" she said, between vodka shots.

"A month or so. We just came back from our last trip to Europe. Dr. Sassoon would have had me arrested if he'd known I was still flying. Sylvie, we spotted Hunter in London. Two weekends ago. He's still madly attractive, madly."

"Paris," I corrected her. "He's in Paris."

"Well, we saw him in London. Ooops."

What was Phoebe talking about? Hunter was in London? Two weekends ago? But . . . my mind whirred back. Was that

. . . was that the weekend I hadn't been able to get hold of Hunter? My breath caught in my throat. I tried to scramble through my mental calendar, piecing together dates . . . it was almost exactly two weeks ago, wasn't it, that I had been unable to track down Hunter . . . although, who knew what two—or was it three by now—vodka shots had done to my diary skills? This was ludicrous. Phoebe was talking nonsense.

"He was in his hotel in Paris all weekend," I said firmly. "Business meetings."

"Absent husbands! Ha ha ha!" laughed Phoebe. "I never see mine either. It's wonderful."

Sensing an awkward atmosphere, Lauren asked, "How's your baby line going, Phoebe?"

"Eeeuuch! It's *such* hard work. My samples are in Shanghai. They should be back next week."

"Excuse me, I'm going to the restroom," I said, and exited quickly.

When I got there I locked myself into a stall. *Had* Hunter been in London? Why would Phoebe say that? More importantly, if he had been there, why hadn't he told me? Suddenly I heard the door to the ladies' room bang open. Someone knocked on the door of the stall, and I came out to find Salome and Lauren peering at me with concern in their eyes.

"There you are," said Lauren. "Don't worry about Phoebe; her brain's totally mushed when she's pregnant. There's no way she saw Hunter in London. She just loves to stir things up."

"Really?" I said. I hoped Lauren was right.

"Yes," said Salome. "The only thing Phoebe ever says is, 'My samples are in Shanghai!' It's her mantra. They've been there two years."

This wasn't quite true. Phoebe was an extremely successful, if notoriously ambitious, baby-wear *creatrice*. But it was sweet of Salome to pretend she was a total loser.

"Come on back out. I want you to meet someone," said Lauren, tugging me by the hand.

The "someone" was Sanford Berman. (His second name had been shortened from Bermothovoski when his family moved from Russia to America in 1939). He was sitting awkwardly on one of the fur poufs in his suit and tie, sipping Perrier. Despite being the ancient, Jello-bodied mogul type, he oozed powerful-man charisma. He seemed to know everyone, and everyone wanted to know him. Phoebe was circling his pouf like a famished lioness when Lauren and I walked over, but as soon as Sanford saw Lauren, his focus shifted. It was as though he'd trained a searchlight on her. He couldn't see anyone else.

"Ah," he said, holding his hands out to Lauren, who took them in hers. Sanford remained pouf-bound, and Lauren sat down next to him. Everyone else stood around, looking down at both of them. "The most beautiful girl in New York." Sanford raised one of her hands to his lips and kissed it.

Sanford was completely and utterly, madly, whatever you want to call it, in love with Lauren.

"Sanford, I want you to meet Sylvie," said Lauren, gesturing toward me.

"Nice to see you," I said, shaking Sanford's hand. It felt like a cold pack.

"If you're Lauren's friend, you're my friend," said Sanford amiably.

Phoebe peered at Sanford expectantly, but he didn't say anything to her. Sanford turned back to Lauren, and said, "My dear, I have a business proposition for you."

"Finally. You want me to find something for your lovely wife?" asked Lauren.

"No, it's for me."

"I hope you're gonna spoil yourself."

"Remember those Fabergé cuff links I lost at auction—"

"—wait!!!" interrupted Phoebe. "The same thing happened to me. When I lost a Lalique gorgon pendant at the Phillips auction, I was physically sick. I went to the doctor and said, I'm going to die. And the doctor said, if you want to live you must buy the gorgon. So I bought it from Fred Leighton after the auction for double the price, and here I am. Alive."

Everyone looked at Phoebe. She suddenly blushed and said, "I'm really focusing on my business. My samples are in Shanghai, you know."

"We know," said Salome. "Let's go get dessert."

Salome and Phoebe disappeared and Lauren and I were left with Sanford. He turned and fixed her with a commanding look.

"I'm serious, Lauren. I want to own the Nicholas II Fabergé cuff links. I haven't a clue who's got 'em now."

Sanford, I learned, had surprisingly exquisite taste. Owners of Fabergé cuff links can barely hold on to them right now, they are so desired, even with price tags of $80,000 and up. If they'd looked Tsar Nicholas, or possibly Rasputin, in the face, they were even more sought after. For Lauren, the more difficult the commission, the more crazed she was about pulling it off. She once told me she usually spends more money on private planes in pursuit of the jewels than she ever makes in profit, but, as she says, what else is she going to do between lunch and dinner?

"I can find them for you," she said, "but, Sanford, there's no knowing if the owner will sell."

"You could persuade a man to give you his entire portfolio just by blinking at him," said Sanford flirtatiously.

Lauren laughed.

"I'll try my best," she said.

"Thank you, my darling," said Sanford. He kissed her on the cheek and wobbled shakily off the pouf to leave. "I have to go, but keep me posted, OK?"

Lauren nodded, and looked after him as he left the room. She seemed a little wistful.

"He's cute," she said.

"He's *completely* in love with you," I told her.

"Pshhht," she said, laughing. "He's such an awesome friend. This is a brilliant project. Those cuff links are so rare. For once I feel really excited about something. Other than my sex life."

⁂

"Darling, it's Sylvie," I said.

"Honey, you're up so late. What time is it there?" said Hunter.

It was 3 A.M. in New York, 9 A.M. in Paris. I was standing in the kitchen, wide awake, phone clenched in my hand. There was no way I could sleep when I got home after Lauren's shower. I was too freaked out about what Phoebe had said, though I couldn't admit it to myself earlier.

"I just got in from Lauren's divorce shower. It didn't even start till midnight."

"Go to sleep and let's speak when you wake up," said Hunter.

"Hunter, I'm missing you masses," I said.

Since that difficult conversation a couple of weeks ago, when Hunter had gone AWOL from his hotel, everything had returned to normal. I had almost forgotten about the whole episode, and Hunter had been sweeter than ever, despite his absence, calling to chat whenever he could. I half didn't even want to mention what Phoebe had said tonight. But I had to.

"I met an old friend of yours tonight. Phoebe?" I said.

"I haven't seen her in years. How was she?" asked Hunter.

Years? What about a couple of weeks ago, I thought. Internally steeling myself, I replied, "Very pregnant. She said she saw you two weekends ago, Hunter." I paused, then added, "On your secret trip to London."

There was a silence at the other end of the phone. I angrily opened the fridge and poured myself a glass of champagne from an open bottle. I took a sip. Nothing happened. I didn't feel delightfully dizzy. Maybe Salome was right about champagne: it didn't work.

Suddenly Hunter said, "Phoebe! She never talks any sense. Her hormones are probably all over the place. I *did* see her, at Chez Georges in Paris, with Peter, her husband. She's huge."

"Why did you say you hadn't seen her for years?" I demanded.

"Sylvie, darling. I love you very much. You have *nothing* to worry about."

Had I mentioned being worried? Why did he suddenly think I was worried? Did that mean I really *did* have something to worry about?

"I'm not worried," I lied.

"Good. So stop worrying and go to bed. Forget about Phoebe. She's just a pregnant flake. Would you mind going out to dinner with her and her husband when I'm back?"

❧

Is it possible, I wondered as I lay in bed that night, for a marriage to be briefer than Liz Taylor and Nicky Hilton's? Six weeks in, and I was already worrying about what my new husband was up to while he was away on business. But you go to a divorce shower, and suddenly the world is full of wicked husbands and boyfriends, and then you wake up (late) the next morning and your husband's a saint. What had I been thinking last night? I was not the next Liz Taylor, and Hunter had not been lying to me. He had made it very clear that he had seen Phoebe, but in Paris. Phoebe had simply made a mistake, due to her pregnancy. Maybe being around all those divorcées had made *my* brain mushy.

Over the next few days I busied myself with work and the finishing touches on the apartment. Milton's team had worked miracles, and we suddenly had a stunningly beautiful apartment. Hunter was due back in a few days' time, and I was dying to see him. He was going to love the apartment, I was sure of it. I could barely think of anything else. Work was a good distraction. I managed to get hold of Salome, who was sweet and gracious when I spoke to her and said she would love to wear Thackeray to Alixe Carter's ball. We arranged an appointment for a week away. Thackeray loved the sound of her, saying, "I've gone beyond Alixe Carter anyway. A Saudi princess is so much more *now*."

A few days later, Milton arrived at the apartment staggering under the weight of two chandeliers he'd brought back from Paris. I helped him set them down in the hallway, and then we did a "walk-thru" of the apartment, as Milton called it. It looked gorgeous, and we ended our tour in my favorite spot, the kitchen. It now had pretty cream cabinets, mirrored back splashes, and a bright red silk blind at the window with a chocolate brown grosgrain trim. There was an old oak farm table in the middle of the room, with vintage bamboo chairs scattered around it. Milton had insisted on little red silk wall lamps instead of those recessed spotlights everyone has.

"You need an Aga in here. The new white one," said Milton. "Then it'll be really cozy." He looked at his watch, seeming rushed. "I can't stay long. I'm leaving for Uzbekistan in the morning. Following in the footsteps of Diane von Furstenberg and Christian Louboutin. Three months on the Nouveau Silk Road. To work on my Target furniture line. I won't be back till January. How do you like the apartment?"

"I love it. I can't wait for Hunter to see it," I said happily.

"Look at you, you're so cute," said Milton. "You're so in love with him, aren't you?"

I blushed a little and nodded.

"No one I know is in love with their actual husband anymore," said Milton. "Even the gay guys."

"That's terrible," I said. "Iced tea?"

I poured two drinks and emptied a bag of chocolate chip cookies onto a plate. Milton grabbed one and perched on one of the chairs.

"Mmmm," grinned Milton.

"Did you have fun in Paris?" I asked, leaning against the countertop.

"Oh, yes. The Sophia family *château* was *a*-mazing."

"Hunter's using it for some scene, right?"

"Yup. He was *very* smart to hire her."

"He *hired* Sophia?" I asked, astonished.

The notorious Husband Huntress was working for the husband? Surely Milton's brain had gone *very* mushy. There is no way Hunter would have hired Sophia, particularly without mentioning it to me. We always discussed everything going on in his company.

"Are you sure?" I gasped.

"Don't look so worried," said Milton.

"I'm not worried," I said, almost choking on my cookie.

Sometimes I think marriage should come with an FDA warning.

"Sylvie, Sophia is dating Pierre Lombarden, you know, that guy who's always in *Paris Match*. He's best friends with the Monacos. I think he's got connections in government. She's not after Hunter. She gets bad press because of her *a*-mazing legs. Everyone's *so* jealous of her. You've got nothing to worry about."

I felt reassured. Milton was right. Amazing legs are nothing to worry about.

8

Paranoia Party

"You've got *everything* to worry about," shrieked Tinsley. "I'm more afraid of Sophia than I am of Saudi Arabia withholding oil, I swear."

I'd just told her the news about Hunter hiring Sophia.

"Hush! Tinsley!" chided Lauren. "The main thing, Sylvie, is, worry, but don't let your husband *know* that you're worried. Just freak out silently inside. Don't spiral into total paranoid fear, even if it means talking to yourself and telling yourself everything's OK when it isn't. That's what I did when my marriage was falling apart."

"But my marriage isn't falling apart," I insisted, wondering, *Is it?*

I was sitting with Lauren and Tinsley in the oval-shaped gallery at the Carlyle Hotel the night before Hunter was due home. This is where Tinsley likes to come for a "paranoia party," as she calls it. She thinks the place is soothing. Indeed, there is nothing as calming as relaxing deep into one of the Carlyle's red velvet armchairs, nor is there a sight more reassuring than that of a white-jacketed octogenarian waiter with a linen napkin thrown at precisely ninety degrees over his left arm. But that night I felt like nothing could calm my sense of mounting anxiety. The only things that vaguely cheered me up that evening were Lauren and Tinsley's outfits. They'd gone nuts at Chanel earlier that day. Tinsley had come away with plus fours and a tweed jacket, and Lauren was wearing a severe black coat fastened tightly at the neck with a huge ruby brooch by James de Givenchy. "I'm channeling Nan Kempner," she said, "and Tinsley's the gamekeeper."

A waitress approached our table. She had an incredible red bouffant hairdo and was wearing a little black dress and high, black patent heels. She walked with a pronounced bounce, as though she were in a Broadway dance troupe.

"What can I get you ladies?" she said.

"Mini-hamburgers," cried Lauren and Tinsley simultaneously.

"I'll have a green salad," I said. I really wasn't hungry. "Shall we get some champagne?"

"Coming up," said the waitress, turning sharply on her heel.

"I don't know if I can *not* say anything to Hunter about Sophia, I mean—" I started.

"—never mention it. He'll think you're being paranoid," said Tinsley. She was fidgeting like mad. "God, tweed is so scratchy. Can you die of itching?"

"*Am* I just being paranoid?" I said.

If I was just being paranoid, that was a good thing. That meant, by definition, that there was actually nothing untoward going on.

"Not necessarily. I remember calling Louis thinking he was in New York, and there he was, in Rio with this fifteen-year-old model!" said Lauren. "If only I had been *properly* paranoid, I might have figured things out sooner."

This was awful. Why had I even told Tinsley and Lauren about Sophia? They were only making things worse.

"I say call in the lawyers now," giggled Lauren. "It's so much easier being divorced."

"Agreed," hooted Tinsley. "By the way, I've made a resolution. I'll take a billionaire or a busboy, but they've got to be under twenty-five. I've got to be trashier now that I'm single. I've been too proper for too long. This outfit is a segue; don't ask me how, but I know it is."

I didn't join in. All this joking around only made me feel doubly depressed. I didn't find Lauren and Tinsley's squealing and laughing at all appropriate under the circumstances. Tinsley prodded me, but when she saw my gloomy expression, she looked mortified.

"God, sorry. We're being terrible," she said, shamefaced.

Just then the waitress appeared with three glasses of champagne, the salad, and the miniature hamburgers. Lauren and Tinsley diligently removed the bun and the mini fries from their plates until they were left with two quarter-size burgers each. It was less food than you'd give a Smurf.

"The only weight-loss junk food in town," said Lauren, nibbling at her beef. "Super-downsize me."

"Mmm," said Tinsley, sipping her champagne. "The thing is, I don't want to confuse you, Sylvie, but you *should* be paranoid. But that doesn't mean there is actually anything *real* to be paranoid about. The truth is all wives have to be *subconsciously* paranoid, if you like. Girls like Sophia are very cunning, you know," she continued. "So even if there is nothing going on, one must always be suspicious just in case there is. A bit like with the Saudis and the oil, to get back to where we began."

"She's absolutely spot on," nodded Lauren. "I couldn't have put it more clearly myself."

⚜

As divorcées, Lauren and Tinsley were bound to be overly suspicious, I told myself as the taxi sped back downtown later that night. Sophia couldn't possibly be after Hunter. If she was as smart as everyone said, she wouldn't be dumb enough to go after him in broad daylight like that, getting a job with him. It was far too obvious.

I let myself into the apartment and went into the drawing room. I lay back on the sofa that Milton had brought over a few days ago. It was lovely, really comfortable, upholstered in faded old Moroccan tapestry. Everything was almost done, and I still had a day until Hunter got back. The only thing missing was a new sink in the bathroom, but that was going to be installed tomorrow. Eventually I got up and headed for the bedroom. I flicked on the light, and suddenly there was Hunter, sitting up in bed, smiling like crazy, and holding a little bunch of white camellias.

"Hello, darling," he said, very cool.

"Eeek!" I screamed.

I dropped my bag and flew over to him. As you can imagine, I totally melted. We had an indecent amount of very, very indecent sex, followed by at least a month's worth of smooching. We had a lot of time to make up for. At about 2 A.M. Hunter got out of bed, opened his bulging suitcase, and took out a stiff white box. When he handed it to me, I saw two delicious words—Sabbia Rosa—printed in black script across the top. Inside was a long nightdress of turquoise silk, trimmed with antique lace. I slipped it on and twirled in front of the mirror. It was very Catherine Deneuve in *Belle de Jour*.

(I say, if you're going to dress like a hooker, she's the one to aspire to.)

"Hunter, it's beautiful," I said, getting back into bed. "Thank you so much." I snuggled up to him and shut my eyes, totally content.

"My darling," said Hunter a few moments later, "where's the basin from our bathroom?"

"What are you doing home one day early?" I replied dozily. "If you'd waited till tomorrow it would have been here."

"The apartment looks amazing," said Hunter. "How did you do it so fast?"

"For the first time in my life, I got a decorator. I'm completely ashamed." I laughed.

"Well, I think it was a brilliant idea. We've got a real home. I love it. And I love you," he said, curling up around me. "Let's get some sleep."

There was absolutely nothing going on. I could tell. Hunter was as cute as ever, and he was very married to me.

⚜

"Darling, you don't have to do this, honestly," said Hunter the next morning.

"I wanted to," I said.

I'd brought him breakfast in bed, and we sat together on top of the duvet munching croissants I'd ordered in from Balthazar bakery. At about a quarter to eight, my cell phone rang. I picked it up.

"Hello, Sylvie. It's Sophia. How are you?"

"Oh. Hi," I said, slightly shocked.

"Can I speak to Hunter? It's really urgent, and his phone must be switched off. I couldn't get through to him."

I reluctantly handed Hunter the phone. Suddenly the bubble of well-being vanished and the doubt of the previous night crept back.

"It's Sophia, for you."

Hunter took the phone. While he listened to Sophia, he started to frown.

"You think there's nothing you can do? Oh God . . . no, actually I don't fancy coming back to Paris next week. I just got back to New York . . . Haven't seen Sylvie for weeks . . . Can it wait until my next trip? . . . I see. Yeah. OK. Let me get back to you," he said, and hung up.

Sophia was trying to get Hunter back to Paris already? I could feel my robe starting to cling to my suddenly clammy skin. Forgetting all Lauren and Tinsley's advice, I blurted, "Darling, why didn't you tell me you'd hired Sophia?" I was trying very hard not to sound horribly jealous.

Hunter looked surprised. "I've only hired her to help with the permits for filming at the chateau. Her boyfriend, Pierre, is something high up in the Paris town hall, and she said she'd get him to help out. We were having so many problems. I thought I ought to pay her something. It was inappropriate her doing all that work for free. She's very connected in Paris, you know."

"So everyone says," I responded a little coldly.

"I hope I don't have to rush back there," sighed Hunter. "Look, if I do, would it make it up to you if we made a very long weekend out of it?"

"Yes, darling, of course it would," I said.

It would, I was sure of it. I shrugged off my slight feeling of irritation. I had absolutely nothing to worry about, I told myself. I quelled an urge to check with Lauren and Tinsley as to whether I should be suspicious about the invitation to

Paris. Was this a bluff? No, they would only convince me that Hunter and Sophia were going to rendezvous. I had to stop listening to them. After all, I was the happy wife, they were the singletons. Marriage was *infinitely* preferable to divorce.

9

The UnGoogle-able Man

Everyone working at A La Vieille Russie, the discreet jeweler on the corner of Fifty-ninth Street and Fifth Avenue, looks like they just died. Inside, the place feels more like a mausoleum than a jewelry boutique, with dusty, meringue-thick moldings and lights trained on glass cases housing "important" Russian gems. Lauren adores the place. She thinks it's the finest jeweler in New York because it's so old-fashioned and un-starry. It was to be her first stop in her search for the Fabergé cuff links, and a few days later, she persuaded me to accompany her there.

"I'm wearing this new perfume called Park Avenue," she said on the way uptown in the car. "I'm trying to seem uptight, to go in there. That's their thing." Having said that, Lauren didn't look uptight: she was wearing a vintage, cerise Giorgio di Sant'Angelo dress that plunged almost to her waist. She was dressed for Studio 54, not Fifty-ninth Street.

After the divorce shower, Sanford had given Lauren specific details about the cuff links he wanted. He said they were "the

mother of all Fabergé cuff links," given to Tsar Nicholas by his
mother, the empress dowager, on Easter 1907. They were egg-
shaped, yellow enamel, with the imperial crown worked in the
center in gold filigree. The genuine pair had an inventory
number scratched on the back with a diamond, which was
only visible with a loupe. Sanford had lost them to an un-
known telephone bidder, but Lauren suspected that the staff
at ALVR could find the buyer or may, possibly, have bought
the cuff links anonymously on behalf of one of their clients.

Sanford had always wanted, being Russian, to own a
piece of Russian history. He'd also heard Tom Ford collected
Fabergé cuff links, which made him feel very much OK
about spending over $100,000 on two pieces of yellow
enamel that each measured less than half a square inch.

"Ah, yes, I do know of the Easter cuff links," whispered
Robert, the corpse-slash-salesperson in the store that morning. He spoke quietly, as though he was afraid of waking the
dead.

"Yeeaay," said Lauren, as quietly as she could. "I knew you
guys would find them for me."

"Miss Blount, we have no idea where the cuff links are
now," said Robert. He started tidying a few things on his desk,
as though that was the end of the conversation.

"Who bought them?" I asked.

"We can't talk about our clients, miss," said Robert with
a disapproving glare.

"Robbie, stop it!" said Lauren. "Come on, please, I have a
very important client who will pay anything for them. He lost
them at auction and he's devastated. I could cut you in on the
deal."

"Miss Blount, the answer's no. Now, if you'll excuse
me—"

"—can I try this?" interrupted Lauren.

She was leaning over a glass case, pointing at an antique turquoise and diamond bracelet that was shaped like a serpent. Robert sighed.

"Certainly, Miss Blount," he replied, unlocking the case and delicately lifting out the object.

Lauren put it on and slid it up her arm as far as it would go, Egyptian-style.

"Oooh," she breathed. "Oooh. Oooh. Oooh."

"It's awesome," I said.

"It's twenty-two awesome big ones as well," she said, looking at the price tag dangling under her arm. "I'm not sure, Robbie—"

"—No doubt we could work something out for you, Miss Blount. You are a regular client," said Robert, watching Lauren like a hawk.

"Could that something include the mysterious Mr. Fabergé cuff links?" Lauren was deadpan, suddenly all business.

Robert huffed. He tipped his head to one side. He glowered slightly at Lauren.

Then he beckoned us to follow him into a back office. It was cramped, with a huge leather desk piled with books, jewel cases, and sketches of gems. Robert somehow squeezed himself behind the desk and tapped at an ancient-looking PC. A photograph of the cuff links appeared on the screen. They were beautiful and delicate, and the yellow enamel was so intense it seemed to glow. Underneath, a few particulars were listed:

Price: $120,000
Client: G. Monterey
Payment type: Bank Transfer

"G. Monterey," I asked. "Who is he?"

"We never met him. Someone called on his behalf, the money was wired, and the cuff links were taken to the Park Hyatt in Moscow. They were very secretive," explained Robbie. "Wouldn't give us contact numbers. That's normal with many of our clients based in Russia. It's so dangerous, no one wants you to know anything about them. Now, Miss Blount, how would you like to pay for the bracelet?"

⁂

"I can't believe you had to buy that bracelet," I said to Lauren when we were in a taxi heading back downtown.

"I'll bill it to 'the client'," said Lauren cheekily. "Sanford wants those cuff links so bad, he doesn't care what it costs him. And I suspect," she said, with a raised eyebrow, "my research is going to be quite costly."

I laughed. Lauren didn't get away with murder, she got away with homicide.

"Sanford is actually an angel, you know," she said. "If he wasn't married—twice—with two small daughters, and God knows how many other stepkids, I might, you know . . ."

"Really?" I said.

"—actually, I just don't know if I could imagine—" Lauren paused. She looked over to the driver to make sure he wasn't listening and then whispered "—it would be like making love to a waterbed."

"Oh, God, Stop," I begged her. "You're totally out of control."

"My sex life is. What I would give for a young, unmarried, weight-loss Sanford. If only he had a son."

As the cab jerked us down Fifth Avenue, I rifled in my bag and pulled out my BlackBerry.

"OK, now I am going to find the mysterious G. Monterey," I said.

Despite the lurches of the cab I managed to type GOOGLE into my BlackBerry, and then the name G. Monterey.

"Why don't we go to Moscow to find him the first weekend of November? It's the ice polo. It'll be fun," said Lauren.

I was tempted. I'd heard Moscow was crazily fun, and that everyone in fashion was doing amazing business there. Maybe I could score some commissions for Thackeray.

"It could be great, but can I let you know? I might go to Paris with Hunter then."

"So everything's good with him?"

"He's been adorable since he's been back," I said.

"So sad you won't be joining our ranks," said Lauren. "Just kidding."

Suddenly a message popped up onto the BlackBerry's screen. It read, *Your search—G. Monterey—did not match any documents. No pages were found containing "G. Monterey."*

"That's annoying," I said.

Lauren looked over my shoulder at the message and frowned. She took the BlackBerry from me and tapped at the little machine a few times, trying several different versions of the name. Nothing came up.

"The UnGoogle-able man. God, how attractive," she said finally. "I must hunt him down in Moscow."

"What's happened to the Make Out plan?" I asked.

"Maybe Monterey can be Number Two," said Lauren.

"What if he's seventy-nine years old?" I asked.

"Of course he's not," declared Lauren. "I can feel the vibe. I'm *madly* in love with him already."

10

Gorgeous West Village Wives

Gorgeous West Village Wives, as an indigenous tribe, are pretty much at the top of the New York food chain right now. Their natural habitat—specifically, the terrace at Pastis, the doorway of the Marc Jacobs store on Bleecker Street, and the stone steps outside their own West Ninth Street townhouse—seems like a little Manhattan paradise all its own. No wonder it's jammed with tourists all weekend now. The out-of-towners just stand there, open-mouthed, gazing at the G.W.V.W.'s blinding white teeth and wonderful hair, which is always shiny and swinging back and forth with the regularity of a metronome.

Liv Tyler, Olatz Schnabel, SJP—you can barely get a lunchtime table anymore at Saint Ambroeus on Perry Street for all the glamorous mommies and their buggies. These girls have fantasy careers (movie star being a fav), wear vintage Spanish ponchos to get coffee at Jack's on West Tenth Street in the mornings, and never seem to leave the house without their epidermis glowing in the manner of a girl who has just had spectacular sex. They ooze happiness and contentment even while pushing a Bugaboo Frog on six-inch Roger Vivier heels.

I can honestly say there is nothing quite as demoralizing for a newlywed than bumping into one of these extraordinary creatures at seven o'clock on a cold night on your way home from work. It hurts, it really does.

A few days after Hunter had gotten back, I'd decided to cook dinner at home. We were both exhausted from work and needed a cozy night in. Thack and I had been working long hours finalizing our spring order book, and Hunter had been locked in script meetings till late at night. I popped into Citarella on the corner of Ninth Street and Sixth Avenue to pick up some delicious Italian food for the evening. Just as I left the meat counter, I remembered that we had run out of Drano, so headed toward the back of the store to get some. As I was scanning the shelves, I started adding some more household items to my cart—Soft Scrub, toothpaste—all the domestic products that seem to be required in ever-increasing quantities once you are married. It was depressing actually, I thought, as I piled detergents and dishwasher powder into the cart.

The fact is, marriage comes with an awful lot of non-sexy, non-romantic projects. Like Drano shopping. However cute my new husband was, he went through way more toilet paper than I did. For every six-pack of Charmin I lugged home, I felt a kilo of energy, that, pre-marriage, would have been allocated to love or sex, dissipate into the void of the supermarket checkout. New wives are never allowed to admit it, but being wed is, sometimes, a grind. Even a few weeks after your wedding. Sorry, but it's the truth.

Last night, for example, I had found myself, against my own free will and better judgment, discussing how to deal with Hunter's laundry over dinner with him. Prior to marriage, the only reason to discuss the washer-dryer over dinner was if you were intending to have sex on it. Then, later on, just as we were falling asleep in bed, Hunter had said to me, "Darling, I love you very much. Where are those hiking socks I got in Telluride?"

Is this really the sort of thing that married couples discuss in bed, I'd thought, miserably. Shouldn't we have been making love? Hmm, I'd thought to myself as I drifted off that night, this wasn't at all like an Eternity ad: the truth is, domestically speaking, being married is more like being in one of those suburban sitcoms like *Everybody Loves Raymond*. No matter how Eternity-ish a husband looks, they all have one or two horrific habits. Hunter's was leaving shaved bristles caked onto the sink. Even more horrific, someone (you) has to point it out and request their removal. No one ever explains that in marriage there is no getting away from chores—even if you are lucky enough to have a housekeeper—and that chores do not put you in the mood for sex.

Sex, I thought wistfully, as I dragged a box of trash bags off the top shelf, *sex* and . . . dry cleaning. I glanced at my watch: 7:30 P.M. I needed to finish up here and get home. There was a whole bunch of Hunter's cleaning being delivered at 8:00 that I needed to pay for.

I schlepped everything to the cash register. I hate to admit it, but my heart sank when I realized I was on line behind Phoebe Calder. The epitome of the G.W.V.W., she looked glowing. She was carrying a chic-looking parcel of French cheese in one hand and one of her own pale yellow PHOEBE BÉBÉ bags in the other. Her bump was hidden by a short tweed cape, and she had impossibly skinny Kate Moss–style jeans on underneath. Her brown hair looked so polished I could virtually see my reflection in it. I had to say hello to her,

I thought, slightly gloomily. It would be rude not to. I tapped her on the shoulder.

"Hi, Phoebe," I said.

Pheobe turned and looked at me. She peered at my overflowing cart. There wasn't even a blink of recognition in her eyes. Suddenly she gasped, "Sylvie! Is that you? I didn't recognize you for a minute there. With all that cleaning stuff."

No wonder I was unrecognizable. I wasn't having nearly as much sex as before. Hunter and I used to make love every day when we were dating, I was sure of it. Now, by my estimation, it was every three nights. Was that bad? Excellent? Average? Was that how often the Eternity couple did it?

"How's married life, Sylvie?" said Phoebe, as we waited on line.

Why is this the only question anyone ever asks you once you are married? What are you supposed to say? Maybe I had post-marital depression, I thought to myself grumpily. Surely if you could get post-natal depression, you could get the married version.

"*Wonderful*," I replied, because that is what you are supposed to say.

Do you have sex with your husband between eating glamorous French cheese and making unaffordable baby wear? I wanted to ask.

"Does Hunter travel as much as he used to for work?" she asked, as the line snaked forward.

"Barely at all," I lied, thinking how little I'd actually seen of my husband since we got married. I didn't want to open up the conversation and have Phoebe regale me with more Hunter-on-the-loose stories.

"I do hope I'll see you tomorrow," said Phoebe, putting her cheese on the counter. The clerk swiped it through.

I looked at her, confused.

"At my new store. The Baby Buggy luncheon? Everyone's coming. Lauren, Marci. Spenderella. It'll be *so much fun*," said Phoebe in a voice that implied everyone *must* have fun, or there would be severe consequences. "Didn't you get the invitation?"

Baby Buggy luncheons are, among a certain set, the most exclusive charity baby events in town, peopled by billionaire mommies and their disciples. Their messiah is Jessica Seinfeld, Baby Buggy chair, mother of three, wife of Jerry. How does *she* have time to wear a different Narciso Rodriguez dress every time she goes out, throw Baby Buggy luncheons, have sex, and get manicures, I wondered.

"Forty dollars, miss," said the girl at the cash register.

Phoebe handed her a hundred dollar bill. Then she said merrily, "This cheese is *sixty-four dollars a pound*. This place is daylight robbery, daylight robbery."

She smiled happily. There is nothing a woman like Phoebe adores more than being daylight robbed in front of a new acquaintance.

"I'll count you in for tomorrow. One o'clock. All the tickets are gone, but you don't need one. You're my guest."

This wasn't an invitation. This was an order.

❧

By the time I got home that night, I had decided, rather than be depressed by Phoebe's glittering wifeliness, to be inspired by it. There was no point, after all, in making myself miserable wondering where exactly one got chic little tweed capelets, or how on earth eight-months-pregnant people could fit into Kate Moss jeans: it was much better to take a leaf out of Phoebe's book and make an effort to be glowing for one's husband rather than gloomy. I would cook Hunter a delicious risotto, and change into a new jersey dress I'd bought a few days ago from Daryl K before he got back. It had a slightly offbeat cut, which made me feel a little avant-garde and sexy. Phoebe was right, I thought to myself, as I slipped the dress on. Being a wife was infinitely more enjoyable in good clothes.

Just as I was starting to chop the onions, the buzzer rang: that must be the dry cleaning. I rifled in my bag for some money and went to open the door. Jim, the Chinese delivery boy from World Class Cleaners on Ninth Street was standing there weighed down with a pile of Hunter's suits and my evening dresses. I helped him in with them, and he laid the whole lot over a chair in the hall.

"Thanks," I said. "How much is it?"

"Eighty-five dollar," replied Jim.

I gave Jim ninety and told him to keep the change.

"Thanks, miss," he said, tucking it in his belt.

"See you next time," I said, holding open the door.

Jim was almost out the door, when he turned and said, "This in Mr. Mortimer pocket, miss."

He shoved something into my hand and disappeared off down the corridor. As I shut the door I looked at what Jim had given me: it was a small, clear plastic Ziploc bag. It looked like it had a bunch of receipts in it. That was nice of Jim, to rescue Hunter's bills, I thought. As I went to put the bag on the hall table for Hunter, something caught my eye on the receipt at the top of the stack. Was that . . . I picked the bag up again and looked closer through the plastic. Was that a £ sign printed on the top receipt?

It couldn't be, could it? Anxiety enveloping me, I tore open the bag and grabbed the receipt. It read,

BLAKES HOTEL
33 Roland Gardens
London SW7
17th September

Room charge: £495.00
Room service: £175.00
Mini bar: £149.00

Mini bar! *Mini bar?* Hunter had drunk three hundred bucks worth of alcohol! In a hotel room! In one of the sexiest hotels in London! I felt myself panic: I checked the date again, wracking my brain. September 17th. Two weeks before Lauren's divorce shower. It was That Weekend, I was sure of it, when Hunter had been impossible to get hold of in Paris. Phoebe *had* seen him in London. Hunter had point-blank lied to me and, worse, blamed an innocent, pregnant woman's mushy brain.

My hands were trembling. Maybe I was getting MS, I feared, regarding my wavering fingers. Maybe my husband had *caused* me to contract MS by his callous hotel-hopping activities. This was hideous. What was I going to do? Should I call Hunter now and tell him I had found him out? Or was I too emotional? Should I call Lauren and tell her what I'd found? Or would she call in the lawyers then and there? Maybe—

"Hello, darling."

I jumped. I had been so wrapped up in my thoughts I hadn't noticed Hunter slip into the apartment. Before I could say anything, he was kissing me hello and stroking my hair, as though he could see I needed to be calmed down.

"Oh, Sylvie, what a great dress this is on you," said Hunter. Noticing the pile of clothes he added, "Thank you for getting the dry cleaning. You really don't need to . . . you're so busy. I could have picked it up."

I didn't say a thing. Anyone ever hear of something called domestic un-bliss?

11

Socialite Baby

$\mathcal{I}$ can't say I was really in the mood for Phoebe's Baby Buggy luncheon the next day: all I could think about was that London hotel bill, and what on earth I was going to say to Hunter. But when I told Thack I was too busy at the office to slip out to Phoebe's lunch, hoping he'd agree, he did quite the opposite and pressured me to go. Alixe Carter was a patron of the Baby Buggy charity, and he wanted me to try and nail her down for another fitting—she had never bothered to call us after not showing for that first fitting, even after I'd met her at the Divorce Shower.

Phoebe Bébé, situated on the corner of Washington and Horatio Streets, right next to the Christian Louboutin boutique, exactly matches the store's shopping bags. All the walls are painted pale yellow, and the trims are dove gray. When I arrived at the shop, it was already crammed with glossy-haired, baby-buggy-mad moms shopping for $750 cashmere bootie and cap sets aimed at the six-week-old demographic. Meanwhile, Phoebe was in the middle of the store with three publicists, who were orchestrating photographs of her and her friends in front of mounds of yellow, logo'd baby product.

"Have you met Armenia?" she hollered at me as I walked up to her.

Phoebe was dressed in a long, gold vintage Halston dress with just enough give for her bulging belly. She had a tiny satin purse in one hand, and in the other was clutched a six-teen-month-old child. Somehow, she was simultaneously sipping a glass of water.

"Ooooh! She's going to be a supermodel," shrieked one of the publicists at the child. "Quick. Photo. Photo? OK. Lemme take that drink from you."

While Casey Silbert, the aforementioned publicist, snatched her glass, Phoebe professionally contorted her face into a maternal but youthful smile for five photographers who appeared, snap-snap-snapped her, and vanished, like human shooting stars.

"Good girl," said Phoebe, jiggling the child on her waif-like hip. "We call her Meni for short."

"What a sweet name," I said.

"Isn't she *amazing*—"

That second there was an explosion of flashes from the back of the store. Phoebe's head swiveled, mid-sentence, in the direction of the glittering light.

"Look! There's Valerie with Baba. I think it's short for Balthazar," said Phoebe, rushing off in the direction of another glamorous girl whose baby was squished photogenically into a fur-lined Baby Björn on her front.

The fact was, the only people anyone was taking any real notice of were the cherubic babies in the crowd, of which more kept arriving. This is, though, the era of Socialite Baby. Rarely older than eighteen months, Socialite Baby attends only the grooviest events—art galas, exclusive movie preview dinners, fashion shows (front row only. What's the point of bringing your baby if you're in the second row and no one can see it?). Before it is barely three weeks old, Socialite Baby has ninety-six Google entries, knows its way around the dressing rooms at Yoya Mart better than its own cot, and has met Kate Winslet's kids at least three times at baby music class at Soho House. The identifying marks of a bona fide Socialite Baby include bluish-black craters beneath the eyes and an exhausted green tinge to the infantile skin. If you don't recognize one at a party, no matter—Socialite Baby is so heavily photographed you can always identify one a few days later by flicking through the pages of *Gotham* or *New York* magazine, in which there are usually at least three Socialite Babies showcased on the party pages.

Hmm, I thought, scanning the room. There was no sign of Alixe Carter. Maybe Phoebe would know where she had gotten to. I headed through the throng of girls toward her, feeling less and less glossy the deeper into the party I got. Judging from the spectacular array of outfits here, I was the only girl who'd come from an office. I had thrown a beautiful embroidered coat of Thack's over my jeans when I'd left work, but I couldn't compete with girls who'd been at Blow all morning getting hair and makeup done.

"Seen Alixe Carter?" I mouthed at Phoebe across the mass of women crowding around her.

"She just went to the restroom. Spenderella's had to take a break!" Phoebe yelled back. "She hasn't even got kids, and she's bought three gold satin diaper bags. She just can't stop herself."

"Thanks," I said, and headed toward the "Powder Room" sign at the back of the store.

Phoebe's powder room looked like a charming guest bed-

room. A small sofa upholstered in white cotton printed with
yellow roses sat invitingly at one end of the room. A heavy,
gilt-framed, antique mirror hung above the basin, and a
huge vase of yellow roses stood in front of it. Piles of yellow
sugared almonds were heaped into little silver dishes. Small
bottles of water had labels printed with the words EAU BÉBÉ
in silver lettering. It was all soft pseudo-French perfection,
even though Phoebe wasn't the slightest bit French. She was
(secretly) from Miami.

There was no sign of Alixe Carter. I was rather relieved.
I was so wound up about the hotel bill that I really wasn't in
the mood for sweet-talking a woman like her right now.
Maybe I could have a break in here from the madness outside, I thought. The bathroom was occupied, so I collapsed
into an armchair, in, I suppose, a sort of personal sulk. What
was I going to do? I kept asking myself over and over. There
was only one outcome if I confronted Hunter, I thought with
dread. But I couldn't *not* confront him . . . or could I? Why
couldn't I just gloss over the suspicious hotel bill, forget it?
Is that what wives did?

It was in this disconcerted frame of mind that I noticed a
giggle-giggle-giggle sound drifting to my ears from behind the
bathroom door. Then a husky, cigarette-hewn voice whispered, "I fucked him standing up in the hallway. Adorable
Nicky. When I asked him how old he is, he said, 'I'm *going* to
be nineteen.'"

My ears, I'm ashamed to admit, perked up.

"Eew! Where does he live?" said another voice.

"On 117th Street, with his mom and dad."

"You are trash. Trash."

"I know. I *love* it."

I couldn't figure out who owned the cigarette voice, but
it was soon obvious who the other party was: Lauren. Slowly,

a silver twist of cigarette smoke crept from under the restroom door.

"Gross!" shrieked the Lauren voice.

The door opened and Lauren tumbled out, followed by
a fog of smoke and Tinsley, who, cigarette between her lips,
was almost unrecognizable. She was wearing tight black
leather trousers and a white blouse, the most noticeable feature of which was the amount of bosom it revealed. She had
a diamond-studded Cartier watch on her left wrist and huge
pale pink diamond studs in her ears. It was a bizarre evolution from her gamekeeper incarnation of a few days ago.

"Sylvie, I'm so glad you're here," said Lauren when she
saw me.

"Look at me." said Tinsley, without removing her cigarette. "I've turned into Kimora Lee Simmons. I'm getting
much younger guys with this look."

"It's worth it, then," I replied, amused.

"This powder room is the best spot in the store. Please,
can we not go back out there? I'm really enjoying fiddling
with my makeup in here," said Lauren. "I adore Phoebe, but
she's insane. I mean yeah, like, there's really fifty zillion kids
who are dying to get their hands on that $20,000 baby-llama-
hair sleeping blanket."

Lauren and Tinsley each grabbed a bottle of baby water
and squished onto the sofa opposite me. Tinsley nonchalantly emptied a dish of the sugared almonds into the trash
bin and flicked her cigarette into the pristine silver tray. She
clocked me clocking her.

"Phoebe likes me being bad. I'm her only outlet. She's so
... *well-behaved*. I don't understand her," she declared, looking confused. Tinsley opened her purse and dug out a mascara wand and a tiny hand mirror. "This looks *très* Kimora

if you load it on like cement," she said, starting to apply the eye makeup.

"You are not going to believe what happened to me last night," said Lauren, looking at me.

"What?" I asked.

"She had five orgasms," interrupted Tinsley.

"How can you be *positive* it was five?" I asked.

A girl has to be sure of the exact amount of orgasms she's potentially missing out on by being married.

"Because last night there were precisely five condoms in the packet. And this morning there were precisely none, and I came every time," declared Lauren, matter of factly. There wasn't a hint of embarrassment about her.

"Who is Five Orgasms? Does he have a name?" I inquired.

"Yes, but I can't remember it. Two down on the Make Out Marathon! I've ordered a new, white Kelly Mu with rose gold hardware to celebrate Number Two. God, he was unbelievable! That was more orgasms in one night than I had in my *entire* marriage," squealed Lauren, opening her makeup purse and rummaging around in it.

"I thought it was a . . . Make Out Challenge," I teased her. "Kissing only?"

"I'm not in high school any more," said Lauren. "Divorcées like . . ."

"Fucking," said Tinsley absentmindedly. "Lauren, have you got that sticky lip gloss I like in your purse? Chanel Sirop? Nicky adores it. It glues me to his face. We've got a daytime rendezvous in half an hour. There's going to be a lot of f—"

"—enough," interrupted Lauren. "Sylvie is a respectable married girl. She'll die if she hears you talk about that one more time. Here." She handed Tinsley a pink stick of lip gloss.

The truth is that in New York wives make love, girlfriends have sex, and divorcées fuck. The opportunities in the city for such activity are endless. After all, there's a luxury hotel every inch of every block, usually with excellent fucking facilities included in the tariff. The Playground, the most expensive suite at Soho House, has a bed the size of France, a bath bigger than the Pacific, plus a shower that is as whooshy as Niagara Falls and shoots water at you from every conceivable angle. It's booked up every Saturday night between now and 2007 by divorcées. Lauren's Make Out Challenge seemed to have evolved in the last twenty-four hours into a lip-gloss and condom-dependent, sex-without-commitment competition with Tinsley.

"It's my fault. I'm a terrible influence," said Tinsley. She was swishing the lip-gloss wand back and forth, back and forth, over her lips. They seemed to visibly swell and pinken every time. When she was done they looked like two plump little cocktail sausages. "This stuff is genius. Doormen, beware! God, am I so tacky or what?"

Tinsley had gone boy-mad, boy being the operative word. She was currently very much "enjoying herself," as she liked to put it, with her eighteen-year-old doorman, the aforementioned Nicky, as well as with her twenty-one-year-old FreshDirect delivery guy, who was generally given access to her building by the aforementioned youthful doorman. Tinsley was thrilled with her Mrs. Robinson–style Love Triangle and relished the logistical complications.

"What about Moscow Make Out?" I asked Lauren, thinking of the UnGoogle-able man. "Does he still count as Make Out potential?"

"I'm obviously still *completely* madly in love with him," Lauren smiled. "I think I'm on to him. His first name is 'Giles.' Isn't that a hot name? He's going to be at the ice polo next month, I'm sure of it—"

"—who's 'Moscow'?" interrupted Tinsley, suddenly alert.

"No one," said Lauren, starting to open her compact and mouthing "Don't say anything" at me.

"So, listen, I have some very unfortunate news about Marci," declared Tinsley.

"I know it already," said Lauren.

"What?" I asked.

"She found Christopher in bed with her *ex-college room-mate*. At least that's the rumor being spread out there by the Baby Buggy chair, Valerie Gervalt," said Tinsley.

"No," I said, shocked.

"All the signs were there. He was really vague about all those business trips, and Marci didn't think anything of it—fool. And she found a locked drawer in his desk—always a *major* indicator of infidelity. Then, he didn't notice her new Rochas gown. *Six thousand dollars on his credit card and he didn't notice!*"

"Is she OK?" I asked. "Maybe I could go visit her. Poor Marci."

"She hasn't eaten in four days. She looks like a prisoner of war. She's thrilled. She hasn't lost that much weight since her bout with anorexia in 1987," said Tinsley.

"Stop being so cruel, T.," said Lauren. "Marci's in terrible shape. She really needs her friends right now. I'm going over there tomorrow. She's well rid of that cheating creep. She'll have more fun as a divorcée anyway."

"Do you think we should go back out there?" I asked. "I'm supposed to be looking for Alixe Carter."

"I wanna see some of those cutie mommies and babies. Lauren, *you* are trash," laughed Tinsley, stubbing out her cigarette. She twirled out the door.

I didn't make any effort to get up; nor did Lauren. I popped an almond in my mouth and crunched it noisily.

"What's wrong?'

"Nothing," I lied. I wasn't sure if it was a good idea to tell Lauren about the hotel bill.

"You look depressed. Was it our conversation? Did it totally disgust you? You look *really* depressed."

Was it that obvious?

"It's Hunter's . . . dry cleaning," I said.

"What are you talking about?" said Lauren.

I sighed, and then told Lauren the truth.

"I found this . . . hotel bill in his dry cleaning. It was from somewhere he said he hadn't been. I think he's been lying to me."

"Oh, God," said Lauren slowly.

"What shall I do?'

"You should come to Moscow with me for the ice polo, and forget all about it. November 6th. Put it in your diary."

"I'm very tempted. But, seriously, what am I going to do?" I continued.

"Maybe its not what it seems—" began Lauren. "It's very un-cool to make a fuss until you're *absolutely* sure. Oh dear, you look a little tearful."

"I feel pretty dreadful," I said, trying not to weep.

This wasn't the moment to collapse in a state of distress about my husband's globe-trotting activities. Still, I felt my eyes starting to well. Pulling myself together, I looked at my watch. It was already 2:30. I decided to walk back through the party once more, and see if I could find Alixe. If not, I would go straight back to the office. The main thing was not to dwell on any of this stuff. Plus, Lauren had a point: I couldn't do anything if I wasn't sure.

"OK, I'm heading out," I said, getting up.

"I'll call you later about everything," said Lauren knowingly. "But don't go saying anything to Hunter about it."

"Good advice. Thanks," I said.

As I walked back through the store, the crowd was thinning out. Suddenly there was a tap on my shoulder.

"Sylvie? Sylvie?"

I turned around. Alixe was standing beside me, a worried look on her face.

"Sylvie, what happened about my fitting?"

How blissful to have a memory so lousy that you can actually forget that you've forgotten stuff. Deciding it was better not to mention that Alixe had missed the fitting, I said, "You can come any time."

"I am *so desperate* for a gown. I was worried Thack had . . . gone and forgotten about me—oh, look!" she said, grabbing a tiny yellow raincoat off a rack. "I've got to have this. It's amazing. Pheobe is amazing."

"I'll call you later, Alixe, and set up a time," I said.

"Lovely. Can't wait."

While I was standing at the door waiting to retrieve my coat, there was suddenly a flurry of activity. While Phoebe and Valerie were kissing everyone good-bye, Marci suddenly arrived, and kissed absolutely everyone hello, as if it were the beginning of the party rather than the end. She was fully made up, with Schiaparelli-pink lips. She was dressed in skinny, black satin pants, high peep-toe shoes revealing red toenails, and a floppy, black silk blouse with a huge bow at the neck. It was exactly like Olivia Newton-John's metamorphosis moment in *Grease*, only for real.

"Marci," I said, "are you OK?"

"I feel *amazing*," she replied. "The scoliosis has completely gone. I'm a size zero."

She was always a size zero, and she never had scoliosis, so no change there.

"Oooh, Valerie, hi—" said Marci swooping on the glamorous mother and child. "Aaah, Baba? Baba—"

There was no response from the exhausted child, so Marci poked her face nearer to it. She pushed her lips into a boiling pink pout, about to kiss Baba.

"Waaahhhhhh!" yelled Baba.

"Baba, it's only Marci—"

Baba started squawking like a chicken and thrashing around. Suddenly he turned toward Marci, at which point she leaned in closer to him. He immediately vomited. The puke globbed lumpily down Marci's silk blouse.

"Eee-uych!" yelped Marci, recoiling. "What is wrong with that child?"

"Your lipstick," said Valerie, turning away from Marci abruptly. "Babies hate . . . makeup. It negatively impacts their brain development. I have to get him away from here."

With that, Valerie exited, and Marci flushed a luminous, embarrassed red. She looked at me, worried. Then she asked, "Did that baby just snub me?"

12

Marci's Meltdown

"*Scram! Screaming Sixteen-Month-Old Snubs Scorned Socialite!*" declared Gawker Stalker the next morning. Socialite Baby can wreak havoc with a grown woman's self-esteem as no adult can. Marci went into hiding. Literally. No one could reach her, and the only person who could have coaxed her out—Lauren—also seemed to have disappeared. There were rumors that Lauren had been spotted the morning after Phoebe's luncheon at 6 A.M. in the lobby of the Mark Hotel wearing workout gear and huge sunglasses, and getting into an elevator. Apparently she pressed P.H. when she got in. The rumor was spreading fast, mainly because it was also rumored that Sanford Berman kept a permanent penthouse suite there. No one had seen her since.

I didn't believe it. The fact was, Lauren never got up before 11 A.M.. Plus, she'd told me categorically that she couldn't have sex with a waterbed. Anyway, aside from all the silly gossip, I desperately needed to speak to her: she was the only person I had mentioned the strange hotel bill to, and for the past few days it had been nagging at me, almost oppressively. Still, the last thing Lauren had said to me was, don't mention it to Hunter. Crazy as she was, I also thought that Lauren had an instinctual wisdom when it came to relationships. I decided not to say anything for now, but it couldn't last: Hunter soon sensed that I was not myself.

One night when we were lying in bed, Hunter said, "Beautiful sheets . . . perfect for . . ." He leaned over and kissed me.

"They're Olatz," I said, turning away from him. "Your cousin sent them as a wedding gift."

It's amazing what a $600, Portuguese linen, lace-trimmed, hand-sewn pillowcase *can't* do to cheer you up sometimes. I felt far too anxious for any sort of romance that night, Olatz sheets or not.

"Darling, what's the matter?" said Hunter sweetly.

"I'm fine," I said, eyes clamped shut. "Tired."

"You seem sad," said Hunter, stroking my back.

"Mmmm . . . not sad," I mumbled. Actually, I was furious. But I didn't know what to do about it.

"I wanted to ask you if you could come to Paris for a week with me, on my next trip. I'm planning to go the first week in November. Would that cheer you up?"

That was a lovely offer. But, the fact was, I was in a state about Hunter. I couldn't let him off that easily.

"I don't need cheering up," I said sulkily, turning on the light and glaring at my husband.

"Why are you frowning in that adorable, grumpy way, then?" said Hunter, looking faintly amused. "What is it?"

Hunter was so cute it made maintaining a fury with him at the level required virtually impossible. And look at him, he looked so delicious, all sleepy and snuggly lying next to me. I kissed him. Maybe I could drop all charges of misconduct, effective immediately? Maybe these overpriced linens were *quite* romantic . . .

"Come on, darling, you've been moody for days," insisted Hunter.

Maybe I *should* say something. Get it over with. Maybe there would be a simple explanation, and I could go to Paris in November with Hunter and have a lovely time. The fact was, I couldn't keep it in any longer, whatever Lauren had advised.

"Well . . . there is . . . something," I said finally. "The other day, when Jim brought back your suits, he gave me a bunch of receipts."

"What do you mean?" asked Hunter quizzically.

I leaned over the edge of the bed and opened the drawer on the side table. There was the Ziploc bag. I took it out, opened it, and fished out the Blakes Hotel bill.

"Please explain," I said, holding out the bill toward him.

Hunter examined the receipt.

"It's a hotel bill," he said. "I should have given it to the accountant weeks ago." He put it on his side table, as if there were nothing odd about it at all. "Now, how about my wife and I make full use of my cousin's over-the-top gift . . . ?"

Hunter started nuzzling my shoulder. It was amazing. He was acting like nothing was wrong. I drew away from him, upset.

"Hunter, I am trying to have a horrible fight with you!" I burst out, shoving him off me.

"What could a newly married couple as happy as we are possibly have to fight about?" he said jokily. He wasn't taking this seriously at all.

"Why did you lie to me about being in London?" I asked. There. I'd said it. Maybe that was the end of our one-minute marriage. I sat bolt upright and glared at him. Why did he look so . . . sexy . . . even when I was so angry with him. It was annoying.

"What?" said Hunter, looking confused. He sat up in bed and rubbed his hand through his hair in a slightly agitated fashion. "I never lie to you. What are you talking about?"

"When Phoebe said she saw you in London, you said her brain was mush and that she'd seen you in Paris," I retorted.

"Er . . . did I?" Hunter hesitated. He seemed to ponder a while, then said, "Hmmm . . ."

Was he trying to get his story straight? Invent an alibi? Or was I being crazily suspicious for no reason? After what seemed an interminable silent interlude, Hunter finally said, "I thought Phoebe said she saw me in . . . London."

"She did!" I said sharply. "But *you* said you had never been in London."

Now I was getting confused. Maybe my brain was the mushy one.

"Darling, I'm sorry. I'm traveling so much right now even *I* don't know where I am half the time. All those European cities merge into one. I don't mean to worry you, sweetheart," said Hunter, taking my hand and kissing it.

How London can merge into Paris I know not.

"What were you doing in London anyway, on a weekend?" I asked crossly.

"I think it was . . ."

Hunter trailed off, as though he was slightly confused. Eventually he said, ". . . that was it. Some last-minute business meeting with the UK distributors. Sorry, I must have forgotten to tell you about it. I was in London for twenty-four hours and then went straight back to Paris."

What was it Tinsley had said, about Marci's husband being "vague" about business meetings? Was this "vague" in the way Tinsley defined "vague"?

"Blakes Hotel isn't a business-meeting kind of hotel," I declared sternly.

"I know, darling. I want to take you there. It's very romantic," said Hunter.

"Please," I said frustrated.

I couldn't believe we were having the row we were having. Surely Christy Turlington never had arguments with that gorgeous guy in the Eternity ad.

"What do you mean?" said Hunter.

"I mean, I'm not a total fool."

"Oh, Sylvie, come on. You know I'm in different hotels all the time. Stop being absurd and let's go to sleep." He was getting annoyed now.

"I am not being absurd! I am justifiably wondering what my husband was doing on a weekend in the sexiest hotel in London—"

"—Sylvie. Stop. I am not even going to dignify that with an answer."

"But—"

"Shush. Now you just want to argue for no reason. I've explained. That's it. OK?"

I always knew Hunter was a man of few words, but now I found it aggravating. I thought it was completely unfair that he now seemed to be furious with me. I tried again.

"B—"

"Darling, enough," said Hunter grimly. "Either you believe me or you don't. I am telling the truth."

Maybe I had been overreacting, I thought, annoyed with myself. I was tired and stressed out from work right now, which occasionally turned me into a little powder keg. And when I really thought about it, Hunter's explanation was completely justifiable: he did travel like crazy right now, and what was one hotel versus another? It was probably all the same to him. Hunter was right, I would just have to trust him. Maybe I should take my husband up on what was a very nice offer, and not obsess so much about the little things. Paris was lovely in the winter without the tourists.

"Darling, I'd love to go to Paris," I said finally. I could definitely do some work while I was over there. We needed some stores in Europe. "I'm sorry I got so cross with you."

"We'll have a lovely time," said Hunter kindly. He never held anything against me; that was one of his finest qualities. "You come for a week, then I have to go to Frankfurt for ten days, then we'll be back in New York together."

I kissed Hunter and burrowed under the comforter to get closer to him. Suddenly I had an idea.

"You know what, I think that's right before the weekend Lauren's going to Moscow. She keeps bugging me to go with her. Maybe I'll meet her there, when you go to Frankfurt," I said. "I could do a little business for Thack, and there's some ice polo match Lauren wants to go to."

"What on earth does Lauren want in Moscow?" asked Hunter, intrigued.

"She calls it a business-pleasure trip. She's trying to acquire this crazy pair of Fabergé cuff links for Sanford, and they happen to be owned by this guy she's decided she's *madly* in love with. The one she's never met. He's called Giles . . . what was his last name? Giles Monterey, that's it. She calls him the UnGoogle-able Man."

Hunter looked at me for a second, with disbelief in his eyes. It was peculiar. Then he laughed, "The debutante divorcée and the UnGoogle-able man! It sounds like the perfect match. I predict a dazzling romance, marriage, and several children, to play with ours. Ha ha ha!"

"Lauren will never marry again," I protested. "She's having way too much fun."

"Being married is *more* fun, my sweet. We must encourage her to marry this poor soul."

"She just wants a hot date," I said. Hunter had no idea.

"Surely everyone would rather be married than divorced," he replied.

"You are the most perfect husband," I said. He was genuinely trying to be sweet.

"No, I'm not. You're the perfect wife."

Maybe we *were* the Eternity couple after all.

⁂

Marci Klugerson, it transpired the next morning, had not gone missing at all. She had been sleeping all day and watching episodes of *Medium* on TiVo all night. When she called me at the office out of the blue at around midday, she sounded so doped up it was like talking to a drug addict.

"Do you know? Where . . . Christopher? . . . is?" mumbled Marci. She sounded like she wasn't even awake.

"Don't you?" I asked, shocked.

"No . . . ," wavered the insufficient voice. "I kicked him out, and he's gone, totally . . . gone . . . away."

It was pathetic. Marci sounded like someone on a Lifetime made-for-TV movie.

"Marci, is it really true about Chris—"

"—Did Tinsley tell you that? He's definitely with someone else. He won't say who. He's said he's gonna end it, but I'm in total shock. Please come over. The only thing I've eaten for the last three days is Seroquel. It's for schizophrenia. But I don't have schizophrenia, I have . . ."

There was a sudden snuffling and rustling of tissues. Marci was weeping uncontrollably.

"Marci, I have a couple of important appointments this

afternoon at work. Can you survive till six? Then I can come over," I said sympathetically.

"Meeewwww," whimpered Marci, sounding like an injured kitten. "Lauren said she's coming in half an hour. She's been hiding out with some guy. Maybe she'll stay with me 'till you get here."

"OK, good, that's great. See you later—"

"—Waaiiit! One more thing, Sylvie . . ." Sniffle-sniffle-sniffle. "Do I get to wear Thack's clothes now that I'm getting divorced?"

❧

Marci's drawing room at 975 Park Avenue would be enough to send anyone into a spiral of Seroquel dependency, missing husband or not. She'd had it done up by Jacques Grange when she got married, which is why she was living in an apartment that looked like the inside of Notre-Dame.

When I arrived just after six, I found Marci perched on a stiffly upholstered, dark green felt sofa in her drawing room. Resting on it was a copy of Maureen Dowd's *Are Men Necessary?* She had a drink in one hand and a remote control in the other. Her eyes were glued to the TV screen. She was maniacally flicking from one channel to the next. She was dressed in an immaculate white Rochas suit with black lace cuffs and a bow at the neck, fishnet stockings, and very high red shoes. Her hair was arranged in blonde curls around her face. The tears from earlier had vanished. Her face was pale, but she looked ghoulishly beautiful, like Nicole Kidman in *The Others*. Her countenance was completely calm. She was quite obviously half out of her mind, because one thing Marci never is when she is all right is calm.

"Sylvie, hi," she said, without moving her eyes from the

screen. "Do you think I can ever go to another party down-town after that kid treated me like that?"

I sat down on the couch next to her and dropped my bag on the floor.

"Marci, I'm really concerned for you. Can I talk to you?" I said gently.

She nodded, mumbling, "Yes."

"Maybe you should be thinking about how to salvage your marriage," I told her, "not . . . party invitations—"

"—parties are important when you're . . ." Marci gulped her drink at alarming speed and then uttered dramatically, "Alone. You wanna vodka shot?"

"Where's Lauren? Shouldn't she be here?"

"She flaked. She's got that Five Orgasm guy installed in her place. She's trying to take her mind off her wedding an-niversary, which is today. She's really depressed too."

"I'm sorry," I said. Lauren's status as flakiest girl in New York obviously hadn't shifted.

"I'm sort of angry with her, but I can never get too angry with her. Lauren was so sweet to me when my mother died. She cleared the whole house out and paid all the movers' bills because I was broke then. Maybe Five Orgasms is the man of her dreams. She deserves someone great."

Suddenly Marci got up and walked over to the huge ma-hogany desk at one end of the room.

"I hate this place. I feel like I live in a Ritz Carlton hotel," she grumbled. She sat down at the desk and picked up the telephone. "Why don't we go down to the knitting café on Bedford Street?"

"Marci, darling, we should stay here," I said. "It's really cold out. Why don't I make us some rose-hip tea?"

"I did something terrible today. I tied all Christopher's

Anderson and Sheppard handmade suits to a brick and threw them into the East River," said Marci.

I had to laugh. That really was terrible. But maybe Christopher deserved it.

"Did you ever suspect Christopher?" I said.

"Of course not. He never came out with me, but I believed him when he said he couldn't socialize that much because of work."

It was true. Marci was never with her husband when she was out. I'd never even met him. All I'd heard about Christopher was that he had bright red hair. Apart from that, he was a blank.

"Never trust a man who's always on a business trip. Men do not work that hard," declared Marci. "I bet Hunter isn't always on a business trip. On the weekends and every night."

"No," I replied, with a sympathetic shudder. "But listen, Marci, you're still married to him, and whatever's been going on, you've got to consider patching it up. That's the whole point of being married. For better or for worse and everything."

"I took the 'for worse' bit out of our vows. Christopher never even noticed." Marci paused and then, brightening up a little, she said, "It's so much fun, Salome wants me to spend all next summer with her in East Hampton. She says her place is like a disco palace all season with . . . uuggghh-ggh-ggh-uuuggh . . ." Marci was suddenly hiccoughing tears, barely able to breathe.

"How about if I order in something for us to eat?" I said. "We can just chat tonight."

"OK, OK . . . yes. No! Why don't we go to Bungalow 8?"

"Marci, it's seven in the evening. Bungalow 8 doesn't even get going till 2 A.M. You're in no state to be going down there tonight. You should take some time to reflect."

"I *hate* Bungalow 8 anyway. I couldn't get in with Christopher. He was too overweight," said Marci, wiping her tears with her lace cuffs. Then, looking at me desperately, she asked, "How long does it take to have reflection, exactly? Three weeks? Could I be done reflecting by Thanksgiving?"

13

Wedding Anniversary F ♥♥♥

To: Sylvie@hotmail.com
From: Lauren@LHB.com
Date: November 1
Re: Wedding Anniversary f ♥♥♥

Darling girl,

Forgive me for disappearing. It was my wedding anniversary last week and I felt like a freakola. I thought Mr. Five Orgasms would sort me out, but try telling a never-married man you need a Wedding Anniversary f ♥♥♥. He came over after some fake-o artists dinner and then, well, put it this way, I've changed his name to The Orgasm Void. Anyway, after ninety minutes of this non-orgasm-ing activity, I'm making I-wanna-sleep-signals, and he goes, "I hope you don't mind, I brought my toothbrush." I almost vomited. It was suddenly a "relationship." It was just like the Seinfeld episode where he has to break up with his girlfriend in person because she brought her toothbrush. So, I told him I

had to discuss the toothbrush with him. I said he had to take
it back. What is the point of being divorced if you have to
have some alien toothbrush messing up your gorgeous white
marble bathroom? I told him I could *lend* him a toothbrush,
but that he couldn't *bring* his own. He didn't really get the
subtle intricacies of that. Regardless, I gave him his back
and lent him a chic one of mine. You know, those ones with
the tortoiseshell handles you get from Asprey. I just knew
that a toothbrush staying over could lead to his clothing
staying over which could lead to him staying over . . . guess
what? I'm still looking for Make Out Number Three!
Have a great time in Paris, and I will see you in Moscow.
Bring major chinchilla. Can't wait.

xxx Lauren

Lauren's email, which arrived just as I was leaving for Paris,
would prove to be a stark contrast to the week I faced ahead.
There is nothing—I swear, nothing—as delicious as being
just-married and in Paris. Between appointments showing
Thackeray's collection to the stores and Hunter's endless
meetings, Hunter and I snuck off for romantic little lunches
in the Marais or met for dinner at cozy Left Bank brasseries,
like D'chez eux on the avenue de Lowendal, where we fed
each other spoonfuls of cassoulet, and held hands all the way
through dinner, the way crazy-in-love people do.

That week everything went right. Two stores—Maria
Luisa and Galeries Lafayette—bought Thack's collection,
even though the weak dollar meant the prices were pretty
astronomical. In the couple of weeks before I'd left New
York, we'd also had some good luck: Alixe Carter had finally
showed up for a fitting and ordered herself an entire couture wardrobe. She seemed to be spreading the word about
Thack's clothes, and we had more and more glamorous

women calling asking to be dressed for various events—there was even a hot young actress, Nina Chlore, whose publicist had called saying she wanted to wear Thack to the premiere of her new movie, *The Fatal Blonde,* in early January. Nina's performance had Hollywood suddenly in awe of this twenty-three-year-old, and her classy, youthful style had the fashion press in a feverish state. They stalked her as though she were a rare breed of leopard. Thack was desperate to dress her, but she still hadn't actually committed to a fitting. We had to hope and pray that the clothes would eventually lure her into the studio—though there was no saying when this might happen.

❦

There is no spot more happy-making for tea in Paris than Ladurée. Right on the corner of the rue Jacob and the rue Bonaparte, the velvet-lined, gilt-trimmed patisserie is the most romantic cake boutique in the world. Everyone should go there once with a brand-new husband. With the waiters in white jackets serving verveine tea in silver pots and fluffy *framboise* macaroons on pastel pink china, the whole thing makes you feel like you're Coco Chanel.

Hunter and I had spent most of the afternoon wandering around the antique shops on the Left Bank. Our favorite shop was Comoglio, an exquisite decorating store selling unaffordable French fabric, including pistacchio silk velvet at €300 a yard. (Only in France, kids, only in France.) By four o'clock we were exhausted, and relieved when we finally found ourselves sitting in two navy damask armchairs at Ladurée.

"I can't believe we've only got one more day, darling!" I said, once we had ordered.

I didn't want to leave Paris at all. We'd had such a lovely time. The argument about the Blakes Hotel bill had faded into a blurred memory. I couldn't believe I'd gotten so wound up about it and that I'd even considered canceling the Paris trip.

"Darling, we're going to be here a lot," said Hunter. "Maybe we'll have to get a place here, I have to be over so much."

"That would be amazing!" I cried, excited.

Just then a waiter appeared with a silver tray loaded with tea and delectable pastries. He set it out on the table and disappeared.

"Darling, have a bite of mine," I said, offering Hunter a piece of my raspberry macaroon.

"Mmm," said Hunter, biting it right off my finger, "I think on our next trip, we should go to the opera. Or maybe the circus. You know the circus here is amazing . . . maybe we *should* get an apartment, on the Quai Voltaire—"

"—With views over the Seine."

"Imagine all the walks around the art galleries we can do. And all those *café crèmes* we'll drink . . ."

"Oh, for a fantasy life in Paris!" I sighed happily.

We carried on like this for some time, in a continuous repetitive cycle that we found terribly romantic but that would have driven an onlooker crazy. It's always the way with being in love. When you're in it, it's beyond thrilling, but when you're sitting next to it in a restaurant it's odious. Luckily the exchange rates are so bad there aren't many Americans in Paris at the moment, so there were no unfortunate English speakers who were forced to suffer our nonsense. This made us very relaxed, and we started doing the kinds of things that you would never dream of doing in your own country, like French kissing across the table, teen-style. The last thing we expected was—

"I hate to interrupt such a cute scene."

Hunter and I looked up, embarrassed. Sophia D'Arlan was standing in front of us with a dazzling smile on her face.

Her mahogany tresses were loose and wavy, and she was dressed very *rive gauche au weekend* in long navy woollen pants, pointy flats, a leather jacket, and a lean scarf that reached down almost to her knees. She looked like Lou Doillon on her day off.

"I'm sorry. I just couldn't resist coming to say hi. I'm here with Pierre," she said, gesturing toward a dark-haired man sitting at a distant table. "Sylvie, I'm *so* glad you're here. I've *so* been meaning to get in touch with you."

"Really?" I said, surprised.

"Yes. Alixe Carter thinks I should wear Thack to the *Fatal Blonde* premiere. I'm Nina's date. We were at pre-school together. We're like sisters."

"Thackeray would love to dress you. Do call me about it. I'm back in New York the middle of next week," I said in a business-like tone.

I handed Sophia my card. It wouldn't be a bad thing if Sophia D'Arlan was seen in Thack: I may not have liked her much, but she was constantly photographed and considered a fashion icon by the glossy magazines.

"Nina's here for two days," said Sophia. "Can I give her your number? She said she's thinking about wearing Thack too."

That would be amazing. But did that mean I was going to have to befriend Sophia in some way? Although I didn't exactly have a specific reason not to like Sophia, I just didn't trust her. But if she was going to encourage Nina Chlore to wear Thack to the premiere, then I needed her. She obviously knew Nina well. Actresses are so fickle with fashion designers you need as many supporters as possible if you want to get them into your clothes. I would have to put my personal feelings aside—this was just too important to our business. I summoned up what I hoped looked like a genuine smile and said, "Sure." There was only a slim chance Nina Chlore would call. She was a meteorite, probably being courted by every designer from Dior to Dolce.

"I'll definitely be in touch. That's so kind of you, I can't believe it," said Sophia.

Sophia pecked Hunter on the cheek. "Bye, darling," she said in a familiar way. I took a sip of tea and resolved not to mind. Business first.

❧

Later that night, Hunter and I were sipping *chocolats chauds* in the bar at the Bristol when my cell rang. To my surprise, Nina Chlore was on the line, all apologies for calling so late. She said she wanted to wear Thack to her premiere in January, and, even more thrilling, she'd just heard she'd officially been nominated for a Golden Globe. Even though she knew it was vain and superficial and Hollywood-ish, of course all she could think about was The Dress. As Sophia had said, Nina was in Paris and wanted to meet the next morning to discuss gowns. I couldn't quite believe my ears, and I signaled a thumbs-up to Hunter.

"I could come to your hotel at eleven," I said, excited.

Though I wouldn't have dreamed of letting on, I could barely contain myself. Sophia D'Arlan's influence had probably helped, I thought, slightly annoyed. I suppose I would just have to put up with her for now.

"No, I'll come to you. I don't want to inconvenience you," Nina insisted.

"Well, if you're sure you can manage."

"I think I can manage to walk over to you from the Ritz." joked Nina, and hung up.

If I were a gorgeous, world-famous starlet who didn't have

to leave the Ritz, I wouldn't. But Nina seemed refreshingly down to earth.

"She seems so nice," I told Hunter, when I recounted the phone conversation to him. "So gracious and charming. Not like a movie star at all."

"She's probably acting," said Hunter. "Actresses do that all the time."

"I think she'd look amazing in Thack," I said.

"Let's see if she shows up tomorrow first," said Hunter.

"You're so cynical."

"I'm just being realistic," said Hunter, getting up and taking me by the hand. "Now how about catching a bit of Paris Première before bed?"

⟡

The next morning, expecting Nina to be the requisite two hours late, I was passing through the lobby at a quarter to eleven, when I spied her sitting in an armchair by the fireplace. I recognized her from endless paparazzi pictures. She was dressed in a fur jacket with a high collar that hid half her face and a tiny denim miniskirt. Her blonde hair was tumbling around her shoulders, and her legs were lightly tanned and bare, even on this wintry November morning. I think they were even longer than Sophia D'Arlan's, if that's possible. They were finished off with a pair of expensive-looking dark green snakeskin pumps. She was reading *Le Monde*. She was early. Nina was the antithesis of the breast-enhanced, latte-hued Los Angeles movie star: she had class. Thack was going to be obsessed when he met her.

"Nina?" I said, walking toward her.

"Sylvie? Hi! God! I'm early. Sorr-eee. I can wait down here if you like," she explained apologetically.

"Come up to the suite now," I said.

"Are you sure I'm not inconveniencing you and your husband?" asked Nina, concerned.

"Not even vaguely."

Hunter was completely and utterly 100 percent wrong about this girl. Nina was *genuinely* genuine, as opposed to fake-genuine. No actress can fake punctuality.

When we got up to the suite I took Nina into the drawing room and ordered two *cafés crèmes* from room service. Just as we were tucking into a plate of *pains aux chocolats,* Hunter put his head around the door and said hello to Nina before going out.

"What a cutie," said Nina, as the door closed.

I smiled. "He's pretty great," I said.

"And so successful. I keep reading about this show he's working on. It sounds amazing," she said.

I spread out one of Thackeray's look books on the table for Nina to peruse. There were eighteen outfits in the collection, of which six were evening gowns. I hoped there was enough choice. Nina picked up the book and studied the photographs intently, moving them this way and that to get a closer look at the details.

"Wow," she breathed. "This one is very *Fatal Blonde,* no?"

She was pointing at a picture of a sky blue, chiffon mousseline dress. It had a tiny waist, and the hem swirled on the floor in a pool of tulle.

"That's the Grace dress. Thackeray based it on one of Grace Kelly's gowns in *To Catch a Thief,*" I told Nina.

"That is literally my favorite movie. Can I really borrow it?" gasped Nina, looking excited.

"We'll make you your own," I said.

"I don't mind borrowing. Young designers can't afford to give away clothes."

"I insist," I said. "We'll make the Grace dress for you, and you should choose another one. You may freak out on the night of the premiere and *hate* the Grace dress suddenly. You need a choice."

Nina did choose another dress—a black duchesse satin cocktail frock with a bow on each shoulder and a sexy split up the front. The trouble was, I had promised it to Salome for Alixe's ball. Feeling slightly guilty, I told Nina she could have it exclusively. Salome would freak if she knew Nina Chlore was going to wear it too. But the cookie always crumbles in favor of the movie star, fashion-wise. That's just the way it is.

The next morning—after a delicious dinner the previous night at Brasserie Vaginaud and a midnight stroll along the river—two cars were waiting outside the Bristol for Hunter and me, our luggage loaded up. Hunter was going to Frankfurt, then on to Denmark and back to New York. I was going to Moscow from a different airport, and then returning to New York. Our blissful Paris week was done, but I didn't feel sad, even though I wouldn't see Hunter for two weeks. In fact, I felt restored. Marriage was heavenly. As I went over to check that the right bags were in the right car, I felt insulated from the pain of our imminent separation by a blanket of love and smoochiness.

"I think everything's in your car, darling," I said, looking into the trunk at Hunter's two ancient navy blue Globetrotter suitcases. "But . . . I don't think this is ours."

There was a tan overnight bag in the trunk of Hunter's car. It definitely wasn't his.

"Excuse me," I called to the busboy. "Can you remove this bag?"

"Oui," he replied, starting to lift the bag from the car.

As he did so, a luggage tag on the side of the bag flipped over. It read SOPHIA D'ARLAN. I froze.

"Hunter—" I started to say, as I turned to look at him, but stopped. There was Sophia D'Arlan, walking toward me, waving. Before I could think any further, Sophia was kissing me hello, saying,"I can't *believe* you're not coming with us. Hunter *promised* me I'd get to hang out with you. I'm *totally* gutted. Hunter's such a pill, forcing me to go to Frankfurt like this just because I speak German. It's an absolute hole there, a hole. By the way, did Nina Chlore choose something? I told her she just *had* to wear Thack."

"She did. Thank you for sending her," I said. What on earth was going on?

Hunter came over. He greeted Sophia in a very offhand way, as though there was nothing untoward about him taking a multi-lingual, Sardinian-legged beauty on a business trip with him. What had Marci said? Never trust a man who's always on a business trip? In an instant, my Parisian glow dissipated, and I felt the familiar twitches of paranoia again. I made a huge effort to appear unruffled. Suddenly Hunter had me in his arms and was giving me a hug.

"God, I'll miss you, darling," he was saying.

"Me too," I whispered.

"What are you doing in Moscow?" interrupted Sophia. "It's a dump, a terrible dump."

Still with my arms wrapped around Hunter—very possessively, I admit—I said, "I'm meeting Lauren, for the ice polo. She's fallen in love with this guy out there."

"Oh?" said Sophia.

"A Mr. Giles Monterey."

Something amazing happened next. Sophia, the cool, I-know-everyone-in-the-world-and-everyone-on-the-moon-too Sophia, was suddenly lost for words.

"Giles Monterey? She *knows* Giles Monterey," whispered Sophia finally, in awe. "My God. I've always wanted to . . . meet him."

From the blush on her face, she may as well have said, *I've always wanted to marry him.* Flustered, she looked at her watch and said, "Oh, we'd better be going. Do report what Monterey's like when you're back . . . God, I can hardly bear it!" said Sophia. "Come on, Mr. H."

Mr. H? She called Hunter by a stupid nickname? This was peculiar. I didn't like it. Even *I* didn't have a nickname for Hunter. Still, there was nothing for it but to wave happily as Hunter and Sophia headed over toward their car. Just before they disappeared inside it, I saw Sophia looking at Hunter in a hungry way. Her gaze lingered on him. She looked as though she hadn't eaten for a week.

14

Mr. Moscow

The girls in Moscow, with their flat, blonde hair, slanting bones, perfect bodies, and dead eyes, behave exactly the way American men think all women should. They sit at dinner, look decorative, smile, and never speak. It's a business deal: the amount a girl is allowed to talk decreases in exact inverse proportion to the amount of dollars or euros her boyfriend has, and the more Versace and Roberto Cavalli dresses he buys her. That's why Russian billionaires are always accompanied by exceptionally beautiful women who chat about as much as Holly Hunter did in *The Piano*.

The night before the ice polo, the lobby of the Park Hyatt Hotel on Neglinnaya Street was buzzing with just such girls and their dates. In the tradition of the new and phenomenally rich, what the crowd lacked in taste it made up for in colored diamonds and white fur. It's not the done thing to remove your sable in Russia, even if you are in a piping-hot hotel lobby. How else would anyone get to see it?

Lauren and I were sitting at the bar observing the scene.

Daylight robbery in New York and Paris is one thing, but in Moscow it's been inflated to meet with billionaire-size expectations. Eighty dollars for a glass of pink champagne at the bar at the Park Hyatt is standard. Even Lauren was appalled.

"Phoebe would love it here." she observed. "By the way. She had her kid. It's called Lila Slingsby, and she wants you to come to the christening. It's about ten days after we get back."

Suddenly Lauren jumped off her stool and exclaimed, "Gerski!"

A rather stout Russian man wearing a thin black leather jacket was striding toward us. He walked as though he were invading a minor nation. When he got close, Lauren kissed him on both cheeks and gave him a long hug.

"Ah! So long! How is your father?" he asked with a tender look in his eyes. Then, winking at both of us, he went on jovially, "You two are the only respectable people in this place. Everyone else has six bodyguards."

Gerksi, who turned out to have numerous bodyguards himself, was to be our "minder" for the weekend. A longtime business associate of Lauren's father, Gerski was a fifty-eight-year-old Siberian who had introduced Mr. Blount to the financial benefits of Russian crouton factories. Gerski oversaw all of Mr. Blount's toasted bread interests. His genius had been to package the croutons, American style, in little plastic bags. Gerski had made Mr. Blount even richer than he already was, and Mr. Blount had made Gerski richer than his wildest dreams.

"Right, Pushkin Café," said Gerski. He ushered us toward the exit, glancing dismissively at the crowd in the bar.

With its roaring fires and waiters dressed in high boots and breeches, the Pushkin Café feels like the kind of place

Chekhov's three sisters would have frequented, if they'd ever gotten out of the house. The building resembles an ornate chateau, wedding-cake deep with molding copied from the Winter Palace in St. Petersburg. You'd never know the whole thing's a total fake, put up about five years ago.

Gerski seemed to know everyone in the restaurant. He had gotten us one of the best tables—downstairs in front of a huge gilt mirror, where we could see the crowd coming in and out. We'd only been seated a few minutes when a young girl—she couldn't have been more than seventeen years old—joined us. Oksana was Gerski's girlfriend—"girlfriend" being a loose term in Moscow, since the richest men prefer to have a different one every night. Oksana was tough, despite her youth. She'd spent two seasons modeling in Milan, which made her a little more outspoken than her peers. She was wearing a daringly cut black satin dress, and two sugar-lump-size brilliant-cut diamond studs in her ears. She looked like she had walked out of a classic Helmut Newton photograph. She rested her left hand on Gerski's right arm throughout dinner, even while they were both eating.

"Eeeuch!" declared Lauren, perusing the menu. "Gerski, are you trying to poison us?"

The menu was deadly. Offerings included a *meriton* of cocks combs and a baked pie stuffed with chicken plucks and liver.

"All very healthy. You must try it," said Oksana. "The chicken plucks keep the skin soft."

"So, your friend Mr. Monterey will definitely be at the ice polo tomorrow afternoon," said Gerski later on in the evening.

"He's not 'my friend,' Gerski. I am here for Fabergé cuff link acquisition only," said Lauren, utterly unconvincingly.

Lauren was, of course, on a mission. She had her sights firmly set on Giles Monterey. For all the flakiness about marriage and love, the debutante divorcée takes her "work" very seriously. Lauren swished the cocks combs around her plate.

"I can't eat this. I feel like I'm in biology class. Well . . . hmmm, Ok . . . *maybe* I can get the jewels and score Make Out Number Three at the same time. That would be convenient."

"How do you know Monterey will be there for sure, Gerski?" I asked.

"Because he's playing. So he better show up or there won't be a game," replied Gerski.

"God, a polo player! How hot! I *can't stand* it," exclaimed Lauren, nearly bursting with excitement. Noticing Gerski scrutinizing her disapprovingly, she quickly added, "You know me, Gerski . . . nothing's ever *all* business with me, is it?"

"I don't want you getting involved with someone like Monterey," said Gerski sharply.

"Why not?" asked Lauren, a smile creeping to the edge of her lips.

Gerski just looked at her and sighed. Then Oksana said, "He's *serdtseyed*. He's a number-one, top-quality, first-class—how do you say it?—heart-eater."

"Heart*breaker*," breathed Lauren. "He sounds *exactly* my type."

⁂

Even gently fluttering snowflakes couldn't disguise the depressing Stalinist architecture of the stadium that Lauren, myself, Gerski, and Oksana drove across town to that Saturday afternoon. Cinder blocks are cinder blocks, snow-covered or not. Still, excited, we trudged in our snow boots across the racetrack, dodging ponies and traps racing around it in the snow.

When we finally arrived at the polo field, it was hardly the romantic, Anna Karenina-esque scene I had expected. Moscow's tower blocks loomed in the distance, and the snow on the pitch was muddied and disheveled. Still, inside the tent alongside, the Russian girls were a glittering diversion. Twenty-first-century *Dallas* is the best way to describe the dress code at the ice polo that afternoon. The uniform consisted of high-heeled snowboots (honestly, and in case you're wondering, they're YSL), reams of yellow diamonds, and as much fox fur as was humanly possible to load onto one female without crippling her.

The tent was packed, and a Russian folk band was performing loudly at the far end. *Sbiten*, a hot wine that tastes like boiling maple syrup, was being handed around. Along with the jewels, the furs, and the noise, one thing was for sure: this was not, thank God, the Bridgehampton polo.

Gerski found some friends, and we joined their table. The polo wasn't due to start for half an hour, so there was much gossiping to be done in the meantime. Suddenly I heard an American voice exclaim, "Sylvie! Hi! Lauren! Ola! It's so *rad* to see you *here*."

I turned to see Valerie Gervalt walking toward us. She was with Marj Craddock, a waspy girl Hunter vaguely knew from New York, and both their husbands. Decked out in pearls and the palest furs, they looked extraordinarily understated next to the Russian girls. Valerie and her gang flopped down at a table next to ours.

"Isn't Ralph Lauren *genius* for wearing in the snow?" said Marj.

"I like it better in Aspen," said Valerie. "Why aren't we in Aspen?"

"I love it here. Where else can you get away with the Ralph white minky?" replied Marj, stroking her coat.

You know what they say. You can take the girl out of Bridgehampton, but you can't take the Bridgehampton polo out of the girl.

"Is your husband here?" asked Valerie, looking at me. "I'm dying to meet him. I keep hearing so much about him."

"He's working in Germany," I replied, shrugging my shoulders.

"He's *never* around, is he? Poor thing, he must get so lonely."

"He's with a colleague," I said, thinking suddenly of Sophia's language skills.

"Could that 'colleague' be one Sophia?" said Marj, giving me a pitying look. "I'm glad she's not my husband's 'colleague'! Ha ha ha!"

Everyone laughed, but I can't say I was enjoying this line of conversation. Sensing my discomfort, Lauren cut Valerie off saying, "They've started! Quick!" and rushed off toward the viewing balcony, which was already getting crowded.

We all watched as eight glistening polo ponies—four on each team—galloped out onto the snowy field. The Moscow Mercedes Team were up against the Cartier International Four.

"There he is, number three," said Lauren, pointing out a man galloping fast up the far side of the field. "He's *so* devastating."

It's amazing. Lauren's the only girl I know who can see if a man is devastating even if his face is completely obscured by a helmet and safety mask.

Half an hour later, Lauren had changed her mind. Maybe number three wasn't so cute, she decided, after his team had lost resoundingly to the opposition. Jack Kidd, an English player in his early twenties, had skidded around the snow-covered arena at terrifying speed, scoring every goal for the

Cartiers. The hero of the game, he was cheered when he stomped into the tent, muddied and sweating, a few minutes later.

Polo kit is designed with one purpose in mind—to make its wearer look like a total hottie. Even Prince Charles used to look like a sex god when he played polo. Tight, spattered white breeches and hand-tooled leather riding boots have a devastating effect on the female. Add a handsome face and a beautiful smile to the look and you have, in Oksana's words, a heart-eater.

"OK, so he *is* cute, after all," said Lauren gazing at Giles Monterey as he walked into the tent. Suddenly she looked flushed. "Oh, God, I've got stomach flutters. Am I getting my nervous rash on my neck?"

Swigging a glass of hot wine, Giles Monterey headed to the far corner of the tent, where he was greeted merrily by a glamorous group of Russians. For someone so elusive he certainly looked very popular. He was conspicuously tall—he must have been six three—and his dark blonde hair was caked to his head with sweat. His face was flecked with dirt from the game, which only made his eyes look bluer and his smile whiter.

"No wonder he's UnGoogle-able," said Lauren. "If you could find him on the internet he'd have more groupies than Elvis. I'm so nervous. I can't possibly just go up to him."

"You have to," I said, egging her on.

"Maybe if I had six tequilas," she said, swiping a glass of wine off a tray and chugging it. "Ooh, this is strong stuff."

She grabbed another one, and finally headed, somewhat anxiously, in Monterey's direction. I went back to our table and joined Gerski and Oksana.

From where we were sitting I could see Lauren's progress from the corner of my eye. Dressed in a 1960s Givenchy

honey-blonde fur cape and matching hat inherited from her
mother, Lauren looked like a very stylish Eskimo. As she approached Monterey, it became quite clear that he had noticed
her well before she arrived. He stopped talking to his com-
panion and watched her approach, captivated. As they spoke,
his face registered first surprise, then delight. They seemed to
chat easily, until, a few minutes later, Lauren put her head
close to his and whispered something in his ear. Suddenly,
Giles Monterey's face darkened. The smile vanished. He
shook his head at Lauren, and they soon parted company.

⚜

"It was *so* weird," said Lauren.

We were installed in the back of Gerski's Mercedes waiting to leave the parking lot in a line of identical black cars. All
of them, including ours, had black, ruched curtains pulled
across the windows. It was like being inside a moving funeral
parlor, only we weren't moving. The traffic was chaos. No one
was getting anywhere.

"What happened?" I said.

"Well, we became absolute best friends in thirty seconds,
but when I suggested he might want to sell his Fabergé cuff
links to Sanford, he freaked. He said, 'Never would I sell anything to that man.'"

"I can't believe you're taking no for an answer, Lauren.
That's not like you."

"You know what? For once, I'm going to quit immediately.
There was something about the look on Giles' face when I
mentioned Sanford. He won't change his mind."

"Really?"

"No way. The only trouble is, you know how I said, a while
ago, that I was madly in love with him?"

"With who?" I asked. I couldn't even vaguely keep up with Lauren's sexual schedule anymore.

"With Giles," she said, clutching my arm. Her expression suddenly became unusually vulnerable and sweet. "Well, I actually *am*. Sylvie, I'm *madly* in love with him. Exactly as I predicted."

"Already?" I said doubtfully.

"It's hopeless. I'm never gonna see him again. And he's got the pick of the most beautiful girls in Moscow. Why would he want a divorcée?" she sighed. "He's UnGoogle-able *and* unmakeout-able. Drat."

For the first time, I saw a little chink in Lauren's party girl armor. It was disarming, actually, although she did her best to disguise it, exclaiming, "I don't care! There's a Make Out Number Three waiting for me somewhere back in New York—"

—Rap-rap-rap.

Someone was banging on the glass. I pulled back the black curtain. Giles Monterey's wild blue eyes were peering right into mine. The snow was swirling about him, and—I have to say, no disloyalty to Hunter—he was devastatingly handsome. He saw Lauren and gestured for me to open the window. I did so, and he said, "Lauren, I need to talk to you."

"Meet my friend Sylvie Mortimer," said Lauren.

"Sylvie?" said Giles. "Sylvie *Mortimer,* you said? You live in New York too?'

"Yes," I replied.

"Ah . . . *you're* Sylvie. Very interesting," he said, staring at me curiously. Suddenly he snapped out of it and said to Lauren, "Look, I know you want the cuff links, and I said I'd never part with them, but, well . . . there is one thing that could cause me to part with them."

"Do tell," said Lauren, pointedly not inviting Giles into the stationary car.

"I want the Princess Letizia diamond. If you can get it for me, I'll sell you the cuff links."

"Are you *crazy*? That's one of the most priceless gems in the world. Sally Rothenburg has owned that blue diamond heart since 1948. She's refused every offer," said Lauren, sounding flabbergasted.

"You're a *very* persuasive girl," said Giles with a charming smile. He was almost as good a flirt as Lauren.

"So are you, Mr. Monterey. Maybe I'll try. It's a challenge. But tell me something, what would a man like you want with a piece of history like that?"

"Well . . . ," said Monterey, looking deep into Lauren's eyes. He trailed off, and just gazed at her. Lauren, never shy, gazed right back, flopping her long eyelashes back and forth, back and forth, like a hypnotist. I felt like I was intruding on a very intimate moment.

"Yes?' said Lauren, breaking the spell.

"Let's just say . . . it would be an engagement present."

With that he turned and walked briskly away. Lauren looked as deflated as a cold cheese soufflé. She leaned over to me and said, dejected, "He's engaged. Of course he is! Why wouldn't he be? He's perfect. She's probably the next Natalia Vodianova, or something like that. Or maybe she's some incredible eighteen-year-old Bolshoi ballerina. I feel even worse than a hog. Alas."

❧

The trouble with Moscow is that there's only one way out: Aeroflot. The only thing to recommend it is that it's the one airline that still takes bribes. A hundred dollars slipped to a hostess facilitates an instant upgrade to first class, which roughly compares with a coach class seat on American.

Our illegal upgrade did little to lift Lauren's spirits. Since Giles Monterey had revealed his engagement, she had taken on the severely disappointed air of a jilted fiancée, who had fully expected to marry the man in question. It was extreme. Lauren had barely removed her sunglasses or her iPod earphones since we'd left the Park Hyatt a few hours earlier. Even coming across a lone issue of *New York* magazine in the airport hadn't cheered her up. One of the cover lines read "NYTV: The city's small screen players." Maybe Hunter's new show would get a mention.

I was just flicking through the magazine to find the story when Lauren took out her earplugs and moaned, "Engaged! I have never met a more beautiful or hot polo player, and just when I decide I want to . . . kiss him, he's all taken. Do you think I can get him back?"

"How can you get a man back if you never had him?" I asked.

Reluctantly, Lauren laughed.

"I guess there *is* that," she said. "My one hope is that heart. It's my only chance of seeing him again. I'm *convinced* he was flirting with me at the polo. But engaged men are always the biggest flirts. Oh! But Sally will never let the heart go. Never. Even if I could get it, how would I find Giles again? I don't even have his email."

It was true. Giles was beyond Un-Google-able. He wasn't even *there* in the normal sense. Secretly, I thought it was a good thing he was taken. He would have driven Lauren crazy.

"Look, there's a photo of Hunter," I said. The *New York* article included a paragraph about Hunter's show, and there was a photo of Hunter in one corner with the caption *Manhattan's Hot TV Guy!!!* underneath it.

"How cute," said Lauren. She took off her dark glasses and examined the photo closely.

"Mmm . . ." she said. "What good taste your husband has. He's coming out of S. J. Phillips on Bond Street. I know it *really* well, believe me. Best jeweler in London. What did he give you?"

"Oh. Well. Nothing," I replied, feeling somewhat perturbed. What had Hunter been doing in a jewelry store in London?

Lauren wasn't really listening. She was holding the magazine about an inch from her nose and examining the photograph closely.

"My god. That operator. I don't believe it. *That,*" declared Lauren, "is Sophia D'Arlan's foot."

I took the magazine from Lauren and looked closely at the picture of Hunter. There was indeed a woman's foot and ankle peeking into the edge of the photograph. The foot was clad in a high-heeled gold shoe with a large cluster of pearls on the toe.

"Lauren, how could you possibly know that is Sophia's foot?" I asked. I tried to sound nonchalant, but I was half-concerned.

"The gold shoes. Couture Bruno Frisoni. I tried to order them, but Sophia got there first. He makes only one pair of each, and he's obsessed with Sophia, so she got first dibs. It made me mad because those are the prettiest shoes ever."

I looked at the photo again. Was that Sophia's ankle in the gold shoes? The leg did look rather slim and tan, just like hers.

"I'm sure it's not her," I said, trying to end the conversation. I was tired and wanted to sleep now. I pulled my mask over my eyes.

"What was Hunter doing in London anyway?" asked Lauren. "Did you ever find out?"

"He said it was some last-minute business meeting," I said with a yawn.

"A last-minute business meeting at a jewelry store?"

I didn't sleep a wink.

15

The Power Christening

The night before Phoebe's daughter's christening, I was restless. I hadn't seen Hunter for almost two weeks, but he was finally coming home the following night. We'd been speaking constantly, but the thought of actually being back together with him was almost too much: I couldn't possibly sleep. At 2 A.M. I was still tossing around unhappily under the comforter. Wide awake, I finally decided to get up for a while and catch up on some emails—there was no point staying in bed any longer. I slipped on my cashmere robe and wandered into the study.

I sat down at Hunter's desk and switched on the study lamp. I had left my laptop in the office, so I turned on Hunter's desktop computer, which I occasionally used when I was home. I was about to type an email when I noticed a file on his desktop I hadn't seen before: underneath it read, sjphillipssketch.jpeg.

S. J. Phillips, I mused to myself. Wasn't that the name of the jewelry store Lauren had mentioned when we were on our way back from Moscow? Feeling tremendously guilty, I clicked on the icon. It popped open, showing a one-page document. The following was written on the page in a curly, old-fashioned typeface:

S. J. Phillips,
Jewellers,
139 New Bond Street,
London, W1
By Royal Appointment

Underneath was an intricate sketch, in pencil, of an oval-shaped, amethyst pendant with an *S* snaking elegantly around it in tiny diamonds. "The necklace will be ready for collection after November 20" was written next to the sketch. I gulped. So that was what Hunter had been up to in London! He had commissioned a special jeweled pendant for me. How sweet of him to pretend he had been at a last-minute business meeting. No wonder he had sounded so vague when I had interrogated him so ferociously about it—he was covering up his beautiful, romantic little love project. Hunter could go on last-minute business trips to S. J. Phillips anytime he wanted. Hopefully, I thought, as I returned to bed, suddenly sleepy and relaxed, Hunter was picking up the jewel while he was in Europe. I could hardly wait to see him. (And not just because of the jewel, honestly.)

❧

Phoebe has more friends-slash-business-associates than the president of the United States. No wonder she had to take out the whole church on the corner of Fifth Avenue and Twelfth Street for the christening of her newborn, Lila

Slingsby. She couldn't possibly *share* a christening like regular people do. Not only would she never have been able to squeeze in everyone she wanted, other parents might have objected to the commercial undertones of the Phoebe Bébé–themed christening: the entire church was decked out with yellow primroses that had been specially grown and white satin ribbons that were tied in bows absolutely everywhere you looked, even around the crucifix at the foot of the altar. Even though I was rather tired that afternoon, I was so excited about Hunter coming back that I felt unusually buoyant. I was in love. It was easy to be pleasantly amused by Phoebe's exhibitionistic display of motherhood.

The unborn Lila Slingsby had been present at so many parties in New York while still womb-bound that the joke at the christening was that she was the first Socialite Fetus of note in the city. Indeed, the little embryo certainly had the best introduction to the world, socially speaking. Lila Slingsby had been born at New York Presbyterian, under the care of Dr. Sassoon. (Everyone wants that hospital because you can bring in your own nurses / chef / manicurist, and everyone wants Dr. Sassoon, because he was rumored to have delivered Caroline Kennedy's children, and every mother in New York wants an introduction to those kids.)

"It's a power christening," whispered Lauren, perusing the crowd from our pew. She was dressed elegantly in a cream, ruffled Oscar de la Renta party dress. A thick rope of oversize black pearls hugged her slim neck. "No one here isn't a some-one. I love Phoebe, but she's sick. I mean, doesn't her kid have grandparents? Or don't old people wear enough Balenciaga to be seen here?"

Lauren had a point. As she and the thirteen other god-parents were summoned to the altar, it was impossible not to notice that not one godfather was not a captain of industry, super-hot hedge fund manager, or a media company owner-operator. The godmothers were wealthy beauties, fashion types, or high-end socialites. Whatever little Lila Slingsby was going to need later in life—an internship at MTV, a front-row seat at Lacroix couture, a permanent table at Pastis—one of her godparents would arrange it, because they probably owned it. It was sweet of Phoebe to prepare her little girl's life so perfectly.

Phoebe's double-width carriage house on West Thirteenth Street between Seventh and Eighth Avenues was bulging with friends when Lauren and I arrived after the service. Lila was fast asleep in her mother's arms, which made it all the easier to show off her outfit to everyone, and whenever anyone congratulated Phoebe, she just looked at Lila and declared, "Lila is a *miracle* . . . doesn't yellow look spectacular on her?"

After a few minutes I spotted Marci on the other side of the crowded drawing room. I hadn't seen her since that dreadful night at her apartment, so I headed over to talk to her.

"Hi Sylvie," she said when I reached her. "I'm feeling *amazing*."

Marci looked fairly amazing. She was wearing a very pretty orange silk dress printed with posies of pink roses.

"I love your dress, Marci," I said.

"Sophia sent it over to me after Christopher went, to cheer me up. I'm rather looking forward to being a divorcée now. Sophia says we'll have such fun. She's become an *incredibly* close friend of mine in the last twelve days. She calls all the time from Europe. She even says she'll talk to Christopher for me now that he's not speaking to me. She's *so* supportive."

"Oh," I said rather unenthusiastically. Still, even a mention of Sophia couldn't dampen my mood that day.

"Hey, I need to discuss something with you," said Lauren, suddenly, pulling me aside.

"What?" I said.

"It's Monterey. I haven't heard a thing. Two weeks and I haven't heard a *thing*! I'm going nuts. I guess I'll have to just wait, right?"

"I don't see what else you can do. He is . . . engaged," I reminded her.

"I guess," moped Lauren. "Anyway, you looked thrilled with life. What's going on? Are you pregnant?"

"No!" I said. "Hunter's coming back tonight. I can't wait to see him." I was so excited about the jewel I couldn't help but tell Lauren about it. "And last night, I found this gorgeous sketch on Hunter's computer from S. J. Phillips of an amethyst pendant with an *S* wrapped around it in diamonds. It's so beautiful. Isn't that sweet of Hunter?"

There was a long pause. Lauren looked pensive, then she said, "Darling, is it for you, or . . . *her*?"

"What?" I said, confused.

"Well, think. *S* is Sylvie, but *S* is also for Sophia."

"Of course the necklace isn't for Sophia!" I cried, upset.

"How can you be sure?" said Lauren in a low voice.

"I'll ask him," I declared, worried.

"Don't do that!" ordered Lauren. "First, it's supposed to be a surprise, so if it is for you, you're screwing things up for yourself by admitting you've been sneaking around your husband's computer. And second, a wife must never, ever confront a husband unless she has concrete proof of misdemeanors. Otherwise he'll think you're neurotic and scary and that will be the end of everything."

"It can't be for Sophia," I said, unsure of myself, ". . . can it?"

"Look, *I'm* probably being neurotic," said Lauren, "But

remember that picture of Sophia's shoe in that *New York* magazine story?"

I suddenly remembered flicking through the magazine on our trip back from Moscow. I felt nauseous.

"I'll have to speak to him," I said. "Tonight—"

"—No," interrupted Lauren. "A one-off Bruno Frisoni shoe isn't enough . . . proof. There was this one time, years ago when I was first married to Louis, and he was spending all his time with my then–best friend, Lucia, and I accused them of being up to no good and . . . they were secretly planning a gorgeous surprise birthday for me! It was completely innocent. Sometimes I think that was one of the things that drove him to cheat on me eventually: I was so suspicious. You have to be sure before you do anything. You can't say a word. *Promise* me you won't mention it."

I nodded reluctantly. "OK," I said. Maybe Lauren was right.

"Good. Then if it turns out he is cheating," said Lauren with a reassuring smile, "at least you can console yourself with the knowledge that you behaved with great dignity and didn't get all neurotic and scary before it was completely appropriate."

16

Christmas Card Envy

That December, the last thing on anyone's mind as they opened Valerie and Tommie Gervalt's Christmas card was Christmas. Valerie had taken the personalized greeting card up a very competitive notch. Smiling from a photograph on the front of the card was her three-year-old daughter, Celeste. She was wearing a pale blue tweed Emily Jane coat, of the type only found at Harrods in London. She had a gray beret on her head, and her feet were clad in black lace-up boots that looked as though they came straight from the costume department of *Little House on the Prairie*. Celeste was standing next to a pillbox-hatted busboy on the front steps of the Ritz Hotel in the Place Vendome. Underneath the photograph were the words:

"Celeste—Paris Couture—Summer"

"Her kid looks like a hobgoblin," chuckled Hunter when he saw it. We were having breakfast together at home the morning after he'd gotten back from Europe, and enjoying opening the pile of cards that had arrived that morning in the mail. "Valerie is New York's finest example of unvarnished social climbing," he declared.

"Here, open this one," I said, handing Hunter a bright red envelope. "And I'll open this."

"Oh my," mused Hunter as he handed me the card he had just pulled out of the envelope. It was a Christmas card from Salome. The cover photograph, of herself in her Christian Lacroix wedding gown, was beautiful. She'd had her ex-husband, and the minister, Photoshopped out of the picture. Inside, she'd had the following words printed, graffiti-style:

> Happy Holidays!
> Love,
> Me, Me, and Me

Next I opened my envelope. Almost as unvarnished as Valerie's card in its display of gorgeousness was the missive inside. It was from Sophia and her five sisters. It featured a shot of the girls (all, naturally, Gwyneth Paltrow lookalikes) waving from the back of a 1960s pickup truck in Colorado.

"How pretty," I said. "They're all so beautiful."

"No one is as beautiful as my wife," said Hunter, looking at me lovingly.

Hunter's return last night had not, through a conscious effort on my part, been marred by the seed of doubt Lauren had planted in my mind about the pendant. (So what if Sophia was sending boho-glam Christmas cards. It didn't mean a thing.) I had decided to remain optimistic about the jewel—and my marriage. Hunter would produce the trinket at Christmas, I was sure of it. He'd gotten home late last night, looking tired but well, and given me a wonderful cream fur stole that he'd bought when he'd stopped off for one day in Copenhagen. We'd sat up late watching *Letterman*, catching up, and making out.

Between kisses, I gave Hunter a rambling account of the Moscow trip, and told him how Lauren had decided to fall in love, inconveniently, with an engaged man. Hunter was intrigued by the story and asked endless questions about why Lauren liked Giles so much and what I thought of the two of them as a potential couple. Of course, I reminded Hunter, they couldn't be a couple—he was getting married. Lauren was right, I thought as I'd drifted off in bed later that night. There was no point saying anything about that photo of him with Sophia in London. I fell asleep, contented, in Hunter's arms.

Now, there's nothing like a Christmas card depicting blissful family life to drive a stake straight through the heart of even the merriest divorcée. About a week after Thanksgiving, Lauren called, completely freaked out. Louis, her ex, had sent out a card with a picture of himself, a strange woman named Arabella, and their newborn son, Christian. Lauren had seen it on Alixe Carter's mantelpiece, and flipped.

"We've only been divorced four months!" she cried. "He hasn't even had time to meet someone, let alone have a child. It must have been going on before we separated. I can't believe it."

What incensed Lauren most was that the photograph had obviously been taken in one of the Royal Suites of the Gritti Palace in Venice. Louis and his new family looked rather like a clan of minor royals posing for *Hello* magazine.

"He just had that kid to upset me," said Lauren, in a moment of monumental self-obsession. She found their blatant display of happiness to be "completely unacceptable. It's so . . . *nouveau riche*. Christmas is ruined."

At this point Lauren went into divorcée crisis mode. Louis's Christmas card so disturbed her that she was rumored to have been spotted wandering down Gansevoort Street in her nightdress and socks at 3 A.M. one night looking for Louis. She received invitations for Christmas to Cuba, Rajasthan, and Palm Beach—and accepted all of them. Finally, she fell into a deep depression because, try as she might, she couldn't complete her challenge: she couldn't seem to nail down Make Out Number Three, or connect her own surround sound, despite spending nine hours one Saturday attempting it.

"Even Sally Rothenburg agreeing to sell me Princess Letizia's heart hasn't cheered me up," she complained miserably to me in a room full of beaded dresses at an uptown Christmas cocktail party one night. "Louis has *wrecked* Christmas for me this year. I'll never recover. I honestly think the stress has given me an incurable disease, like polio. Can you get me another glass of champagne?"

⚜

For a girl with polio, Lauren's recovery was miraculous. The day after the cocktail party, Lauren received a hand-delivered note from Giles Monterey. It read:

> I am in town. Meet you Grand Central Oyster Bar one o'clock Thursday to exchange. Regards, G. M.

A meeting with Giles was just the thing to cheer Lauren up, though I hoped her infatuation with him was passing. He was not available, and even if he had been he was too elusive for my liking.

Lauren's aesthetic preparations for her business meeting,

as she called her assignation with Giles, were, she said, more labor-intensive than those for her own wedding had been. Her main obsession was that her makeup artist achieve perfect "Hooker Eyes," the secret of which was black kohl flown in from Egypt. After careful consideration, the outfit selected consisted of Lauren's favorite skinny cream pants, a feather-light black knitted mink jacket, and, underneath, a cobweb-light tulle top. She left her hair loose and wavy, having decided, on the basis of no evidence at all, that a blow-out wouldn't appeal to Giles. She called me every thirty minutes that morning to report her progress, makeup-, outfit- or mood-wise, the latter of which I can report was violently upbeat. She left her house at 12:15, accompanied by a discreet security guard hired to protect the jewel. Lauren was convinced she was headed for a professional and romantic success: she was determined to get the Fabergé cuff links and score Make Out Number Three simultaneously.

You can imagine my surprise when Lauren showed up at Thack's studio at five that afternoon, her face pale and smudged with traces of mascara. She had been crying.

"So much for Hooker Eyes. I look like any old call girl," she said when she arrived.

"God, you're dramatic, I love it," said Thack when he saw her. "It's so inspiring. I could make you a dress just for weeping in. Emmy," he called out to his assistant, "make a note: Hooker Eyes for the next show."

"Thanks, Thack, you're a dear," sighed Lauren, dabbing at her eyes with a scrap of fuchsia silk from the cutting table. "Gosh, this would make lovely handkerchiefs. Hi everyone," added Lauren, waving at the group of interns embroidering in one corner. They shyly nodded back and stared at Lauren, no doubt just as inspired as Thack by her particular brand of glamour.

"What happened?" I asked, getting up from my desk. It was piled with a stack of paperwork, and I needed a break. "I'm going to order tea for everyone," I said, dialing the deli downstairs.

"He didn't show," said Lauren weakly. She flopped onto the only sofa in the studio, which was overflowing with sample fabrics and the odd sleeve and ruffle.

"Can you send up tea for everyone in the studio? It's Sylvie . . . OK, thanks," I said, putting down the phone. Then I turned to Lauren. "What are you going to do with the heart?" I asked.

Lauren sighed. Her face was wracked with disappointment.

"Oh, he has the heart, all right. I guess his lucky fiancée will have it soon."

A lone tear squeezed itself from Lauren's eye. It rolled along the side of her nose and stopped on her lip, where it perched, tragically.

"Sorry, I'm such a loser." She half-cried, half-laughed, wiping the tear away. "I don't even know the guy, and look at me!"

Monterey, it turned out, had sent an envoy to collect the jewel. As we drank our tea, Lauren recounted how an immaculately groomed Russian man, probably in his late twenties, Lauren thought, had appeared, claiming he was to take the heart on behalf of Monterey. He had produced the Nicholas II cuff links from a velvet pouch inside his jacket, plus a letter stating the change of plan. Lauren's security guard had handed over the jeweled heart. The whole transaction was over in five minutes, and Lauren hadn't even gotten a raw oyster, let alone a Make Out, out of it.

"I hope Sanford liked the cuff links after all that thwarted romance," mumbled Thack through a mouthful of pins. He was carefully pinning a piece of lilac paper tafetta to a dressmaker's dummy.

"That's the awful thing. I go to all this trouble, and then I show up at Sanford's suite at the Mark and everything just . . . it was absolutely . . . awful, awful."

Lauren had, slightly showing off, told Sanford about the escapade to Moscow to acquire the cuff links, but Sanford had cut short Lauren's excited account of Monterey at the polo match.

"It was so weird . . . like he was jealous or something," said Lauren. "Can I smoke?"

"Just this time," said Thack. "If I can have one too."

Lauren pulled out her little green lizard case and handed Thack a platinum.

"How divine," he said, regarding it and lighting Lauren's cigarette and then his own. He took a drag, then, exhaling, went on, "Of course he's jealous. Sanford's infatuated with you, and you're infatuated with someone who isn't Sanford. Moguls can't take rejection like normal men."

"Then he kissed me," continued Lauren, wrinkling her nose at the thought of it. "Against my will. He was shaking, like he was *afraid*. But I guess if you've been married for twenty years, you probably haven't made out in forever . . . it must be terrifying. The whole thing was so embarrassing. He just moved his tongue from left to right, and right to left, horizontally. It was this mechanically weird kissing, and all I could think of was, did he have garlic mashed potatoes tonight? I guess every girl should have a Mogul Make Out once in her life just so she knows what she's *not* missing."

By this stage, everyone in the studio was hooting with laughter. But suddenly Lauren's cheeky demeanor vanished.

"What happened?" I said, sensing her bleak mood.

"He said if I didn't agree to have an affair with him, the friendship's off."

"How bizarre," I said.

"It's really sad," said Lauren. "I thought he was a really . . . you know . . . solid friend."

At this, Thack tutted, shaking his head.

Lauren took a long drag of her cigarette. She looked at me wistfully and said, "He says he wants to divorce his wife and marry me! I can't bear it. I can never see Sanford again. I was so naïve, letting Sanford hang with me, and thinking he was cool with only that. He's such a great man, but he's not . . . Giles Monterey, is he? There's nothing worse than romantic disappointment, is there? I was hoping for a make out session in Grand Central with Mr. Moscow and all I got was a lousy pair of Fabergé cuff links and a kiss with a waterbed. This is the worst Christmas ever."

⁓⁂⁓

I, on the other hand, found Christmas enchanting this year. It wasn't always so. Christmas as a single girl had become grimmer and grimmer, but now the season seemed delightful, charming. This year I found the midtown traffic gridlock caused by the lighting of the Rockefeller Center tree enchanting, the endless *"jingle-bell-jingle-bell-jingle-bell-TARGET!!!"* tune on TV filled me with festive spirit, and the prospect of *Barbara Walters' Ten Most Fascinating People* gave me a warm and mushy feeling inside. Being married made the whole thing bearable: there were no lonely Christmas parties, no wrapping presents alone, no who-am-I-going-to-kiss-on-New-Year-type anxieties. The only thing that occasionally marred my mood was wondering about that sketch of the S. J. Phillips jewel: Hunter had never even mentioned it. Not so much as a hint. As the lights went up all across the city, twinkling white up Park Avenue, glowing a chic pink in the windows of Bergdorf Goodman, I told myself—again and again—that it was destined to be my Christmas present.

Although it was a little early for a tree, I'd bought ours a few days after Thanksgiving from a Vermont family selling trees on lower Fifth Avenue. Hunter and I merrily spent the first Sunday in December decorating the pine with pale pink grosgrain ribbons, old-fashioned clear glass balls, and white vintage canaries. (Can you believe ABC Carpet now has a whole section devoted to antique tree ornaments? Obviously, irresistible. Obviously, daylight robbery.) As we did so, I recounted Lauren's latest romantic disaster.

"I feel a little sorry for Lauren now," I said. "I think she really likes this Giles Monterey guy. Can you pass me that silver tinsel?"

Hunter handed me the glittery decoration, saying, "*Very* interesting. You think she wants to marry him?"

"She says she isn't interested in marriage and that it's all about business and her Make Out Challenge, but you should have seen her when he didn't show up that day at the Oyster Bar. She was beside herself. I honestly think she'd marry him. If he wasn't engaged."

I sat back and regarded the tree. "Doesn't it look pretty," I said.

"It's lovely, darling. I thought you said Lauren would never marry again," said Hunter.

"This guy, I don't know, it's different. Mind you, if he got all interested and was suddenly available, she'd probably freak out and say she *wasn't* interested."

"Really," mused Hunter, gazing at the crystal ball he'd just hung on a branch. He seemed distracted, as though he was pondering something. "So Lauren's the type where the more engaged a man is, the more she likes him."

"Exactly," I agreed.

"I don't think she should give up on him. Engaged is not married," said Hunter. "Oh, Christ—I just remembered, I have to call someone."

He left the room, and through the door I heard him mumbling, as if in some conspiracy. Obviously some work call. At seven o'clock he finally reappeared in the drawing room, where I was tying the last bow on the tree, holding a jacket in his hand, saying,

"Listen, Sylvie, something's come up. I have to go out tonight."

"But what about *Barbara Walters*," I responded, disappointed. We'd planned a cozy evening in, watching TV with Japanese takeout. "Can't you rearrange? What do you have to do so urgently on a Sunday evening?"

"My old college friend's in town, and I'd arranged to have dinner with him ages ago. I must have forgotten to tell you."

"Not the guy you wanted to set Lauren up with?" I asked.

"Actually, it is him," Hunter replied. He started to pull the jacket on.

"Well, why don't I call Lauren and we'll all go out? It'd really cheer her up. Take her mind off Monterey—"

"I don't think it's a good idea," said Hunter quickly.

Why was Hunter being so strange? Why didn't he want me to go with him?

"You did say once that you wanted to introduce Lauren and your friend. Christmas is the perfect time for dating and—"

"There's no point. Blind dates never work. People who are meant to fall in love do it very well all by themselves."

"But he sounds so cute. Who is he?" I asked.

"He's only here for a few hours, I better run. See you later darling, and sorry about tonight," said Hunter, dashing out.

❦

That was all very rushed, I thought later, as I ate my Japanese alone in front of the television. I usually find Barbara Walters to be compelling viewing. Her choices are so bizarre (remember the year Karl Rove was Most Fascinating Person?), her questions so wonderfully polite, that you can enjoy the whole thing immensely if you pretend it's a *Saturday Night Live* spoof. Then, the way Barbara's hair stays the same each year is endlessly comforting. But tonight I felt distinctly uncomfortable, despite Ms. Walters' reassuringly immobile coiffure.

My appetite disappeared. I couldn't even seem to digest my favorite tuna sashimi. Why was Hunter suddenly refusing to introduce Lauren to his perfect college friend? He'd been so excited a few weeks ago about his mysterious buddy meeting Lauren. And why wouldn't he tell me his name? When I thought back over the past few days, the fact was, Hunter had been acting strangely. He'd been spending hours at a time on the Internet. There were whispered phone calls that were suddenly cut off whenever I walked into the room. He responded vaguely when I asked him what he'd been doing. Even stranger, there was no sign of the S. J. Phillips jewel. Whenever I hinted at it, he acted as though he had no idea what I was talking about. When I went around the tree that evening shaking the Christmas boxes (as I do most years), it was apparent that it wasn't there. He *must* have picked up the necklace by this time, I thought. But where was it? And now this: standing up Barbara W. and his wife, whom he'd barely seen in the past few weeks, in favor of dinner with an anonymous college "friend." On a Sunday! No one ever had anything important to do on a Sunday.

Just as Barbara was about to introduce her Most Fascinating Person, I forced myself to take a bite of the tuna sashimi. Not eating would only make things worse. Just then, my cell phone rang.

"Sorry, Sylvie! You must think I'm the worst, most unreliable movie star ever."

It was Nina Chlore. Predictably, she had failed to follow up on our meeting in Paris and actually be fitted for her dresses, which were hanging in the studio waiting for her.

"Filming in Morocco took an extra two weeks, and there's literally not a phone *anywhere* in the desert. Can I come into the studio tomorrow for the fitting? With Sophia? We've been missing you *so much*!"

I almost choked on my tuna. Sophia was back in town. And my husband had just rushed out to meet a "college friend." Maybe Christmas wasn't going to be so warm and mushy after all.

⚜

"Sophia's *really* sorry she can't make it," said Nina when she arrived, on time, the next day at the studio for the fitting. I, on the other hand, was not sorry. She was the last person I wanted to see. "I am so stressed out! I've been offered *seven* movies! I feel like I'm going to die," Nina went on from behind a screen in the studio as she changed. "I'm twenty-three years old and I feel like I'm sixty-two, I'm so tired."

A few moments later Nina appeared wearing the ruched Grace dress that we'd made up for her in oyster-colored chiffon. It drifted around her body like a breath of air: she looked soft and old-fashioned in it. She gazed at herself in the mirror and then said, "Oh, look at *this*. This is The Dress for the premiere. Can I take it with me now?"

When Nina was snapped by a paparazzo leaving Thack's studio carrying one of his bags, two things happened: first, the supermarket tabloid magazines went crazy calling us, trying to find out which dress Nina was wearing to her premiere. (The truth was, even I didn't know. Nina had ended up taking four dresses, two of which were loans to be returned immediately after the event, and two of which were gifts from us. She was so secretive she wouldn't even tell Thack which one she was most likely to wear.) Second, every girl in New York suddenly wanted to be dressed by Thack for Alixe's Winter Ball, which was only a couple of weeks after Christmas.

Neiman's sold out of our dresses, and Bergdorf Goodman called and offered Thack a trunk show. If this was the result of a photo of Nina carrying one of our shopping bags, it was clear that an actual photo of Nina in the Grace dress could change Thack's business dramatically. Designers around actresses are a sorry sight. Thack, normally so blasé, started twitching every time he opened a magazine and saw a photo of Nina. He perspired when her name was mentioned on TV. His temperature shot up to feverish levels when she appeared in another designer's gown. The Nina Effect, as Thack called it, had hit him worse than avian flu.

17

Jailbait Make Out

There is nothing more chic, I swear, than a white Eres one-piece worn on the deck of a 1920s ski chalet in the French Alps. Tanning when there's two feet of snow on the ground, the sky is electric blue, and the sun is beating down at 70 degrees has to be the most luxurious thing ever. I think it's the white-on-white thing. It's insanely flattering, especially when there's a mountain of terry toweling robes and matching slippers to add to the effect.

When Hunter had announced, just a few days before Christmas, that one of his French partners had offered him his ski chalet in Megève over the holiday, I'd packed in a heartbeat. The quaintest village in the Alps, Megève makes Aspen look like the Mall of America. There are twisting cobbled streets, scrumptious patisseries, charming boutiques, and an immaculate church square. Our journey had been exhausting—we'd taken an overnight flight to Paris and an early flight the next morning to Geneva, but it was worth it when we finally arrived.

Thick with icicles, our little chalet looked like something from *Hansel and Gretel*. Inside, the drawing room was furnished with faded sofas and sheepskin rugs, and our bedroom was so romantic I wondered if we would ever leave it. The bed was made up with antique linen, and a fur coverlet was thrown across it. It was better than being in a Ralph Lauren Ski ad. Who cared that I couldn't actually ski?

"It's divine, Hunter," I said, as we dropped our things in the bedroom. We'd finally arrived in mid-afternoon, and the sun was casting its last silvery rays across the pristine mountainside.

A happy smile on his face, Hunter enveloped me in his arms, saying, "Aren't you glad we're out of New York for Christmas?"

"Yes, I am," I replied, excited.

Hunter had been so sweet over the last few days, and looked after me so well on our trip over, that the whole mysterious Barbara Walters episode started to seem unimportant. Now that we were here, in this beautiful spot, the concerns of the last few months dissipated. Just then there was a knock at the bedroom door. A maid appeared with two *chocolats chauds* on a tray and an envelope addressed to me. I opened it and read,

> *Darling Sylvie and Hunter,*
> *You won't believe it. I am next door in Camille de Dordogne's chalet. Come for cocktails tonight?*
>
> *xxx Lauren*

Lauren, predictably, had flaked on all three of her Christmas invitations. At the last minute she'd decided to spend the week with Camille, a beautiful, thirty-seven-year-old French countess. Camille was famously happily married to Davide de

Dordogne, a banker, to whom she'd lost her virginity at seventeen in the Palace Hotel in Gstaad ("I wouldn't consider mislaying it anywhere else," she always says). She married him six weeks later, and her three children were now virtually adults. She ran a chic porcelain store in Paris and loved matchmaking her friends. With Camille's help Lauren was determined to complete her Make Out Challenge on the slopes.

"I'm hoping Camille can hook me up with the Monaco son," Lauren told her friends. "Don't you think Andrea Casiraghi would be the perfect Number Four? I *may* even consider marrying him. One offer I can't turn down is Princess Lauren of Monaco."

❧

Hunter and I drove over to Camille's chalet early that evening—we were tired, and to be honest, fond as I was of Lauren, I didn't much feel like socializing after our long flight. We decided to drop in briefly, and then go back and snuggle up together in that heavenly, fur-covered bed. Chalet Dordogne had been built by Davide's family in the 1920s and was half hidden up a steep mountain lane.

Camille greeted us at the door. She was petite, and dressed in wide tweed pants and a pale blue satin blouse, which hinted at a milky décolleté. How do French women pull off that bourgeois-sexy thing so well, I thought, as I regarded her wonderful outfit. She was an oxymoron—so conservative, yet so provocative at the same time, like a modern Romy Schneider.

"Ah, *bon soir.* Mwah. Mwah. Mwah. Mwah," she said, clutching my shoulders and kissing me twice on each cheek. She then repeated the exercise with Hunter. "Welcome."

The drawing room had a high, arched ceiling with an ornate galleried balcony leading to the bedrooms. The house was bulging with guests and children who were gathering around the fireplace for pre-dinner drinks. Just as we arrived, Camille's husband, Davide, appeared. Neatly dressed in a white shirt, moleskin pants, and loafers, he was the very picture of the suave European banker on vacation—BlackBerry on hand at all times.

"*Vin chaud?*" he asked.

"Mmm! *Merci,*" said Hunter.

Davide poured a couple of glasses, and we all lounged on sofas by the fire.

"Lauren brought that *amie* Marci with her, which is no good at all," said Camille, with a little frown.

"Why?" I asked, sipping my wine. It was warming and delicious.

"Marci isn't a good influence. She just wants to party, like a teenager. I have told Lauren, she's been through enough. She must make an executive decision to marry a rich man. None of her friends want to see her suffer."

"Lauren would hardly suffer if she didn't marry a rich man," Hunter remarked.

"No one suffers *more* than a rich woman with a man who isn't—"

"—Sylvie! Hunter!" came a voice from above us.

We all looked up: Marci was leaning over the balcony from the gallery upstairs, waving madly. She looked completely amazing but completely inappropriate in an orange velvet Lela Rose cocktail dress with a huge silk ruffle at the neck. "We're having the best time. Absolutely no one from New York's here," she said. "They're all in Antigua, poor tragic things."

Just then Lauren strolled in, trailed by a tall, good-looking teenage boy. He was in ski pants, with the straps pushed nonchalantly off his shoulders. His matted blonde hair grew straight into his eyes, half-covering his face, which added to his cool allure. He couldn't have been more than fifteen years old.

"Have you met Henri?" said Lauren, with a wink. She was wearing faded corduroy pants and a huge cashmere sweater. She seemed extraordinarily relaxed, compared with the last time I'd seen her. "Ooh! Glühwein! Mmmm. Henri's going to introduce me to all the cute underage guys out here."

"*Non!* I forbid it!" objected Camille.

"*Maman,*" huffed Henri. He poured a *vin chaud* for Lauren and one for himself, and stretched lazily into an armchair. From there he glared possessively at Lauren while chewing his blonde forelock.

"Sylvie, why don't you come up and see my new ski outfits," said Marci from the balcony.

"Sure," I said. "Will you be OK without me for five minutes, Hunter?"

"I'll survive, but *only* five minutes," he replied sweetly.

I followed Marci upstairs. When we were in the bedroom she said, "What are you guys going to do for Hunter's birthday?"

Hunter's birthday! It was on Christmas Eve, and I had completely forgotten about it. I felt terrible. I had vaguely planned to do a surprise party back in New York, but with the last-minute Megève trip it had completely slipped my mind.

"Well, maybe I could do a surprise party out here," I said. "Our chalet's perfect for a fun cocktail."

"It would be so cute. We'll help you," said Marci. "We've got three days till the twenty-fourth, which is enough time. It's going to be *amazing*. I've met so many new people here already."

I was worried about Marci. Her mood was relentlessly upbeat, but it seemed forced. Surely she must be missing Christopher?

"Don't you love the off-vanilla of the ski jacket?" said Marci, showing off a piece of the gorgeous ski gear that she had bought at Jet Set in St. Moritz. Marci squished the jacket with her fingers. "Isn't the down filling so . . . mmm . . . goodgey. Look, it has this little red star on the collar, which is *very* Jet Set, and the matching pants have another red star right on the sexy part of your butt—"

"Are you OK, Marci? Have you seen Christopher?"

"I am sure I saw that gorgeous Swedish Princess Victoria at Jet Set. It's the only place in the world that makes chic ski stuff. There isn't anywhere else you can get chinchilla snowboots," continued Marci, holding up a cloud-colored fur boot. "Aren't they *to die*?"

"Marci, what is happening with you and Christopher?" I said, serious.

"Sylvie, you are so sweet to be concerned, but actually, everything is . . . proceeding."

"What do you mean, proceeding?" I asked.

"I've changed my mind, about becoming a divorcée. It's seeing all those pictures of movie stars shrinking into a swizzle stick when they've become single again. It's really put me off. I'm trying to gain weight now, can you imagine? Christopher's saying he wants to come back. So we're in . . . negotiations. Sophia's organizing the whole thing. She's been so sweet, talking to him and so on."

"Sophia?" I hoped Marci didn't sense my lack of enthusiasm.

"Yes. She told me to get these. Look."

With that Marci popped a pair of huge, Jackie O style sunglasses on her nose. They looked even bigger than Nicole Richie's eyewear, if that's possible.

"From the Hermès store down in the Place de l'Église. They're the only polarized Jackie sunglasses *in the world*. You can ski in them. You can see three miles in them. Four hundred and fifty euros! But you feel *so good* skiing in them. I won't regret these. No."

"Four hundred and fifty euros is a lot for a pair of sunglasses."

"I'm worth it." Suddenly Marci took the Hermès shades off and looked at me with a mischievous smile. "Listen, don't tell a soul this, but Sophia told me something."

I looked at Marci, my eyebrows raised.

"She's having an affair," she said.

"Sophia's *always* having an affair," I remarked, blasé.

"With a married man." Marci put the glasses back on and turned back to the mirror, admiring herself. "Hasn't she got the best taste?"

⚜

Who cared that I couldn't ski, I said again to myself as I regarded the Alps from the deck of the chalet the next morning. They really *do* look as fresh and clear as the pale blue mountains on an Evian bottle. I couldn't wait to be up there in the clear air.

"You're going to love it," said Hélène, the ski instructor Hunter had hired to teach me. She was twenty-three years old, with dark hair and intensely freckled skin. She'd appeared at 9 A.M. that morning to pick me up, wearing a bright yellow instructor's jacket, and a headscarf printed with strawberries.

"I'm excited," I said.

We'd arranged to meet Hunter, who'd left very early that morning to ski a black run, at a mountainside restaurant, La P'tite Ravine, at midday for lunch.

Three hours later, a burning pain shooting into my foot,

and with my right ankle wedged at a sharp right angle to my calf, I couldn't have been more desperate to get off the slopes. Why people called skiing a vacation I could no longer fathom: this wasn't a vacation, it was like being the guy who almost died in *Touching the Void*, I thought miserably as I tried to move. Two toddlers shot past me on mini-skis. How were they doing that, and why were they smiling? Didn't they know they were about to die? God, being married is a nightmare, I thought, feeling the agony sear up into my ankle. Suddenly, just because you're married, you have to join in a husband's life-threatening pursuits, like skiing, while they do not have to join in on your life-enhancing ones, like Pilates classes.

"We must go up," said Hélène. "Your husband is expecting us, and there's no way to find him now."

"I can't," I wailed miserably. Maybe I had fractured my ankle.

"Then we have to go back down in the car," said Hélène.

"I just . . . can we just stay here and . . ." I burst into tears.

Suddenly I felt a tap on my shoulder. I twisted my stiff neck to find myself looking up into a man's mirrored sunglasses. They belonged to Pierre, Sophia's ex-boyfriend from Paris.

"Pierre," I groaned.

"Oh my God, are you all right?" he asked, concerned.

"She won't get up," said Hélène, with a frustrated sigh.

"Are you in pain?"

"Yes, and I promised to meet Hunter at P'tite Ravine. I can't even move."

"Here," he said, gently pulling me up with Hélène's help. I managed to stand, shakily.

"You should go home. I'll go find Hunter."

"Really?" I said gratefully.

Pierre nodded. Why Sophia had let this one go for a married man I knew not.

"You must come to Hunter's surprise birthday party at the chalet," I said, regaining my composure a little. "It's on the twenty-fourth."

"I'd love to," said Pierre. "Now, you should be going."

❧

Melania Trump wouldn't get on at all well, clothes-wise, in Megève. There are only two nights of the year when one is allowed to dress up—Christmas and New Year's. The rest of the time, the dress code is strictly informal, or smart-casual at the dressiest. The most important accessory at a Megève party, I soon realized, is a cell phone with a camera. As the drawing room filled up with guests the night of Hunter's birthday, all they did between sips of champagne or bites of *raclette* was compare pictures of each other mid-ski jump. By ten o'clock the chalet was packed, and Hunter seemed to be having a great time. There was only one person missing: Marci. She hadn't appeared, and endless people she'd invited were showing up asking for her. Where was she?

I spotted Camille, her seventeen-year-old daughter, Eugenie, her son Henri, and Lauren sprawled on the sheepskin rugs picking at bowls of *flocon de Megève* by the fire. Maybe they would know where Marci had got to. Hunter and I went over and joined them.

"There's an eighties moon-boot revival going on," Camille was saying. She was sporting a giant pair of fluffy white boots. They looked like enormous marshmallows on her feet.

"They're a little *out*, Mom," said Eugenie, regarding her mother as one would a loser cousin. "All the Monaco kids were wearing the pink and violet puffy boots après-ski *last* year. Now it's all about seventies snowboots."

Eugenie got up and headed over to her friends, who were all clad in skin-tight jeans, fur gilets, and vintage boots of pony skin or tan suede. Their look was very Ali MacGraw in Colorado.

"She's unbelievably cute," I said, as she walked off. I sat down next to Camille.

"Isn't she?" said Camille, looking fondly over at her daughter. "Now, Sylvie, please encourage your friend to re-marry."

"I'm not sure if I can under the circumstances. Husbands make you do things like ski," I joked.

"Husbands are terrible, darling, aren't they?" said Hunter, kissing my hand affectionately.

Everyone laughed. My ankle had been so inflamed by my fall that I'd avoided the slopes and spent the last few after-noons at the spa at Les Fermes de Marie getting physiother-apy. Today I'd stopped by the Hermès boutique, where I, like Marci, had been seduced by the Jackie O ski glasses. When I'd gone to pay for them I realized that Marci had wildly under-estimated the price tag: they were actually €650, a price based on Hermès' rule that anything by Hermès costs at least seven times as much as it would anywhere else. Still, the glasses were so fabulous I was sure they would speed my recovery. I wouldn't regret them.

"Lauren," continued Camille, "you are spoiled. You are rich. You like incredible homes, a lot of travel. You should marry an older man. Otherwise you'll be bored—"

"Camille, I'm not interested in marriage. Old, rich guys are boring. The only one I could do is Barry Diller," joked Lau-ren. She looped her arm over Henri's shoulders and sighed, with an exaggerated wistfulness. "But this little Henri here! *Soooo* cute!"

She took Henri's hand and dragged him off into the crowd. Camille rolled her eyes and groaned.

"Camille, have you seen Marci yet?" I asked.

"She's having dinner with Pierre," she said. "Then they're picking up Sophia D'Arlan and coming late—"

"But I didn't invite Sophia D'Arlan tonight," I interrupted, slightly annoyed.

"You don't get Pierre without Sophia," said Camille.

"But Sophia isn't dating Pierre anymore," I said.

Just then, I saw Marci squishing into the crush on the far side of the room. She looked flushed and excited from the cold night air. Behind her followed Pierre, and after him, Sophia. Why was she *always* around? Wherever Hunter was, Sophia was, it seemed. Or . . . maybe I was being unfair. Maybe she was just here with Pierre, by chance. After all, I had invited Pierre myself. As it turned out, Sophia immediately disappeared into the guest bedroom with Pierre. No one saw either of them again all night. I didn't even get to say hello to her that evening, which was a relief.

Christmas day in Megève is like something from *The Snow Queen*. A heavy overnight snowfall made the village look like it had been dipped in Chantilly cream, the church providing a meringue-like spire. After a charming church service, Hunter and I bought *chocolats chauds* in the main square, then went home and spent most of the afternoon relaxing in the hot tub on the deck.

"Thank you for organizing the party, Sylvie," said Hunter as we sat in the steaming bubbles. "It was so wonderful, and so different from New York."

"I loved it too," I said, wrapping my dripping arms around him and kissing him. Everything was so sexy and romantic here. "You are the *best* husband—"

Just then, I heard my BlackBerry beeping. I'd left it on the side of the tub, knowing that my family would send a few emails today. Gingerly avoiding covering it with water, I picked it up and read the email out loud:

To: Sylvie@hotmail.com
From: Lauren@LHB.com
Re: Jailbait Make Out

Darling Sylvie,
    Henri is so growth-spurty and awkward. That geeky teen thing is so cute. He thinks he fell in love with me last night, which might be a bit tricky with his mom and dad. I'm not in love, but I highly recommend making out with someone less than half your age at least once in your lifetime.
    Just to make gross generalizations, which you know I love to do, the thing about fifteen-year-old men is that all they want to do is f ♥♥♥, because they're so young and virile and they don't know what else to do. It all started when we were dancing. Henri was so tall, and he did this really weird thing where he would keep holding my hands up in the air, high above my head, and then finally I realized what was going on and I said, "Stop looking at my breasts! Stop it!" Then, I don't know, I thought it was kind of adorable that he was so into my breasts like that—after all, he hasn't really gotten to see any yet, and literally a second later he was on top of me on the deck. He came after five minutes, and then he blacked out. I took that as a compliment actually. I always used to black out at that age at Studio 54 when I was having the best time. Thanks for a great party. Four down!

"Oh, Jesus," laughed Hunter. "What about her big love with Giles Monterey? Has she forgotten about him?"

"Listen to this," I said. I read the end of the email:

> You will be pleased to hear that Henri's youthful butt has started to erase the haunting memory of Mr. Moscow's beautiful blue eyes. If I don't hear from Monterey soon there is real hope for me that I can completely forget about him. Here's to moving on to number five.

"I think he'd better make a move on her soon," said Hunter.

"He's engaged, darling, you seem to keep forgetting that."

"So he is. Now," said Hunter, coming close to me, "I think we should go and make full use of that incredible bedroom we have in there."

Later that evening we lounged lazily in front of the fireplace, chatting about the rest of our trip. It was perfect—cozy, sexy, everything. Camille was right. I should encourage Lauren to get married. There was no other way to get this feeling.

"Why don't we open the gifts now?" I said, just before dinner. "I'm so excited about my pressie."

"Oh, darling, my gift for you is very humble, I'm afraid. Don't get all excited."

It was sweet the way Hunter was pretending he hadn't bothered at all. I couldn't wait to see the necklace. While Hunter disappeared off into the guest bedroom, where he had been storing his gifts, I went to find mine from under the bed in our room. I had wrapped up two books and a photograph of Hunter and me in Paris that I'd had framed and engraved. I retrieved them and went back into the drawing room.

I put them in front of Hunter, who was sitting cross-legged on the rug by the fire. He had a small square box in front of him, wrapped in bright red paper with a silver bow. Ooh. It was definitely jewel-size.

"You open mine first," I said, trying to act casual.

"How adorable, darling," said Hunter, when he saw the photograph. He kissed me on the lips. "I'm very touched. Now why don't you open this?"

He handed me the little package. He was looking edgy, I thought. That was a good thing. He must be nervous about whether I was going to like the jewelry. I picked up the little red box and started unwrapping it. The layers of red paper came off. Underneath was a black leather box.

"Oooh!" I said, looking up at Hunter.

He swallowed, worried. It was very endearing. I lifted the lid of the velvet box to see several layers of white tissue paper.

"I'm so thrilled, darling . . ." I said, as I lifted the layers of tissue. There was something glinting underneath. I took it out and looked at it. "A . . . silver napkin ring?" I exclaimed, trying to sound ecstatic.

"I thought you'd like the roses engraved on it," said Hunter. He looked upset. Maybe he could tell I was disappointed. I didn't want to hurt him, so, trying to sound happy, I said, "I love roses," planting a kiss on his nose. "They look so . . . romantic . . . on a napkin ring."

Where, oh, where was my necklace?

❧

"Do *not* confront him. It's not hard evidence of an affair," said Lauren.

"Affair," I repeated horrified. The word completely freaked me out.

"The only thing that counts as real proof of extra-marital activity is finding thong underwear that's not yours. And not getting a piece of jewelry you expected isn't exactly . . . well, it wouldn't stand up in court. Maybe he just forgot it."

I'd met Lauren for lunch the next day on the terrace of L'Idéal. It was so sunny that the skiers stripped down to their T-shirts while they ate their plates of *pela*. It was however, not a good choice of venue for such a conversation: everyone in Megève came here for lunch, if they could get a table.

"Lauren! Shhhhh!" I hissed, looking around at the other diners anxiously. No one was taking the slightest notice of us. "What am I going to do—"

At that moment, call it coincidence, or just call it skiing— Sophia herself appeared on the far corner of the terrace. She was dressed in a cream ski outfit. As she bent over to loosen her boots, I noticed a red star on the butt of her pants. She had the same ski gear as Marci. She removed her jacket and tied it around her waist. She was wearing a thin pink T-shirt underneath, which showed off her tan beautifully. Just then a cry went up from a table of six Frenchmen two tables away from us. They all had George Hamilton tans, which, in Megève, are still very in.

"Sophia! *Viens nous voir!*" they called when they saw her. Sophia waved and made her way toward them.

"Oh, God, she's coming this way," I said.

"Be cool, say hello. In fact, let's be *over-friendly*," commanded Lauren. "Hello, Sophia!" she called out loudly, as Sophia made her way across the terrace.

Sophia turned and saw us. She smiled and walked across to our table. When she arrived she said,

"Lauren! Hi! Sylvie! Thank you so much for last night. Pierre loved the party . . . such a lovely place . . . I heard Eugenie did a striptease . . . in your hot tub. . . ."

Something caught my eye. If I wasn't mistaken, there, hanging just below the edge of Sophia's tee was a pendant.

Each time she made a little movement, I glimpsed it, swinging against her skin. The necklace consisted of a platinum chain, with a large, translucent mauve stone attached. Sure enough, the letter *S* snaked around it in diamonds. It was exquisite. *It couldn't be*, I thought. I looked again, hoping I wasn't being too obvious, but Sophia registered my gaze. She smiled right at me and said, "Have you seen my Christmas present, Sylvie?" As Sophia regaled us with details of Eugenie's antics, she twirled the lovely jewel in her fingers, and then popped it in her mouth and chewed on it. Was she *flaunting* it in front of me?

Hoping to hide the distress in my eyes, I grabbed my new Hermès sunglasses off the table and put them on. Suddenly the necklace came into slightly sharper focus with the aid of the polarized lenses. As I feared, it was indeed identical to the S. J. Phillips sketch. Never, ever, had I regretted a pair of €650 ski glasses so much.

18

Valley of the Dolls, the Sequel

"My God, Sylvie, when did you last eat?" bellowed Tinsley. "You look like a prisoner of war."

It couldn't have mattered less to Tinsley that she was shrieking through a private movie screening at Soho House, but then, everyone does that in New York. It's not considered particularly sophisticated to actually *watch* the movie at a private screening. All anyone cares about at those things is each other's outfits, even though it's too dark to see them.

"I'm just tired. Ssshhh," I whispered, gesturing at the screen.

The truth was, I had barely slept since we'd gotten back from Megève. The last few days there had been a nightmare, with Hunter enjoying himself more and more, while I seethed behind those wretched sunglasses. I was so flabbergasted by what had occurred that day at L'Idéal, that I decided to wait until I got home to decide what to do next. The flights home were exhausting, and by the time I got back to

New York I was so stressed out and fatigued that I looked grimmer than the Corpse Bride.

That night in early January Thack was hosting the screening of *The Women*. It was a comedy of divorcées, which was the last thing I felt like seeing. But I couldn't get out of it: it was a big night for Thack, and I hoped that by arriving at the last minute, when the lights were already down, no one would notice how weary I looked. Unfortunately, the only seat left was on one of the leather armchairs at the back of the room. I had Tinsley on one side, Marci on the other. Phoebe was a little farther down from me.

"Anxiety?" said Tinsley, loud enough for the entire audience to hear.

I nodded. Just then Phoebe leaned across Marci and said, "I always take a Xanax for that. You should try it."

"Actually, Atavan is a better anti-anxiety medication," declared Marci. "I mean, look at me. Things are *horrible*, but I feel *amazing*."

"I pop an Ambien one night and a Valium the next," said Tinsley. "That way you don't get addicted to either of them." She looked delighted, as though she'd unraveled the mystery of life.

Just then a red-headed girl in the row in front of us turned around and said, very matter of fact, "If you're not sleeping, don't take Ambien. It's like an alarm clock. It wakes you up after four hours. I lick a Remeron tablet before bed. It's the strongest anti-depressant on the market. One lick knocks you out for twelve hours."

"Atavan just feels like you are wrapped in one big blanket of love," said Marci. She laughed a lot when she said it, and her eyes lit up.

Was *everyone* in New York on pills, I wondered with horror. Was that how Phoebe always looked so perky? How else do you manage three kids and a lifestyle business? God, maybe Kate Spade's on medication too, I thought. She always looks so bouncy, with her hair defying gravity like that. The fact is, *all* New York wives should look like the Corpse Bride. I was so tired my hair ached. Did everyone else's too? Or did the medicine take care of that? I felt like I was living in a chapter of *Valley of the Dolls*.

❦

When the movie was over, I snuck quickly to the cloakroom and hurriedly wrapped myself in my fur coat. It was bitter outside. Hopefully I could escape without anyone noticing.

"Sylvie? Is that you or the yeti?"

It was Marci. My heart sank.

"Me," I sulked, walking past Marci toward the elevators. "I've got to go."

"Wait," she said. Then she looked at me with a sad expression. It was weird. "There's something I *have* to tell you."

"What?" I asked.

Marci glanced behind her surreptitiously. No one else had come out of the screening room yet.

"I hate to be the messenger ... but ... it's Hunter. It's *him*."

"What are you talking about?" I said.

"Sophia's 'married man.' It's your husband. She says he's madly in love with her, like when they were at Dalton."

I looked at her with disbelief. What was she saying?

"How do you know?" I croaked. All I could utter was a broken whisper.

Marci cast her eyes downward, as though studying the giant daisies in the groovy Soho House carpet, and then back at me.

"I feel *soooo ba-a-a-a-d*. She was over at mine. I overheard her on the phone."

"What did she say, *exactly*?" I dreaded Marci's answer.

"It was something about having gotten some jewelry from him, and they were going away together."

"*Away?* Where?" I gasped.

"I don't know, but I'm furious with her . . . behaving like this. After I *lent* her, *so generously,* my Jet Set outfit with the red star. The only other person in the world who has that outfit is Athina Roussel. It makes your torso look like Giselle's. And I sacrificed all that and loaned it to Sophia, and then she betrays me like this, stealing one of my best friend's husbands, when I trusted her so much. Can you *imagine*?"

I looked at Marci with horror.

"I know. I was speechless too. To treat someone like that after they've lent you the holy grail of snow looks."

"OK, well, I'm going home to . . . brood, I don't know," I sighed miserably. I started to leave.

"Just a second, I have something for you," said Marci, grabbing my arm. "Don't think I'm a drug dealer or anything, but this is for you."

Marci pressed a folded white handkerchief into my palm. I unwrapped it. Inside was a single tablet. I snapped my hand shut.

"Marci!"

"It's a Klonopin. Also known as the gay man's valium. For emergencies."

"Marci, I don't take pills," I insisted.

"Darling, don't be embarrassed. Everyone's drugged twenty-four-seven in New York," whispered Marci, pulling me off into a dark corner. "It's not Botox that's smoothing their brows, it's anti-anxiety medication."

"Are you coming upstairs?" sang out Phoebe's voice from behind us. "We've got the table by the window—"

Ignoring Phoebe, I fled through the fire exit and down the back stairs. Secretly, I was glad I had Marci's Klonopin: in a crisis there's nothing wrong with a chemically induced blanket of love.

⤜⥊⤛

"Can you believe Henri sent me a *llama* for Christmas? What am I supposed to do with a llama? It's going to die of homesickness here. And then Juan keeps faxing pictures of this stallion to me. It's in a field in Spain, waiting for me. I can't stand it." Lauren sighed, as if in frustration. "I suppose you do get better gifts as a divorcée. Five Orgasms sent me a mink-lined Yves Saint Laurent trench coat." Lauren fingered the oversized pearl, gold, and turquoise choker that was flat around her neck, as if to check it was still there. The stones were so large and extraordinarily shaped that it reminded me of a Picasso sketch. "Tony Duquette. It's my me-me gift celebrating Jailbait Make Out and Mogul Make Out. I had to *really* cheer myself up after Sanford. Do you like it?"

"Its incredible," I replied, trying to sound enthusiastic.

"You don't think I look like Elizabeth Taylor wearing it with this lace dress? Do you want to borrow it? Anytime, just ask."

Lauren and I were sitting in one of the double booths at Rescue getting a pedicure the night after the Soho House screening. I'd recounted what Marci had told me the night before, and I suppose she was trying to cheer me up. I'd gone home last night, seen Hunter, and tried to pretend nothing was wrong. I needed time to figure out my next move. When

Hunter had asked me why I looked so exhausted, I'd lied and told him it was the stress of organizing the outfits for Alixe's Winter Ball, which was only a few days away. In the meantime I had tortured myself all night, brooding obsessively and dreading the inevitable confrontation with Hunter. Strangely, he'd seemed as affectionate as ever, which almost made it all the more painful. The fact was, I really loved him.

"I don't understand why he's being so attentive. When I got home last night, he saw I was cold and made me hot ginger tea. Why would he do that if he's seeing Sophia? I love him. I really adore him," I said hopelessly.

"Don't be deceived," said Lauren grimly. "Husbands are always most attentive and sweet when they're up to something."

"Maybe you could take me to see your divorce lawyer," I said.

"Not right now. You shouldn't be speaking to lawyers. You should be figuring things out with your husband," said Lauren, changing tack.

"But—"

"—divorce isn't all it's cracked up to be," Lauren interrupted me. "It's over-rated. And who knows? Maybe Marci's made a mistake."

"But, Lauren, you seem so . . . well, you have fun. I'm miserable. I just want to have fun again."

"Shouldn't you hear Hunter's side first? I think it's time to confront him. Do it tonight," replied Lauren. "*Occasionally* husbands admit the truth."

⋆⋇⋆

I am going to ruin tonight, I thought guiltily when I got home after the pedicure. Hunter had made reservations to see Eartha Kitt at Café Carlyle weeks ago. When he'd suggested it, I thought it had sounded like a very romantic night out. I was due to meet him there at eight. As I got dressed, in a rather somber black velvet cocktail dress that matched my mood, I wondered whether I could delay telling him what Marci had told me: did I really have to do it tonight, of all nights? Or would it be better to get it over with? I couldn't keep pretending nothing was wrong just because there was this thing or that thing we were supposed to be doing. As I headed uptown in a taxi, I tried to steel myself for what was to come: tonight was going to be hell, but if I put it off, I would only be delaying the hell and making things even worse.

When I arrived at the Carlyle, Hunter was already at our table. There was a glass of champagne waiting for me, which I drank in three seconds flat. Gloomy as I felt, I couldn't help but notice what a nice atmosphere there was in the place: it was glitzy but cozy, a welcome relief from the freezing January weather outside.

"Are you all right, darling?" said Hunter, immediately sensing my mood.

"Actually, I'm not . . . feeling too good," I said, eyes lowered. Was I supposed to do this now, I wondered? Or should we order first? Oh God, oh God.

"I think I can cheer you up—"

"I don't think so," I said sadly. I drew in a long breath and started, "Hunter I—"

Just then, Hunter placed a small, purple suede box on my plate. The words S. J. Phillips were stamped across the top in gold. I just stared at it, baffled. What was this supposed to mean?

"Don't you want to open it, darling?" said Hunter. He had a huge smile across his face.

I carefully lifted the lid of the box. There, sitting on a puffy bed of pale blue satin was the pendant from the sketch. It was spectacular: the amethyst glimmered magnificently, as though it was lit from inside, and the diamonds entwined around it twinkled like a galaxy of glittering stars. It was such a romantic gift. But . . . was this the same pendant I had seen on Sophia? It couldn't be! But then, why hadn't Hunter given it to me at Christmas? Should I say something to Hunter now, or not? Maybe Marci *had* made a mistake . . . or . . . oh, God. I didn't know what to do.

"Don't you like it?" said Hunter, looking worried.

"Oh, yes, it's . . . amazing," I said. "Absolutely exquisite."

"I meant to give it to you at Christmas, but the clasp wasn't right. They had to redo it."

Was that true? Had Sophia worn it first? I was mystified.

"Aren't you going to try it on?"

I took the necklace out of the case and fastened it around my neck. I turned and looked in the mirror behind me. The amethyst hung in exactly the right spot, just below my clavicle. It gleamed and sparkled in such a seductive way. It would be lovely to wear to Alixe Carter's ball.

"Hunter, it's lovely, but—"

"—*grrrrrrr!*" purred Eartha Kitt, as she started her set.

Hunter suddenly got up and came and sat on the banquette next to me. He put his arm around me and kissed me affectionately. This wasn't the moment to start accusing him of all sorts of craziness. Maybe I would delay, just for tonight.

When I told Lauren and Marci what had happened, they were just as puzzled as I was. We were having breakfast the next morning at a quiet corner table at Jack's on West Tenth Street.

"But I saw Sophia last night, at Alixe's. *She* was wearing the pendant," said Marci.

"No," I shuddered, unable to hide my worry. "That's impossible. Look," I added, showing her the pendant, which was still around my neck.

"It's identical to the one she was wearing," declared Marci. "That's so bizarre. Weird."

"Marci, you have to find out what's going on," ordered Lauren. "Get Sophia on the phone, *now*."

Marci got up from the table and headed over to a secluded nook. Lauren and I watched anxiously as she dialed Sophia. A few seconds later Marci mouthed "it's her" and spent the next five minutes whispering down the line. I was so nervous I could feel a piercing headache coming on above my left eye.

Eventually she hung up and came back to the table. She looked troubled.

"What did she say? Come on," said Lauren bossily.

"Well . . . I think she said . . ." Marci looked confused. She put her hand to her forehead and pressed it hard as though solving a complicated algebraic equation. Finally she went on, "OK, this is what I think happened. I told Sophia that I loved the necklace she was wearing last night. So, I asked her where it was from. Anyway, she just said '*He* gave it to me.' I think. Yes. That's what she said, or . . ."

"Get on with it," scolded Lauren.

"Don't stress me out. I'm trying to get the story right," replied Marci anxiously.

I drew in a large breath and held it, terrified.

"So, I told Sophia '*He's* given his wife the same necklace.' So Sophia said that *He* had to do that after his wife saw her wearing it in Megève. She thinks you don't have a clue, Sylvie, and she said she felt sorry for you. Anyway, she made me promise not to say a thing but she said that necklace was always meant for her. Always."

"I can't believe it," I whispered, "How can you be sure?"

Marci looked bleak. "Because, darling, Sophia went and got the necklace with him. They went to some jewelry store together in . . . Italy, or, no . . . in London! That's it! Some jewel store in London the Queen likes—"

"Shut up about the Queen! What else," demanded Lauren.

"She says he's leaving you for her. She thinks people are already talking about it. She told me that Hunter has been in love with her since high school and that it's hard for you to compete when you've only known him for two months . . . Or did she say six months?"

Marci paused as though she had lost her thread. Then she continued, "Or something like that. I can't remember *every exact* word she said. I'm really sorry, Sylvie. I don't know how I'm going to get my Jet Set outfit back now, since I will never speak to Sophia again."

I felt very very ill. Then Lauren said, "Did she say anything else at all?"

"She asked if I'd seen some blind item about her and Hunter in Page Six yet."

Lauren was silent. I was in a state of shock. Suddenly Marci grabbed an abandoned copy of that morning's *New York Post* off a neighboring table. She opened it at Page Six and we all crowded over the page. Under a small headline reading "Which Husband . . . ?" were the words ". . . likes to give his wife and girlfriends the same very expensive jewels?"

"*Girlfriend-s*!" I snapped. "There's more than one? Oh, God."

"Sylvie, *you* have to be the one to leave," said Lauren. "Don't let him leave you. It's better to be the leaver than the leavee, self-esteem-wise."

"I agree," said Marci. "I felt really good kicking Christopher out. *Really* good. Look how happy I am now."

"Marci, stop it," said Lauren. "The fact is, we need to get Sylvie into a hotel. You shouldn't speak to Hunter or see him for at least a week. Plan your exit. Only see him when you're not so emotional. Then you can start thinking about your divorce."

All I could do was mumble agreement, my eyes heavy with tears.

⊱※⊰

"Oh, my God," said Lauren grimly. "You're so pale. You're the same color as that Limewash paint everyone's getting from London now. You *totally* clash with the walls. Here's the one thing you've got to do when you leave your husband: get an illegal vitamin drip from Dr. Bo Morgan. You know the high you get from buying a fur coat? It's way better than that. And it makes your skin look like Sophie Dahl's. I'm calling him *now,*" she added, flipping out her cell phone and dialing.

The Pucci Suite at the St. Regis Hotel on East Fifty-fifth Street is not the ideal color scheme for a girl transparent with grief. The place is meant for tan, happy, rich Italian people under the age of twenty-five, like those gorgeous Brandolini sisters you see everywhere. The walls of the drawing room, which looked right over Fifth Avenue, are upholstered in the famous hot pink Venus silk. Even another of Marci's Klonopins hadn't put me to sleep last night. Forget the Corpse Bride; this morning I looked paler than *The Grudge.*

It hadn't been difficult, logistically, to get out of the apartment with a small hold-all last night before Hunter got home. Emotionally, however, I was in meltdown. As I'd snuck out past the doorman, hoping he wouldn't notice my full bag and my tear-stained face, I'd felt as though I'd become sick with a disease from which I'd never recover. As the evening had worn on, there were more and more messages on my cell from Hunter, asking where I was, but I didn't call back. I felt horribly guilty, but Lauren was right. I couldn't speak to him until I'd figured things out, calmed down. But how, I had wondered as I unpacked my little case in the suite, would I calm down from this? Did one *ever* calm down from this kind of thing? How would I ever erase the sight of Sophia in that necklace from my mind? How had I gotten Hunter so wrong? Didn't Phoebe once say he used to be quite a player? The only thing that had gotten me through the night was watching *E! True Hollywood Story: The Barbi Twins.* Late-night TV always put things in perspective: I might be about to get a divorce, but at least I wasn't a bulimic porn sister, I reminded myself, trying to feel grateful.

"I feel feverish," I said to Lauren. I was lying on the drawing room sofa, which was upholstered in lime linen. It made me feel slightly delirious. My body seemed to be pulsating with emotional inflammation. I was as furious as I was devastated. "What am I going to do?"

"You are going to eat breakfast, and then Bo will come and inject you, and then you are going to go to the office, as usual," replied Lauren, dialing room service. "Two orders of scrambled eggs and fruit salad please . . . no, *with* yolks . . . and the toast in a *toast rack . . .* thanks." She came and stood over me. "Finding a silver toast rack in a hotel is harder than locating a Democrat in Texas."

"I think I'm going to call Hunter," I said. "He'll be going out of his mind with worry."

"Absolutely not. I'm going to get an attorney on standby," insisted Lauren.

"Shouldn't I find out what's really going on?"

Lauren ignored my question and just said, "You've got to get up and get ready for work."

"I can't go to work," I objected. I was far too overwrought to go to the studio.

"Sylvie, there are a million girls going to the studio today for fittings for Alixe's ball. You've got to be there. Particularly for *my* outfit."

Lauren had a point. Alixe's imminent party had become a fashion project unto itself. Then there were Nina's movie premiere looks to work on. The premiere of *The Fatal Blonde* was tonight, and although Nina already had those four dresses, she was bound to demand something completely different at the last minute.

"I can't. Thack will have to cope by himself. Do you have any more Klonopin tablets?"

"Wait!" said Lauren excitedly. "I've got the best idea. Get Thack uptown, have the fittings in here. I mean, this is the most beautiful suite in all of New York. Everyone will think Thack is *so* glam . . ." Lauren handed me a glass of water and two little pills.

"Here, take these."

⚜

"It's sick," said Marci. "I love it. I feel *très* C. Z. Guest." She was wearing a pale lemon lace column dress that swirled into a giant puff at her feet. She was focusing hard on her reflection in the gilt deco mirror above the fireplace while I pinned the hem. "I look *so* . . . Palm Beach in a good way." Then she lowered her voice and whispered, "Are you doing OK, Sylvie?"

I shook my head and carried on working.

"Lauren made me get some intravenous drip this morning. I felt like my blood was on fire," I said.

The aforementioned Dr. Bo Morgan had appeared at 9 A.M., dressed like a rock star in Paper Denim & Cloth jeans and a white shirt so well starched it rustled when he moved. From a Goyard case he'd produced a drip and a bottle of brown liquid labeled Pirateum. While he hooked me up to the drip and the liquid seeped into my veins, he told me all about his super-model clients. He didn't seem like a doctor at all. When I told him how young he looked, he'd smiled and said, "I take my own advice."

"Bo! I love Bo," said Marci. "Did he tell you your immune system is blown out?"

"Yes, he said my adrenal system is on over-drive, but I know why I feel so wiped out. I'm furious about everything. Lauren won't even let me call my husband," I said.

"She's right. He needs to know what he's lost—"

"—Is this *actressy* enough for me?" interrupted Tinsley. She was floating toward us in a red ball dress with thick frills at the shoulders. "How will people know I've decided to become an actress? I look like a flamenco dancer."

"All actresses dress to look like flamenco dancers, so there's no problem there," said Marci dismissively.

"My wrists look . . . *fat* in this . . . *thing."* Salome was standing at the door to the bathroom wearing a silver satin charmeuse dress with long, billowy sleeves and black grosgrain bows that tied at the cuff. "Ugh . . . I'm *disgusting,"* she added.

"Wrists can't put on weight," said Tinsley, nudging Marci out of her way so she could get a better view of herself in the mirror. "You look great. Now, Sylvie, what about me—"

"Sylvie, I want the dress I had on hold before. The black satin," Salome declared.

Oh, God! Nina had that dress in L.A. Mind you, the premiere was tonight, Wednesday, and Alixe's party was on Friday. I could easily get the dress back from Nina by then.

"It's out . . . on a fashion shoot," I lied.

"Oh, OK," said Salome grumpily. She wandered into the bedroom, where Thack was working on Alixe, who'd demanded total privacy.

"What are you all doing in there?" asked Tinsley suspiciously. She followed Salome into the bedroom, Marci followed her, and I was finally alone.

I let the dress I was working on fall to the floor and stared listlessly out of the window. All this seemed so superficial and unimportant. Who cared about some stupid party outfits and whether or not Salome had put on half an ounce on her wrist? How was I going to survive this craziness without my husband? I wiped a tear from my face. I just had to get through the next couple of hours. Sometimes, even the most exclusive illegal vitamin drip can't make you smile.

⚜

"HELLO!!! MISCHA! BARTON! You! Look! STUNN!-ING! Tonight!" shouted *Access Hollywood*'s Nancy O'Dell in the booming awards voice required on red carpets. She sounded like she had a loudspeaker installed in her neck.

I was watching the show from the hotel suite. Thack was so excited about Nina appearing in his outfit that he had organized an early-evening screening at his studio for staff and friends. Feeling bleak, I'd decided to watch alone. Hunter had left more messages today, but Lauren and Marci had convinced me that calling him back would be unwise at this point. Maybe I should get Marci to let him know I was OK, I thought. I hated the thought of Hunter worrying about me like this. It made me feel terrible. But, if Marci called, she'd tell him where I was. She couldn't even vaguely keep a secret. This was awful. I turned my attention back to the TV: maybe *Access Hollywood* would take my mind off things.

"JUST STUNNING!!!!" yelled Nancy, who was dressed in a blue gown covered in white rhinestones. She looked exactly like one of the chandeliers downstairs in the St. Regis lobby. "Can you tell us all what you're *wearing*!!!!"

"Chanel couture," replied Mischa, looking bored.

"Chanel!!! *Koo-tooor*!!!" repeated Nancy. "IN! CRED! IBLE! You look lovely!!! I understand the lace is from—Oh!!! I see Nina Chlore! Coming over!" Now Nancy looked bored with Mischa Barton. "ThankyouMischagoodbye—" she said, in the your-time-is-up tone of voice TV hosts reserve for evicting celebrities from their turf.

On the screen, Nina floated toward Mary in a cloud of chiffon. Despite everything, I couldn't help but be excited. I was suddenly glued to the screen, inspecting every last detail of Nina's look.

"Here is Nina Chlore!!! The star of *The Fatal Blonde* . . ." Nancy was saying as she approached. "Nina! Chlore! You! Are! Amazing!"

"Stop!" said Nina sweetly as she arrived at the *Access Hollywood* stage. "*You* are amazing, Nancy. How *are* you?"

"I'm good! Whose is this . . . *magical* gown, Nina?"

"The designer made it specially for me," smiled Nina.

"How wonderful!!!!" screamed Nancy, over the yells for Nina behind her.

"It's Versace," said Nina. "There's no one I love more than Donatella."

I couldn't believe it. Thack would be devastated. And I was in no state to cheer him up. Just then, my phone started beeping. I looked at the screen. Alixe was calling. I decided not to take her call. The last thing I wanted now was a change of dress before Friday. After a few seconds her call went to voicemail.

A few moments later, the phone started ringing again. Alixe was obviously desperate to get through.

I picked up. Alixe sounded blocked up, like she was sick with a cold.

"Is the dress OK?" I asked.

"I love the . . . d-d-dress," stuttered Alixe. God, was she weeping?

"Alixe, are you OK?"

"It's not me. It's S-s-s-ugh-sanford. He's dead."

"How awful."

I'd had no idea Alixe was so close to him. She sounded cut up.

"God, I'm so sorry, Alixe. You sound so distressed," I added.

"I a-a-a-amm!" she howled. She sounded hysterical. "It's so *incons-s-s-iderate! D-d-d-ying!* Like that! Two days before my lovely ball! If only he could have died on Saturday. Then I could still have had the party. Now everyone's got to go to the wake on Friday," she wept. A sound like a pig hoovering a trough of swill shuddered down the line. Alixe had uttered a long, ugly snivel to clear her nose. Finally, brightly, she said, "Now, can we discuss my outfit? For the funeral?"

19

The See-and-Be-Seen-Funeral

"What a *fabulous* place to be dead," breathed Lauren.

A glamorous funeral at Saint Thomas Church, the Gothic pile on the corner of Fifth Avenue and Fifty-third Street, presided over by a minister who happens to be an Orlando Bloom look-alike, is enough to send even the most superficial New York girl straight around the religious bend. For a start, it's right opposite the Gucci store, so it's convenient, and, secondly, there was more brain candy at Sanford's funeral (Charlie Rose / Bloomberg / Oprah) than at one of Rupert Murdoch's Sun Valley summits.

Sanford Berman had died of vanity. One minute he was at the dentist being fitted for a new gold crown for a lower right molar—an item for which he had an aesthetic passion—the next he was choking on it, and dead.

Lauren had begged me to accompany her to the funeral. Her sense of regret—regret that she'd argued with Sanford, regret that they hadn't remained friends, regret that she hadn't said *au revoir*, regret that she hadn't had an affair with him (in her grief she even wished she had slept with the waterbed after all)—hit her, she said, almost as badly as a Marquee Club hangover. She was so headachey on the morning of the funeral that she was completely unable to choose between her black Chanel shift and her black Dior shift, despite the fact that there was zero difference between them. She'd ended up in the Dior and had pinned a giant Verdura sapphire brooch at her neck. I, meanwhile, was so traumatized by not having spoken to Hunter for three days that I was equally inept that morning. The only thing I could pull myself out of my gloomy retreat for was a funeral. I had even pinned a black veil to my hair, hoping that no one would be able to see the distress in my eyes. Inevitably, we both arrived at Saint Thomas so late there weren't even any service sheets left.

No wonder Sanford had wished for a funeral here, I thought, as we stepped inside. The place is so cavernous you could fit Disneyland inside it—and 600 friends. As the giant oak door echoed closed behind us, the frenzy of Fifth Avenue was replaced by the comforting hush peculiar to a church.

"Over here," came a voice from our left.

Marci, Salome, and Alixe had saved us a spot in their pew. We squeezed in. Salome was looking particularly devastating today in a knife-sharp, black silk faille skirt suit from Roland Mouret. She even had black gloves and a black lace handkerchief to complete her look. Marci was in a black crepe-de-chine, tiered-ruffle shift dress, and Alixe was wearing one of Thack's boxy jackets with a short skirt, and had a black rose pinned to her lapel. They looked like three very glamorous extras from *The Godfather*.

"I am the resurrection and the life, saith the Lord; he that believeth in me, though he were dead, yet he shall live—" began the minister solemnly.

"—that minister can resurrect me *any* time," murmured Marci, flushing a hot pink.

"—and whosoever liveth and believeth in me, shall never die—"

"Do you think ministers are allowed to have girlfriends?" said Marci in a low voice.

"I thought you were getting back with Christopher," I whispered.

"I am!" said Marci, affronted. "It's in negotiation, I told you that before."

"Oh," I said. "That's really good news."

The minister continued.

"We brought nothing into this world and it is certain . . ." (he paused, regarding the congregation to make sure they were paying particular attention to a passage relevant to themselves) . . . "and I repeat, it is *certain* we carry nothing out . . ."

"It's a shame they don't tell you this stuff *before* you're dead," said Alixe. " It's *such* good advice. What am I going to do with all the stuff I've bought when I croak?"

"Let us pray," ordered the minister.

The congregation knelt as one, and silence fell. Suddenly from behind us I heard the church door creak open. Who could be this late? I turned to look. Dressed in long, flowing black chiffon, Sophia D'Arlan appeared. I literally felt my intestines curdle at the sight of her. I tapped Lauren on the shoulder, and we both followed Sophia with our eyes. She walked silently up the aisle, her dress flowing romantically behind her. I think everyone in the congregation looked at her.

"This is *not* her wedding," said Lauren disapprovingly. "How inappropriate." She sighed, exasperated, and bent her head in prayer again.

I, on the other hand, couldn't help but watch while Sophia

walked brazenly to a pew right at the front. Everyone was forced to shuffle up to allow her to sit down. God, she was selfish! She took a seat next to a man in a dark suit who looked, from behind, vaguely familiar, but it was too far away for me to really see who it was. He leaned in to talk to her. Maybe I *could* see who it was. NO! Was that—

"Lauren," I nudged her. "Is that . . . *Giles*?"

Lauren's head shot up. She stared at the man in question, transfixed.

"What is he doing . . . in the family pew . . . and . . . is that *Sophia* whispering to him?" she said crossly.

". . . Amen," said the minister. "Now we continue with our first reading, the psalm read by Giles Monterey."

"*What?*" gasped Lauren, as Giles made his way silently up to the pulpit.

"Oooh. The cute stepson. We see him at last!" giggled Salome. "My God, he's *adorable*."

"Salome, did you just say that is Sanford's *stepson*?" uttered Lauren, amazed. "Are you *sure*?"

"His mom—Isabel Clarke Monterey—was a model with my mom in the seventies in London. I used to play with him when we were three. He was hot even then," said Salome. "It was a whole huge scandal. My mom says Giles never forgave Sanford for breaking up his mom's marriage and then leaving her two years later. I guess he's here with his mom—look, there she is."

Salome pointed at a woman sitting in Giles' pew. When she turned to the side, I could see that she was beautiful, if fragile-looking. Lauren meanwhile had turned ashen, as though the blood had drained from her body. She was obviously madly in love. She didn't move her eyes from Giles while he read: "The Lord is my shepherd, therefore can I lack nothing."

He paused, and regarded the congregation, as though looking for someone.

"He shall feed me in green pastures,"

He paused again, and seemed to catch Lauren's eye. For a moment the two of them seemed locked in each other's gaze.

"And lead me forth beside the waters of comfort—"

THUNK!

Lauren had fainted.

"Yeah," sighed Salome unsympathetically, as she regarded Lauren collapsed on the pew. "He had that effect on all the girls at pre-school too."

⚜

"It's *so* 1987 here, I love it," declared Salome, as she walked into Swifty's. "If nothing else we are guaranteed an Ivana sighting. Is that Bill Clinton?"

Swifty's, on Lexington and Seventy-second Street, isn't the most obvious spot for a wake. Still, Sanford Berman had lunched there three times a week, and had decreed in his will that his wake would take place there, mainly because he thought the Swifty's caviar would cheer up the mourners.

While Lauren recovered from her love-faint in the restroom, Marci, Alixe, Salome, and I had promised to observe the UnGoogle-able man and Sophia D'Arlan on Lauren's behalf. She was convinced Sophia had designs on Giles. The trouble was, none of us could see either of them. The restaurant was so crowded it was impossible to see where anyone was.

"This is *almost* better than my New Year's ball," huffed Alixe, as she surveyed the crowd. "If it wasn't a funeral I'd be having the most amazing time. "Look, there's Margarita Missoni." She looked over at a willowy girl dressed in a floor-length knitted black dress with silver leaves embroidered around the hem. She was surrounded by older men. "I'm so desperate to get her to use the Arancia bubble bath. Do you think it's a sin to network at a wake?" Alixe didn't wait for an answer. She bounded straight after her.

"Girls! She's over there!" said Salome suddenly. She nodded discreetly toward an alcove on the far side of the room, in which were framed the silhouettes of Sophia D'Arlan and Giles. "They're . . . *chatting*." She looked piqued. "It's *outrageous*. Grave-side flirting is unforgivable."

"Is Sophia wearing . . . sequins with that chiffon?" asked Marci, with slight disdain. She craned her neck to get a better look at her outfit. "That is a woman interested only in perpetuating the *myth* that she wears Valentino."

Marci obviously loathed Sophia at this point. I, meanwhile, observed the scene pensively. What was Sophia up to, flirting with Giles like that, while planning to run off with my husband too? The girl was unbelievable.

"OK, I'm going over there to break it up," said Salome, marching off in the direction of Giles and Sophia. She had an enormous grin on her face, as though she was enjoying herself immensely.

"Shall we sit down for a moment?" said Marci, suddenly looking serious. "I need to talk to you."

We ventured out of the main room and wandered along a side corridor. Two little armchairs perched invitingly at the end of it, and we headed straight for them.

"Uggh!" sighed Marci, collapsing into one of them.

Marci waited for me to be seated and then said, "Listen, I heard something I thought you might want to know. Hunter and Sophia are meeting tomorrow at MOMA."

"They are?" I whispered. "You're *sure*?"

She nodded.

"I'm really sorry, Sylvie. I overheard something yesterday. Apparently Sophia was having tea at The Mark with Phoebe when she suddenly got a phone call. I'm told that she made a plan for a sexy rendezvous with a married man. She's picked the most romantic spot in the museum: she's meeting him at six o'clock in front of the Monet on the mezzanine."

20

MOMA Madness

*L*ater on that afternoon—it must have been four o'clock—Hunter finally got me on the phone. I hadn't meant to pick up my cell, and when I heard Hunter's voice, I became so jittery I felt a chill come over my body.

"Darling, where on earth are you? I've been out of my mind," said Hunter.

I couldn't believe Hunter had finally gotten ahold of me. My friends had been sworn to secrecy about my whereabouts, and I'd barely turned on my cell phone for the last few days. But there was a little part of me that was secretly relieved that my husband had sought me out.

"Away from you!" I cried.

"What on earth is the matter, Sylvie?"

"You know exactly what the matter is!" I said. "Sophia—"

"What are you talking about?" said Hunter.

I paused before I spoke. How was I going to put this? Finally, I took a long breath and said angrily, "Marci told me that it's an open secret that you and Sophia are having an affair."

There was a shocked silence.

"What?"

"The fact is, you *were* with Sophia in London that weekend. You took her to that jewelry store. She told Marci—and half of New York apparently. And then I saw her in Megève wearing my necklace. I can't believe you!"

"I never gave Sophia that necklace. I can explain—"

"She's still wearing it." My voice rose as my angst level increased. "No more 'explanations.' I know what you're up to. You've been lying to me for months—"

"Darling, it's not what you think—"

"Just leave me alone, Hunter. I don't want this." I could hear my words coming faster and faster, as though I may not have time to get it all out. "I've never been so unhappy. I want a divorce. I'd rather be the leaver than the leavee," I said, echoing Lauren's words.

"The what?"

"Leav-*er*!" I yelled at him, and hung up in a fury of misery and melancholy.

I stared at the cell phone in my hand. Now I was full of doubt. Hunter sounded genuinely shocked. Not at all guilty. But no doubt guilty men cultivate non-guilty tones of voice, I told myself. And then, Lauren had said something terrifying about men being more affectionate toward their wives when they are being ultra-devious elsewhere. I had to see for myself.

❧

You can imagine my state when I arrived at MOMA at ten before six and saw a line that snaked all the way along Fifty-third Street as far back as Sixth Avenue. Hundreds of eager art-lovers were patiently—no, *happily*—standing in line to see inside the great glass box. Just then, a bus spewed out a full load of French tourists. I looked at my watch: 5:55 P.M.

"How long does the line take?" I asked a guard hopefully.

"Forty-five minutes," he replied, automaton-like.

"But—" *I've got to catch my husband cheating on me in five minutes*, I wanted to say. God, it was depressing.

"Can I buy a ticket somewhere else?" I asked.

It was deathly cold out here. My hands were slowly turning a ghastly shade of lilac. Devoid of Christmas lights, chilling its inhabitants to the bone, and drowning in slush— nothing is crueler than New York in January. Especially when your husband's on the loose with a crazy Husband Huntress.

"Yeah. Internet," replied the guard.

What a lot of help that was. I looked at the guard helplessly.

"Or Ticketmaster. 212-555-6000."

"Thank you," I said gratefully.

Thank God. I could call Ticketmaster and book for 6 P.M.—two minutes hence. I dialed the number on my cell phone. Naturally, my call was answered by a computer. Ugh.

"Welcome to Ticketmaster. Please. Listen. Carefully. The Menu. Has. Changed—"

So slow! Impatient, I pushed zero. Maybe that would get me to an operator.

"—sorry. I. Did. Not. Understand. Welcome to Ticketmaster . . ."

This time, I listened, and pushed 5 for ticket sales.

"Hello. What show?" said a voice. Hurrah! A person.

"MOMA," I gabbled.

"Is that a Broadway production?"

Jesus Christ.

"Museum of Modern Art," I said, trying not to get hysterical. I mean, it wasn't the minimum-wage person on the other end of the phone's fault that I was late for a spying session on my husband's mistress.

"Please call the dedicated reservations for MOMA at 212-555-7800."

I looked at my watch. It was already after six. This was hopeless. Still, dejectedly, I started to dial the new number. As I did so, I felt a tap on my shoulder. I whipped around: it was Marci.

"I can't get in," I wailed.

Marci, her face unusually grim, flashed a card reading MEMBER:MOMA in front of me. She took my hand and led me straight into the museum.

"I thought you might need moral support," she said.

MOMA always reminds me of a giant glass candy jar buzzing with flies. The works of art look like giant bonbons invisibly suspended in the air, and the visitors are reduced to tiny black dots swarming *en masse* from de Kooning to Warhol to LeWitt. Where, oh, where was the peaceful, zen-like space I had read about in all those *New York Times* stories? This place was more like Times Square.

"Marci, it's six ten." I said anxiously looking around.

We were standing in the vast white atrium that stretches from Fifty-third Street all the way across the block to Fifty-fourth. Straight ahead was a huge staircase leading up to the mezzanine, which now, controversially, according to those who worry about art controversy, houses Monet's *Reflections of Clouds on the Water-Lily Pond*. A huge glass balcony allows those below to gaze up to the crowds above, and to the giant green plastic helicopter that hangs above the staircase.

"Sophia's never on time. It's part of her man-killing allure."

With that, Marci slipped into the throng surging toward the giant staircase leading up to the mezzanine. I followed her in a state of numb expectation: all that lay ahead was hideous dreadfulness. For once, I was relieved to be invisible, cloaked in the swell of tour groups and school parties: I didn't want anyone to notice me ever again. What could be more embarrassing than a cheating husband? From this moment forward, I thought, I would hide: I would live on the sidelines of life, like the tourists and the out-of-town visitors around me. No doubt I would be in a very bad temper for the rest of my life.

I followed Marci up to the mezzanine, where we were confronted by a giant, steel pin in the center of the room. Like two schoolgirls on the run, we concealed ourselves behind it. From there we could view the Monet and the austere black-leather viewing benches positioned in front of it.

"There she is," whispered Marci. "Alone. Weird."

Sophia was sitting with her back to us, but it was unmistakably her. Who else would be wearing a gold sequin jacket at six o'clock in the evening in a public art gallery?

"This is so odd," said Marci. "It's a quarter after six. No! Wait! She's answering her cell . . ."

Indeed Sophia was now talking into her cell phone. She stood up and started walking right toward the steel pin. Oh, God. She stopped just the other side of the artwork. We could make out little bits of her conversation.

"Yes, darling . . . I saw her at the funeral, poor thing . . . yes, three minutes . . . in the sculpture garden? It's freezing out there. You know I can't bear those giant blue triangles . . . I'd much rather meet you by the Matthew Barney . . ."

With that, she snapped her phone shut, turned on her heel, and headed away from us toward the contemporary galleries.

"I don't know if I can go on," I said to Marci. Hearing Sophia refer to me as a "poor thing" made me so mad, I just wanted to leave. I knew as much as I needed to know already, didn't I? Did I really have to put myself through more agony?

"Sylvie, you have to go through with it. Come on, we'll watch from behind the Dan Flavin. Let's go," she said, following Sophia discreetly.

Sophia had chosen the most popular gallery in the museum for her secret assignation. The room was so crowded, we could barely see her. Hidden from view behind the giant multi-colored Dan Flavin wall, there was no chance of Sophia noticing us. Once we were safely installed, we peeked out from the left side. Sophia was standing peering at Matthew Barney's weird installation, *The Cabinet of Baby Fay La Foe 2000*, a plexiglass coffin containing a top hat and an operating table. What a macabre spot for a romantic tryst.

"Where is he?" whispered Marci.

"Maybe . . . maybe he's not coming," I said hopefully.

Suddenly Sophia waved across the room. As she did so her gold bangles jangled sexily—and my nerves jangled painfully. I could hardly bear to look. But I did. I barely breathed, I was so anxious. After a few seconds, a red-headed, rather short, slightly balding man made his way toward Sophia. Marci took a sharp breath.

"Oh, my good Lord!" she cried, as Sophia and the red-headed man hugged and then kissed in a way that you don't usually see in art galleries, to say the least.

A smile slapped itself across my face: it felt like it would last forever. It felt big enough to wrap around the globe.

"I'm so happy!" I breathed. "That *definitely* isn't my husband. I've made the *best* mistake."

I turned to Marci. She was sheet white.

"What?" I asked her, suddenly sober. "Do you know who that guy is?"

"It's . . ." Marci couldn't speak. Her chirpy voice was reduced to a breathless whisper. "It's *my* husband."

"That's *Christopher*?" I asked.

"I've made the most ghastly mistake," wailed Marci.

"So have I," I mumbled. What a mess.

With that, Marci rushed out into the mezzanine and headed toward the staircase. I chased after her. When she got to the top of the staircase, she stopped under the giant helicopter. She looked up above her, and then crossed herself twice over.

"Dear God, when I go home and shoot myself tonight," she prayed, "please, *don't* resurrect me."

"Marci, calm down, don't do anything silly," I said grabbing her arm.

"I'm going to kill him. Who was Ivana's lawyer again?"

21

The Disappearing Husband

While Marci *was* being resurrected against her will by Salome, who had come, saint-like, and picked her up at MOMA, I flew down Fifth Avenue by cab. I couldn't get to the apartment quickly enough: I was desperate to see Hunter and make amends. Why had I been so vile to him earlier? Why hadn't I let him explain his side of the story? How could I have not trusted him! What a fool I'd been, I chastised myself. Why had I ever thought things were as obvious as they seemed: Sophia was far too clever to have been doing what she *seemed* to be doing. She had tormented me with her flirting with Hunter while distracting Marci and me from her real mission—nailing Christopher. Maybe I had been hanging out with the debutante divorcées far too much and they'd influenced me for the worse. They were paranoid about men, unsurprisingly, and it had made me paranoid too. Certainly, I had not been imagining Sophia's behavior— she *had* been making a play for my husband, whatever her other motives were—but no less than she was after every innocent husband in New York. Poor Marci. What a wicked game Sophia had played.

What on earth was I going to say to Hunter, I wondered frantically, as the cab swerved down past the corner of Fifth and Twenty-third Street. I couldn't believe that three hours ago I had been demanding a divorce, and now there was nothing I wanted less. I had been wrong about everything, but, however wrong one is, it's hideous having to admit it. "I'm sorry" was a feeble antidote from a wife who had accused her husband of the ultimate marital crime. I felt terrible, completely ashamed of myself. Panicked and anxious, I could feel my lungs puffing faster and faster: I felt as though I was going to suffocate with shame and embarrassment.

When I finally reached One Fifth I paid the driver and ran toward my building. By now icy rain was coming down in flat, cold sheets, and by the time I got inside I was half-soaked and hyperventilating.

"Is Mr. Mortimer home?" I asked the doorman, Luccio, as I flew past him.

"He left for the airport an hour ago," said Luccio. "Where's he going?"

I stopped, dead still, in the middle of the lobby. Hunter had gone? Had I driven him away with my accusations? If so, I could hardly blame him.

"You all right?" asked Luccio.

"Yes . . . no . . . I just . . ."

I scrabbled in my bag for my phone. When I finally found it, I called Hunter's cell. It went straight to voicemail. I left a frantic message telling him how much I loved him and begging him to call me. Next I called his office. Hopefully someone would still be there. After a few rings, one of the interns, Danny, picked up.

"Where's Hunter?" I asked. "It's his wife."

"Oh, he went off to . . ." Danny trailed off. "Hang on. Let me ask someone."

I heard voices in the background, and then he came back on the line.

"We're not sure where he is now. He left a couple of hours ago. He said he was going to Zurich . . . or was it Geneva? Er . . ."

"When's he due back?" I asked, desperate.

"He's taken his diary from his desk . . . We don't really know how long this trip is going to be."

I hung up. Where was Hunter? How was I going to find him? Was I going to be the leavee after all? Maybe, maybe . . .

I ran out into the street. It was still pouring. Maybe I'd go over to Lauren's. She'd know what to do. Tears streamed down my cheeks as I started walking up Fifth Avenue in search of a cab. Suddenly I heard a familiar voice from behind me.

"Sylvie! Sylvie!"

I turned to see Milton standing behind me. He was tan and dressed in an Afghan hat and a yak-hair cape. He must have just gotten back from his Silk Road.

"Hi," I said falteringly.

"What's happened? Sylvie, are you crying?"

"It's Hunter. He's gone," I replied, my shoulders juddering.

"OK, let's get you home," said Milton, putting a comforting arm across my shoulder.

Half an hour later, Milton and I were installed in the apartment eating Belgian truffles ordered in from the Chocolate Bar. Without drawing breath, I told him the whole story, and I cried my whole guts out, or so it felt. As I talked, it occurred to me that whatever I had seen earlier, with Christopher and Sophia, it still didn't explain the two identical necklaces. Why had my husband given Sophia and me the same jewelry? It was so strange, especially if Sophia was cheating with Christopher. I felt so sorry for Marci! I hoped that Salome was cheering her up.

"Sophia D'Arlan is *unbelievable*. If I'd been here I could have told you exactly what was going on," said Milton, who was languishing on the drawing room sofa in the red silk shalwar kameez that was revealed when he slipped off his cloak.

"What do you mean?" I said, dabbing my eyes with a handkerchief. I was sitting cross-legged on the floor, trying to dry myself out in front of the fire.

"Sylvie, Hunter bought that necklace for *you*. You only."

"How do you know?"

"Because, darling, I was there. We were all in London that weekend, staying at Blakes—"

"But, Milton!" I interrupted angrily. "Why didn't you tell me? I remember asking you specifically if you had seen Hunter that weekend when I couldn't get hold of him, and you said you hadn't."

Milton roused himself from the sofa with a swish of his crimson robes. He sat up and leaned toward me conspiratorially. Then he said in the hushed tones he reserved for spreading the most valuable gossip, "I shouldn't even be telling you this, but we were all sworn to secrecy. It was so romantic."

"What was so romantic? Why has Sophia got the same necklace as me?"

"Well . . . mmm . . . the pendant was Sophia's idea."

"No! What do you mean?" I jumped up and started pacing back and forth in front of the fireplace.

"Well, we were all sitting around at dinner that Friday night in London at Le Caprice—love Le Caprice, *love*—and Hunter—who is so sweet, Sylvie, and loves you so much— asked us how he could make up for the canceled honeymoon.

So Sophia screams, "Jewelry!" So Hunter said he wouldn't know what to get you. Sophia pulls out this great pendant with an *S* on it from under her blouse and tells him to get the same thing made for you."

"The *same*?" My voice rose at least three octaves.

"That's what *I* said. But Sophia told Hunter you'd never know. I think he was so desperate to make up for the honeymoon fiasco that he just plunged in. Sophia even took him to S. J. Phillips herself to commission the piece."

That explained the photograph in *New York* magazine. But Milton wasn't finished. He continued, "It was a rather sweet-slash-stupid straight man's attempt to tell you he was sorry. You know what husbands are like. They never quite know what to buy for their wives. They don't have a clue about jewelry, which I find rather charming, actually."

"But then why did Sophia tell Marci that Hunter had given *her* the necklace?" I protested.

"Because, darling, Sophia wanted Hunter for herself," said Milton. "She wanted you to think that necklace was for her, and by flaunting hers in front of you, she achieved exactly what she wanted—chaos. It doesn't help that Marci is such a hopeless rumor-monger. Sophia's been playing her like a piccolo."

"But what about Christopher?" I asked, confused.

"She obviously went after both husbands and settled for the easiest catch."

"Stop it!" I managed a laugh. "But, what about that Page Six item?"

"Sophia likes nothing more than planting a story about herself in a gossip column. Listen to me, any rumors that get around about Sophia are created by her, and her only. She says *everyone's* in love with her, especially the married guys. I actually heard she was hospitalized for it at one stage. That necklace was *always* for you."

"Oh, Milton. I've wrecked everything," I said, feeling daunted. "What am I going to do?"

"Why don't you have another truffle?"

"You won't believe where I am!"

It was 4 A.M. the same night. Lauren was wide awake on the other end of the line and, presumably, on the other side of the world.

"Where?" I said sleepily.

"Narita Airport, Tokyo."

I sat up in bed and switched on a lamp. Maybe Lauren's adventures would distract me from my own worried state.

"What are you doing in Tokyo, Lauren?" I asked.

"G.M. What can I say? We kissed in the Japan Airlines first-class spa. It's all very *Lost in Translation*. I think he's *madly* in love with me, don't you?"

"Are you in love with him?" I asked.

"God, no! Remember the goal: five Make Outs by Memorial Day, zero commitment," she giggled. "But . . . it was the *Make Out* of *Make Outs*, if you know what I'm saying. I mean . . . compared with all the others, this was like kissing God, honestly. Giles has the best kissing methods of any man I have ever made out with. It was so delicious I thought I was having a near-death experience. Everything went white, and I think I actually fainted for two seconds. Do you know that feeling?"

"Sort of . . ." I trailed off. I couldn't summon up the energy to laugh with Lauren. All I could do was muster up a heavy sigh.

"You sound like hell. What happened?' said Lauren.

I told her the whole sorry story, about Marci and Sophia, and Christopher and Sophia, and me and Hunter.

"What a mess. Jesus. I'll be back tomorrow. Giles wants me

to stay, but . . . I don't want to be disappointed. He has got a
fiancée. I have to remember that."

Lauren's love bubble had suddenly burst. She sounded
deflated.

"I thought you said you didn't want a relationship."

"I don't but . . . I guess now I've completed the Make Out
Challenge, I don't know, I feel a little flat. Where has it gotten me? I'm having a moment of clarity: I mean, I've reached
my goal, but . . . I've gotten nowhere . . . nowhere."

"You've had fun," I said, trying to cheer her up. "You're
not wretched, like me. I don't even know where Hunter is!"

I felt panicked. What was I going to do?

"We'll find Hunter. My father can find *anyone*, he's best
friends with everyone at the FBI. Don't worry. I'll see you tomorrow. Salome says there's some party she's working on that
we both have to be at. Be there. No excuses."

22

Glamela

"Glamela" Grigione (real name:—Pamela) is the epitome of the raven-haired Italian *contessa* set living in New York. She earned her moniker by literally dripping herself in glamour over the years, and particularly by being a constant guest as a teenager on *Stealth,* which was Gianni Agnelli's favorite boat. Glamela is one of the most offbeat women in New York. If you call and ask her "How are you?" she gives one of only two replies: either "I'm divine" or "I'm a little insane." At cocktail parties, arriving in a dazzling outfit of vintage Missoni or Pucci, she always declares, "I'm ugly; take me home," immediately endearing herself to the entire crowd, despite her envy-inducing, Monica Bellucci–style beauty and bust.

She was a clever choice for the hostess of Salome's Revenge—as Salome code-named the cocktail party at which she was planning to avenge Sophia on Marci's behalf. In the twenty-four hours since the Sophia–Christopher scandal had broken, Salome had pulled together an event at Glamela's loft on Grand Street. The place was so famous for its contemporary art that no one could refuse the invitation, even Sophia. The pretext was a cocktail for Prince Angus, as he was known, an avant-garde installation artist from Glasgow. His show was opening the next night at Gagosian. No one knew Prince Angus's real name, but in New York no one cares what British people are really called.

"What an amazing space!" I gushed, when Glamela opened the door to me that night. I was being overly enthusiastic in an effort to hide my desperate mood: it had been twenty-four hours since Hunter had disappeared, and I hadn't heard a word from him. When I'd called his office again this morning, Danny had told me that Hunter had not checked in to the hotel in Zurich where he was supposed to be staying. No one knew where he'd gone.

"Isn't it hilarious?" agreed Glamela, as she led me through the loft. She was wearing a paisley chiffon gown that floated behind her as she walked, barefoot, through the vast space. Her only jewelry was an emerald-and-gold bracelet that she wore on her left ankle, like an Indian princess. "Can you believe it was once Manhattan Mini Storage?"

Of course the loft had been Manhattan Mini Storage: it was big enough to store the entire eastern seaboard in here. The drawing room alone must have been fifty feet long, with floor-to-ceiling windows looking across the pretty rooftops of SoHo. Everywhere you looked there was art: a giant Jeff Koons poodle here, a Cecily Brown oil there, a Tracey Emin rug on the floor. With its dark floors and white lacquered walls, the room was the perfect backdrop for the work. The only furnishings in the room were two white leather stools and a white baby grand piano.

"Everyone's in the library," said Glamela, chiffon swooshing quickly ahead of me.

The "library" was much cozier than the rest of the apartment, but still ultra-modern. All the "books," wrapped immaculately in brown paper, were, on close examination, revealed to be old-school videotapes. The room was crowded with art types.

"Over here!" said Tinsley.

She was lounging on a huge sofa draped in a goatskin rug, dressed in a red velvet puff-sleeved frock that looked like it was intended for a four-year-old. She was chatting with Prince Angus. Dressed in slashed tartan drainpipes with safety pins holding them together, and with a long fringe of bleach-blonde hair, he looked like a cross between Sid Vicious and David Hockney. He was strangely sexy, in that way that creative types just are, even though they are totally weird-looking. I went over and joined them, grabbing a glass of champagne on the way.

"'Ello!" said Prince Angus, when I sat down by Tinsley. He spoke exactly like one of the Beatles.

"Isn't he *divine?*" said Tinsley, looping a long arm around Prince Angus's neck. "Salome's got the most savage crush on him already."

"She's tasty!" said Prince Angus.

"Isn't she?" I agreed. "What's your show about?"

"I shipped a Tudor hovel from Penrith to New York, and I've painted the outside to look like a cartoon of a Mock Tudor mansion in Beverly Hills. The show's called *Mock Mock Tudor*. Haaahhhhaaa!" he chuckled. "Is the lovely Salome single?"

"She could be, for the right . . . Muslim," said Tinsley, looking at Prince Angus a little dubiously. "She'd decided to date within her religion now. Too much angst with her parents otherwise."

"Oh," said Prince Angus, a little wistfully.

Just then I saw Sophia from the corner of my eye. Ugh! I loathed the sight of her. However, for the sake of Salome's plan, which I assumed was devilishly clever, I attempted to appear calm. Sophia was standing by the fireplace at the other end of the room, with one arm resting on the mantelpiece. She was dressed head to toe in white cashmere and a cream fur gilet. She seemed to be laughing hysterically with . . . Salome. What *was* Salome up to? A little way off, Valerie and Alixe were standing together chatting. What *was* going on? And where was Lauren? Wasn't she supposed to be here?

I headed over toward Alixe and whispered, "What is Salome up to?"

"I *love* your necklace, Alixe," interrupted Valerie, before she could answer.

"Lanvin. I'm so dull. Everyone's got these already," said Alixe, fingering the long skein of black pearls wrapped in delicate net. "The trouble is, if I buy a necklace I have to have the ring *and* the bracelet *and* the earrings. I can never *just* get the necklace. You can't imagine the trouble I'm in with myself," she huffed. "*Adore* your dress."

"I just wanted to stay under the covers tonight, so this is my under-the-duvet dress," replied Valerie.

This was completely disingenuous on Valerie's part. She was wearing a searingly tight black cocktail dress with a white ribbon tied in a bow at the waist. She couldn't have looked less like someone who was in bed.

Suddenly there was yelling and waving from the fireplace.

"Faisal! Darling! Over here!" sang Salome, who was dressed in a chocolate-brown-and-white polka dot cocktail dress.

She was gesturing at someone. Everyone turned to see who it was. An extraordinarily beautiful Persian man, dressed in an immaculate dark suit and a red keffiyeh, was strolling into the library. He looked like a modern Omar Sharif, with eyes like black diamonds. I swear I could hear a collective intake of female breath as he strode across to where Salome was waiting at the fireplace.

"Salome. The Beauty," declared Faisal as he took Salome's outstretched hand and kissed it. "And who is this . . . *flower*?" he asked, turning toward Sophia.

"I'm Sophia D'Arlan," said Sophia, dredging up her most seductive expression for Faisal.

I couldn't quite see how all this was going to punish Sophia—it seemed far too pleasant. What was Salome thinking? Was this man Salome's ex-husband? And where was Lauren? There was still no sign of her. Meanwhile Sophia, in inimitable style, moved in on Faisal like a tiger killing its prey. Twenty minutes later they left the party together, arm in arm, much to the shock of the guests gathered at the party. The only person who didn't seemed freaked out was Salome, who was happily perched on the sofa, snuggling up to Prince Angus all the while. As the door closed behind Sophia and Faisal, Salome literally fell off the sofa and lay on the floor giggling like an exotic wind-up doll.

"I'm a genius!!! *Haahhheeeehhahhahaha!*" tittered Salome madly.

"What do you mean?" I asked.

"Wait and—*giggle-giggle-hahaaha*—see! I am *completely* evil."

Aside from the generally peculiar nature of Salome's revenge party, there was something else that struck me as odd that night: Lauren had never shown up. Since she was obviously in on whatever plan Salome was pursuing, it seemed strange— but not overly so. After all, Lauren *always* didn't show up for things she was supposed to show up at. But when, the next day, I still hadn't heard from her and she failed to come to Thack's studio for a fitting she'd scheduled, that really *was* strange. Lauren had been invited to attend the Oscars by one of the Warner kids, and had given Thack a huge check to pay for a dress she wanted made. Even Lauren was impressed by the Oscars: I couldn't imagine her not being obsessed by her outfit. Aside from all this, I was desperate for someone to talk to about Hunter: it was the last thing I wanted to analyze with Marci or Tinsley. It had been two days, and there was still no word from Hunter. Even his office had started to get concerned. What had happened to him?

That day, when I called Lauren's cell it was dead. When I called the house, the line went straight to voicemail. What was even odder was Thack's reaction: for a kid whose business was in deep trouble, who was banking on Lauren being photographed in his gown at the Oscars, he didn't seem at all panicked, even after the Nina-gate fiasco, as he called it.

"Isn't the *toile* delicious?" he said, gazing at Lauren's gown with a dreamy look on his face. "The silhouette is totally John Singer Sargent."

The *toile* was a desperately romantic shape. Corseted sharply on the bust, pinching into a tiny waist and floating out into a dreamy skirt, it was a dress far chicer than anything you see at the Oscars now.

"Thack, she's not here," I protested in vain.

"Ha!" he giggled cheerfully. "The dress is killer."

"Thack, the accounts are not even vaguely killer this month," I pointed out.

"Everything will be fine, Sylvie, stop fretting. Now, who else am I dressing for the Oscars?"

I didn't have the heart to tell him: no one.

❧

"Miss Sylvie! Mii–sss!" wailed Lauren's maid, Agata, on the phone two days later. Her voice was choked with tears, hysterical. "She's gone! Gone!"

"What do you mean?" I asked. Agata sounded incredibly upset.

"Lauren came home from Tokyo. Then she said she was going out for five minutes and . . . and she never came back. Her passport is gone, b-b-but . . ." she cried, barely intelligible.

"Well, maybe she's on vacation," I suggested, trying not to betray my own worry.

"She never goes away without me packing a case for her. Never. She doesn't even *know* how to pack a case. Uggghhh! I think she's dead!"

"Agata!" I gasped. "That's not true—"

"But, Miss, she left her jewels," gulped Agata. "She always takes her jewels on vacation!"

Without a bagful of diamonds a vacation simply wasn't a vacation if you were Lauren Blount. Agata was right: the jewels said it all. Lauren had officially disappeared.

23

Revenge Is Iran

THEY MET AT A COCKTAIL PARTY, and were married within three days. On Saturday, Sophia D'Arlan, of Paris and New York, and Sheikh Faisal Al-Firaih, of Jeddah, Saudi Arabia, and Geneva, Switzerland, said to be worth $17 billion, wed in a civil ceremony in the tiny European principality of Luxembourg. (Faisal already has four wives, and this was, apparently, one place in Europe he could re-marry legally.) They plan to live between his palace in Jeddah and his vacation ranch in Iran.

"I can't stand it! I married the Husband Huntress off to the only man I know who can be four other women's husband and hers at the same time." Salome laughed as she read the story out loud from the "Vows" section of the *New York Times* several days later. "Ranch in Iran? What about a harem in Iran? Ever heard of Sharia law, Sophia?"

Faisal Al-Firaih was Salome's ex-husband's uncle ("every-one in the family's called Faisal, even the daughters," she ex-plained). He was apparently thrilled with his new Western wife. Salome, meanwhile, was thrilled with herself. She had achieved her goal. Salome was convinced that Sophia was never going to be allowed to set foot in the land of the infidels again. Meanwhile, Marci had hired Ivana's aforementioned divorce lawyer and was claiming that she was going to go through with a divorce. Her sex life had gone crazy. She was determined to complete a Make Out Challenge more demanding even than Lauren's.

The news on Lauren wasn't as hopeful. She had properly vanished. It was reported in the newspapers, and Lauren was newly dubbed the *Disappearing Debutante Divorcée* in the press. She seemed to become as famous as Princess Diana overnight, with the disappearance written up as a desperately glamorous tragedy. Even Dominick Dunne had gone on the trail for his *Vanity Fair* column, to no avail. Some press items suggested she had been spotted boarding a small plane alone at Teterboro a few days ago, others that she had been seen wandering, drunk, around duty-free shops in Geneva airport buying Swiss cuckoo clocks. You can imagine the whispers at dinner parties: "She was dreadfully unhappy"; "Too much money"; "No, it was the diamonds. Far too many diamonds at a young age brings on early madness"; "If she'd stuck to Pilates this would never have happened"; "Louis kidnapped her, and she's locked in his cabin in Alaska. He couldn't bear to see her having such a good time"; "She wasn't drinking enough water. If she'd drunk two liters of Evian a day she'd be here now." My favorite was, "She's gone into hiding at Brigitte Bardot's place in France."

I was very depressed. Lauren might have been spoiled, she might have been the flakiest of all the New York flakes, but she was fun and a great friend, and underneath it all, she had a heart of gold. She really cared about Marci, Salome, and all her girlfriends, and, selfishly, I hated not having her around to care about me. What if something terrible had happened to her? I kept wondering. Lauren's disappearance only exacerbated my anxiety about Hunter's absence. Yesterday Hunter's office had called asking me if I had heard from him. They had found his BlackBerry under a pile of papers on his desk and were very worried. It had been at least five days now, and not a word. Even when Milton tried to reassure me by telling me that it sounded like Hunter had gone into "the straight man's cave" I didn't feel any better. I felt very much alone, and even slightly envious of Sophia—at least she knew the whereabouts of her husband.

⋘⋙

The following Monday morning I wandered disconsolately into Café Rafaella for breakfast, regretting that I wasn't there with Hunter. When the waitress brought two lattes and two croissants, as she usually did for Hunter and me, I felt so dejected I couldn't even face telling her there was no need for two of everything anymore. As I sipped my coffee and regarded the other cup, I felt like I was breaking bread with a ghost. I dismally picked up a copy of the *New York Post*.

I got the shock of my life.

"What?" I blurted to no one in particular.

There, screaming at me in bright red ink from the cover of the paper was the splashy headline:

DEBUTANTE DIVORCÉE'S SECRET WEDDING!
See Page 3 for Dress, Details and Dish!!!

I turned to page 3. There, radiant, Lauren smiled out from a black-and-white photograph. Snow was swirling around her, and a wedding gown of white organdie was blowing behind her . . . Was she in . . . *Russia?* I peered more closely at the photograph. There were little gold turrets in the back-ground . . . It looked exotic and wintry. The dress was as slim as could be at the bust and then flowed out around her legs and feet, with a huge train . . . no way! It was Thack's dress. It looked to die for. Had he known all along? Of course he had! No wonder he was so relaxed that day when she hadn't shown up at the studio. Next I looked at Lauren's face: her eyes were immaculately lined in black eyeliner, slightly sixties-style, and her hair was falling in soft, loose waves around her face. She seemed to be wearing some kind of huge jewel around her neck, although it was hard to see exactly what it was. In one hand she had a bouquet of white camellias, and in the other a cigarette. It was very her, that particular touch. Her eyes were sparkling as though she was bursting with happiness. But where was the groom?

I quickly scanned down to the text on the page. I gasped as I read:

NEW YORK'S MOST GLAMOROUS DIVORCÉE, Hamill heiress Lauren Blount, who once declared she would never remarry and coined the phrase "debutante di-vorcée" to describe herself and her fun-loving girlfriends, was spotted tying the knot in Saint Isaac's Cathedral, St. Petersburg. The bride wore a gown of organdie and silk by young New York designer Thackeray Johnston. It is rumored there were 200 yards of hand-rolled hems on the dress, and 17,000 seed pearls embroidered on the train. She carried a stole of white ermine fur, and a blue diamond heart hung at her neck, thought to be the famous Princess Letizia of Spain's heart. The stone was a gift from the groom, Giles Monterey, about whom little is known. It is thought the couple met over a pair of Fabergé cuff links on show at the Hermitage in St. Petersburg. The cou-ple have known each other for five weeks. Several days ago Miss Blount disappeared from her New York residence. She was feared dead or kidnapped. When asked for a comment, the new Mrs. Monterey, radiant despite the minus-twenty-degree weather, said, "Say hi to all my girlfriends in New York for me," and disappeared into a blacked-out Mercedes. The couple departed immediately on a four-month honeymoon.

A tear trembled down my nose: everyone was getting married, which only highlighted my lonely plight. I stared down at the newspaper as drop after drop splashed onto it. Just then something white came into view: a handkerchief was being pushed toward me. How embarrassing. I looked up, flushed: there was Hunter.

"I've done something terrible," he said. "I'm so sorry."

24

Silver Linings

"Stop," I protested, wiping my tears with Hunter's handkerchief. "*I've* done something awful. Darling, I've made the most ghastly mistake. I thought you were having an affair with Sophia, and then I discovered she was cheating with Marci's husband, and . . . I can't believe I didn't trust you. I've been so dumb, demanding a divorce, which is the last thing I want. Can you ever forgive me?"

"No," said Hunter, looking me straight in the eye.

I froze. I had gotten what I deserved. I just stared at Hunter, horrified at what I had done.

Next something strange happened. Hunter sat down at the table, and took my hand in his. Then he said,

"I don't have to forgive you . . . It's not your fault. I made a very silly mistake."

He had a strange expression on his face. Oh God, was he going to say he *had* been with Sophia after all? This was too horrible for words. I stared back at him, swallowing anxiously, waiting.

"What?" I finally stammered.

"Hiring that ghastly Sophia. I mentioned to her on that trip to London that I wanted to get you something special, to make up for canceling the honeymoon, and she offered to help me choose something for you. She told me it wouldn't matter if I copied her necklace. I was a fool. I know what she's like. I should have known that she would engineer things to her advantage. I wish I'd never hired her. She's been a man-eater since high school. Always whipping up these affairs around herself that are usually lies—"

"Shush," I said, holding my hand up to Hunter's lips. "I never want to hear another thing about that wretched girl."

Although I was relieved to have Hunter back, I still felt incredibly angry at even the briefest mention of Sophia's name. She had caused so much damage. My only consolation was that I knew she would never escape her Saudi life.

"I promise Sophia will never be allowed anywhere near us again," said Hunter.

"Really? You really mean that?" I said stiffly.

Much as I wanted to embrace my husband, I still couldn't quite relax after everything that had happened. Hunter noticed my reluctant air. Trying to reassure me, he said, "When do I not mean what I say, darling?" with a little twinkle in his eye.

I paused. When I really thought about it, the fact was Hunter didn't go back on his promises. Finally I just said, "Never, darling."

Hunter looked relieved and put his hand up to stroke my cheek. Then he said, "I can't bear that you saw Sophia wearing that gorgeous necklace. I'm going to get you something even more beautiful, my darling."

"Actually I love it—"

"That's too bad because I have already commissioned something so exquisite you won't believe it."

I melted faster than an ice cream on a hot Fourth of July.

Suddenly I felt a delicious mix of laughter and tears bubbling up inside me. Hunter leaned across the table and kissed me for a long time on the lips. Then he got up and came and sat next to me on the banquette with his arm looped around my neck. With the other hand he dabbed at my tears with a handkerchief. It felt divine, just the way things should be.

"Where have you been these past few days?" I asked, although I wasn't really concerned about it anymore.

"Thinking."

"Where?"

"It doesn't matter."

"Darling, I have to ask you something else," I said. "No vague answers, please."

"OK. I will be completely clear and transparent. What do you want to know? Anything."

"Why are you so secretive? Always disappearing? All those secret phone calls, and all that time you're on the Internet, and you'll never let me know what you are doing. If you weren't having an affair with Sophia, what were you up to?"

Hunter just smiled and opened his briefcase. He took out a flat brown envelope and handed it to me. HONEYMOON #2 was written across the top.

"Eeek!" I cried, delighted. I handed the package back to Hunter.

"Aren't you going to look at where we're going?" he said, pushing it back toward me.

"No. A new bride never knows where she's going on her honeymoon. It should be a surprise."

"Absolutely. I'm glad you trust me to take you somewhere nice."

"I do, darling, I do," I said. But I couldn't resist needling my husband a little. "Even after you canceled our last honeymoon."

"You're very brave," he said, tearing off a piece of croissant and popping it into my mouth. "You look like you haven't eaten for a week."

"I couldn't eat while you were gone," I said through my mouthful of breakfast. "By the way, can you believe Lauren got married?"

I pointed to the *Post* story. Hunter didn't seem surprised at all.

"Didn't I always tell you she'd be married with three kids in no time?" he said.

"But . . . to Giles Monterey? He was engaged!"

"I told you they'd be the perfect couple, didn't I?"

It was true. Hunter had an uncanny sense for Lauren's love life that even I couldn't fathom.

"Darling, can I just ask one more question, and then I promise that's it?" I said.

"Go ahead," he replied. "Anything you want."

"Who is that lousy college friend you're always running off to visit? It's really been bugging me."

"Oh, he's . . . well, can you wait until the honeymoon? Then I promise I'll tell you. Actually, you'll meet him."

"Even better!" I said. "But I hope this is not a honeymoon with all your college buddies . . . OK?"

Hunter came closer. He put his lips close to my ear and whispered, flirtatiously, "Now, my darling, I haven't seen you for a few days, why don't we go home and . . . you know what?"

"It's Monday, what about work . . . ," I said, mildly protesting. But . . . Hunter looked so cute. He had that sort of slightly rumpled, just-got-off-a-plane look about him this morning that I found irresistibly sexy. And I had missed him so much. I couldn't help but be tempted. "Actually, I think we should . . . you know what too."

25

Honeymoon—For Real

I wrote pretty much the same thing in my diary every day of our honeymoon:

Honeymoon. Boat. Husband. Divine.

Honeymoons are bliss. They just are. From dawn to dusk, dinner to breakfast, and all the time in between, you actually do feel like the Eternity couple. Unlike attempted Honeymoon #1, Honeymoon #2 was dreamy. In late January, Hunter and I left a snow-covered New York, and about seven hours later (it seemed like seven minutes—which everything does when you're on honeymoon; it all goes far too quickly) we kicked off our shoes and stepped onto the teak deck of a very beautiful, truly immaculate, sailing sloop, named—very appropriately, I thought—*Happiness*. It was moored in Gustavia Harbor in St. Bart's, a pretty little bay surrounded by lush green hills dotted with pink and yellow beach houses.

A wind-burned Italian captain, Antonino, greeted us. He was dressed in tan Bermuda shorts, an immaculate white polo shirt, and tortoiseshell sunglasses. He matched the boat exactly, as did the six crew members. Every chair and lounger was upholstered in the same tan as Antonino's shorts, and the woodwork was either lacquered a glossy white or polished to a deep walnut. You literally couldn't move for tan and white on that boat: it was like being inside a coffee ice cream. There were tan terry toweling robes, monogrammed with a white *H*, matching striped Bernardaud china and even custom swimming shoes in the same colors.

We spent the next couple of days sailing lazily around the bays and coves of St. Bart's. We did the same things every day: swim, smooch, and sunbathe. Seriously, that's all we did. It wasn't like we needed any variety. We'd anchor in a charming cove, get off the boat, stroll around the little village, and then drink *citron pressés* in an outdoor café while reading the *Herald Tribune*. In the afternoon we would sail to a secluded bay for swimming and waterskiing.

Occasionally, another boat would glide into the bay and anchor far enough away to not disturb us, but close enough to be observed through binoculars. Spending hours peering through long lenses at someone else's deck is considered, on boats, an acceptable sport. It's endlessly fascinating speculating who the black specks on the far-off deck are, and what they're up to.

Other activities included an awful lot of eating, frequent mid-afternoon honeymoon sex, which, I can confirm, is way better than non-honeymoon sex, and—God, how delicious—freshly baked cakes for tea. I think tea and cake was my favorite honeymoon meal. There is something comfortingly old-fashioned—yet glamorous—about throwing an emerald green Allegra Hicks kaftan over a hot pink bikini and sitting in the shade drinking tea and eating fresh ginger cake while on board. The cakes were accompanied by silly, romantic, honeymoon-ish chats. Our teatime conversations mainly consisted of me veering from how much I loved Hunter in his new Villebrequins to what type of cake I could get tomorrow, and Hunter telling me I looked cuter fatter.

Then, one afternoon, something happened. We'd anchored in a small bay close to a quaint fishing village called Corossol. The cliffs surrounding the bay were thick with hummingbird trees and frangipani, and the water below looked as though it was almost glowing a neon blue—a perfect spot. On the far side of the bay was a completely empty rocky beach. After lunch I lay on a soft lounger on the deck and shut my eyes while Hunter read a book. Apart from the lap-lap-lap of the water against the sides of the boat, and the faint buzzing of the cicadas on shore, it was quiet. We had the whole bay to ourselves—the most private beach you could ever find. Occasionally a seagull would flap by, swerving as though peering at our deck. The only sound was the pleasing voice of an occasional crew member asking, "Would you like a drink?"

"Oh, hello?" said Hunter suddenly.

"What?" I said lazily. I couldn't possibly make the effort to open my eyes. It was too delicious, lying there half asleep in the heat.

"You might want to see this," said Hunter.

Reluctantly I cracked open my eyes and put on my sunglasses. I sat up. A little way off, in the direction of the beach, we could see a very large sailing yacht sweeping silently into the bay.

"Aren't they a little close?" I said, as I heard the sound of the other boat's anchor and chain unraveling into the sea. One gets very protective about one's bay: about five minutes after entering it, it somehow becomes your own private property.

"It's a beautiful boat," said Hunter, picking up a pair of binoculars and looking through them. "Have a look." He handed the goggles over.

Framed by the large black circle of the binoculars, the boat came into sharp focus: it must have been 150 feet long, with two huge masts at the front. Super-elegant, the sleek hull had a navy mirror finish that reflected the glistening ocean as clearly as a looking glass.

"I don't mind sharing our bay with this boat. It's gorgeous," I decided on viewing it.

I looked a little closer. The boat was immaculate, with two decks, its furniture upholstered in crisp navy and white cotton. I pointed the binoculars at the stern. There, I could just make out her name.

"*Au Bout de Souffle,*" I said out loud. "*Breathless*! What a cool name for a boat."

"Isn't it?" said Hunter. "What else is going on over there?"

"Well, I can see a ton of crew shammying the upper deck," I said, squinting.

"And then, oh, that looks like a man wandering about on the lower deck . . . and here's his wife . . . she looks incredibly glamorous . . . She's wearing the most incredible mini kaftan with gold embroidery . . . wow, her legs are so brown, and her bottom's perfect."

I moved the binoculars up the girl's body. She was wearing enormous black sunglasses that hid most of her face, and she had a turquoise silk scarf wound tightly around her head like a turban. She looked even more glamorous than Lee Radziwill on holiday in Capri in the sixties. I continued with my fashion commentary for Hunter, who seemed very amused by all the details.

"Oh, look, she's lighting a cigarette. Gosh, what gorgeous gold bangles she's wearing. I love girls who wear jewelry on the beach. It's so decadent. That's funny . . . she's got the most beautiful pearls around her neck . . . wait! Hunter!" I yelled, passing the binoculars over to him. "Is that Lauren over there? With Monterey? I'm *sure* it's her."

Hunter smiled and took the binoculars.

"Hmm. That's definitely her with some sort of husband in tow," he said.

He didn't seem in the slightest bit surprised. I, on the other hand, was bursting with over-excitement.

"Come on," said Hunter taking my hand. "Let's get in the tender and go over and say hi."

Twenty minutes later the French skipper of *Au Bout de Soufle* was helping us on board. Lauren and Giles were standing arm in arm on the deck waiting for us. It was unbelievable: Lauren, married! The newlyweds seemed to be literally glowing with happiness. Giles was incredibly tan, and wearing pastel pink swimming shorts; Lauren had already changed outfits—and jewelry. She was now wearing a chocolate brown and white zebra-striped bathing suit that was completely backless. She had a huge ebony and topaz cocktail ring on her wedding finger, and her hair was swept into a sleek pony tail. Marriage obviously agreed with Lauren. She looked more dazzling than ever, particularly against the backdrop of one of the most glamorous boats I'd ever seen.

"Hiiii!" exclaimed Lauren, giving me a huge hug. Then she turned to Hunter and said, "Hunter, you *star*."

Meanwhile, Hunter and Giles hugged like old friends. How peculiar, I thought.

"Good to see you again, Hunter," said Giles.

"It's been far too long," said Hunter, giving Giles a manly pat on the back.

That was odd. These two weren't supposed to be friends.

They weren't even acquainted, as far as I knew. I looked at Hunter quizzically.

"Wait a minute, do you two *know* each other?" I asked suspiciously.

Hunter had an unspeakably mischievous smile on his face.

"Darling, I've got something funny to tell you." Hunter looked at me and winked. "Giles is that old college friend I was telling you about."

"*What?!*" I cried.

"*Best* college friends," added Lauren with a grin. "They're so into each other sometimes I worry . . . didn't he tell you yet?"

I looked at Lauren. Then I looked at Giles, then back at Hunter. I was completely out of the loop. Seeing the look on my face, Giles and Hunter were immediately in fits of laughter.

"I told you I'd set them up and they'd get married, didn't I?" said Hunter.

Giles Monterey was that mysterious college friend? I couldn't believe I hadn't figured it out ages ago.

"But Hunter, at Christmas, when you said your old college friend was in town again and I suggested bringing Lauren to meet him, I distinctly remember you saying no," I remarked, piqued.

That was during the height of my Sophia paranoia. I remember thinking Hunter must be seeing her. I'd obviously completely misread the situation.

"Darling, it was too late. They'd already met in Moscow. I'm afraid Giles and I had been plotting away for months by that time," replied Hunter. "It would have ruined our strategy if she'd come out that night."

"It's true," giggled Lauren. "They've been absolutely terrible to us!" She started heading off toward a spiral staircase in the middle of the deck. "Come on up to the top deck. There's the most fabulous hammock up there."

We all followed. The top deck was slightly more bohemian, with a huge tented area under which were low white sofas. The hammock rocked gently in the wind a little way toward the bow. It was *almost* as romantic as the *Happiness*, although I secretly decided that *Au Bout de Souffle* was too large to be truly intimate. We all sat around on the sofas except Giles, who remained standing, asking, "Drinks for anyone?"

"I'd love a mojito," I said.

"Homemade lemonade, please, darling," said Lauren, blowing him a kiss.

With that, Giles disappeared off to get the drinks, and I was left with Hunter and Lauren.

"I can't believe you, Hunter!" I protested. "Why didn't you tell me? How could you have let me worry about Lauren and this whole thing with Giles for so long? And what about his fiancée? What happened to her? It's too much!"

As pleased as I was for Lauren, I was slightly annoyed about being duped.

"Sylvie, I *conjured* that fiancée out of nowhere," said Lauren.

"What do you mean you conjured her?" I asked.

"Don't you remember? That day at the polo, when I asked Giles who Princess Letizia's heart was for, he said, 'Let's just say it would be an engagement present.' He didn't actually say he had a specific fiancée in mind," explained Lauren. "I just started imagining he had the most gorgeous wife-to-be, but he didn't. He told me later that he'd decided to marry me when he saw me walking toward him in the polo tent. Isn't that so romantic? It doesn't even sound real, does it?"

"But, Hunter, all those times when I told you about Lauren being in love with this man who was engaged, why didn't you tell me that he was available?" I asked.

Hunter didn't reply immediately. He looked out to the ocean as he contemplated his answer. Everything was quiet, except for the occasional ripple of a crystalline wave against the boat.

"If I'd set you straight, you would have run right back and told Lauren everything, and we wouldn't have this beautiful love story," said Hunter finally with a chuckle. "Giles swore me to secrecy. He was mad about her. He was always going to give her the blue heart, but he knew if he seemed too interested she'd bolt. Plus, you gave me marvelous information about the state of your friend's heart, which of course went straight back to Giles. I'm sure you wouldn't have told me so much if you had known what we were planning."

I couldn't quite believe what I was hearing. If I was not mistaken, Hunter had allowed Lauren and me to think that Giles Monterey was engaged, while he was quietly reporting Lauren's passionate feelings back to him, so that Monterey had a better chance of marrying her.

"Your husband has me figured out, and I'm very grateful to him," nodded Lauren resignedly. "An engaged man is *far* more attractive than a single one, I always say. And it was so romantic when Giles said the blue heart was for his future wife and I thought, *that won't be me*. I fell for him immediately."

Hunter was right. It was a beautiful love story. Just then Giles reappeared with a tray of drinks.

"The lemons are local, you know," said Lauren, taking a glass of lemonade. As Giles handed around the drinks, she said, "I *never* would have married you if I thought you were actually available for marrying, would I, darling?"

Giles smiled and smoothed his hand over his wife's hair. He genuinely adored her. Then he said, "I owe all my happiness to Hunter. He planned the whole thing. It's amazing. Your husband is our cupid."

"Agreed. My husband is a saint," I said. "OK, enough."

Just then Lauren turned and looked right at me. Her ponytail fluttered about her shoulders in the ocean breeze.

"You see, Sylvie, when your husband says you must trust him that everything is OK, you can," she said.

I glanced over at Hunter. He gazed back at me, with a very gentle look in his eyes. In that short moment, it was suddenly as though we understood each other perfectly. I had never trusted my husband more.

"I know," I said, feeling happiness glide across my face. I was so joyful, so truly content, that I could feel delight stretching into every fingertip.

Lauren drained her glass of lemonade. "Now, who feels like a four o'clock tequila?" she said, looking around for a crew member.

What a relief: despite being married, Lauren hadn't changed a bit.

❧

"God, I love being on my second honeymoon. It's *sooo* much better than my divorce honeymoon," sighed Lauren.

It was sunset, and we were both lying in the huge hammock, being rocked gently by the soft evening wind. Giles and Hunter were taking advantage of the flat water of early evening and had gone wakeboarding out in the bay. At one point, Hunter skimmed by on the wakeboard and somehow managed to blow me a kiss while jumping a wave.

"What a show-off," I said, secretly proud.

"You know, Sylvie, Hunter is the best husband ever—after my own, of course. You shouldn't be annoyed with him," said

Lauren. "All that time he knew exactly what was going on, but he didn't say a word, so as not to spoil things for anyone. I'm a much better friend for you now that I'm married."

"I couldn't understand it when you were suddenly married and he didn't seem surprised. He's such a dark horse."

"Do you feel like a *mille-feuille*? You know, we have a French pastry chef on board."

"I think I'm too hot for a patisserie now," I answered sipping at my cool mojito. "Your wedding dress was divine."

Lauren closed her eyes for a moment as if remembering the bliss of the gown. "It was a shame no one got to see it for real," she sighed. "Thack is a genius. He texted me. He's had zillions of new orders from that picture in the *Post*."

"And get this, Nina Chlore wants to wear a blue version of it to the Oscars. You don't mind, do you?" I asked.

"I'm flattered that a fashion icon like Nina is inspired by someone as shabby as myself," she said wryly. "Shall we go up to the front of the boat and look for dolphins?"

With that, Lauren launched herself out of the hammock, and I followed. We strolled up to the bow, where we hung over the edge of the boat, staring down at the blue depths, silent. Suddenly Lauren pointed to a gray shadow moving through the water to her left.

"Look," she whispered. "It's a turtle. I *love* turtles. They're so ugly and cute. Do you think I'd wreck this Thomas Maier bathing suit if I did a back flip off the front of the boat?"

Just then a dolphin's nose splashed powerfully out of the water as it came up for air. Just as suddenly, it disappeared into the distance.

"Oh, it's gone," said Lauren. "Did I tell you about Salome?"

"What?" I said, lifting myself from the edge of the boat and looking at Lauren.

"She's getting married."

"Stop it! Who to?"

"Angus McConnell, that Scottish guy. It turns out he *is* an actual prince. He's, like, one of the Macbeths or something. The whole made-up name thing was just made up. Her family is *totally* talking to him. Her father said she could definitely marry an infidel if he was royal. She'll be 'Princess Angus' from now on."

"No!"

"It's true. And Tinsley's eloped with the FreshDirect guy, *while* engaged to her doorman, who is devastated. He picked her up from her building in a white limo that stretched from here to next week. Tinsley loves him so much that she's pretending not to be embarrassed. Oh! Another dolphin, look!" said Lauren craning her neck downward.

"Did you hear that Marci is thinking of getting back with Christopher?" I asked.

"Really?" said Lauren.

She seemed pensive suddenly and looked out to sea for a moment. Then she looked back at me and said, "I hope she does. Whatever anyone says, being married is a million times sexier than being divorced. It's the intimacy. Now I know what I was missing, I feel like all those parties, all those vacations, all those . . . orgasms"—here Lauren couldn't help but burst out laughing—"as I was saying, all those orgasms weren't so great after all, even the multiple ones. There's nothing better, you know, than being a *former* Debutante Divorcée. Of course, I'm a little disappointed in myself."

"Why?" I asked.

Lauren fiddled with the cocktail ring on her wedding finger, sliding it back and forth before she answered me. She had a mischievous look in her eye. Then she said, deadpan. "I *totally* failed at the Make Out Challenge."

I looked at her quizically.

"What do you mean you failed?"

"I wasn't planning to land a new husband . . ." she said. "*And* be madly in love with it."

"I wouldn't exactly call that a failure," I told her.

"And I *still* can't fix the surround sound," insisted Lauren stubbornly. "It's so inconvenient."

Lauren was completely and utterly, madly, whatever you want to call it, in love with her husband. It was a shock. I never thought I'd say this, but it's true. Divorced girls in New York these days put almost as much effort into finding husbands as they once did into losing them.

The End

Acknowledgements

I could not have written *The Debutante Divorcée* without being inspired by some incredibly glamorous, wonderfully witty, and quite extraordinary New York girls. I thank all those fabulous, real-life Debutante Divorcées who whispered me their secrets and cooperated with me for this book with such great humor. To all of you—and you know who you are—your anonymity remains intact and my thanks are sincere.

I would also like to thank my editor in New York, Jonathan Burnham, for his line-by-line editing, without which this book might not be quite as readable. To Juliet Annan at Penguin U.K., many thanks. To my agent, Eric Simonoff at Janklow Nesbit, I owe a debt for his marvelous agenting. I also thank Luke Janklow for his support. At Miramax Books, Harvey Weinstein, Rob Weisbach, Kristin Powers, and Judy Hottensen have been a great team to work with. Sandi Mendelson has been a fantastic publicist.

For their incredible help on the inspiration and detail

for this book—from the art on Lauren's walls to the jewels she wore in bed—I would like to thank the following: Bob Cohen, Pamela Gross, Susan Campos, Miles Redd, Daniel Romauldez, Dr. Genevieve Davies, Blaire Voltz-Clarke, Jeoffrey Munn at Wartski, the staff at A La Vielle Russie, Gulia Costantini, Samantha Gregory, Antony Todd, Tinsley Mercer-Mortimer, Beth Blake, Kara Baker, Miranda Brooks, Milly de Cabrol, Holly Peterson, Cleopatra, NG, Muffy Potter Aston, Vicky Ward, Charlotte Sprintus, and Samantha Cameron.

I also thank Anna Wintour for her support for my work, both in and out of *Vogue*, the huge Sykes family for their loyalty and support, Carly Fraser for her amazing fact checking, Anna-Louise Clegg for her help with organizing my edits, and Emily Berkeley at Louis Vuitton for finding the beautiful Epi leather suitcases for the cover.

Most of all, I thank my husband, Toby Rowland, for reading *The Debutante Divorcée* over and over again, and for taking me to extraordinary places that inspire me.

Letters to a Young Novelist

Letters to a Young Novelist

MARIO VARGAS LLOSA

TRANSLATED BY NATASHA WIMMER

PICADOR
FARRAR, STRAUS AND GIROUX
NEW YORK

www.picadorusa.com

Picador® is a U.S. registered trademark and is used by
Farrar, Straus and Giroux under license from Pan Books Limited.

For information on Picador Reading Group Guides, as well as ordering,
please contact the Trade Marketing department at St. Martin's Press.
Phone: 1-800-221-7945 extension 763
Fax: 212-677-7456
E-mail: trademarketing@stmartins.com

Portions of this book have appeared in *Literary Review, Partisan Review,
Tin House,* and *The Yale Review.*

Library of Congress Cataloging-in-Publication Data

Vargas Llosa, Mario, 1936-
  [Cartas a un joven novelista. English]
  Letters to a young novelist / Mario Vargas Llosa; translated by Natasha
Wimmer.— 1st Picador ed.
      p. cm.
  ISBN: 978-0-312-42172-4
  1. Fiction—Authorship. 2. Imaginary letters. I. Wimmer, Natasha.
II. Title.

PN3365.V2713 2003
808.3—dc21   2003041337

First published in Spain
under the title *Cartas a un joven novelista*
by Ariel/Planeta.

P1

Contents

Letters to a Young Novelist

The Parable of the Tapeworm

Didn't Know Where to Start (handwritten)

DEAR FRIEND,

I was moved by your letter because in it I saw myself at fourteen or fifteen, in gray Lima under the dictatorship of General Odría, aflame with the desire to one day become a writer yet disheartened because I didn't know what steps to take, how to begin channeling my ambition, which I experienced as an urgent prompting, into the creation of real works; how to write stories that would dazzle my readers as I had been dazzled by the writers I was beginning to install in my personal pantheon: Faulkner, Hemingway, Malraux, Dos Passos, Camus, Sartre.

Many times it occurred to me to write to one of them (they were all still alive) and ask for their advice on how to be a writer. I never dared, out of shyness or out of the kind of defeatism—why write, if I know no one will deign to respond?—that so often thwarts the ambitions of young people in countries where literature means little to most and survives on the margins of society as an almost underground activity.

3

You do not suffer from that kind of paralysis, since you've written to me. That's a fine beginning to the adventure you wish to set out on and from which you expect—as I'm sure you do, though you don't tell me so in your letter—many marvelous things. I venture to suggest that you not expect quite so much and that you not count too much on success. There's no reason why you shouldn't be successful, of course, but if you persevere in writing and publishing, you'll soon discover that prizes, public acclaim, book sales, the social standing of a writer all have a sui generis appeal; they are extraordinarily arbitrary, sometimes stubbornly evading those who most deserve them while besieging and overwhelming those who merit them least. Which means that those who see success as their main goal will probably never realize their dreams; they are confusing literary ambition with a hunger for glory and for the financial gains that literature affords certain writers (very few of them). There is a difference.

Prizes are Bogus

The defining characteristic of the literary vocation may be that those who possess it experience the exercise of their craft as its own best reward, much superior to anything they might gain from the fruits of their labors. That is one thing I am sure of amid my many uncertainties regarding the literary vocation: deep inside, a writer feels that writing is the best thing that ever happened to him, or could ever happen to him, because as far as he is concerned, writing is the best possible way of life, never mind the social, political, or financial rewards of what he might achieve through it.

Best reward is to write

Vocation seems to me the inevitable starting point for our talk about what is exciting and troubling you: namely, how to become a writer. It's a mysterious business, of course, veiled in doubt and subjectivity. But that doesn't stop us from trying to explain it rationally, rejecting the religious fervor and pride of the self-important myths the romantics spun around it, according to which the writer was the chosen one of the gods, a being singled out by a transcendent superhuman entity to write divine words that, once breathed, would effect the sublimation of the human soul and allow the writer, thanks to his brush with Beauty (capitalized, of course), to achieve immortality.

Today nobody talks that way about literary or artistic vocation, but even though the definition offered in our times is less grandiose, less steeped in fatefulness, it is still fairly elusive: a predisposition of murky origin that causes certain men and women to dedicate their lives to an activity that one day they feel called, almost obliged, to pursue, because they sense that only in pursuing this vocation—writing stories, *feel complete* for example—will they feel complete, at peace with themselves, able to give the best of themselves without the nagging fear that they are wasting their lives.

I don't believe that the destinies of human beings are programmed in the womb by fate or by a mischievous divin- *but pre-determined* ity that distributes aptitudes, ineptitudes, likes, and dislikes among brand-new souls. But neither do I believe, as once I did under the influence of the French existentialists—especially Sartre—that vocation is a *choice*, a free expression of individual will that decides a person's future. Indeed, in spite of my conviction that literary vocation is not governed by fate or inscribed in the genes of future writers, and despite my belief that discipline and perseverance may sometimes produce genius, I've come to be convinced that it cannot be explained solely in terms of free choice. Free choice is essential, in my opinion, but only at a second stage, following an initial subjective inclination, innate or forged in childhood or earliest adolescence, that rational choice serves to strengthen but is unable to manufacture from scratch.

If I'm not mistaken in my supposition (though I very well may be), a man or a woman develops precociously in childhood or early in his or her teenage years a penchant for dreaming up people, situations, anecdotes, worlds different from the world in which he or she lives, and that inclination is the first sign of what may later be termed literary vocation. Naturally, there is an abyss that the vast majority of human beings never cross between the propensity to retreat from the real world and real life into the imagination and the actual practice of literature. Those who do cross and who become creators of worlds with the written word are writers, the minority who have reinforced their penchant or tendency with an exertion of the will Sartre called *choice*. At a given moment, they decided to become writers. That's what they chose to be. They arranged their lives to make the written word the focus of the drive that at first they contented themselves with harnessing for the elaboration, in the misty realms of the mind, of other lives and worlds. This is where you are now: at the difficult and thrilling moment when you must decide whether you will go beyond amusing yourself with the creation of fictional realities, whether you will set them down in writing. If that's what you choose, you will certainly have taken a very important step, though your future as a writer will still be far from assured. But the decision to commit yourself, to orient your life toward the achievement of your purposes, is already a way—the only possible way—of beginning to be a writer.

What is the origin of this early inclination, the source of the literary vocation, for inventing beings and stories? The answer, I think, is rebellion. I'm convinced that those who immerse themselves in the lucubration of lives different from their own demonstrate indirectly their rejection and criticism of life as it is, of the real world, and manifest their desire to substitute for it the creations of their imagination and dreams. Why would anyone who is deeply satisfied with reality, with real life as it is lived, dedicate himself to something as insubstantial and fanciful as the creation of fictional realities? Naturally, those who rebel against life as it is, using their ability to invent different lives and different people, may do so for any number of reasons, honorable or dishonorable, generous or selfish, complex or banal. The nature of this basic questioning of reality, which to my mind lies at the heart of every literary calling, doesn't matter at all. What matters is that the rejection be strong enough to fuel the enthusiasm for a task as quixotic as tilting at windmills—the sleight-of-hand replacement of the concrete, objective world of life as it is lived with the subtle and ephemeral world of fiction.

Nevertheless, despite the evanescence of fiction, and the subjective, figurative, extrahistorical nature of its execution, it comes to have long-term effects on the real world—in other words, on the lives of flesh-and-blood people.

This questioning of real life, which is the secret raison d'être of literature—of the literary vocation—ensures that literature offers a unique vision of a given period. Life as described in fiction (especially in superior fiction) is never just life as it was lived by those who imagined, wrote, read, or experienced it but rather the fictional equivalent, what they were obliged to fabricate because they weren't able to live it in reality and, as a result, resigned themselves to live only in the indirect and subjective way it could be lived: in dreams and in fiction. Fiction is a lie covering up a deep truth: it is life as it wasn't, life as the men and women of a certain age wanted to live it and didn't and thus had to invent. It isn't the face of History but rather her reverse or flip side: what didn't happen and therefore had to be fabricated in the imagination and in words to fulfill the ambitions real life was unable to satisfy, to fill the voids women and men discovered around them and tried to populate with ghosts they conjured up themselves.

This rebellion is relative, of course. Many story writers aren't even conscious of it, and it's possible that if they were to become aware of the seditious roots of their calling, they would be surprised and frightened since in their public lives they certainly don't imagine themselves as plotting secretly to dynamite the world they inhabit. On the other hand, theirs is ultimately a fairly peaceful rebellion. What harm is there, after all, in pitting vaporous fictional lives against real life? Where is the danger in such a contest? At first glance, there is none. It's just a game, isn't it? And games aren't supposed to be dangerous, so long as they don't threaten to overflow their boundaries and mingle with real life. Of course, when a person—Don Quixote or Madame Bovary, for example—insists on confusing fiction with life and tries to make life resemble fiction, the consequences can be disastrous. Those who behave in such a way tend to suffer terrible disappointments. *Cont mix.*

So the game of literature is not innocuous. The fruit of a deep dissatisfaction with real life, fiction is itself a source of discomfort and dissatisfaction. Those who, through reading, *live* a great story—like the two tales I've just referred to, by Cervantes and Flaubert—return to real life with a heightened sensitivity to its limitations and imperfections, alerted by these magnificent fantasies to the fact that the real world, and life as it is lived, is infinitely more mediocre than life as invented by novelists. When readers are faced with the real world, the unease fomented by good literature may, in certain circumstances, even translate itself into an act of rebellion against authority, the establishment, or sanctioned beliefs.

That's why the Spanish Inquisition distrusted works of fiction and subjected them to strict censorship, going so far as to prohibit them in the American colonies for three hundred years. The pretext was that these wild tales might distract the Indians from the worship of God, the only serious concern of a theocratic society. Like the Inquisition, all governments and regimes aspiring to control the life of their citizens have shown a similar distrust of fiction and have submitted it to the kind of scrutiny and pruning called censorship. None of these authorities have been mistaken: innocent as it may seem, the writing of stories is a way of exercising freedom and of quarreling with those—religious or secular—who wish to do away with it. That's why all dictatorships—fascist, communist, or Islamic fundamentalist regimes, African or Latin American military tyrannies—have tried to control literature by forcing it into the straitjacket of censorship.

But these general reflections have caused us to stray a little from your particular case. Let's get back to specifics. Deep down, you've felt a certain predilection, and you've bolstered it with an exertion of will and decided to devote yourself to literature. Now what?

Your decision to claim your literary leanings as your destiny must lead you into servitude, into nothing less than slavery. To put it graphically, you've just done what some nineteenth-century ladies, concerned about their weight and determined to recover their slender silhouettes, were reputed to do: you've swallowed a tapeworm. Have you ever come across anyone who sheltered that terrible parasite in his gut? I have, and I assure you those ladies were heroines, martyrs to beauty. In the early sixties in Paris, a great friend of mine, José María, a young Spanish painter and filmmaker, was invaded by such a creature. Once the tapeworm establishes itself inside an organism, it merges with it, feeds off it, grows and is nourished at its expense; the worm is very difficult to expel from the body it thrives on and effectively colonizes.

José María kept getting thinner, even though he was constantly forced to eat and drink (milk, especially) to satisfy the gnawing of the creature housed inside him, since if he didn't, his suffering would become intolerable. But everything he ate and drank was for the tapeworm's benefit, not his. One day, when we were talking in a little Montparnasse bistro, he surprised me with the following confession: "We do so many things together. We go to theaters, exhibitions, bookstores, we spend hours and hours discussing politics, books, films, friends. And you think I do these things for the same reason you do, because I enjoy them. But you're wrong. I do them all for it, for the tapeworm. That's how it seems to me: that my whole life is lived no longer for my sake but for the sake of what I carry inside me, of which I am now no more than a servant." Bizarre

Ever since then, I've liked to compare the lot of the writer to that of my friend José María when he had the tapeworm inside him. The literary vocation is not a hobby, a sport, a pleasant leisure-time activity. It is an all-encompassing, all-excluding occupation, an urgent priority, a freely chosen servitude that turns its victims (its lucky victims) into slaves. Like José María's tapeworm, literature becomes a permanent preoccupation, something that takes up your entire existence, that overflows the hours you devote to writing and seeps into everything else you do, because the literary vocation feeds off the life of the writer just as the tapeworm feeds off the bodies it invades. As Flaubert said: "Writing is just another way of living." In other words, those who make this enchanting and engrossing vocation their own don't write to live but live to write.

This idea of comparing the writer's vocation to a tapeworm is not original. I've just come across it reading Thomas Wolfe, who described his vocation as the lodging of a worm in his very being:

> For sleep was dead forever, the merciful, dark and sweet oblivions of childhood sleep. The worm had entered at my heart, the worm lay coiled and feeding at my brain, my spirit, and my memory—I knew that finally I had been caught in my own fire, consumed by my own hungers, impaled on the hook of that furious and insensate desire that had absorbed my life for years. I knew, in short, that one bright cell in the brain or heart or memory would now blaze on forever—by night, by day, through every waking, sleeping moment of my life, the worm would feed and the light be lit,—that no anodyne of food or drink, or friendship, travel, sport or woman could ever quench it, and that never more until death put its total and conclusive darkness on my life, could I escape.
>
> I knew at last I had become a writer: I knew at last what happens to a man who makes the writer's life his own.*

* "The Story of a Novelist," *The Autobiography of an American Novelist*, ed. Leslie Field (Cambridge, Mass.: Harvard U. Press, 1983), pp. 68–69.

I think that only those who come to literature as they might to religion, prepared to dedicate their time, energy, and efforts to their vocation, have what it takes to really become writers and transcend themselves in their works. The mysterious thing we call talent, or genius, does not spring to life full-fledged—at least not in novelists, although it may sometimes in poets or musicians (the classic examples being Rimbaud and Mozart, of course). Instead it becomes apparent at the end of many long years of discipline and perseverance. There are no novel-writing prodigies. All the greatest, most revered novelists were first apprentice writers whose budding talent required early application and conviction. The example of those writers who, unlike Rimbaud, a brilliant poet even as an adolescent, were required to cultivate their talent gives heart to the beginner, don't you think?

If you are interested in the subject—the fostering of literary genius—I recommend that you read the voluminous correspondence of Flaubert, and especially the letters he wrote to his lover, Louise Colet, between 1850 and 1854, the period in which he wrote *Madame Bovary*, his first masterpiece. I read them while I was writing my first books, and they were very helpful. Although Flaubert was a misanthrope and his letters are full of tirades against humanity, his love for literature was boundless. That is why he pledged himself to his vocation like a crusader, surrendering himself to it day and night, working with fanatical conviction, pushing to surpass himself. In this way, he managed to overcome his limitations (very evident in his early works, which are as formal and ornate as the romantic models then in fashion) and write novels like *Madame Bovary* and *A Sentimental Education*, perhaps the first two modern novels.

Another book you might read on the subject addressed by this letter is one by William S. Burroughs, a very different kind of author: *Junky*. Burroughs doesn't interest me at all as a novelist: his experimental, psychedelic stories have always bored me, so much so that I don't think I've ever been able to finish one. But *Junky*, the first book he wrote, a factual and autobiographical account of how he became a drug addict and how his addiction to drugs—free choice augmenting what was already doubtless a certain proclivity—made him a willing slave, furnishes an accurate description of what I believe to be the literary vocation, of the utter interdependence of the writer and his work and the way the latter feeds on the former, on all he is and does or does not do.

But, my friend, this letter has gone on longer than it should, belonging as it does to a genre—the epistolary—of which the primary virtue is precisely brevity, and so I'll take my leave.

Fondly,

The Catoblepas

DEAR FRIEND,

I've been so busy in the last few days that I haven't written back as soon as I should have, but I've been thinking about your letter ever since I received it. Not only because I share its enthusiasm, believing as you do that literature is the best thing ever invented to combat misfortune, but also because the questions you ask—"Where do stories come from?" and "How do novelists come up with their ideas?"— still intrigue me as much as they did in the early days of my literary apprenticeship, even now that I've written a good many novels.

I have an answer for you, which will have to be very nuanced if it is not to be entirely false. All stories are rooted in the lives of those who write them; experience is the source from which fiction flows. This doesn't mean, of course, that novels are always thinly disguised biographies of their authors; rather, that in every fiction, even the most freely imagined, it is possible to uncover a starting point, a secret

15

node viscerally linked to the experiences of the writer. I'd venture to claim that there are no exceptions to this rule and that, as a result, scientifically pure invention does not exist in literature. All fictions are structures of fantasy and craft erected around certain acts, people, or circumstances that stand out in the writer's memory and stimulate his imagination, leading him to create a world so rich and various that sometimes it is almost impossible (and sometimes just plain impossible) to recognize in it the autobiographical material that was its genesis and that is, in a way, the secret heart of all fiction, as well as its obverse and antithesis.

ironic

At a youth conference, I tried to explain this process as a backwards striptease. Writing novels is the equivalent of what professional strippers do when they take off their clothes and exhibit their naked bodies on stage. The novelist performs the same acts in reverse. In constructing the novel, he goes through the motions of getting dressed, hiding the nudity in which he began under heavy, multicolored articles of clothing conjured up out of his imagination. The process is so complex and exacting that many times not even the author is able to identify in the finished product—that exuberant display of his ability to invent imaginary people and worlds—the images lurking in his memory, fixed there by life, which sparked his imagination, spurred him on, and induced him to produce his story.

As for themes, well, I believe the novelist feeds off himself, like the *catoblepas*, the mythical animal that appears to Saint Anthony in Flaubert's *The Temptation of Saint Anthony* and that Borges later revisited in his *Book of Imaginary Beings*. The *catoblepas* is an impossible creature that devours itself, beginning with its feet. Likewise, the novelist scavenges his own experience for raw material for stories—in a more abstract sense, of course. He does this not just in order to re-create characters, anecdotes, or landscapes from the stuff of certain memories but also to gather fuel from them for the willpower that must sustain him if he is to see the long, hard project through.

I'll venture a little further in discussing the themes of fiction. The novelist doesn't choose his themes; he is chosen by them. He writes on certain subjects because certain things have happened to him. In the choice of a theme, the writer's freedom is relative, perhaps even nonexistent. In any case, it is nothing when compared with his freedom to choose the literary form of his work; there, it seems to me, he enjoys total liberty—and total responsibility. My impression is that life—a big word, I know—inflicts themes on a writer through certain experiences that impress themselves on his consciousness or subconscious and later compel him to shake himself free by turning them into stories. We need hardly seek out examples of the way themes from life thrust themselves on writers, because all testimonies tend to concur: a story, a character, a situation, a mystery haunted me, obsessed me, importuned me from the very depths of my self until I was obliged to write it to be free of it. Of course, Proust's is the first name that comes to anyone's mind. A real writer-*catoblepas*, wasn't he? Who ever consumed themselves more thoroughly or profitably, digging like an archaeologist in all the nooks and crannies of memory, than the industrious creator of *In Search of Lost Time*, that monumental artistic re-creation of Proust's daily life, family, surroundings, friendships, relationships, speakable or unspeakable appetites, likes, and dislikes — and, at the same time, of the subtle and mysterious charms of the human spirit in its painstaking efforts to collect, sort, unearth and bury, associate and dissociate, polish, or deface the images that memory retains of time past. Proust's biographers (Painter, for example) have been able to come up with long lists of real experiences and people concealed in the sumptuous inventions of the Proustian saga, demonstrating beyond a doubt that this prodigious literary creation was assembled out of raw materials from the life of its author. But what those lists of autobiographical data unearthed by the critics really prove to us is something else: the creative capacity of Proust, who, exploiting his introspection and his immersion in the past, transformed the incidents of his fairly conventional existence into a splendid tapestry, a stunning representation of the human condition perceived from the point of view of a consciousness turned inward to view the unfolding of life itself.

This brings us to another realization, no less important than the previous one. Although the starting point of a novelist's invention is what he has lived, that is not, and cannot be, its ending point. The invention's end is located at a considerable distance — sometimes a cosmic distance — from its origin, because as a theme is embodied in language and narrative, the autobiographical material is transformed, enriched (some-

Cannot have lived ending

times leached of value), integrated with other remembered or invented materials, and manipulated and structured—if the novel is a real creation—until it achieves the complete autonomy that fiction must assume to live of its own accord. (Those stories that never cast off from their authors and that serve only as biographical documents are, of course, failed fictions.) The task of the novelist is to transform the material supplied by his own memory into an objective world constructed of words: the novel. Form is what allows the text to cohere, to take concrete shape; and it is in the manipulation of form, if my conception of the literary project is correct (and I repeat, I have my doubts), that the novelist enjoys complete freedom and therefore responsibility for his results. If what you are reading between the lines is that, in my opinion, fiction writers are not responsible for their themes (since life assigns them) but are responsible for the way they convert them into literature and that as a result it is possible to say that they are ultimately responsible for their success or failure—for their mediocrity or genius—that is indeed exactly what I mean to say.

Why, of all the infinite occurrences in a writer's life, do some stimulate creativity so vigorously and so many others filter through the memory without rousing the imagination? I don't know for sure. All I have is a suspicion. And that is that the faces, anecdotes, situations, and conflicts that impress themselves on a writer and lead him to dream up stories are precisely those representing that dissent from real life, from the world as it is, which, as I noted in my previous letter, is the root of the novelist's vocation, the hidden impulse that drives him to defy the real world by replacing it symbolically with fiction.

Of the many examples that might be cited to illustrate this idea, I choose that of a minor writer—though he was prolific to the point of incontinence—of eighteenth-century France, Restif de la Bretonne. I don't choose him for his talent—he didn't have much—but for the clear-cut nature of his particular rebellion against reality, his discomfort in the real world, which drove him to engineer fictional realities designed to mimic the world as he would have liked it to be.

In the many novels written by Restif de la Bretonne (the best known is his lengthy novelistic autobiography, *Monsieur Nicolas*) eighteenth-century France, rural and urban, is documented by a painstaking sociologist and rigorous observer of human types, customs, daily routines, work, festivals, superstitions, attire, and beliefs, in such a way that his books have become a veritable treasure trove for researchers: historians, anthropologists, ethnologists, and sociologists have helped themselves liberally to the information excavated by the tireless Restif from the quarry of his era. Nevertheless, in being transposed into his novels, this social and historical realism so copiously described undergoes a radical transformation, and that is why it is possible to speak of the novels as fiction. In the teeming world he creates, similar in so many details to the real world that inspired it, men fall in love with women not for the beauty of their faces, the slenderness of their waists, their good breeding, or spiritual charms but ultimately for the beauty of their feet or the elegance of their boots. Restif de la

Bretonne was a fetishist, something that in real life made him an eccentric among his contemporaries, an exception to the rule, that is to say, a "dissident" from reality. And that dissidence, surely the driving force of his vocation, is revealed to us in his works, in which life is corrected, reworked in the image and likeness of Restif himself. In the world as Restif experienced it, it was natural and normal that the principal female attribute, the object of pleasure coveted by men—*all* men—should be that delicate extremity and, by extension, its coverings, stockings and shoes. Few writers make it possible to grasp so plainly the process by which fiction transforms the world through the subjective urges—desires, appetites, dreams, frustrations, grudges, et cetera—of novelists as this instructive Frenchman.

All creators of fiction are embroiled in the same process, though less thoroughly and blatantly. There is something in their lives like the fetishism of Restif—a noble craving for justice, an egotistical drive to satisfy the most sordid masochistic or sadistic urges, a reasonable human longing to live a life of adventure, an undying love—that makes them wish passionately for a world different from the one they live in, a world that they are then compelled to construct of words and upon which they stamp, usually in code, their questioning of real life and their affirmation of that other reality which their selfishness or generosity spurs them to set up in place of the one they've been allotted.

Perhaps, my budding young novelist friend, this is the right moment to speak of a notion dangerous when it is

Be authentic

applied to literature: authenticity. What does it mean to be an authentic writer? What is certain is that fiction is, by definition, fraud—something that is not real yet pretends to be—and that all novels are lies passing themselves off as truth, creations whose *power of persuasion* depends entirely on the novelist's skill at performing conjuring and sleight-of-hand tricks, like a circus or theater magician. So does it make sense to speak of authenticity in fiction, a genre in which it is most authentic to be a trickster, a swindler? It does, but in this way: the authentic novelist is the novelist who docilely obeys the rules life dictates, writing on those themes born out of experience and possessed of urgency and avoiding all others. That is what authenticity or sincerity is for the novelist: the acceptance of his own demons and the decision to serve them as well as possible.

The novelist who doesn't write about what deep down stimulates and inspires him and who coldly chooses subjects or themes in a rational manner because he believes that way he'll have a better chance at success is inauthentic and most likely a bad novelist (even if he is successful—the best-seller lists are crowded with very bad novelists, as you are well aware). But it seems unlikely to me that anyone will become a creator—a transformer of reality—if he doesn't write encouraged and nourished from the depths of his being by those ghosts (or demons) who've made us novelists determined protesters and reconstructors of life in the stories we tell. I think that to accept that imposition—to write about what obsesses us and excites us and is viscerally though often mysteriously part of our lives—is to write "better," with more conviction and energy, and to be better equipped to undertake the exciting but also arduous and sometimes disappointing and harrowing task of composing a novel.

Those writers who shun their own demons and set themselves themes because they believe their own aren't original or appealing enough are making an enormous mistake. In and of itself, no literary theme is good or bad. Any themes can be either, and the verdict depends not on the theme itself but rather on what it becomes when the application of form—narrative style and structure—makes it a novel. It is the form a theme is couched in that makes a story original or trivial, profound or superficial, complex or simple; that lends its characters depth, ambiguity, credibility or turns them into lifeless caricatures, the creations of a puppet master. That is another of the few rules of literature that, it seems to me, brook no exceptions: the themes of a novel themselves promise nothing, because they'll be judged good or bad, appealing or dull solely in view of what the novelist does to turn them into a reality of words ranged in a certain order.

Well, my friend, I think that's all for now.

Fondly,

The Power of Persuasion

DEAR FRIEND,

You're right. My first few letters, with their vague hypothesizing on the literary vocation and the origin of novelists' themes, not to mention their zoological allegories—the tapeworm, the *catoblepas*—were overly abstract, their suppositions sadly unverifiable. Which means that the moment has come for us to move on to less subjective matters, ones more specifically rooted in literary practice.

Let us speak, then, of form, which, paradoxical as it may seem, is the novel's most concrete attribute, since it is form that gives novels their shape and substance. But before we set sail on waters so alluring for those who, like you and me, love and practice the narrative craft, it's worth establishing what you already know very well, though it is not so clear to most readers of novels: the separation of form and content (or theme and style and narrative structure) is artificial, admissible only when we are explaining or analyzing them; it never occurs in reality, since the story a novel tells is inseparable from the way it is told. This *way* is what determines whether the tale is believable or not, moving or ridiculous, comic or dramatic. It is of course possible to say that *Moby-Dick* is the story of a sea captain obsessed with a white whale that he pursues across all the world's oceans and that *Don Quixote* tells of the adventures and misadventures of a half-mad knight who tries to reproduce on the plains of La Mancha the deeds of the heroes of chivalric literature. But would anyone who has read those novels recognize in such plot descriptions the infinitely rich and subtle universes of Melville and Cervantes? To explain the mechanisms that bring a tale to life, it is permissible to separate content from form only on the condition that it is made clear that such a division never occurs naturally, at least not in good novels. It does occur, on the other hand, in bad ones, and that is why they're bad, but in good novels what is told and the way it is told are inextricably bound up together. They are good because thanks to the effectiveness of their form they are endowed with an irresistible *power of persuasion*.

If before reading *The Metamorphosis* you had been told that it was about the transformation of a meek little office worker into a repulsive cockroach, you probably would have yawned and said to yourself there was no reason to read such a ridiculous tale. However, since you've read the story as Kafka magically tells it, you "believe" wholeheartedly in the terrible plight of Gregor Samsa: you identify with him, you suffer with him, and you feel choked by the same despair that destroys the poor character, until with his death the ordinariness of life as it was (before his unhappy adventure dis-

26

turbed it) is restored. And you believe the story of Gregor Samsa because Kafka was capable of finding a way to tell it—in words, silences, revelations, details, organization of information and narrative flow—that overwhelms the reader's defenses, surmounting all the mental reservations he or she might harbor when faced with such a tale.

To equip a novel with *power of persuasion*, it is necessary to tell your story in such a way that it makes the most of every personal experience implicit in its plot and characters; at the same time, it must transmit to the reader an illusion of autonomy from the real world he inhabits. The more independent and self-contained a novel seems to us, and the more everything happening in it gives us the impression of occurring as a result of the story's internal mechanisms and not as a result of the arbitrary imposition of an outside will, the greater the novel's power of persuasion. When a novel gives us the impression of self-sufficiency, of being freed from *real* life, of containing in itself everything it requires to exist, it has reached its maximum capacity for persuasion, successfully seducing its readers and making them believe what it tells them. Good novels—great ones—never actually seem to tell us anything; rather, they make us live it and share in it by virtue of their persuasive powers.

You're undoubtedly familiar with Bertolt Brecht's famous theory of the alienation effect. He believed that to succeed in writing the kind of epic and didactic theater he proposed, it was essential to develop a way of staging plays—reflected in the movement or speech of the actors and even

27 form = life

the construction of the sets—that would gradually destroy the "illusion" and remind the audience that what they were seeing was not real life but theater, a fabrication, a performance, from which, nevertheless, conclusions should be drawn and lessons learned promoting action and reform. I don't know what you think of Brecht. I believe he was a great writer, and that, although he was often hampered by his propagandistic and ideological aims, his plays are excellent and, thankfully, much more persuasive than his theorizing.

In its persuasive efforts, the novel aims for exactly the opposite effect: to reduce the distance that separates fiction from reality and, once that boundary is elided, to make the reader live the lie of fiction as if it were the most eternal truth, its illusions the most consistent and convincing depictions of reality. That is the trick great novels play: they convince us that the world is the way they describe it, as if fiction were not what it is, the picture of a world dismantled and rebuilt to satisfy the deicidal urge to remake reality, the urge that fuels the novelist's vocation whether he knows it or not. Only bad novels foster the alienation Brecht wanted his spectators to experience in order to learn the political lessons he meant to impart along with his plays. Bad novels lacking in the power of persuasion, or possessing only a weak strain of it, don't convince us that the lie they're telling is true; the "lie" appears to us as what it is: a construction, an arbitrary, lifeless invention that moves ploddingly and clumsily, like the puppets of a mediocre puppet master whose threads, manipulated by their creator, are in full sight, exposing them as caricatures of living beings. The deeds or sufferings of these caricatures will scarcely be able to move us: do they, after all, experience anything themselves? They are no more than captive shades, borrowed lives dependent on an omnipotent master.

Naturally, the autonomy of fiction is not a truth—it is a fiction, too. That is to say, fiction is autonomous only in a figurative sense, and that's why I've been very careful when referring to it to speak of an "illusion of autonomy," "the impression of self-sufficiency, of being freed from *real* life." *Someone* is writing these novels. That fact, that they are not the product of spontaneous generation, makes them dependent, connects each of them by an umbilical cord to the rest of the world. But it's not just having an author that links novels to real life; if the storytelling inventions of novels did not reflect on the world as it is lived by their readers, the novel would be something remote and mute, an artifice that shuts us out: it would never possess any power of persuasion, it could never cast a spell, seduce readers, convince them of its truth, and make them live what it relates as if they were experiencing it themselves.

This is the curious ambiguity of fiction: it must aspire to independence knowing that its slavery to reality is inevitable, and it must suggest through sophisticated techniques an autonomy and self-sufficiency as deceptive as the melodies of an opera divorced from the instruments or the throats that voice them.

Form works these miracles—when it works. It is in practical terms an indivisible entity, made up of two equally important components that, though they are always inter-twined, may be isolated for purposes of analysis and explica-tion: style and order. *Style* refers, of course, to words, to the way a story is written; *order* to the organization of the story's elements. To simplify greatly, order concerns the great axes of all novelistic construction: narrative space and time.

So as not to make this letter too long, I'll leave for next time some thoughts on *style*, the language of fiction, and the workings of that *power of persuasion* on which the life (or death) of all novels depends.

Fondly,

Style

DEAR FRIEND,

Style is an essential element, though not the only element, of narrative form. Novels are made of words, which means that the way a writer chooses and orders his language largely determines whether his stories possess or lack the power of persuasion. Of course, a novel's language cannot be disassociated from what it relates—words shape their subject. The only way to know if a novelist has succeeded or failed in his narrative undertaking is to decide whether, through his writing, the fiction lives, liberates itself from its creator and real life, and impresses itself on the reader as an autonomous reality.

It is, therefore, what a text relates that determines whether it is efficient or inefficient, life-giving or lifeless. To identify the elements of style, perhaps we should begin by eliminating the idea of *correctness*. It doesn't matter at all whether a style is correct or incorrect; what matters is that it be efficient, or suited to its task, which is to endow the stories it tells with the illusion of life—real life. There are novelists who write very

efficient off style

correctly, obeying the grammatical and stylistic imperatives of their times, like Cervantes, Stendhal, Dickens, García Márquez, and there are others, no less great, who break all the rules and make all kinds of grammatical mistakes, like Balzac, Joyce, Pío Baroja, Céline, Cortázar, and Lezama Lima. Their style is full of improprieties from the academic point of view, but that does not prevent them from being good or even excellent novelists. The Spanish writer Azorín, who was an extraordinary prose stylist (and nevertheless a very boring novelist), wrote in a collection of autobiographical essays titled *Madrid*: "The man of letters writes prose, correct prose, classical prose, and yet that prose is worth nothing without the leavening of grace, worthy intent, irony, disdain, or sarcasm." It is a sharp observation: on its own, stylistic correctness does not guarantee either the success or the failure of a work of fiction.

On what, then, does the success of a novel's language depend? On two qualities: its internal coherence and its essentiality. The story a novel tells can be incoherent, but the language that shapes it must be coherent if the incoherence is to be genuinely and convincingly simulated. An example of this is Molly Bloom's monologue at the end of Joyce's *Ulysses*, a chaotic torrent of memories, feelings, thoughts, and emotions. Its power to bewitch derives from a prose that is seemingly ragged and fragmented but that retains beneath its unruly and anarchic surface a rigorous coherence, a structural consistency that follows a model or original system of rules and principles from which it never deviates. Is the monologue an exact *description* of consciousness in motion? No. It is a literary creation so powerfully convincing that it seems to us to mimic the meandering of Molly's consciousness when really it is inventing it.

Julio Cortázar boasted in his later years that he was writing "worse all the time." He meant that in order to express what he longed to express in his stories and novels he was increasingly obliged to search out forms of expression further and further from classic forms, to defy the flow of language and try to impose upon it rhythms, patterns, vocabularies, and distortions in such a way that his prose might more convincingly represent the characters or occurrences he invented. In truth, Cortázar's bad writing was very good writing. His prose was clear and fluid, beautifully imitating speech, incorporating and assimilating with perfect assurance the flourishes, quirks, and phrasings of the spoken word: he made use of Argentine colloquialisms, of course, but also French turns of phrase, and he invented words and expressions with such ingenuity and such a good ear that they didn't stand out in his sentences but rather enriched them with the "leavening" that Azorín believed was required of a good novelist.

The credibility of a story (its power to persuade) doesn't depend solely on the coherence of the style in which it is told—no less important is the role played by narrative technique. But without coherence there is no credibility, or it is reduced almost to nil.

A writer's style may be unpleasant and yet, thanks to its coherence, effective. Such is the case of someone like Louis-

Ferdinand Céline, for example. You may not agree with me, but I find irritating his short, stuttering little sentences, plagued with ellipses and packed with exclamations and slangy expressions. And yet I have no doubt that *Journey to the End of the Night* and also, though not so unequivocably, *Death on the Installment Plan* are novels possessed of an overwhelming power of persuasion. Their sordid outpourings and extravagance hypnotize us, making irrelevant any aesthetic or ethical objections we in good conscience might raise.

I have a similar reaction to the Cuban writer Alejo Carpentier, without a doubt one of the greatest novelists of the Spanish language. Taken out of the context of his novels, his prose is exactly the opposite of the kind of writing I admire (I know it's impossible to make such a distinction, but I make it to clarify my point). I don't like his stiffness, his academicism, and his bookish mannerisms, which always give me the sense that they are informed by meticulous searches in dictionaries, a product of that old passion for archaisms and artifice that seized the Baroque writers of the seventeenth century. And yet this same prose, when it tells the story of Ti Noel and Henri Christophe in Carpentier's 1949 novel *The Kingdom of This World*, an absolute masterwork that I've read at least three times, cancels out my reservations and antipathies with its contagious and overwhelming power and dazzles me, making me believe wholeheartedly everything it has to tell. How does the starched and buttoned-up style of Alejo Carpentier accomplish such a thing? Through its unflagging coherence and its aura of indispensability. His style has about it a conviction that makes its readers feel that he tells the story *only way it could be told*

the only way it could be told: in *these* words, phrases, and rhythms.

It is relatively easy to speak of the coherence of a style and harder to explain what I mean by *essentiality*, a quality required of the language of a novel if that novel is to be persuasive. Maybe the best way of describing essentiality is to explain its opposite, the style that fails in telling a story because it keeps us at a distance and lucidly conscious; in other words, a style that makes us conscious of reading something alien and prevents us from experiencing the story alongside its characters and sharing it with them. This failure is perceived when the reader feels an abyss that the novelist does not successfully bridge in writing his tale, an abyss between what is being told and the language in which it is told. This bifurcation or split between the language of a story and the story itself annihilates the story's power of persuasion. The reader doesn't believe what he is being told, because the clumsiness and inconvenience of the style make him sense that between word and deed there is an unbreachable divide, a fissure that exposes all the artifice and arbitrariness that fiction depends on and that only successful fictions manage to erase or hide.

Such a style fails because we don't feel it is necessary; indeed, as we read we realize that the same story told in a different way or in other words would be better (which in literary terms simply means more persuasive). We never feel any dichotomy of language and content when we read Faulkner's novels or the stories of Borges or Isak Dinesen. The styles of these authors—each so very different—persuade us because in them words, characters, and things constitute an indissoluble unity; it is impossible to conceive of the parts in isolation. It is this perfect integration of style and content that I am alluding to when I speak of the quality of *essentiality* any creative writing must possess.

The *essentiality* of the language of great writers is detected, by contrast, in the forced and false writing of their epigones. Borges is one of the most original prose stylists of the Spanish language, and perhaps the greatest Spanish stylist of the twentieth century. For that very reason, he has exerted a great influence and, if I may say so, an unfortunate one. Borges's style is unmistakable and functions extraordinarily well, giving life and credibility to a world of sophisticated intellectual and abstract ideas and curiosities. In this world, philosophical systems, theological disquisitions, myths and literary symbols, reflection and speculation, and universal history (contemplated from an eminently literary perspective) are the raw material of invention. Borges's style adapts itself to its subject matter and merges with it in a powerful alloy, and the reader feels from the first sentences of his stories and of many of his essays that these works have the inventive and sovereign quality of true fictions, that they could only have been told in this way, in this intelligent, ironic, and mathematically precise language—not a word too few, not a word too many—with its cold elegance and aristocratic defiance, privileging intellect and knowledge over sensation and emotion, playing with erudition, making a technique of presumption, eluding all forms of sentimentality, and ignoring the body and sensuality (or noting them at a great distance, as lower manifestations of existence). His stories are humanized thanks to their subtle irony, a fresh breeze that lightens the complexity of the arguments, intellectual labyrinths, and baroque constructions that are almost always their subject matter. The color and grace of Borges's style lies first and foremost in his use of adjectives, which shake the reader with their audacity and eccentricity ("No one saw him disembark in the *unanimous* night"), and in his violent and unexpected metaphors, whose adjectives and adverbs, besides fleshing out an idea or highlighting a physical or psychological trait, often serve to foster a Borgesian atmosphere. Precisely because it is essential, Borges's style is inimitable. When his admirers or literary followers copy his way of using adjectives, his irreverent sallies, his witticisms and poses, their stylings are as out of place as badly made wigs that fail to pass as real hair, proclaiming their falseness and bringing ridicule down on the unhappy heads they cover. Jorge Luis Borges was a formidable creator, and there is nothing more irritating or bothersome than the "mini-Borges" imitators whose imitations lack the essentiality of the prose they mimic, making what was original, authentic, beautiful, and stimulating something caricaturish, ugly, and insincere. (The question of sincerity or lack of sincerity in literature is not an ethical issue but an aesthetic one.)

Something similar has happened around another great prose stylist, Gabriel García Márquez. Unlike Borges's style, his is not sober but exuberant and not intellectualized at all; rather, it is sensory and sensual. Its clarity and correctness reveal its classical origins, but it is not stiff or old-fashioned—it is open to the assimilation of sayings and popular expressions and to neologisms and foreign words, and it possesses a rich musicality and conceptual purity free of complications or intellectual wordplay. Heat, taste, music, all the textures of perception and the appetites of the body are expressed naturally and without fuss, and fantasy draws breath with the same freedom, casting itself unfettered toward the extraordinary. Reading *One Hundred Years of Solitude* or *Love in the Time of Cholera* we are overwhelmed by the certainty that only in these words, with this grace and rhythm, would these stories be believable, convincing, fascinating, moving; that separated from these words they would not have been able to enchant us as they have: his stories *are* the words in which they are told.

And the truth is that words are also the stories they tell. As a result, when a writer borrows a style, the literature that is produced sounds false, like mere parody. After Borges, García Márquez is the most imitated writer in the language, and although some of his disciples have been successful— that is to say, they've attracted many readers—the work, no matter how diligent the disciple, fails to take on a life of its own, and its secondary, forced character is immediately evident. Literature is pure artifice, but great literature is able to hide the fact while mediocre literature gives itself away.

Although it seems to me that now I've told you everything I know about style, in view of your letter's demands for *practical* advice, I'll give you this: since you want to be a novelist and you can't be one without a coherent and essential style, set out to find a style for yourself. Read constantly, *Read* because it is impossible to acquire a rich, full sense of language without reading plenty of good literature, and try as hard as you can, though this is not quite so easy, not to imitate the styles of the novelists you most admire and who first taught you to love literature. Imitate them in everything else: in their dedication, in their discipline, in their habits; if you feel it is right, make their convictions yours. But try to avoid the mechanical reproduction of the patterns and rhythms of their writing, since if you don't manage to develop a personal style that suits your subject matter, your stories will likely never achieve the power of persuasion that makes them come to life.

It is possible to seek out and find a style of your own. Read Faulkner's early novels. You'll see that from the mediocre *Mosquitoes* to the estimable *Flags in the Dust*, as the first version of *Sartoris* was called, Faulkner found *his* style, the labyrinthine and majestic language, part religious, part mythical, and part epic, that animates the Yoknapatawpha novels. Flaubert also sought and found his style between the first version of *The Temptation of Saint Anthony*, written in a torrential, unmoored, lyrically romantic fashion, and *Madame Bovary*, in which that unbridled style was severely curtailed and all the emotional and lyrical exuberance in it sternly repressed in favor of an "illusion of reality," which he managed to perfect in five years of superhuman labor, the same amount of time it took him to compose his first masterpiece. As you may know, Flaubert had a theory about style, that of the mot juste. The right word was the one word—the only word—that was able to express an idea aptly. The obligation of the writer was to find that word. How did he know when he had? A whisper in his ear: the word was right when it *sounded* right. The perfect correspondence between form and content— between word and idea—translated itself into musical harmony. That is why Flaubert submitted his sentences to "*la gueulade*," the shouting test. He'd go outside to read aloud everything he had written, out to an avenue of lime trees that still exists near what used to be his house at Croisset: the "*allée des gueulades*," the shouting allée. There he'd read as loudly as he could what he'd written, and his ear would tell him if he'd succeeded or if he'd have to keep trying out words and sentences until he achieved the artistic perfection he pursued with such fanatic tenacity.

Do you remember the line by Rubén Darío "My style in search of a form"? For a long time, I was disconcerted by it: aren't style and form the same thing? How is it possible to search for form when it is there in front of you? Now I understand better because, as I mentioned in one of my earlier letters, writing is only one aspect of literary form. Another, no less important, is technique, since words alone do not suffice in the telling of good stories. But this letter has gone on too long, and I'd better leave that discussion for next time.

Fondly,

The Narrator and Narrative Space

DEAR FRIEND,

I'm glad you encourage me to discuss the structure of the novel, the framework that sustains the fictions that dazzle us as harmonious and living entities, their persuasive power so great they seem all-encompassing, self-generated, and self-contained. But we already know that that is only what they seem. Ultimately, it is not what they are: the magic of their prose and the dexterity of their construction only manage to give that illusion. We've already discussed narrative style. Now we must consider the ways in which the elements of the novel are organized and the techniques the novelist employs to invest his inventions with the power of suggestion.

The variety of problems or challenges that those who set out to write fiction must confront may be divided into four major categories, as follows:

a. narrator
b. space

c. time

d. level of reality

That is to say, the ability of a story to surprise, move, uplift, or bore us depends as much upon the choice and handling of the narrator and three points of view, all closely interwoven, as upon the effectiveness of the story's style.

Today I'd like to discuss the narrator, the most important character in any novel and the one upon whom, in a way, all the rest depend. But first of all we must clear up a common misunderstanding: the narrator—that is, the person who tells the story—must not be confused with the author, the person who writes it. This is a very serious error, made even by many novelists who, having decided to tell their stories in the first person and deliberately taking their own biographies as their subject matter, believe that they are the narrators of their fictions. They are mistaken. A narrator is a being made of words and not of flesh and blood, as authors tend to be; the former lives only within the confines of the story that is being told, and only while he is telling it (the boundaries of the story are those of his existence). The author has a much richer and fuller life, which predates the writing of a particular novel and survives it. Even while he is writing a novel, it does not entirely occupy his existence.

The narrator is always a made-up character, a fictional being, just like all the other characters whose story he "tells," but he is the most important because the way he acts—showing or hiding himself, lingering or surging ahead, being explicit or elusive, talkative or taciturn, playful or serious—decides whether we will be persuaded of the reality of the other characters and whether we will be convinced that they are not puppets or caricatures. The behavior of the narrator establishes the internal coherence of a story, which, in turn, is an essential factor in determining its power to persuade.

The first problem the author must resolve is who will tell the story. The possibilities seem endless, but in general terms they may be reduced to three: a narrator-character, an omniscient narrator outside and separate from the story he tells, or an ambiguous narrator whose position is unclear—he may be narrating from either inside or outside the narrative world. The first two types of narrator are the most traditional; the last, on the other hand, has only very recently been established and is a product of the modern novel.

To determine which the author chose, one must just check which grammatical person the story is told in: whether it is a *he* or *she*, an *I*, or a *you*. The pronoun tells us what space the narrator occupies in relation to that of the story. If the narration is from the point of view of an *I* (or a *we*, a rare case, but not unheard of; remember *Citadelle* by Antoine de Saint-Exupéry or many passages in John Steinbeck's *The Grapes of Wrath*), the narrator is inside the narrative, interacting with the characters of the story. If the narrator speaks from the third-person singular, he is outside the narrative space and is, as in so many classic novels, an omniscient narrator modeled on an all-powerful God, since he sees everything—no matter how big or small—and knows everything but is not part of the world he proceeds to show us from the outside perspective of his soaring gaze. And what space is occupied by the narrator who narrates from the second-person *you*, as the narrator does, for example, in *Passing Time* by Michel Butor, *Aura* by Carlos Fuentes, *Juan the Landless* by Juan Goytisolo, *Five Hours with Mario* by Miguel Delibes, and many chapters of *Galíndez* by Manuel Vázquez Montalbán? There's no way of knowing beforehand; the answer may only be sought by examining the way the second person is employed. The *you* could be spoken by an omniscient narrator from outside the fictional world who goes about giving orders and commands and imposing his word as law, causing everything to happen in obedience to his will and the fully fledged, limitless powers he enjoys as an imitator of God. But the narrator might also be a consciousness turned inward and speaking to itself through the subterfuge of the *you*, a somewhat schizophrenic narrator-character who is involved in the novel's action but disguises his identity from the reader (and sometimes from himself) through the device of the split personality. In novels narrated by second-person narrators, there is no way to know for sure, and the answer must be deduced from internal narrative evidence.

The relationship that exists in all novels between the space the narrator occupies and the narrative space is called the *spatial point of view*, and we say that it is determined by the grammatical person in which the novel is narrated. The possibilities are three:

a. a narrator-character who narrates in the first-person singular, a point of view in which the space of the narrator and the narrative space coincide;

b. an omniscient narrator who narrates in the third person and occupies a space independent of and separate from the narrative space; and

c. an ambiguous narrator, concealed behind the second person, whose *you* might be the voice of an all-seeing and all-powerful narrator decreeing from outside the narrative space the course of fictional events or the voice of a narrator-character involved in the action who, whether timid or conniving or seized by schizophrenia or mere whim, reproduces himself and talks to himself as he addresses the reader.

Broken down in this way, I imagine the *spatial point of view* seems very clear, something identifiable by a simple glance at the first few sentences of a novel. That is true if we limit ourselves to abstract generalizations, but when we consider specific cases we discover that multiple variations fit within the scheme, permitting each author, having chosen a certain spatial point of view from which to tell his story, to avail himself of a wide range of innovations and variations, thereby assuring his originality and freedom.

Do you remember how *Don Quixote* begins? No doubt you do, since its first line is one of the most memorable in literature: "In a village of La Mancha the name of which I have no desire to recall . . ." Following our system of classification, we see that the narrator of the novel occupies the first-person singular, that he speaks as an *I*, and that he is therefore a narrator-character whose space is the same as the story's. Nevertheless, we soon discover that although this first-person narrator makes an appearance every so often (as in the first sentence) and speaks to us as *I*, he is not at all a narrator-character but rather an omniscient, God-like narrator who, from a lofty exterior perspective, narrates the action as if he were narrating from the outside, as a *he*. In fact, he does narrate as a *he*, except in a few instances in which he shifts to the first person and reveals himself to the reader, speaking from the perspective of an exhibitionistic and distracting *I* (since his sudden appearance in the middle of a story in which he plays no part is a gratuitous spectacle and distracts the reader from what is happening). These shifts or leaps in spatial point of view—from an *I* to a *he* and an omniscient narrator to a narrator-character or vice versa—alter the narrator's perspective or distance from the narrative and may or may not be justified. If they aren't justified—if the shifts in spatial perspective only serve as a self-congratulatory demonstration of the narrator's omnipotence—then the incongruity introduced conspires against illusion, weakening the persuasive power of the story.

But these shifts also give us an idea of the versatility a narrator may enjoy and the *transformations* he undergoes, modifying with his leaps from one grammatical person to another the perspective from which what is narrated unfolds.

Let's have a look at some interesting cases of versatility, of those spatial shifts or transformations of the narrator. Take the first sentence of *Moby-Dick*, "Call me Ishmael." Extraordinary beginning, isn't it? In just three words, Melville manages to awaken in us a lively curiosity regarding the mysterious narrator-character whose identity we can only guess at, since it's not even certain whether Ishmael is his name. The spatial point of view is certainly very well defined. Ishmael speaks in the first-person singular; he's a character in the story, though not the most important one—that role is reserved for the fanatical, possessed Captain Ahab or perhaps for his enemy, the maddening, ever-present absence that is the white whale he pursues—but he either witnesses or participates in most of the adventures he recounts (those he doesn't, he hears of secondhand and transmits to the reader). This point of view is rigorously respected by the author throughout the tale, but only until the final episode. Up until that point, the coherence of the spatial point of view is complete because Ishmael only tells (and only knows) what he is able to know as a person involved in the story, and this coherence strengthens the persuasive power of the novel. But in the end, as you'll recall, there comes the terrible moment when the fearsome sea beast becomes aware of Captain Ahab and the sailors on the *Pequod*. From an objective point of view, and to preserve the internal coherence of the story, the logical conclusion would be for Ishmael to succumb along with his companions. But if the logic of this development had been respected, how would it be possible for someone to be telling us a story when he dies at the end of it? To avoid this incongruity and to keep *Moby-Dick* from turning into a ghost story told by a narrator speaking from beyond the grave, Melville has Ishmael survive (miraculously) and informs us of his fate in a postscript to the tale. This postscript is not written by Ishmael himself but by an omniscient narrator, separate from the world of the narrative, an omniscient narrator who occupies a different, greater space than the narrative (since from it he can observe and describe the space in which the narrative unfolds).

I hardly need point out something you've surely already realized, which is that these shifts in narrator are not unusual. On the contrary, it is common for novels to be told (though we might not always notice it at first) not by one narrator but by two or sometimes several, who relieve each other every so often, like runners in a relay race.

The most obvious example of this narrative handing off—of spatial shifts—that occurs to me is *As I Lay Dying*, the novel in which Faulkner describes the Bundren family's trip across Mississippi to bury their mother, Addie Bundren, who wanted to be laid to rest in the place where she was born. The trip has biblical and epic qualities, since the cadaver begins to decompose under the merciless sun of the Deep South, but the family presses on undaunted in their journey, animated by the fanatical conviction that Faulkner's characters tend to possess. Do you remember how the novel is told, or, to be more precise, who tells it? Many narrators: all the members of the Bundren family and others as well. The story passes along through the consciousness of each of them, establishing peripatetic and multiple points of view. The narrator is, in all cases, a narrator-character, involved in the action and settled in the narrative space. But although in this sense the spatial point of view remains unchanged, the identity of the narrator changes as the narrative is transferred from one character to the next, so that in this novel—unlike in *Moby-Dick* or *Don Quixote*—the shift is not between one spatial point of view and another but between one character and another, and requires no exiting of the narrative space.

If these shifts are justified and lend the novel a denser and richer verisimilitude, they are invisible to the reader, who is caught up in the excitement and curiosity awakened in him by the story. On the other hand, if they don't work, the effect is the opposite: their artifice is laid bare, and they seem forced and arbitrary to us, straitjackets squeezing spontaneity and authenticity out of the story's characters. This is not the case with *Don Quixote* or *Moby-Dick*, of course.

And neither is it the case with the marvelous *Madame Bovary*, another cathedral of the novel genre, in which we also witness a fascinating spatial shift. Do you remember the beginning? "We were in class when the headmaster came in, followed by a new boy, not wearing the school uniform, and a school servant carrying a large desk." Who is the narrator? Who is speaking to us in the person of that *we*? We'll never know. All we know for sure is that it is a narrator-character whose space is the same as the narrative's space and who is a witness to what he is telling since he tells it in the first-person plural. Since the narrator is a *we*, the possibility cannot be discounted that it is a collective character, perhaps the group of students whose class the young Monsieur Bovary joins. (If you'll allow me to cite a pygmy alongside the giant Flaubert, I once wrote a novella, *The Cubs*, from the spatial point of view of a collective narrator-character, the group of neighborhood friends of the protagonist, Pichulita Cuéllar.) But it could also be a single student, who discreetly, modestly, or timidly speaks as "we." In any case, this point of view is maintained for only a few pages, over the course of which we hear that first-person voice relating an episode two or three times and presenting himself or herself unequivocally as a witness to it. But at a moment difficult to define—the subtlety is evidence of another technical feat—the voice ceases to be that of a narrator-character and shifts to that of an omniscient narrator, distant from the tale, located in a different space, who no longer narrates as *we* but in the third-person singular, as *he*. The shift is from one point of view to another: in the beginning, the voice is that of a character, and then it becomes that of an omniscient and invisible God, who knows all and sees all and tells all without revealing or describing himself or herself. This new point of view is rigorously sustained until the end of the novel.

Flaubert, who developed a whole theory of the novel in his letters, was an unflagging champion of the invisibility of the narrator, since he maintained that what we have termed the autonomy or self-sufficiency of a fiction requires the reader to forget that what he's reading is being narrated; he must be under the impression that it is coming to life in the act, as if generated by something inherent in the novel itself. To create an invisible omniscient narrator, Flaubert invented and perfected many techniques, the first of which was an adherence to the neutrality and impassibility of the narrator. Commentary, interpretation, and judgment represent intrusions of the narrator into the story and are signs of a presence (in space and reality) different from the presences that make up the reality of the novel; the intrusion of the narrator destroys the illusion of self-sufficiency, betrays the accidental, derivative nature of the story, and shows it to be dependent on something or someone external to itself. Flaubert's theory of the "objectivity" of the narrator—objectivity being the price paid for invisibility—has long been followed by modern-day novelists (though often they do not realize it) and that is why it is perhaps no exaggeration to call Flaubert the first writer of the modern novel, tracing between it and the romantic or classical novel a technical divide.

That is not to say, of course, that because the narrators of romantic or classical novels are less invisible and sometimes all too visible, those novels seem defective or awkward to us or lacking in power of persuasion. Not at all. It means that when we read a novel by Dickens, Victor Hugo, Voltaire, Daniel Defoe, or Thackeray, we must resituate ourselves as readers, adapt ourselves to a different spectacle from the one we're used to in the modern novel.

This difference has to do especially with the different ways in which an omniscient narrator manifests himself in modern novels and in novels that we call romantic or classical. In the former, he tends to be invisible, or at least discreet, and in the latter, a distinct presence, sometimes so overbearing that as he narrates he seems to tell his own story and sometimes even takes what he is telling us as a pretext for unbridled exhibitionism.

Isn't that what happens in *Les Misérables*? One of the most ambitious narrative creations of the nineteenth century—the golden age of the novel—*Les Misérables* is steeped in all the great social, cultural, and political events of its time and in all of Victor Hugo's personal experiences over the nearly thirty years he spent writing it (he returned to the manuscript several times after abandoning it for long intervals). It is no exaggeration to say that the novel includes a formidable display of exhibitionism and egomania on the part of its narrator. The narrator is omniscient, technically separate from the world of the narrative, observing from outside the space where the lives of Jean Valjean, Monseigneur Bienvenu, Gavroche, Marius, Cosette, and the other abundant human fauna of the novel intersect. But in truth, the narrator is more present in the tale than the characters themselves: possessed of a proud and overbearing nature and seized by an irresistible megalomania, he can't keep from constantly revealing himself as he presents the story to us. Often he interrupts the action, shifts into the first-person singular from the third to weigh in on whatever he likes, pontificates on philosophy, history, morality, and religion, and judges his characters, mercilessly condemning them or praising them to the heavens for their civic-minded and spiritual inclinations. This narrator-God (and the epithet was never better employed) not only gives us constant proof of his existence and of the lesser and dependent status of the narrative world but also reveals to us—besides his convictions and theories—his phobias and sympathies, proceeding without the slightest discretion or precaution or scruple, convinced of the truth and justice of everything he thinks, says, or does in the name of his cause. In the hands of a less skillful and powerful novelist than Victor Hugo, these intrusions would entirely destroy the novel's power to persuade. The intrusions of an omniscient narrator constitute what contemporary critics call a "rupture of the system," a series of incursions introducing incoherencies and incongruencies liable to vanquish all illusion and strip the story of credibility in the reader's eyes. But that's not what happens in *Les Misérables*. Why not? Because the modern reader rapidly becomes accustomed to the intrusions and feels them to be an intrinsic part of the narrative system, of a fiction that is really two stories intimately intertwined and inextricably bound up together: the narrative that begins with Jean Valjean's theft of silver from the home of the bishop Monseigneur Bienvenu and concludes forty years later when the ex-convict, redeemed by the sacrifices and virtuous deeds of his heroic life, steps into eternity; and the story of the narrator, whose embellishments, exclamations, reflections, judgments, whims, and sermons constitute the intellectual context, an ideological-philosophical-moral backdrop to the text.

Might we, in imitation of the egocentric and impulsive narrator of *Les Misérables*, pause here to summarize what has been said about the narrator, the spatial point of view, and the space of the novel? I don't think the digression is unwarranted, because if everything has not been made clear I'm afraid that what I have to say next, encouraged by your interest, commentary, and questions, will seem confusing and even incomprehensible—and it's hard to make me stop in the middle of any discussion of the fascinating form of the novel.

In order to tell a story in writing, all novelists invent a narrator—their fictional representative or agent—who is as much a fiction as the other characters whose story he tells, since he is made of words and only lives for and as part of the novel he inhabits. This character, the narrator, may be situated inside the story, outside it, or in an uncertain location, depending on whether he narrates in the first, third, or second person. The choice is not random: the narrator's distance from and knowledge of the story he is telling will vary depending on the space he occupies relative to the novel. It is obvious that a narrator-character cannot know—and therefore, cannot describe or relate—matters other than those credibly within his reach, while an omniscient narrator can know everything and be everywhere in the narrative world. Whichever point of view is chosen, therefore, it is accompanied by a set of conditions, and if the narrator fails to abide by those conditions, the novel's power to persuade is impaired. Conversely, the closer the narrator keeps to the limits the spatial point of view imposes, the stronger the power of persuasion and the more real the narrative will seem to us, imbued with the "truth" that all great lies passing as good novels seem to possess.

It must be stressed that the novelist enjoys absolute freedom when he sets out to create his narrator. In other words, the distinction between the three possible types of narrator does not in any way indicate that their spatial placement limits their attributes or personalities. In a few examples we've seen how omniscient narrators—the all-seeing, God-like narrators of a Flaubert or a Victor Hugo—differ from one another, never mind narrator-characters, who are as infinitely variable as fictional characters in general.

We've also seen something that should perhaps have been mentioned explicitly from the start, something that for the sake of expository clarity I didn't bring up but that you likely already know, or have discovered reading this letter, since it is evident in the examples cited. Namely: it is rare and almost impossible for a novel to have only one narrator. Most common is that it should have many, a series of narrators who take turns telling the story from different perspectives, sometimes from the same spatial point of view (that of a narrator-character, in books like *La Celestina* or *As I Lay Dying*, which function like stage plays), sometimes from shifting ones, as in the examples from Cervantes, Flaubert, or Melville.

We can push our analysis of the spatial point of view and the spatial shifts of narrators a little further still. If we move in with a magnifying glass and make a meticulous freeze-frame examination (this is a terrible and unacceptable way to read a novel, of course), we discover that shifts take place not only in a general manner and over long stretches of narrative time as in the examples I've used. They can be swift and very brief, lasting barely a few words, in which the narrator undergoes a subtle and inconspicuous spatial shifting.

For example, whenever dialogue between characters lacks formal attribution, there is a spatial shift, a change of speaker. If, in a novel featuring Pedro and María and narrated by an omniscient narrator outside the story, this exchange is suddenly inserted:

"I love you, María."

"I love you too, Pedro."

then in the very brief instant in which Pedro and María declare their love for each other there is a shift: the narrator ceases to be omniscient and becomes a narrator-character involved in the narrative (Pedro and María), and within the spatial point of view of the narrator-character there is another shift between the two characters (from Pedro to María), after which the story returns to the spatial point of view of the omniscient narrator. Naturally, these shifts would not have occurred if that brief dialogue had been formally attributed ("I love you, María," *said Pedro*. "I love you too, Pedro," *replied María*), since then the story would have been consistently narrated from the point of view of the omniscient narrator.

Do these infinitesimal shifts, so rapid that the reader doesn't even notice them, seem insignificant to you? They are not. In fact, nothing is without importance in the formal domain, and it is the sum of these tiny details that decides the excellence or lack of merit of a work of art. What is evident, in any event, is that the author's unlimited freedom in creating and manipulating his narrator (moving him, hiding him, exhibiting him, bringing him into the foreground, pushing him into the background, turning him into different narrators or multiple narrators within a single spatial point of view, or leaping between different spaces) is not, nor can it ever be, arbitrary, but must find its justification in the novel's power of persuasion. The shifts in point of view can enrich a story, give it depth, give it subtlety, make it mysterious, ambiguous, multifaceted; or they can smother and crush it if instead of causing events to multiply of their own accord in an illusion of life these displays of technique—mechanical tricks in this case—give rise to incongruities and gratuitous complications or confusions that destroy the story's credibility and make evident to the reader its origins as mere artifice.

I'll hear from you soon I hope.

Fondly,

Time

Dear Friend,

I'm glad that these reflections on the structure of the novel are yielding you a few clues, pointing you the way into the depths of fiction as if you were a spelunker venturing deep into the heart of a mountain. Now that we've touched on the characteristics of the narrator in relation to the space of the novel (which in disagreeably academic language I termed the *spatial point of view*), I propose that we examine time, a no less important aspect of narrative form, the treatment of which is as crucial as the treatment of space in determining the persuasive power of a story.

On this subject we must also first dispel some prejudices, venerable yet false, in order to understand what a novel is and how it works.

I refer to the naive equation that is often made between real time (to be called, redundant though the definition may be, the chronological time we readers and authors inhabit) and fictional time, a time or passage of time as imaginary as the narrator and characters trapped in it. As with the spatial point of view, huge doses of creativity and imagination go into the creation of the temporal point of view of all the novels we read, although in many cases their authors don't realize it. The time novels take place in is a fictional creation, just like the narrator and the setting; it is one of the elements the novelist manipulates to liberate his invention from the real world and give it the (apparent) autonomy upon which, I repeat, his power of persuasion depends.

Although the theme of time, a source of fascination for so many thinkers and creators (among them Borges, who made it the subject of many of his works), has given rise to a number of different and divergent theories, all of us, I think, can agree on at least one simple distinction: there are two kinds of time, chronological and psychological. The former exists objectively, independent of human subjectivity. It is in chronological time that we measure the movement of heavenly bodies in space and the positions the planets occupy with respect to one another; it is chronological time that eats away at us from the moment we are born until the moment we die and presides over the fateful life curve of all sentient beings. But there is also a psychological time, of which we are conscious depending on what we are doing or not doing and which figures very differently in our emotional lives. This time passes quickly when we are enjoying ourselves and when we are immersed in overwhelmingly intense, absorbing, or distracting experiences. On the other hand, it drags and seems infinite—the seconds like minutes, the minutes

like hours—when we are waiting or suffering and our circumstances (loneliness, a long vigil, catastrophe, a wait for
something that may or may not happen) give us a sharp
awareness of the passing of time, which, precisely because we
desire it to speed up, seems to sputter, slow, and stop.

I assure you that it is the rule (another of the very few
binding rules in the world of fiction) that time in the novel is
based not on chronological time but on psychological time,
a subjective time to which the novelist (the *good* novelist) is
able to give the appearance of objectivity, thereby setting the
novel apart from the real world (which is the obligation of all
fiction that desires to live of its own accord).

An example might make this clearer. Have you read the
wonderful short story by Ambrose Bierce called "An Occurrence at Owl Creek Bridge"? It takes place during the American Civil War. Peyton Farquhar, a southern planter who has
tried to blow up a rail line, is about to be hanged from a
bridge. The story begins as the rope tightens around the poor
man's neck; he is surrounded by the soldiers in charge of his
execution. But when the order that will end his life is given,
the rope breaks and the condemned man falls into the river.
Somehow he manages to swim to shore and dodge the bullets
of the soldiers on the bridge and the banks of the river. The
omniscient narration is nearly at one with Peyton Farquhar's
consciousness as he flees through the woods toward the safety
of his home and the woman he loves, recalling episodes from
his past as he runs with the soldiers at his heels. The narrative
is harrowing, as is Farquhar's perilous flight. The house is

there, within sight, and when the fugitive crosses the threshold, he at last glimpses his wife's profile. Just as he is about to embrace her, he is choked by the rope that had begun to tighten around his neck at the beginning of the story one or two seconds before. All of this occurs in the briefest flash; it is an instant, fleeting vision prolonged by the narrative, which creates its own separate time composed of words and different from real time (the objective time of the story's action, of which barely a second elapses). Doesn't this example make clear the way in which fiction constructs its *own* time out of psychological time?

A variation on this theme is a famous story by Borges, "The Secret Miracle." At the moment a Czech poet named Jaromir Hladik is about to be executed, God grants him another year of life, allowing him to complete—mentally— the drama in verse he had been planning to write all his life, *The Enemies*. Over the course of this year he successfully completes his ambitious work in the intimacy of his own mind, but the year he experiences is squeezed in between the order of "Fire" given by the head of the firing squad and the impact of the bullets as they riddle their target; that is to say, it lasts barely a fraction of a second, a mere instant. All fictions (and especially good ones) occupy their own time, a temporal system exclusively their own, different from the real time their readers inhabit.

To identify the basic characteristics of novelistic time, the first step is to divine the *temporal point of view* of the novel in question, which should never be confused with the spatial point of view, although in practice the two are viscerally linked.

There being no way to escape definitions (I'm sure they vex you as much as they do me, since they seem alien to the unpredictable world of literature), let's venture this one: the *temporal point of view* is the relationship that exists in all novels between the time the narrator inhabits and the time of what is being narrated. As with the spatial point of view, the novelist has only three to choose among (although the variations are many), and they are determined by the tense in which the narrator tells the story:

a. The time the narrator inhabits and the time of what is being narrated may coincide and be one and the same. In this case, the narrator narrates in the present tense.
b. The narrator may situate himself in the past to narrate events taking place in the present and the future. And, finally,
c. The narrator may situate himself in the present or the future and narrate events that have taken place in the (near or middle) past.

Although in their abstract form these distinctions may seem a little complicated, in practice they are quite obvious and easy to spot once we stop to check what tense the narrator has chosen to tell the story from.

Let's take as an example not a novel but a story, perhaps the shortest (and one of the best) in the world. "The Dinosaur," by Guatemalan writer Augusto Monterroso, is one sentence long:

"When he woke up, the dinosaur was still there."

A perfect story, is it not? Unbeatable power of persuasion, remarkable concision, perfect drama, color, suggestiveness, and clarity. Suppressing in ourselves all the very rich *other* possible readings of this minimalist narrative gem, let's concentrate on its temporal point of view. In what tense is it narrated? In a simple past tense: "he woke up." The narrator is situated, then, in the future, narrating something that happened—when? In the near or middle past from the narrator's future point of view? In the middle past. How do I know that the time of the story is a middle and not a near past in relation to the time of the narrator? Because between those two times there is an unbridgeable abyss, a gap, a barrier that abolishes all link or continuity between the two. This is the determining characteristic of the tense the narrator employs: the action is confined to a closed-off past, split from the time the narrator inhabits. The action of "The Dinosaur" takes place, therefore, in a middle past with respect to the time of the narrator; this is an example of case c.

Let us avail ourselves of "The Dinosaur" again to illustrate case a, the simplest and most obvious of the three: in it, the time of the narrator and the time of what is narrated coincide. This temporal point of view requires that the narrator narrate from the present tense:

"He wakes up and the dinosaur is still there."

The narrator and what is being narrated inhabit the same temporal space. The story is *happening* as the narrator tells it to us. This tale is very different from the previous one, in which we noted two tenses and in which the narrator, because he was situated in a later time than that of the narrative events, had a full-fledged and complete temporal vision of what he was narrating. In case a, the knowledge or perspective of the narrator is narrower: it only covers what is happening as it is happening; that is to say, as it is being told. When the time of the narrator and the time of the narrative are confused in a present tense (as is usually true in novels by Samuel Beckett or Alain Robbe-Grillet), the immediacy of the narrative is maximized; immediacy is minimal when the narrator narrates in the past tense.

Let's examine case b now, the least common and certainly the most complex: the narrator is situated in the past and narrates events that haven't taken place yet but will take place in a near or middle future. Here are examples of possible modes of this *temporal point of view*:

a. "You'll wake up, and the dinosaur will still be there."
b. "When you wake up, the dinosaur will still be there."
c. "When you have woken up, the dinosaur will still be there."

Each case (others are possible) constitutes a slight shading, establishing a different distance between the time of the narrator and the time of the narrated world, but the common denominator is that the narrator is narrating events that haven't taken place yet, that will take place when he has finished narrating them, and over which, as a result, an essential indeterminacy hovers: there is no certainty that they *will occur*, as there is when the narrator locates himself in a present or future tense to narrate events that have already occurred or that are occurring as they are narrated. Besides shading his story with relativity and uncertainty, the narrator located in the past who narrates events that will occur in a middle or near future reveals himself more aggressively, exhibiting his God-like powers in the fictional universe. Through the use of future tenses, his story becomes a series of imperatives, a sequence of orders commanding that what is being narrated must occur. The dominance of the narrator is absolute and overwhelming when a fiction is narrated from this *temporal point of view*. Hence a novelist can't use it without being conscious of it; he can't use it if he doesn't mean to manipulate uncertainty and allow the narrator a show of force in order to tell something that *only told in this way* will achieve power of persuasion.

Once the three possible temporal points of view have been identified, along with the variations permitted by each, and once we have established that the way to decide which point of view is being used is to check the tense that the narrator narrates from and the tense the story is narrated in, it is necessary to add that it would be very strange if a story were told from only one *temporal point of view*. Although in general one point of view dominates, the narrator usually moves from one *temporal point of view* to another, in shifts (changes of tense) that are more effective the less they call attention to themselves. This effectiveness is achieved by ensuring the coherence of the temporal system (the shifts in time must keep within certain boundaries) and the essentiality of the shifts, which should not seem whimsical or flashy but rather should lend an extra dimension—density, complexity, diversity, depth—to the characters and the story.

Without getting too technical, we may say, above all when speaking of modern novels, that a story flows in time just as it does in space, since novelistic time is something that stretches, lags, freezes, or suddenly speeds precipitously ahead. The story moves in fictional time as if in a physical territory, coming and going across it, moving forward in leaps and bounds or at a shuffle, leaving blank (wiping out) big chronological periods and going back later to pick up the thread of that lost time, leaping from the past to the future and back to the past with a freedom denied beings of flesh and blood in real life. This fictional time is therefore a creation just like the narrator.

Let's take a look at some examples of original constructions (or more obviously original constructions, I should say, since all are original) of fictional time. Instead of moving from the past to the present and then back to the future, the Alejo Carpentier story "Journey to the Seed" proceeds in the exact opposite direction: at the beginning of the story, Carpentier's protagonist, Don Marcial, the Marqués of Capellanías, is a dying old man and we watch him slip through maturity, youth, and childhood and finally retreat into a world of pure, unconscious sensation ("sensorial and tactile") where the character has yet to be born; he is still a fetus in the womb. The story isn't being told backwards; in this fictional world, time moves backwards. And, speaking of prenatal states, perhaps we should make reference to Laurence Sterne's *Tristram Shandy*, the first several dozen pages of which relate the prebirth biography of the narrator-protagonist, including ironic details about his complicated conception, his development in his mother's womb, and his arrival in the world. The twists, turns, spirals, and contortions of the tale make *Tristram Shandy*'s temporal structure a very odd and elaborate creation.

The coexistence in fiction of two or more tenses or temporal systems is also common. For example, in Günter Grass's *The Tin Drum*, time passes normally for everyone except the protagonist, the renowned Oskar Matzerath (he of the glass-shattering voice and the drum), who decides not to age, to abolish time. He succeeds, since by sheer force of will he stops growing and lives a kind of eternal life in a world that ages, perishes, and renews itself all around him, subjected to the inevitable decay imposed by the god Chronos. Everything and everyone fades away, except Oskar.

The theme of the abolition of time and its consequences (disastrous, according to fictional testimony) is a recurring one in fiction. It appears, for example, in a not very successful novel by Simone de Beauvoir, *All Men Are Mortal*. Julio Cortázar, playing a technical trick, engineered his best-known novel to explode the inexorable law of expiration that all living things must obey. The reader who reads *Hopscotch* following the rules suggested by the narrator in the Table of Instructions will *never* finish reading it, since the last two chapters refer endlessly back to each other, and in theory (not in practice, of course) the obedient and disciplined reader must spend the rest of his life reading and rereading those chapters, trapped in a temporal labyrinth with no hope of escape.

Borges liked to quote from *The Time Machine* by H. G. Wells (an author who was also fascinated by the theme of time), in which a man travels to the future and returns with a rose in his hand as proof of his adventure. This impossible displaced rose impressed Borges as a paradigm of the fantastic object.

Another case of parallel times is a story by Adolfo Bioy Casares, "The Celestial Plot," in which an aviator disappears in his plane and reappears later, telling an extraordinary tale that no one believes: he landed in a different time from the one he took off in. In his fictional universe many different parallel times mysteriously coexist, each with its own features, inhabitants, and rhythms, and the times never meet except in unusual instances like this pilot's accident, which reveals to us the structure of a universe that is like a pyramid of ascending temporal floors without connection to one another.

The opposite of these multiple temporal universes is a time so intensified by the narrative that the chronology and the passage of time slow down until they almost stop: as we recall, Joyce's huge novel *Ulysses* covers just twenty-four hours in the life of Leopold Bloom.

At this point in this long letter, you must be eager to interrupt me with an observation you are barely able to contain: "But in what you've written so far on the temporal point of view, I note a mix of different things: time as theme or plot (in the examples by Alejo Carpentier and Bioy Casares) and time as form, a narrative construction in which the plot unfolds (true of *Hopscotch* and its eternal time)." Fair enough. The only excuse I have (and it is relative, of course) is that I confused things on purpose. Why? Because I believe that it is precisely when you are examining the temporal point of view in fiction that you are best able to notice how inseparable "form" and "content" really are, though I've dissociated them in a brutal way to reveal the secret anatomy of the novel.

Time in all novels is, I repeat, a formal creation, since in fiction the story unfolds in a way it never could in real life; at the same time, the passing of fictional time, or the relationship between the time of the narrator and what is being narrated, depends entirely on the story's being told from a particular temporal perspective. This could be expressed the other way around, too: the story the novel tells *depends* on the temporal point of view. Actually, it all boils down to the same thing when we abandon the theoretical plane of our discussion and take a look at concrete novels. In them we discover that "form" does not exist (whether it is spatial or temporal or has to do with levels of reality) independently of the stories that give (or fail to give) the novels life and shape through the words in which they are told.

But let's move on and discuss something else that is common to all fictional narratives. In every story we note moments when time seems to be condensed, revealing its passage to the reader in a tremendously vivid way, seizing his or her full attention, and periods in which intensity flags and the vitality of the episodes lessens; distanced from us, these latter episodes fail to capture our attention and seem ordinary and predictable—they transmit information or commentary that is intended merely as filler and that serves only to link characters or events that would otherwise be left dangling. We may call the former episodes *cruxes* (*live time*, with a maximum concentration of occurrences), and the latter episodes *dead time*, or transition time. Nevertheless, it would be unfair to reproach a novelist for the existence of dead time, of episodes in his novels with nothing more than a linking function. They are useful too, since they establish continuity and create the illusion of a world, of beings immersed in a social setting, which novels must foster. Poetry may be an intensive genre, distilled to the essentials, without waste. The novel may not. Novels are long, unfolding over time (a self-created time), and they play at being "histories," following the path of their characters within a certain social context. This requires that the novel present *informative*, connective, inevitable subject matter, as well as the cruxes or episodes of maximum energy that propel the story (and that sometimes change its nature, swerving it into the future or the past, revealing in it unexpected depths or ambiguities).

The combination of cruxes or live time, and of dead or transition time, determines the configuration of time in the novel—that is, the particular chronological system of written stories, which may be broken down into three varieties of *temporal point of view*. But let me assure you that though what I've said about time has advanced us a little in our examination of the nature of fiction, there is still much to be discussed. That will become evident as we address other aspects of the novelistic enterprise. Because we are going to keep unwinding this interminable skein, are we not?

There you see, you've got me started, and now there's no stopping me.

Fondly, and until next time,

Levels of Reality

DEAR FRIEND,

I very much appreciate your quick response, and I'm pleased you want us to continue exploring the anatomy of the novel. It's good to know, too, that you don't have too many objections to my presentation of the spatial and temporal points of view.

I'm afraid, however, that the point of view we're about to explore won't be so easily explained, though it is just as important as the ones we've already discussed; we are venturing now into a much more nebulous realm than that of space or time. But let's not waste time on introductory remarks.

To begin with what is easiest—a general definition—let's say that the point of view in terms of level of reality is the relationship between the level, or plane, of reality on which the narrator situates himself to narrate the novel and the plane of reality on which the story takes place. As with space and time, the planes occupied by the narrator and by the story may coincide or they may be different, and it is their relationship that determines the kind of fiction that is produced.

I can imagine your first objection. "It may be easy to establish the three possible spatial points of view—the narrator within the narrative, outside of it, or in an uncertain location—and the temporal points of view, too, given the conventional division of time into present, past, and future, but aren't we faced with a boundless infinity when we consider reality?" That may be true. In theory, reality can be divided and subdivided into a boundless number of planes, giving rise to infinite points of view in fictional realities. But, my friend, don't let yourself be overwhelmed by that dizzying possibility. Fortunately, when we move from theory to practice (here, too, is an example of two sharply distinct planes), we find that fiction only really negotiates a limited number of levels and that, as a result, we may identify the most common expressions of the point of view in terms of level of reality (I don't like this formulation either, but I haven't been able to come up with anything better) without presuming to cover all of them.

Perhaps the most distinct and clearly opposed of the options are the "real" world and the "fantastic" world. (I use quotation marks to emphasize the relativity of these concepts, though without such terms we wouldn't be able to understand one another, and perhaps wouldn't even be able to use language.) I'm sure that although you may not like it much (I don't either), you'll agree that we should call real or realist (as opposed to fantastic) all persons, things, or occurrences that we are able to recognize and define through our own experience of the world, and call everything else fantastic. The notion of the fantastic, then, covers a whole range of levels: the magic, the miraculous, the legendary, the mythical, et cetera.

Now that we are provisionally in agreement, I can tell you that this juxtaposition of the real and the fantastic is one of the associations of opposed or identical planes that may occur in a novel between narrator and narrative. And to make it clearer for you, let's move on to a concrete example, making use once again of Augusto Monterroso's brief masterpiece "The Dinosaur."

"When he woke up, the dinosaur was still there."

What is the point of view in terms of level of reality in this story? You'll agree that *the narrative* is situated in the plane of the fantastic, since in the real world you and I inhabit it is improbable that prehistoric animals that appeared in our dreams—or in our nightmares—would turn up in an objective reality and that we would encounter them in the flesh at the foot of our beds when we opened our eyes. It's clear, then, that the level of reality of the narrative is an imaginary or fantastic reality. Is the narrator (omniscient and impersonal) situated on the same plane? I'd venture to say that he is not, that he establishes himself instead on a real or realist plane—in other words, one that is essentially opposite and contrary to that of the narrative. How do I know this? By the tiniest but most unmistakable of indications, a signal or hint that the careful narrator gives the reader as he tells his pared-down tale: the adverb *still*. The word doesn't just define an objective temporal circumstance indicating a miraculous occurrence (the passage of the dinosaur from a dreamworld to objective reality). It is also a call to attention, a display of surprise or astonishment at the remarkable event. Monterroso's *still* is flanked by invisible exclamation points and implicitly urges us to be surprised by the amazing thing that has happened. ("Notice, all of you, what is going on: the dinosaur is *still* there, when it's obvious that it shouldn't be, since in true reality things like this don't happen; they are only possible in a fantastic reality.") This is how we know the narrator is narrating from an objective reality; if he weren't, he wouldn't induce us through the knowing use of an amphibious adverb to take note of the transition of the dinosaur from dream to life, from the imaginary to the tangible.

I have here, therefore, the point of view in terms of level of reality of "The Dinosaur": it belongs to a narrator who, situated in a real world, relates a fantastic occurrence. Can you recall other, similar examples of this point of view? What happens, for example, in Henry James's long story, or short novel, *The Turn of the Screw*? Bly, the grim country house that serves as the setting of the tale, is haunted by ghosts, which appear to two poor children and their governess; it is the governess's testimony—transmitted to us by another narrator-character—that is the source of all the information we are given. As a result, there is no doubt that the story takes place—as far as theme and plot are concerned—on a fantastic plane. And on what plane is the narrator situated? Things begin to get a little complicated, as always with Henry James, who was a magician greatly skilled in the combination and manipulation of points of view, which means that his stories always radiate a subtle ambiguity and lend themselves to multiple interpretations. Remember that in the story there are *two* narrators, not one (or are there three, if we include the invisible and omniscient narrator who always precedes the narrator-character?). There is an unnamed primary or principal narrator who informs us that he has heard his friend Douglas read a story aloud written by the very governess who tells us the ghost story. That first narrator is plainly situated on a "real" or "realist" plane in order to relate the fantastic tale, which perplexes and amazes him as much as it does the reader. Then, too, it is clear that the other narrator, the second-level narrator, the governess who "sees" the ghosts, is not on the same plane of reality but inhabits a fantastic plane unlike the world we know from personal experience, where the dead return to earth to "grieve" in the houses they inhabited when they were alive and to torment the new inhabitants. So far we could say that this story's point of view in terms of level of reality involves a narration of fantastic events featuring two narrators, one situated on a realist or objective plane and the other—the governess—narrating from a fantastic perspective. But when we examine the story even more carefully, we perceive a new complication in this point of view. Most likely, the governess hasn't seen the famous ghosts but only believes she has seen them or has imagined them. If this interpretation is correct (in other words, if the reader chooses it as the correct interpretation)—and it has been advanced by a number of critics—it transforms *The Turn of the Screw* into a realist tale, though one narrated from a plane of pure subjectivity (that of hysteria or neurosis) of a repressed spinster who is probably naturally inclined to see things that are not and have never been part of the real world. The critics who propose this interpretation of *The Turn of the Screw* read it as realist fiction, since the real world also encompasses a subjective plane, home to visions, illusions, and fantasies. It is not the story's content but the subtlety of its telling that makes it seem fantastic; its point of view in terms of level of reality is the pure subjectivity of a psychologically unbalanced person who sees things that don't exist and mistakes her fears and fantasies for objective reality.

So we have here two examples of point of view in which there is a relationship between the real and the fantastic; this opposition is the kind of radical contradiction that characterizes the literary genre we call fantastic (into which we lump, I repeat, texts that differ quite significantly from one another). If we set out to examine this point of view in the writings of the most distinguished authors of fantastic literature of our time (Borges, Cortázar, Calvino, Rulfo, Pierre de Mandiargues, Kafka, García Márquez, Alejo Carpentier, to supply a quick list) we would discover that the matching up of these two separate universes—the real and the unreal or the fantastic, as they are embodied or represented by the narrator and the narrative—leads to an infinity of gradations and variations, to the point that it is perhaps not an exaggeration to say that the originality of a writer of fantastic literature depends above all on the way in which the point of view in terms of level of reality is manifested in his fiction.

Now, the opposition of planes that we have observed so far—the real and the unreal, the realist and the fantastic—is a fundamental opposition between different kinds of universes. But real or realist fiction also consists of separate planes—although each of them may exist and be recognizable to us through our objective experience of the world—and realist writers are able, as a result, to take advantage of many options regarding the level of reality in the fictions they invent.

Perhaps the most obvious discontinuity within the bounds of a realist universe is between the objective world—of things, events, and people existing in and of themselves—and the subjective, interior world of emotions, feelings, fantasies, dreams, and the psychological motivations of much behavior. If you make an effort, you will immediately be able to dredge up the names of a good many writers who fit—according to this arbitrary system of classification—into the category of objective writers, and others who may be called subjective writers, depending on whether their fictional worlds tend to be principally or exclusively situated on one or the other of those two sides of reality. Isn't it obvious that Hemingway would be grouped with the objectives and Faulkner with the subjectives? That Virginia Woolf figures among the latter and Graham Greene among the former? But I know, don't worry: we are in agreement that the objective-subjective dichotomy is too general and that writers grouped into either of these two broad, generic classes may be very different from one another. (And of course we agree that it is always the individual case that matters in literature, since generic models can never tell us what we would like to know about the particular nature of a certain novel.)

Let's take a look at some specific works, then. Have you read *Jealousy* by Alain Robbe-Grillet? I don't believe it's a masterpiece, but it is a very interesting novel, perhaps Robbe-Grillet's best, and one of the best produced by the movement that briefly caused a stir on the French literary scene in the sixties, *le nouveau roman*. Robbe-Grillet was its standard-bearer and theoretician; in his book of essays *For a New Novel*, he explains that his intention is to purge the novel of all psychologizing and, beyond that, of all subjectivity and introspection; he intends to focus on the exterior, physical surface of an objectivized world, whose reality resides in things that are "resistant, stubborn, present in the moment, irreducible." In adhering to this (very limiting) theory, Robbe-Grillet wrote some incredibly dull books, if you'll allow me the discourtesy, but also some texts whose undeniable interest resides in what we might call his technical dexterity. For example, *Jealousy*. The title isn't very objective—quite a paradox!—since in French it means both "window blind" and "jealousy," an amphibiology that disappears in Spanish [and English—*Tr.*]. The novel is, I'll venture to say, the description of an icy, objective stare, and the anonymous and invisible human behind the stare is presumably a jealous husband spying on his wife. The novelty (the action, you might call it, if you were making a joke) of the work isn't its plot, since nothing happens, or, more accurately, nothing worth remembering happens; there is only the tireless, distrustful, insomniac stare with which the woman is besieged. She is entirely defined by the point of view in terms of level of reality. It's a realist story (since there's nothing in it that doesn't correspond to our experience of the world), told by a narrator outside the narrative world but so close to the observer-character that we sometimes tend to confuse their voices. The novel keeps so rigorously to a single level of reality that the effect is sensory; the narrative evokes a pair of reddened eyes that are always observing, watching, missing nothing about the person they are monitoring or her surroundings, and thus it can only capture (and transmit) an exterior, sensory, physical, and visual impression of the world, a world that is all surface—a plastic reality—without emotional, psychological, or psychic depth. This point of view is quite original. Of all the possible planes or levels of reality, Robbe-Grillet confines himself to one—the visual—to tell us a story that, for that very reason, seems to take place exclusively on a plane of total objectivity.

It's clear that the plane or level of reality that Robbe-Grillet's novels (especially *Jealousy*) inhabit is different from that generally occupied by the works of Virginia Woolf, another of the great revolutionaries of the modern novel. Woolf wrote a fantastic novel, of course—*Orlando*—in which we witness the impossible transformation of a man into a woman, but her other novels may be called realist, because they are lacking in similar marvels. Their "marvel" is the delicate and finely grained texture of the "reality" they portray. This is due to Woolf's refined and subtle style, its ethereal lightness, and its great power to suggest and evoke. On what plane of reality does one of her most original novels, *Mrs. Dalloway*, take place, for example? On that of human deeds and behavior, as in Hemingway's stories? No—on an interior and subjective plane, on the plane of feelings and emotions imprinted on the human spirit by life experience, in the intangible but demonstrable reality in which we register what takes place around us, what we see and do, and either rejoice in it or lament it, are moved or frustrated by it, and finally judge it. This level-of-reality point of view is another proof of Virginia Woolf's originality; she managed, thanks to her prose and the lovely, keen perspective from which she described her fictional world, to spiritualize all reality, dematerialize it, infuse it with soul. Exactly the opposite of a Robbe-Grillet, who developed a narrative technique with the aim of objectifying reality and described everything contained in it—including sentiments and emotions—as if they were things.

Through these few examples, I hope that you've come to the same conclusion I came to some time ago regarding point of view in terms of level of reality: that the originality of the novelist often resides in it. In other words, by uncovering (or throwing into relief, at least) one aspect or function of life or human experience previously overlooked, ignored, or suppressed in fiction and resurgent now as the dominant feature, the novelist grants us a pristine, refreshing, unfamiliar vision of life. Isn't this what happens in the work of a Proust or a Joyce? For the former, what is important is not what goes on in the real world but the way memory retains and reproduces lived experience, the way the human mind works to rescue and order the past; you couldn't ask for a more subjective reality than that in which the episodes and characters develop and evolve in *In Search of Lost Time*. And, speaking of Joyce, wasn't *Ulysses* a cataclysmic innovation? In it, reality is "represented" by the very motion of human consciousness as it notices, critiques, judges worthy, treasures or discards, and reacts emotionally and intellectually to the experiences lived through. By privileging planes or levels of reality once ignored or barely noted over more conventional planes, certain writers expand our understanding of human existence, not just quantitatively but in a qualitative sense too. Through writers like Virginia Woolf or Joyce or Kafka or Proust, we can say that our intellect has been enriched, as has our ability to identify—from within the infinite vertigo of planes or levels of reality—the mechanisms of memory, the absurd, the flow of consciousness, the subtleties of emotion and perception that we used to disregard and have a simplistic or stereotyped idea of.

All these examples demonstrate the very broad spectrum of shadings that may differentiate one realist author from another. The same is true of the writers of fantastic fiction, of course. Though this letter is in danger of running longer than it should, I'd like to examine the level of reality that predominates in *The Kingdom of This World* by Alejo Carpentier.

If we try to situate this novel in either the realist or the fantastic camp, there's no doubt that it should be assigned to the latter: in the story that Carpentier tells—which has much in common with the story of the real-life Haitian Henri Christophe, the builder of the celebrated Citadelle—extraordinary things take place, inconceivable in the world we know through firsthand experience. But no one who has read Carpentier's lovely tale will be content to see it classified simply as fantastic literature. Its fantastic passages are not as explicit and obvious as parts of stories by writers like Edgar Allan Poe, the Robert Louis Stevenson of *Dr. Jekyll and Mr. Hyde*, or Jorge Luis Borges, whose fiction flagrantly breaks with reality. In *The Kingdom of This World*, the unusual occurrences seem unusual because of their proximity to real life, to history—it so happens that the book very closely mirrors episodes and characters from Haitian history—and because they contaminate realist happenings. How can this be? It is possible because the narrative of Carpentier's novel is grounded in a plane of unreality associated with myth or legend; in this plane, "real" historical acts or characters undergo an "unreal" transformation when acted upon by faith or beliefs that give the fantastic text a kind of objective legitimacy. Myths explicate reality in terms of particular religious or philosophical convictions; all myths possess, besides their imaginary or fantastic element, an objective historical context. This determines their place in a subjective group consciousness that pretends to impose (and often succeeds in imposing) itself on reality, in the same way that a fantastic planet is superimposed on the real world by the members of a secret society in Borges's story "Tlön, Uqbar, Orbis Tertius." The incredible technical achievement of *The Kingdom of This World* is the point of view in terms of level of reality that Carpentier creates. The story often unfolds on a mythical or legendary plane—the first level of fantastic literature or the last of realism—and is narrated by an impersonal narrator who, though he doesn't establish himself entirely on that same level, comes very close to it, brushing up against it, so that the distance he maintains from his material is small enough to *almost* make us live inside the myths and legends of his story and yet unequivocal enough to make us realize that what we are being told is not objective reality but rather a reality undone by the credulity of a town that has not given up magic, witchcraft, or irrational practices, although on the outside it seems to have embraced the rationalism of the colonizers from whom it is emancipated.

We could go on forever trying to identify original and unusual points of view in the world of fiction, but I think that these examples are more than enough to show how various the relationship between the narrative and the narrator can be and how a discussion of levels of reality allows us to speak—if we're inclined to classify and catalog, which I'm not and I hope you're not either—of realist and fantastic novels, mythical and religious novels, psychological and lyrical novels, action-driven and analytical novels, philosophical and historical novels, surrealist and experimental novels, et cetera, et cetera. (The establishment of systems of classification is an insatiable vice.)

It's not important to know exactly where the novel we analyze fits on a series of pedantic and innumerable charts. What's important is to notice that in every novel there is a spatial point of view, a temporal point of view, and a level-of-reality point of view; to understand that the three are essentially independent of and different from one another, though their boundaries are often unclear; and to realize that the way the three points of view mesh and harmonize lends the novel the internal coherence that determines its power of persuasion. This ability to persuade us of "truth," "authenticity," and "sincerity" never comes from the novel's resemblance to or association with the real world we readers inhabit. It comes exclusively from the novel's own being, from the words in which it is written and from the writer's manipulation of space, time, and level of reality. If the words and the structure of a novel are efficient, and appropriate to the story that the novel intends to make persuasive, that means that its text is perfectly balanced. Theme, style, and points of view are so perfectly harmonized and the reader is so hypnotized and absorbed by what is being told that he completely forgets the *way* it is being told and is under the impression that technique and form have nothing to do with it, that life itself animates the work's characters, landscapes, and events, which seem to the reader nothing less than reality incarnate, life in print.

This is the great triumph of technical skill in novel writing: the achievement of invisibility, the ability to endow a story with color, drama, subtlety, beauty, and suggestive power so effectively that no reader even notices the story exists; under the spell of its craftsmanship, he feels that he is not reading but rather living a fiction that, for a while at least and as far as he is concerned, supplants life.

Fondly,

Shifts and Qualitative Leaps

Dear Friend,

You're right: throughout our correspondence as we've discussed the three points of view that are common to all novels, I've used the expression *shifts* several times to refer to certain conversions a narrative undergoes, but I haven't really stopped to explain this common fictional device as carefully as I should. I'm going to describe the process now; it is one of the most ancient used by writers in the composition of their stories.

A "shift" is an alteration in any of the points of view we've examined. There may, therefore, be spatial shifts, temporal shifts, or shifts in level of reality. Frequently, especially in the twentieth century, novels have multiple narrators: sometimes various narrator-characters, as in Faulkner's *As I Lay Dying*, sometimes an omniscient, exterior narrator and one or more narrator-characters, as in Joyce's *Ulysses*. Each time, then, that the spatial perspective of the story changes—and it changes whenever there is a shift in narrator, which is evident when the grammatical person switches from *he* to *I*, from *I* to *he*, or otherwise fluctuates—a spatial shift is taking place. In some novels these shifts are frequent and in others they are rare, and only the end result indicates whether they are helpful or counterproductive and whether they reinforce or undermine the story's power of persuasion. When spatial shifts are effective, they manage to give a broad, variegated, even global and totalizing vision of a story (and thereby produce the illusion of independence from the real world that, as we've already noted, all fictional worlds secretly aspire to). If the shifts aren't effective, the result may be confusion: the reader is disoriented by the sudden and arbitrary leaps in perspective.

Perhaps less frequent than spatial shifts are temporal shifts, the movements of the narrator in time that cause a story to unfold simultaneously before our eyes in the past, present, or future. If the technique is well applied, they lend the story an illusion of chronological totality, of temporal self-sufficiency. There are writers who are obsessed with the subject of time—we've discussed a few—and that is evident not only in the subject matter of their novels but also in their construction of unusual and sometimes incredibly complex chronological systems. One example out of thousands: D. M. Thomas's novel *The White Hotel*, which was much discussed in its time. The novel tells the story of a terrible massacre of Jews in the Ukraine; the confessions that the protagonist, the singer Lisa Erdman, makes to her Viennese analyst, Sigmund Freud, are its slender backbone. From the temporal point of view, the novel is divided into three parts, which correspond to the past, present, and future of the chilling collective crime, the novel's crux. The temporal point of view shifts twice: from the past to the present (the massacre) and to the future of the narrative's central event. But this second shift, to the future, is not just temporal: it is also a shift in level of reality. The story, which until this moment had existed in a "realist," historical, objective plane, shifts after the massacre in the last chapter, "The Camp," into a fantastic reality, a purely imaginary plane, an ethereal, spiritual territory inhabited by beings shed of physical existence, shades or ghosts of the human victims of the slaughter. The temporal shift is also a qualitative leap, causing the narrative to change in nature. As a result of the shift, the story shoots from a realist world to a purely fantastic one. Something similar happens in Hermann Hesse's *Steppenwolf* when the immortal spirits of the great creators of the past appear to the narrator-character.

It is shifts in level of reality that give writers the best opportunity to organize their narrative materials in a complex and original fashion. In saying this I don't mean to denigrate shifts in space and time, where the possibilities are, for obvious reasons, more limited; I merely wish to emphasize that, given the existence of innumerable levels of reality, the possibility of shifts is correspondingly immense, and writers of all eras have learned to exploit this very versatile resource.

But before we venture deep into the rich terrain of shifts, it might perhaps be convenient to make a distinction. Shifts are defined, on the one hand, by the points of view in which they occur—spatial, temporal, or level of reality—and, on the other hand, by their supplementary or substantive (peripheral or essential) character. A mere temporal or spatial change is significant, but it doesn't entirely alter the substance of a story, whether the story is realist or fantastic. The kind of shift that occurs in a novel like *The White Hotel*, however, does change the nature of the tale, transferring it from an objective ("realist") world to a purely fantastic one. The shifts that provoke this ontological cataclysm—since they change the *being* of the narrative—may be called *qualitative leaps*, a term borrowed from the Hegelian dialectic; according to Hegel, quantitative accumulation triggers "a leap in quality" (like that of water, which becomes a gas when it boils long enough or is turned to ice when its temperature drops low enough). A narrative undergoes a similar transformation when a radical shift in the point of view in terms of level of reality occurs, constituting a *qualitative leap*.

Let's take a look at some striking examples from the rich arsenal of contemporary literature. In two contemporary novels published a good many years apart, for example, one Brazilian and the other English—*The Devil to Pay in the Backlands* by João Guimarães Rosa and *Orlando* by Virginia Woolf—the sudden change in sex of the main character (from man to woman in both cases) causes the entire narrative to undergo a qualitative shift, relocating the narrative from a plane that until that point seemed "realist" to one that is imaginary and even fantastic. In both instances, the shift is a crux, a central upheaval in the body of the narrative, an episode of maximum concentration of experiences that confers on its setting a quality it didn't seem to possess before. There is no such crux in Kafka's *Metamorphosis*, in which the remarkable event—poor Gregor Samsa's transformation into a horrible cockroach— takes place in the story's first sentence, positioning the story from the start in the realm of the fantastic.

These are examples of sudden and rapid shifts, abrupt acts that, because they are miraculous or extraordinary, skew the coordinates of the "real" world and give it a new dimension, a secret and marvelous configuration conforming not to rational or physical laws but rather to dark, fundamental forces that are only possible to understand (and, in some cases, control) through divine mediation, witchcraft, or magic. But in Kafka's most famous novels, *The Castle* and *The Trial*, the shift is a slow, involved, and stealthy process, the result of the accumulation or intensification in time of a certain state of things; in the end, the narrative world is emancipated from the objective reality—the "realism"—it pretended to imitate, and reveals itself as a different brand, a different species of reality. The mysterious Mr. K., the anonymous surveyor of *The Castle*, tries many times to reach the massive edifice that looms over the district where he has come to work and where he is the supreme authority. The obstacles he encounters are trivial at first; for a good stretch of the tale, the reader has the sense of being submerged in a tightly realist world, a world that appears to mirror the most ordinary, everyday aspects of reality. But as the story progresses and the unlucky Mr. K. seems more and more defenseless and vulnerable, confounded by obstacles that, we come to understand, aren't fortuitous or the by-product of a mere administrative inertia but the manifestations of a sinister secret mechanism that controls human actions and destroys individuals, we readers are seized with the consciousness—besides the mounting anguish we feel at the impotence in which humanity is mired in the story—that the novel's level of reality is not the objective and historical one familiar to us but another kind of reality, a symbolic and allegorical (or simply fantastic) imaginary version. (This, however, should not be taken to suggest that "fantastic" novels are any less capable of imparting illuminating lessons about human existence and our own reality.) The shift takes place, then, between two magnitudes or levels of reality much more slowly and tortuously than in *Orlando* or *The Devil to Pay in the Backlands*.

The same thing happens in *The Trial*, in which Mr. K. finds himself trapped in the nightmarish labyrinth of a political and judicial system that initially seems "realist" to us, a somewhat paranoid interpretation of the inefficiency and absurdities that lead to the excessive bureaucratization of justice. But then, as absurd occurrences become increasingly frequent and intense, at a certain moment we begin to realize that there is something more sinister and inhuman behind the administrative tangle that traps the protagonist and is gradually destroying him: an ominous system of a perhaps metaphysical nature in which a citizen's free will and ability to react vanish; a system that uses and abuses individuals like a puppet master manipulating puppets on a stage; an order that it is impossible to rebel against, one that is omnipotent, invisible, and deeply ingrained in human consciousness. Symbolic, metaphysical, or fantastic, this level of reality becomes evident gradually and progressively in *The Trial*, as in *The Castle*, so that it is impossible to determine the precise moment the metamorphosis takes place. The same is true of *Moby-Dick*, isn't it? The endless chase across the sea in pursuit of a white whale that, by virtue of its very absence, acquires an aura of evil legend and is seen as a mythical animal—doesn't it, too, undergo a shift or qualitative leap that transforms what was at first a realist novel into a tale classifiable as imaginary, symbolic, allegorical, metaphysical—or simply fantastic?

At this point, your head is probably full of memorable shifts and qualitative leaps from your favorite novels. And the truth is, writers from every age have made frequent use of the device, especially in fantastic fictions. Let's think back on some of the shifts that are still vivid in our memory, shifts that serve as reminders of the books we've enjoyed. I know! I'm sure I've guessed right: Comala! Isn't the name of that Mexican village the first that comes to mind when we think about shifts? And the association is an excellent one, since it's unlikely that anyone who has read Juan Rulfo's classic 1955 novel *Pedro Páramo* will ever forget the shock of discovering deep into the book that all the characters in the story are dead and that the fictional Comala is not part of "reality"— or not, at least, the reality the reader inhabits—but belongs to a literary reality, where the dead do not disappear but continue to live. This is one of the most effective shifts (of the radical, qualitative-leap kind) of contemporary Latin American literature. The way it is achieved is so masterful that if you set out to establish where it occurs in the space or time of the story, you're faced with a real dilemma. Because it is rooted in no precise episode, event, or moment but reveals itself little by little, gradually, insinuatingly, announcing its progress in vague signs and faint traces that we barely notice when we come across them. Only later, retroactively, do the string of clues and the accumulation of suspicious events and incongruities allow us to see that Comala is a town not of live beings but of ghosts.

But it might be a good idea to move on to other literary shifts less macabre than Rulfo's. The most engaging, exuberant, and amusing one I can think of takes place in the story "Letter to a Young Lady in Paris" by Julio Cortázar. An amazing shift in level of reality occurs when the narrator-character, the author of the letter in question, lets us know that he has the unfortunate habit of vomiting up bunnies. This is a serious qualitative leap in the middle of what is generally a lighthearted story, though there is a chance it ends in tragedy; the last sentences of the letter insinuate that the protagonist, overcome by the constant stream of bunnies, kills himself at the end of the tale.

This is a procedure Cortázar often employs in his stories and novels. He uses it essentially to unsettle things in his invented worlds, shifting from a fairly simple, everyday reality of predictable, banal, ordinary elements to another, fantastic world where extraordinary things happen, like humans vomiting bunnies, and in which there is often a hint of violence. You must have read "The Maenads," another of Cortázar's great stories, in which the narrative world undergoes a psychic transformation, this one progressive and exponential. At what first seems a harmless concert at the Corona Theater, the musicians' performance elicits the almost excessive enthusiasm of the audience; this enthusiasm degenerates into an explosion of savage, incomprehensible animal violence, a collective lynching or struggle to the death. At the end of this unexpected slaughter, we are discomfited and ask ourselves whether it all really happened or whether it was a horrible nightmare, an absurd occurrence taking place in "another world," a world governed by an unusual mix of fantasy, hidden terrors, and the darker impulses of the human spirit.

Cortázar knows how to use shifts better than almost any other writer, whether those shifts are gradual or sudden, and in space, time, or level of reality: in the unmistakable geography of his world, poetry and the imagination are linked with his infallible sense of what the surrealists called the incredible everyday, and the apparent simplicity and conversational ease of his clean, fluid prose, entirely free of mannerisms, disguise complex arguments and a great inventive audacity.

Now that we're recalling literary shifts that linger in memory, I must cite one (and it's a crux) that occurs in *Death on the Installment Plan* by Céline. I have no personal sympathy for Céline: his racism and anti-Semitism inspire repugnance in me; nevertheless, he wrote two great novels (the other is *Journey to the End of the Night*). In *Death on the Installment Plan*, there is an unforgettable episode in which the protagonist crosses the English Channel on a ferry full of passengers. The sea is rough, and the rocking of the little boat makes everyone on board — crew and passengers alike — seasick. And of course, in the kind of sordid and threatening atmosphere that so fascinated Céline, everybody starts to vomit. Up until this point, we are in a natural world — an incredibly vulgar and petty world, perhaps — but our feet are firmly planted in objective reality. However, the vomit that begins to fall on the reader, splashing him with all the filth and waste one can imagine Céline's organisms expelling, is so painstakingly and effectively described that the tale becomes detached from reality and turns into something nightmarish and apocalyptic, until finally it is not just a handful of seasick men and women but all the humans in the universe who seem to be coughing up their guts. As a result of this shift, the story changes levels of reality and moves into a visionary, symbolic, and even fantastic plane; everything in the narrative is affected by the extraordinary transformation.

We could keep on discussing shifts indefinitely but that would mean repeating ourselves, since the examples cited more than explain the way the process (with its different variations) works and the effects it has on the novel. It may be worth insisting on something I haven't tired of repeating since my first letter: in and of themselves, shifts don't guarantee or indicate anything, and their success or failure in terms of power of persuasion depends on the particular way in which a narrator uses shifts in a specific story: the same process may strengthen a novel's power of persuasion or destroy it.

To conclude, I'd like to remind you of a theory of fantastic literature developed by the great French-Belgian critic and essayist Roger Caillois (in the prologue to his *Anthologie du fantastique*). According to Caillois, true fantastic literature isn't created deliberately; it isn't the result of a conscious effort by an author who sets out to write a fantastic tale. In Caillois's opinion, true fantastic literature requires the spontaneous revelation of incredible, prodigious, fabulous, rationally inexplicable acts, unpremeditated and possibly even unnoticed by the author—it is literature in which the fantastic appears *motu proprio*, as one might say. In other words, these fictions don't tell fantastic stories; they themselves *are* fantastic. This is a very debatable theory, of course, but it is original and rich in possibility, and it provides us with a good way of ending this reflection on shifts, one of whose versions might be—if Caillois isn't too far off track—the autogenerated shift: a shift that would bypass the author, take possession of the text, and set it along a path its creator could never foresee.

Fondly,

Chinese Boxes

DEAR FRIEND,

Another tool that narrators use to endow their stories with power of persuasion is what we might call the "Chinese box" or *matryoshka* technique. How does it work? The story is constructed like those traditional puzzles with successively smaller and smaller identical parts nestled inside each other, sometimes dwindling to the infinitesimal. It should be noted, however, that when a central story begets one or more subsidiary stories, the procedure can't be mechanical (although often it is) if it is to be successful. A creative effect is achieved when a construction of this kind contributes something to the tale—mystery, ambiguity, complexity—that makes it seem necessary, not merely a juxtaposition but a symbiosis or association of elements with a mutually unsettling effect on each other. For example, though one might say that the Chinese box structure of *The Thousand and One Nights*—the collection of famous Arabian stories that upon being discovered and translated into English and French were the delight of

Europe—is often mechanical, it is clear that the puzzle box structure of a modern novel like *A Brief Life* by the Uruguayan writer Juan Carlos Onetti is enormously effective since the extraordinary subtlety of the story and the clever surprises it offers its readers depend almost entirely upon it.

But I'm getting ahead of myself. It would be better to start at the beginning and discuss this technique or narrative device at leisure, moving on later to examine its variants, applications, possibilities, and risks.

I think the best example of the method is the work already cited, a classic of the narrative genre: *The Thousand and One Nights*. Allow me to remind you how the stories are pieced together. To save herself from being beheaded like the other women possessed by the terrible Sultan, Scheherazade tells him stories, scheming so that each night the story is interrupted in such a way that his curiosity about what will happen next—the suspense—makes him prolong her life one more day. In this way, the renowned storyteller manages to survive for a thousand and one nights, and finally the Sultan (won over to the point of addiction by the tales) spares her life. How does the skillful Scheherazade manage to tell so steadily and continuously the interminable series of stories that her life depends on? By using the Chinese box method: fitting stories inside stories through narrative shifts (in time, space, and level of reality). For example: four merchants appear in the story of the blind dervish that Scheherazade tells the Sultan, and one of the merchants tells the other three the story of the leper of Baghdad; in that story, an adventurous fisherman turns up and proceeds to regale a group of shoppers in a market in Alexandria with tales of his maritime exploits. Like Chinese boxes or nesting dolls, each story contains another story subordinate in a first, second, or third degree. Thus, the stories are connected in a system and the whole of the system is enriched by the sum of its parts; each part—each particular story—is enriched, too (or at least affected), according to its dependent or generative role in relation to the other stories.

You yourself can no doubt think of a number of works that feature stories within stories, since the device has long been in use and is very popular; despite being so common, it is always fresh in the hands of a good narrator. At times, as I've said of *The Thousand and One Nights*, the Chinese box method is applied in a somewhat mechanical manner, and the generation of stories by other stories does not trigger significant reverberations within the mother stories (let's call them that). These reverberations occur, for example, in *Don Quixote* when Sancho tells the story—periodically interrupted by Don Quixote's commentary on the way Sancho is telling it—of the shepherdess Torralba (a Chinese box tale in which there is an interaction between the mother story and the daughter story), but other Chinese box narratives, like the excerpt from the novel *The Curious Impertinent* that the priest reads at the inn while Quixote is sleeping, don't work the same way. When speaking of such an episode, it makes more sense to speak of *collage* than of Chinese boxes, since (as is true of many daughter stories or granddaughter stories in *The Thousand and One Nights*) the story has an autonomous existence and doesn't exert a thematic or psychological effect on the story it is contained within (the adventures of Don Quixote and Sancho). Something similar may be said, of course, about another Chinese box classic, *A Captain's Tale*.

The truth is that a lengthy essay could be written on the diversity and variety of Chinese box stories in *Don Quixote*, since Cervantes's genius gave the device a formidable utility, first evident in the invention of the supposed manuscript of Cide Hamete Benengeli of which *Don Quixote* is said be a version or transcription (whether or not this is true is left purposefully unclear). One could say this was a convention worked to death in chivalric novels, all of which pretended to be (or to derive from) mysterious manuscripts discovered in exotic locales. But not even the use of conventions in a novel is empty: it has consequences, sometimes positive, sometimes negative. If we take the existence of Cide Hamete Benengeli's manuscript seriously, the structure of *Don Quixote* is a *matryoshka* of at least four levels of connected histories:

a. The manuscript of Cide Hamete Benengeli, only made known to us in a partial and fractured state, would be the first box. The box immediately subordinate to it, or the first daughter history, is

b. The story of Don Quixote and Sancho, so far as we are allowed to observe it, a daughter story that contains many granddaughter stories (third box), although of a different kind:

c. Stories told among the actual characters, like Sancho's story about the shepherdess Torralba, and

d. Stories incorporated in collage-like fashion and read by the characters; these are freestanding, written stories not intimately linked to the story that contains them, like *The Curious Impertinent* or *A Captain's Tale*.

Now, despite the fact that Cide Hamete Benengeli, quoted and mentioned by the omniscient narrator, appears only outside the bounds of the narrative in *Don Quixote* (though he is still involved in the text, as we noted in our discussion of the spatial point of view), we must step back even further and point out that since he is quoted, his manuscript can't be discussed as the first level, the foundational reality of the novel—the progenitor of all the other stories. If Cide Hamete Benengeli speaks and airs his opinions in the first person in his manuscript (which he does, according to the quotations cited by the omniscient narrator), it is obvious that he is a narrator-character, which means he is part of a story that only in rhetorical terms may be considered self-generated (this, of course, is a structural fiction). All stories told from a point of view in which the narrative space and the narrator's space coincide are also contained by an initial Chinese box outside fictional reality: the hand that writes, inventing (in a first instance) its narrators. Once we become conscious of that first hand (and only hand, since we know Cervantes had only one arm), we must accept that the Chinese boxes of *Don Quixote* are actually four superimposed realities.

The passage from one of these realities to another—from a mother story to a daughter story—constitutes a shift, as you will have noticed. When I say "a" shift, though, I must immediately contradict myself, since the reality is that in many cases a Chinese box story is the result of several simultaneous shifts: in space, time, and level of reality. Let's take a look, for example, at the impressive Chinese box system that *A Brief Life* by Juan Carlos Onetti is built on.

From a technical point of view, this magnificent novel, one of the subtlest and most artful ever written in Spanish, revolves entirely around the artifice of the Chinese box, which Onetti manipulates masterfully to create a world of delicate superimposed and intersecting planes, in which the boundary between fiction and reality (between life and dreams or desires) is dissolved. The novel is narrated by a narrator-character, Juan María Brausen, who lives in Buenos Aires and is tormented by the idea that his lover, Gertrudis, who has cancer, has lost a breast; he also spies on and fantasizes about a woman, Queca, and is trying to write a screenplay. All of this makes up the basic reality or first box of the story. The tale slides in a surreptitious manner, however, toward Santa María, a small provinicial city on the banks of the Río de la Plata, where a doctor in his forties, a shady character, sells morphine to one of his patients. Soon we discover that Santa María, the doctor Díaz Grey, and the mysterious morphine addict are all figments of Brausen's imagination and represent a second level of reality in the story; Díaz Grey is really a kind of alter ego for Brausen, and his morphine-addict patient is a projection of Gertrudis. This is how the novel unfolds, shifting (in space and level of reality) between these two worlds or Chinese boxes and swinging the reader from Buenos Aires to Santa María and back again. Though disguised by the realist-seeming prose and the effectiveness of the technique, these comings and goings are a voyage between reality and fantasy, or, if you prefer, between objective and subjective worlds (Brausen's life and the stories he elaborates). This Chinese box setup isn't the only one in the novel. There is another, parallel one. Queca, the woman Brausen is spying on, is a prostitute who receives clients in the apartment next door to his in Buenos Aires. The story involving Queca takes place—or so it seems at first—on an objective plane like Brausen's own, although it reaches the reader through the medium of the narrator's testimony, and the narrator is a Brausen who must imagine much of what Queca is doing (he hears her but can't see her). And then, at a certain moment—one of the cruxes of the novel and one of its most effective shifts—the reader discovers that the crooked Arce, Queca's pimp, who ends up murdering her, is also really another of Brausen's alter egos, just like Dr. Díaz Grey, a character (partially or totally—this is unclear) created by Brausen—that is to say, someone who exists on a different plane of reality. This second Chinese box is parallel to the Santa María box and coexists with it but it isn't identical, because unlike the Santa María subplot, which is entirely imaginary—the place and its characters existing only in Brausen's imagination—the second box is halfway between reality and fiction, between objectivity and subjectivity: Brausen has added invented elements to a real character (Queca) and her surroundings. Onetti's formal mastery—his writing and the architecture of the story— makes the novel seem to the reader a homogenous whole without internal rifts, even though it is composed, as we've noted, of different planes and levels of reality. The Chinese boxes of *A Brief Life* aren't mechanical. Thanks to them we discover that the true subject of the novel isn't Brausen's story but something vaster, involving shared human experience: the way people retreat into fantasy and fiction in order to enrich their lives, and the way fictions created in the mind are built on the little occurrences of daily life. Fiction is not life as it is lived but a different life, conjured out of the materials supplied by life; without fiction, real life would be a paler and drearier affair.

More later,

The Hidden Fact

DEAR FRIEND,

Ernest Hemingway says somewhere that at the beginning of his writing career it suddenly occurred to him that he should leave out the central event of the story he was writing (his protagonist hangs himself). And he explains that with this decision he discovered a narrative technique that he would later use often in his stories and novels. In fact, it is no exaggeration to say that Hemingway's best stories are full of significant silences; the narrator causes pieces of information to vanish, managing nonetheless to give the missing data an eloquent and insistent presence in readers' imaginations, contriving it so that readers fill in the blanks with their own hypotheses and conjectures. I'll call this technique "the hidden fact" and quickly make clear that although Hemingway gave it a personal twist and used it often (and sometimes masterfully), he hardly invented it, since it is a process as old as the novel itself.

But the truth is that few modern authors have employed it with the same audacity as the author of *The Old Man and the Sea.* Remember "The Killers," an excellent story and perhaps Hemingway's most famous? At its heart is a big question mark: Why do the two outlaws with sawed-off shotguns who come into a little lunchroom called Henry's in the middle of nowhere want to kill the Swede Ole Andreson? And why, when the young Nick Adams warns him that there are a pair of killers after him, does the mysterious Andreson refuse to flee or inform the police, resigning himself calmly to his fate? We'll never know. If we want answers to those two crucial questions, we have to make them up ourselves on the basis of the few facts allotted us by the omniscient and impersonal narrator: before moving to town, Andreson seems to have been a boxer in Chicago, where he did something (something wrong, he says) that sealed his fate.

The hidden fact, or narration by omission, can't be gratuitous or arbitrary. It is vital that the narrator's silence be meaningful, that it have a definite influence on the explicit part of the story, that it make itself felt as an absence, and that it kindle the curiosity, expectations, and fantasies of the reader. Hemingway was a great master of technique, as is evident in "The Killers," a model of narrative economy. Its text is like the tip of an iceberg, a small visible outcropping that gives a glimpse in the lightning flash of its appearance of the complex mass of detail it rests on and is then immediately snatched from the reader's view. To tell by keeping quiet, through allusions that turn the trick into a promise and force the reader to actively intervene in the construction of the story with conjectures and suppositions: this is one of the most common ways narrators succeed in bringing their stories to life and thereby endow them with power of persuasion.

Remember the piece of information hidden in *The Sun Also Rises*, Hemingway's best novel as far as I'm concerned? Yes, the impotence of narrator Jake Barnes. It is never explicitly referred to but grows gradually evident—I'd almost say that the reader, goaded by what he reads, imposes it on the character—out of a telling silence, a strange physical distance, Jake's chaste relationship with the beautiful Brett, whom he clearly loves and who without a doubt also loves him or could have loved him if not for some obstacle or impediment of which we are never precisely informed. Jake Barnes's impotence is an implicit silence, an absence that becomes striking as the reader notices and is surprised by the unusual and contradictory way Jake Barnes relates to Brett, until the only way of explaining it is by realizing (or inventing?) his impotence. Although it is silenced, or maybe precisely because it is silenced, that hidden bit of information bathes the story of *The Sun Also Rises* in a very particular light.

Jealousy is another novel in which an essential element—the main character, no less—is omitted from the story, but in such a way that his absence is projected in the book and felt at every instant. *Jealousy*, which doesn't really have a plot, exhibits the signs or symptoms of a story that we can't quite grasp. We are obliged to reconstruct it the way archaeologists reconstruct the palaces of Babylon from a handful of stones that have been buried for centuries, the way zoologists piece together prehistoric dinosaurs and pterodactyls from a clavicle or a metacarpus. We may safely say that the novels of Robbe-Grillet—all of them—are based on hidden facts. In *Jealousy*, though, the procedure works particularly well, since in order for the story to make sense it is essential that the absence in question, the central abolished self, make itself present and take shape in the consciousness of the reader. Who is this invisible being? A jealous husband, as the title of the book ambiguously suggests: someone who, possessed by the demon of suspicion, spies assiduously on his wife's movements without being noticed. The reader doesn't know this for sure; he deduces it or invents it, taking his cue from the narrator's obsessive, deranged stare devoted to the mad minute scrutiny of the woman's smallest movements, gestures, and errands. Who is this mathematical observer? Why does he subject his wife to this visual harassment? The novel does not reveal the hidden information as it progresses, and the reader must clear up the mystery on his own, with the few clues the story provides. These key hidden facts—eliminated forever from the novel—may be called *elliptic*, to differentiate them from facts that are only temporarily hidden from the reader, displaced in the novel's chronology in order to create anticipation and suspense, as in mystery novels, which reveal the identity of the assassin only at the end. These facts that are only hidden for a while—or temporarily relocated—may be called *anastrophic*, anastrophe, as you'll recall, being a poetic device in which a word in a line of poetry is displaced for reasons of euphony or rhyme. ("Let

me not to the marriage of true minds / admit impediments"
instead of the usual order: "Let me not admit impediments
to the marriage of true minds.")*

The most remarkable piece of hidden information in a
modern novel might be the information omitted from Faulkner's gothic *Sanctuary*, in which the crux of the story—the
deflowering of the young and foolish Temple Drake by Popeye, an impotent, psychopathic gangster who uses a corn-
cob—is displaced and dissolved into rivulets of information
that allow the reader, little by little and retroactively, to piece
together the terrible scene. It is out of this abominable silence
that the atmosphere of *Sanctuary* radiates: a climate of sav-
agery, sexual repression, fear, prejudice, and barbarism that
gives symbolic significance to Jefferson, Memphis, and the
story's other settings, marking them as places of evil and asso-
ciating them with the ruin and fall of man, in the biblical
sense of the term. When faced with the horrors of the novel—
the rape of Temple is only one of them; there is also a hanging, a lynching, several killings, a wide-ranging display of
moral degradation—we understand that they arise not from
the transgression of human laws but from the victory of infer-
nal powers, from the defeat of good by a spirit of perdition
that has taken over the earth. *Sanctuary* seethes with hidden
information. Besides the rape of Temple Drake, important

---

*Shakespeare's Sonnet 116 is quoted here in place of Spanish Golden Age
poet Luis de Góngora's first eclogue ("Era del año la estación florida . . .").
[*Tr.*]

incidents like the killing of Tommy and Red or facts like Popeye's impotence are silences at first: only retroactively are these blanks filled in. Then, supplied with the information hidden in anastrophe, the reader begins to understand what has happened and to establish the true chronology of events. Not just in this story but in all his stories, Faulkner was the consummate master of hidden information.

For a final example, I'd like to skip back five hundred years to one of the best medieval novels of chivalry: *Tirant Lo Blanc* by Joanot Martorell, a book I keep by the side of my bed. In it, Martorell manipulates hidden information—anastrophic or elliptic—as dexterously as the best modern novelist. Let's see how the narrative material is structured at one of the cruxes of the novel, the "silent marriages" celebrated by Tirant and Carmesina and Diaphebus and Stephanie (in an episode that stretches from the last half of chapter 162 to the middle of 163). This is what happens: Carmesina and Stephanie lead Tirant and Diaphebus into a room of the palace. There, not realizing that Pleasure-of-My-Life is spying on them through a keyhole, the two couples spend the night engaged in love play, innocent in the case of Tirant and Carmesina, much less so in that of Diaphebus and Stephanie. The lovers separate at dawn, and hours later, Pleasure-of-My-Life reveals to Stephanie and Carmesina that she has been witness to their silent marriages.

In the novel, these events appear not in "real" chronological order but discontinuously, the information concealed and revealed in temporal shifts and anastrophic leaps; as a result, the episode is extraordinarily enriched by anecdote. The plot supplies the setup—Carmesina and Stephanie's decision to bring Tirant and Diaphebus into the room—and explains how Carmesina, suspecting that there will be a "celebration of silent marriages," pretends to sleep. The impersonal and omniscient narrator proceeds in "real" chronological order to describe Tirant's astonishment when he sees the beautiful princess, and how he falls to his knees and kisses her hands. Here the first temporal shift or rupture in chronology occurs: "And they uttered many amorous words. When they thought it was time, the knights returned to their quarters." The story leaps into the future, leaving in the gap, the abyss of silence, a sly question: " . . . between love and grief, who could sleep that night?" The narrative next brings the reader to the following morning. Pleasure-of-My-Life gets up, goes into the princess Carmesina's room and finds Stephanie "in no mood to be disturbed." What happened? Why Stephanie's voluptuous abandon? The insinuations, questions, jokes, and gibes of the delicious Pleasure-of-My-Life are really directed at the reader, whose curiosity and prurience are roused. And at last, at the end of this long, clever preamble, Pleasure-of-My-Life reveals that the night before she had a dream in which she saw Stephanie escorting Tirant and Diaphebus into the room. Here the episode's second temporal shift or chronological leap takes place. There is a retreat to the evening before, and through Pleasure-of-My-Life's supposed dream, the reader discovers what happened in the silent marriages. The hidden information is revealed, restoring the episode's integrity. Full integrity? Not quite. As you will have observed, there has been a spatial shift, or change in spatial point of view, as well as a temporal shift, since the voice narrating the silent marriages no longer belongs to the impersonal and eccentric original narrator. It belongs to Pleasure-of-My-Life, a narrator-character whose testimony is not intended to be objective but rather charged with subjectivity (her frank, jocular commentary doesn't just subjectivize the episode; most important, it defuses what would otherwise be the violent story of Stephanie's deflowering by Diaphebus). This double shift—in time and space—therefore turns the episode of the silent marriages into a series of Chinese boxes; that is to say, an autonomous narrative (by Pleasure-of-My-Life) is contained within the general narrative of the omniscient narrator. (Parenthetically, I'll note that *Tirant Lo Blanc* often makes use of the device of Chinese boxes or nesting dolls. The exploits of Tirant over the course of the year and a day that the festivities last in the English court are revealed to the reader not by the omniscient narrator but through the story that Diaphebus tells the count of Vàroic; the capture of Rhodes by the Genoans is made known in a story that two knights of the French court tell Tirant and the duke of Brittany; and the adventure of the merchant Gaubedi is revealed in a story with which Tirant regales the Widow Reposada.) In this way, then, after examining just one episode of a classic narrative, we discover that resources and processes that often seem as if they must be modern inventions because of the showy use contemporary writers make of them are really part of our novelistic heritage, since classic narrators were already using them with assurance. What the moderns have done in most cases is to polish, refine, or experiment with new possibilities implicit in narrative systems that are often manifest in the most ancient written samples of fiction.

Before finishing this letter, I think it might be worthwhile to make a general observation—relevant to all novels—about an innate characteristic of the genre, from which the Chinese box technique is derived. The written part of any novel is just a piece or fragment of the story it tells: the fully developed story, embracing every element without exception—thoughts, gestures, objects, cultural coordinates, historical, psychological, and ideological material, and so on that presupposes and contains the *total* story—covers infinitely more ground than is explicitly traveled in the text, more ground than any novelist, even the wordiest and most prolific, with the least sense of narrative economy, would be capable of covering in his text.

To underscore the inevitably partial nature of all narrative discourse, the French novelist Claude Simon—intending to poke fun at realist literature's conviction that it could reproduce reality—set out to describe a pack of Gitanes. What qualities should the description include in order to be realist? he asked himself. The packet's size, color, content, inscriptions, and the material it was made of were necessary, of course. Would that be enough? In a totalizing sense, no. In order not to leave out any important piece of information, the description would also have to include a meticulous report on the industrial processes involved in the making of the packet and the cigarettes it contained, and—why not?—the systems of distribution and marketing that got them from the producer to the consumer. Once this was done, would the description of the pack of Gitanes be complete? Not even close. The consumption of cigarettes isn't an isolated act: it is the result of the evolution of habits and the introduction of fashions; it is inextricably bound up with social history, mythology, politics, lifestyle. And on the other hand, it is a practice—a habit or vice—on which publicity and economic life exert a definite influence and that has certain effects on the health of the smoker. Following the thread of this demonstration as it progresses to ridiculous extremes, it is not difficult to conclude that the description of even the most insignificant object, if extended in a totalizing manner, leads purely and simply to a utopic proposition: the description of the universe.

Something similar may doubtless be said about fiction. If, theoretically, a novelist didn't impose certain limits when he set out to tell a story (if he didn't resign himself to hiding certain bits of information), his story wouldn't have a beginning or an end but would somehow end up connecting itself with all possible stories and become that chimeric totality: the infinite imaginary universe where all fictions coexist and are intimately linked.

If you accept the supposition that a novel—or rather, a fiction set down in writing—is just a part of a full story from which the novelist finds himself inevitably obliged to eliminate much information because it is superfluous, dispensable, or because it gets in the way of information that he does make explicit, one must nevertheless differentiate between information excluded because it is obvious or useless and the hidden information I refer to in this letter. That is, *my* hidden information isn't obvious or useless. On the contrary, it has a function and plays a role in the narrative scheme, and that is why its elimination or displacement has an effect on the story, producing reverberations in the plot or points of view.

Finally, I'd like to repeat a comparison I once made in discussing Faulkner's *Sanctuary*. Let's say that the *full* story of a novel (including all selected and omitted facts) is a cube and that, once the superfluous pieces of information and the bits omitted deliberately in order to obtain a specific effect are carved away, each particular novel takes on a certain form. That object, that sculpture, is an expression of the artist's originality. It has been shaped with the help of many different tools, but there is no doubt that the hidden fact (if you can't come up with a more appealing name for the device) is one of the most valuable and widely used instruments for cutting away material until the desired beautiful and persuasive form emerges.

Fondly, and until next time,

Communicating Vessels

DEAR FRIEND,

In order for us to discuss this final procedure, involving "communicating vessels" (later I'll explain what I mean by the term), I'd like us to revisit together one of the most memorable episodes of *Madame Bovary*. I refer to the agricultural fair of chapter 8 in the second part of the novel, a scene that is in fact composed of two (or even three) different story lines braided together, each shadowing and in a certain fashion modifying the others. Because of the way the scene is structured, the different events, joined in a system of communicating vessels, exchange material, and an interaction is established among them, causing the episodes to merge into a whole that makes them something more than mere juxtaposed story fragments. A system of communicating vessels operates when the sum of an episode is something more than its parts—and that is true of Flaubert's fair.

Here we have, in scenes interwoven by the narrator, a description of the day the farmers exhibit produce and animals from their farms and celebrate the harvest; the authorities make speeches and award medals; and at the same time, in the council chamber on an upper floor of the town hall, which overlooks the festivities, Emma Bovary listens as Rodolphe woos her with fiery declarations of love. The seduction of Madame Bovary by her noble suitor is perfectly able to stand alone as a scene, but, interwoven as it is with the speech of the councillor Lieuvain, a complicity is established between it and the minor goings-on of the fair. The episode acquires another dimension, another texture, until it might just as well be said that the villagers' celebration takes place below the window where the soon-to-be lovers exchange vows of love: presented alongside their encounter, the fair seems less grotesque and pathetic than it would without the softening effect of such a delicate filter. We are pondering here a very nuanced subject, one that has nothing to do with simple action but rather with finely calibrated ambiance and the emotional and psychological essences that emanate from a story. It is in this context that the system of communicating vessels is most effective, so long as it is handled well.

The whole description of the agricultural fair in *Madame Bovary* is witheringly sarcastic, underscoring to the point of cruelty the human stupidity (*la bêtise*) that fascinated Flaubert, his scorn reaching its height with the appearance of Catherine Leroux, a little old woman who receives an award for her fifty-four years of work in the fields and announces that she will give the prize money to the priest so he will say masses for her soul. If all the poor farmers seem, in Flaubert's description, to be mired in a dehumanizing routine that strips them of sensitivity and imagination and makes them dull figures, thoroughly common and conventional, the authorities are shown in an even worse light as garrulous, blatantly ridiculous nonentities in whom hypocrisy and spiritual duplicity seem primordial character traits, as expressed in the empty and trite utterances of the councillor Lieuvain. But this picture, painted so dark and remorseless that it is hardly credible (and suggests a possible failure of the episode's power of persuasion), only emerges when we analyze the agricultural fair on its own, disassociated from the seduction to which it is viscerally linked. In reality, tangled up as it is with an episode that serves as an escape valve for its vitriolic irony, the sarcastic ferocity of the fair scene is considerably tempered. The sentimental, light, romantic air that is introduced by the seduction establishes a subtle counterpoint, which fosters verisimilitude. And the sunny element of the country fair, presented with exaggerated and humorous irony, also has, reciprocally, a moderating effect, correcting the excesses of sentimentalism—especially the rhetorical excesses—that characterize the episode of Emma's seduction. Without the presence of a very powerful "realist" factor—the presence of the farmers and their cows and pigs in the square down below—the lovers' dialogue, brimming with the clichés and commonplaces of the romantic lexicon, would perhaps dissolve into fantasy. Thanks to the system of communicating vessels that merges the two scenes, the rough edges that might have interfered with each episode's power of persuasion are smoothed and the narrative unity is actually enriched by the resulting amalgam, which gives the chapter a rich and original character.

At the heart of the whole created by the communicating vessels linking the country fair and the seduction, it is possible to establish still another subtle counterpoint—this one on a rhetorical level—that contrasts the mayor's remarks in the square with the romantic words that Emma's seducer whispers in her ear. The narrator weaves the speeches together intending (entirely successfully) that the two—which unspool in a double strand of political and romantic stereotypes—should alternately drown each other out, introducing an ironic perspective without which the tale's power of persuasion would be reduced to a minimum or vanish completely. We may therefore conclude that a second set of specific communicating vessels is enclosed within the general set, reproducing in miniature the overarching structure of the episode.

Now we may attempt a definition of communicating vessels. Two or more episodes that occur at different times, in different places, or on different levels of reality but are linked by the narrator so that their proximity or mingling causes them to modify each other, lending each, among other qualities, a different meaning, tone, or symbolic value than they might have possessed if they were narrated separately: these are communicating vessels. Their mere juxtaposition is not enough, of course, for the procedure to work. The decisive factor is a "communication" between two episodes set side by side or merged in the text by the narrator. The communication may be minimal, but if it doesn't exist at all it is impossible to speak of communicating vessels, since, as we have noted, the unity that this narrative technique establishes makes an episode composed this way always more than the sum of its parts.

The most subtle and daring case of communicating vessels may be that of Faulkner's *The Wild Palms*, a novel that tells, in alternating chapters, two separate stories: one a tragic tale of passionate (and ill-fated adulterous) love and the other that of a convict who in the wake of a devastating natural disaster, a flood that lays waste a vast region, struggles mightily to return to prison, where the authorities, since they don't know what to do with him, sentence him to even more years in prison—for trying to escape! The plots of these two stories never mix, though at a certain point in the story of the lovers there is a reference to the flood and the convict; nevertheless, because of the physical proximity of the protagonists, the language of the narrator, and a certain climate of excess—passionate love in one case, and in the other the fury of the elements and the suicidal integrity that drives the convict to keep his word and return to prison—a kind of resemblance is established. Borges, with the intelligence and precision that never failed him in his literary criticism, put it best: "Two stories that never intersect but somehow complement each other."

Julio Cortázar experiments with an interesting variation on the system of communicating vessels in *Hopscotch*, a novel that takes place, as you may recall, in two settings, Paris

("From the Other Side") and Buenos Aires ("From This Side"), between which it is possible to establish a certain chronology (the Parisian episodes precede the Buenos Aires episodes). At the beginning of the book, there is an author's note suggesting two different possible readings: one (let's call it the traditional one) begins with the first chapter and proceeds in the usual order; the other skips from chapter to chapter, following the directions given at the end of each episode. Only if the reader chooses this second option does he or she read the whole text of the novel; if the first is chosen, a full third of *Hopscotch* is excluded. This third—"From Diverse Sides (Expendable Chapters)"—is not made up of episodes created by Cortázar or narrated by his narrators; it consists of texts and quotations from other sources or, when the material is by Cortázar, of freestanding texts without a direct plot relationship to the story of Oliveira, La Maga, Rocamadour, and the other characters of the "realist" story (if it is not incongruous to use that term to describe *Hopscotch*). They are pieces of a collage that, in its communicating vessel relationship with the novelistic episodes, is intended to add a new dimension—a dimension we might call mythical or literary, an extra rhetorical level—to the story of *Hopscotch*. This, very clearly, is what the counterpointing of "realist" episodes and collage is meant to achieve. Cortázar had already used this system in his first published novel, *The Winners*. In it, he interweaves the adventures of the passengers of the ship on which the story is set with some odd monologues by Persio, a principal character—abstract, metaphysical, sometimes abstruse reflections meant to add a mythical dimension to the "realist" story (though in this case too, as always with Cortázar, it is inadequate to speak of realism).

But it is above all in some of his stories that Cortázar uses the communicating vessel scheme with true mastery. Allow me to remind you of the small marvel of technical craftsmanship that is "The Night Face Up." Remember it? The protagonist, who has been in a motorcycle accident on the streets of a big modern city—almost certainly Buenos Aires—undergoes an operation and, in what at first seems merely a nightmare, is transferred in a temporal shift from the hospital bed where he is convalescing to a precolonial Mexico in the throes of a *guerra florida*, when Aztec warriors hunted for human victims to sacrifice to their gods. From this point on, the story is built on a system of communicating vessels, alternating between the hospital ward where the protagonist is recovering and the remote precolonial night in which in the guise of a Moteca he first flees and then falls into the hands of his Aztec pursuers, who bring him to the pyramid where he is sacrificed with many other victims. The counterpoint is achieved by subtle temporal shifts that, in what we might call a subliminal way, cause the two realities—the present-day hospital and the precolonial jungle—to approach and somehow contaminate each other. Until, at the final crux—which involves another shift, this time not just temporal but in level of reality—the two times merge and the character is in fact not the motorcyclist being operated on in a modern city but a primitive Moteca who, seconds before the priest rips his heart out to appease the bloodthirsty gods, has a visionary glimpse of a future of cities, motorcycles, and hospitals.

Another narrative gem by Cortázar, "The Idol of the Cyclades," is a very similar story, though it is structurally more complex. In it Cortázar uses communicating vessels in an even more original way. Here, too, the story takes place in two different temporal realities, one contemporary and European (a Greek island in the Cyclades and a sculpture workshop on the outskirts of Paris) and one ancient, at least five thousand years old (the primitive civilization of the Aegean, a society of magic, religion, music, sacrifices, and rites that archaeologists have long been trying to reconstruct from the fragments—utensils, statues—that have come down to us). But in this story, past reality filters into the present in a more insidious and unobtrusive way, first through an Aegean statuette that two friends, the sculptor Somoza and the archaeologist Morand, find in the valley of Skoros. Two years later, the statuette sits in Somoza's workshop, and Somoza has made many copies of it, not for aesthetic purposes but because he believes that by doing so he'll be able to transport himself to the time and culture that produced it. In the story's present, in which Morand and Somoza confront each other in the latter's workshop, the narrator seems to insinuate that Somoza has gone mad and that Morand is the sane one. But all of a sudden, at the story's amazing conclusion, when Morand winds up killing Somoza, performing ancient magic rituals on his cadaver, and preparing to sacrifice his own wife, Thérèse, we discover that in fact the little statue has possessed both protagonists, turning them into men of the age and culture that made it, an age that has burst violently into a modern-day present that believed it had buried it forever. In this case, the communicating vessels aren't symmetric as they are in "The Night Face Up," with its balanced counterpoint. Here, the incursions of the remote past are more spasmodic, fleeting, until the splendid final crux—when we see the cadaver of Somoza naked with the ax sunk in his forehead, the little statue smeared with his blood, and Morand, naked too, listening to wild flute music and waiting for Thérèse with his ax raised—makes us realize that the past has entirely subsumed the present, subjecting it to its barbaric and ceremonial magic. By linking two different times and cultures in a narrative unity, the communicating vessels of both stories cause a new reality to be born, one qualitatively different from the mere composite of the two that are merged in it.

And although it seems impossible, I believe that with this explanation of communicating vessels we may conclude our discussion of the tools and principal techniques that novelists use to construct their fictions. There may be others, but I, at least, haven't come across them. The ones that leap out at me from the page (and the truth is, of course, that I don't go searching for them with a magnifying glass, since I'd rather read novels than autopsy them) seem to me likely to be related to one or another of the methods of composition of the stories that have been the subject of these letters.

Fondly,

By Way of a P.S.

DEAR FRIEND,

Just a few lines as a kind of farewell, to reiterate something I've already expressed many times in the course of our correspondence as, spurred on by your stimulating missives, I've tried to describe some of the tools that good novelists use to cast the kind of spell that keeps readers in thrall. And that is that technique, form, discourse, text, or whatever you want to call it (pedants have come up with many names for something that any reader could identify with ease) is a seamless whole. To isolate theme, style, order, points of view, et cetera, in other words, to perform a vivisection, is always, even in the best of cases, a form of murder. And a corpse is a pallid and misleading stand-in for a living, breathing, thinking entity not in the grip of rigor mortis or helpless against the onset of decay.

What do I mean by this? Not, of course, that criticism is useless and unnecessary. On the contrary, criticism can be a very valuable guide to the world and ways of an author, and sometimes a critical essay is itself a creative work, no less than a great novel or poem. (Off the top of my head, here are a few examples: *Studies and Essays on Góngora* by Dámaso Alonso, *To the Finland Station* by Edmund Wilson, *Port Royal* by Sainte-Beuve, and *The Road to Xanadu* by John Livingston Lowes: four very different kinds of critical works, but all of them equally valuable, illuminating, and original.) At the same time, it seems to me of the utmost importance to make it clear that criticism in and of itself, even when it is most rigorous and inspired, is unable to entirely account for the phenomenon of creation, to explain it in its totality. A successful fiction or poem will always contain an element or a dimension that rational critical analysis isn't quite able to encompass. This is because criticism is a labor of reason and intelligence, and in literary creation other factors, sometimes crucial to the work—intuition, sensitivity, divination, and even chance—intervene and escape the very finest nets of literary criticism. That is why no one can teach anyone else to create; at most, we may be taught to read and write. The rest we must teach ourselves, stumbling, falling, and picking ourselves up over and over again.

My dear friend: what I am trying to say is that you should forget everything you've read in my letters about the structure of the novel, and just sit down and write.

Good luck to you.

LIMA, MAY 10, 1997

Index of Names and Works

CPSIA information can be obtained
at www.ICGtesting.com
Printed in the USA
LVHW02s2257290818
588525LV00003B/216/P